FROGKISSER!

by

GARTH NIX

SCHOLASTIC PRESS
· NEW YORK ·

Library of Congress Cataloging-in-Publication Data
Names: Nix, Garth, author.
Title: Frogkisser! / Garth Nix.
Description: New York, NY : Scholastic Press, [2017] | Summary: Princess
Anya has a big problem: Duke Rikard, her step-stepfather is an evil wizard
who wants to rule the kingdom and has a habit of changing people into
frogs, and her older sister Morven, the heir, is a wimp—so with the help
of the librarian Gotfried (who turns into an owl when he is upset), and the
Royal Dogs, she must find away to defeat Rikard, save her sister, and
maybe even turn Prince Denholm back into a human being.
Identifiers: LCCN 2016026559 | ISBN 9781338052084 (hard jacket cover)
Subjects: LCSH: Princesses—Juvenile fiction. | Sisters—Juvenile fiction. |
Wizards—Juvenile fiction. | Magic—Juvenile fiction. | Dogs—Juvenile
fiction. | Adventure stories. | CYAC: Princesses—Fiction. | Sisters—
Fiction. | Wizards—Fiction. | Magic—Fiction. | Dogs—Fiction. |
Adventure and adventurers—Fiction. | GSAFD: Adventure fiction. |
LCGFT: Action and adventure fiction.
Classification: LCC PZ7.N647 Fr 2017 | DDC 823.914 [Fic]—dc23
LC record available at https://lccn.loc.gov/2016026559

10 9 8 7 6 5 4 3 2 1   17 18 19 20 21

Printed in the U.S.A. 23

First edition, March 2017

Book design by Christopher Stengel

To Anna, Thomas, Edward,
and all my family and friends

And particularly to Samwise Gamgee Nix, the
Labrador who unexpectedly joined our family some
three months after I started writing about Ardent
the Royal Dog, and to Yumdi and Bytenix, the dogs
who have gone ahead on the longest of all walks

Ten Years Before

It was the middle of an ice storm, the wind howling across the frozen moat to hurl hailstones against the walls of the castle and its tightly shuttered windows. But despite wind and hail and the full chill panoply of winter, it was deliciously warm in the Great Hall.

All four fireplaces were burning high, loaded up with double handfuls of small fir cones atop the great year-end logs. The scent of the cones was like incense, delicate wreaths of smoke leaving the fires to swirl above the wriggling mound of puppies that occupied the most comfortable place of all, on the carpet in front of the biggest fire.

There were at least two dozen puppies in the constantly moving pile, and one young human. A princess, though you'd never know it to look at her, since she was dressed like one of the garden boys. Unlike the puppies, she was sound asleep.

The puppies became quiet as a great old dog, her muzzle silvered, stalked into the hall and approached them. She sat down heavily on the carpet and gave a soft, low bark. Instantly, the puppies broke out of the pile and ordered themselves into two lines, ears up, all at attention.

The princess stirred a little at all the movement, and rolled onto her side. One of the puppies nudged her with his snout, and was about to nip her awake when the older dog spoke.

"Let the princess sleep. She is too young to hear what I am to tell you, and she needs to live without fear as long as may be. We will all need her courage in time to come."

"What about her sister?" asked the oldest puppy, who often took it on herself to ask questions. "Should I fetch her?"

"No," said the old dog. She sighed and paused to sniff at something that rolled out of the fire. As it wasn't food, she continued. "No. For now we keep this between ourselves. It is a matter for the Royal Dogs, and no others."

The puppies barely restrained themselves from leaping up and wrestling with one another. This was exciting! But the old dog fixed the most wrigglesome with her sheep-stunning gaze and they settled once more.

"The new Duke is a sorcerer," said the old dog. "A real one. Not just a dabbler. His heart is cold now, and will only grow colder."

The puppies growled and showed their teeth.

"He is allied with other sorcerers," continued the old dog. "The most evil, the most scheming, the most dangerous sorcerers around. They are not yet powerful enough to act upon their plans, but in time . . ."

"What do we do?" asked the next-oldest puppy, one who rarely spoke. "What can we do?"

"Watch. Wait. Protect the princesses. Keep them cheerful and unafraid. They will need whole hearts and the memory of happiness, at least, to have any chance of doing what must be done."

The old dog spoke of both princesses, but she looked at the younger one, asleep on the carpet. The puppies all turned their heads and looked at her too, with love and adoration.

Perhaps their combined gaze had some peculiar energy, for the little princess woke up. She saw the old dog and squealed with delight, leaping up to hug her very energetically, receiving several welcoming licks to the face in return.

"A story!" exclaimed the princess. "Tell us a story!"

CHAPTER ONE

In Which Morven's Denholm Is Turned into a Frog

The scream was very loud and went on for a very long time. Princess Anya, who was reading in the castle library, ignored it at first but eventually lifted her head from her book to listen.

"That sounds bad," said Gotfried, the librarian, in his quavering, high-pitched voice. Disturbed by the sound, he immediately turned into an owl and began to vomit up a nicely packaged parcel of bones from the mouse he'd had for breakfast. It was something he did when under stress. Turning into an owl, that is. The vomiting just came with the shape.

"It does." Anya frowned. It was her older sister Morven screaming, which was not unusual, but the intensity and duration of this particular scream were quite out of the ordinary.

Anya shut her book with an emphatic thump and latched it closed, since it was a copy of *The Adventures of a Sorcerous Typesetter's Apprentice* and the words inside would otherwise climb off the page and go wandering around the library. In fact there were still several words missing from an earlier reading, including the particularly troublesome pair of *instantly* and *forthwith*, which Gotfried now believed had escaped the castle altogether . . . or had been eaten by one of the dogs.

The screaming continued as Anya hurried out of the library, across the inner courtyard to the main part of the castle, and up the private stair to her sister's rooms. Morven was the heir to the kingdom—at least theoretically—so she had more space than Anya's little room. The sisters had not one but two stepparents, so the matter of lineage was a complicated one.

This was one of the most frequent questions Anya was asked later in life: *How is it possible to have two stepparents and no actual parents?* The answer ended up being rather straightforward: Their mother, who had been the ruling queen of the little kingdom of Trallonia, had died when Morven was six and Anya was three. Their father remarried a year later, to Countess Yselde.

So they had a stepmother, who was expected to be quite evil but mainly turned out to be a very enthusiastic botanist. She was not interested in the children at all, for good or ill. Only in plants.

But then their father died a year after his marriage to Countess Yselde, and their stepmother married Duke Rikard.

So the girls had two stepparents. Their stepmother the botanist wasn't a huge problem, but as it turned out, their stepstepfather *was* evil and wanted to be the king. Though Morven should by rights be crowned when she turned sixteen, in three months' time, it was fairly certain Duke Rikard would somehow prevent this from happening.

Perhaps he already has, thought Anya as she knocked on Morven's door. Not waiting for an answer, she went straight in. As expected, her sister was lying on a lounge in her receiving room, screaming at the ceiling and kicking her legs. Her maid, Bethany, was sitting on a stool nearby knitting. Large strands of the wool she'd stuffed in her ears hung down her neck.

Anya leaned over her sister and waited until two things happened at the same time: Her presence was registered through the veil of tears and Morven needed to take a breath.

"What's happened?" asked Anya.

Morven stopped screaming and started sobbing.

"Ste . . . ste . . . step—"

"Stepstepfather," guessed Anya. It was far more likely to be *stepstepfather* than *stepmother*. Anya hadn't even seen Yselde for the past month. She'd gone somewhere far-off to collect a rare shrub or a sapling.

"Tur . . . tur . . . tur . . . tur . . ."

Anya raised an eyebrow. She could normally translate Morven's sobbing speech but this was beyond her.

"Turned," said Morven at last.

"Turned?"

"Denholm." Morven started crying even harder, so hard the tears were flying horizontally out of her eyes. Anya stood back a bit, impressed that this was even possible.

"In . . . in . . . into . . . a . . . a . . ."

"Rikard has turned Denholm into something," translated Anya.

One of the greater disadvantages of having Duke Rikard as an evil stepstepfather was that he was an accomplished sorcerer. Prince Denholm was the latest total-amazing-love-beyond-any-possibility-of-measuring of Morven's life. The son of one of the kings from the petty kingdoms near the coast, Denholm was a thoroughly nice young man, one of the better princes in the continuous cavalcade that came to the castle to woo Morven.

Anya liked Denholm, and thought he was unlucky to have soft, wavy blond hair and blue eyes of the sort that made Morven fall in love with people. As Morven was remarkably beautiful herself, with her raven hair and snow-white skin and warm chocolate eyes, young men she fell in love with usually fell in love back, at least until she decided she liked someone else better.

The spurned princes usually retired to their homes to write bad poetry and brood by the fire. Or they went on a quest and in the process discovered that they also liked someone else better. Or they got eaten by a dragon. Whether at home writing poetry, embraced by a new love, or in a dragon's stomach, they didn't come back.

Getting turned into something was unusual. Denholm must have been foolish enough to try to talk to Rikard over breakfast, or maybe even ask for Morven's hand in marriage, which to the Duke would have been the equivalent of volunteering for immediate transformation. If Morven was married, she would have allies and it would be even more difficult to get rid of her. And with her around, Rikard could never become the king.

"What has Rikard turned Denholm into?" asked Anya.

"A fr . . . fr . . . fr . . . fr . . ."

"Frog," said Anya. "How unimaginative. Typical. Stop crying, Morven. It's not the end of the world. Just kiss him and turn him back."

Morven turned her great tear-swamped eyes to Anya. Her plump rose-petal lips quivered as if she had a fever. She made a choking noise.

"Can't," said Bethany, who had pulled the wool out of her ears when Anya had started talking. "He jumped out the window into the moat."

"Go and fetch him," said Anya. "Then kiss him."

"Thousands of frogs in the moat," Bethany pointed out cheerfully.

"Morven will recognize him," said Anya. "Princess. True love. All that."

Bethany rolled her eyes.

"The Duke has decreed the princess is not to leave her chambers for a week," she said.

"You . . . you . . . you," sobbed Morven.

Anya rolled her eyes too, and sighed.

"I know, I know. You want me to do it, right?"

Morven sobbed, hiccupped, and nodded.

"How am *I* supposed to find him amongst all those frogs? I'm not in love with him," Anya went on . . . in the process answering her own question, which was just as well, for Morven would have no idea. "I'll have to get a dowsing rod and tune it with a lock of his hair. I suppose you've kept one?"

Bethany snorted. "Tufts and tufts. Locket."

Morven continued to sob, but she managed to lift a chain from her neck and pull a crystal locket out of her bodice. It was heart shaped and had so much hair stuffed in it that some was escaping around the edges.

"I'm very busy right now, though," Anya prevaricated. The last thing she wanted to do was to go and find a transformed prince in the moat.

"Puh . . . puh . . . please," sobbed Morven. *"Please."*

"Stop crying, Morven!"

Morven held out the locket mournfully, her shoulders shaking.

"Pro . . . promise me you'll find my Dennie. I'll duh . . . duh . . . die without him!"

Anya sighed, reached forward, and took just a few hairs out of the locket, carefully placing them in the belt purse of her kirtle.

"All right! I *promise!*"

"Sister promise?" asked Morven. She tilted her head to one side and blinked her large tear-filled eyes beseechingly.

"Yes! Sister promise. I'll find him and you can kiss him and . . . all will be well."

All would *not* be well, but Anya knew there was no point in tasking Morven with the larger political situation. If Morven's current love was back in human form, she would be able to forget their stepstepfather was planning to do something horrible to both of them. Duke Rikard would have long since turned them into swans or maybe even geese if it hadn't been for the protective devotion of everyone else in the castle, from the stable girls to the kitchen boys.

And, of course, the Royal Dogs. Rikard wasn't a powerful enough sorcerer yet to go up against the dogs. They were intensely loyal and largely immune to his magic. Dogs were so very confident of their own identity they resisted transformation magic.

One legend told the story of a dog who *had* been successfully transmogrified into a duck, but simply refused to believe it and carried on as a hunting dog. After a few days with the hunting pack, the duck brought down a small deer and the spell broke immediately.

"Thank you!" Morven smiled. "You are the bestest sister. The bestest!"

"There's not much competition," muttered Anya on her way out, but she didn't say it loud enough for Morven to hear. It might start her thinking about their dead parents, or her lack of more siblings to help her out, and then she might start screaming again. Quiet sobbing was much to be preferred.

"I do hope Gotfried is back to normal," Anya said to herself as she returned to the library. She would need his help with the dowsing rod and it was very difficult to keep his attention when he was an owl. Despite what she had said to her sister, Anya was rather worried about finding Denholm. There were thousands of frogs in the moat, yes, but there were also hungry frog-eating pike and ravenous frog-eating storks . . .

The more Anya thought about it, the more concerned she got. There was also the man from the village who gathered frogs to eat . . . and the snakes that liked to devour frogs in one gulp . . . and though it was an outside chance the moat monster would bother with a single frog, it might swallow a dozen or so just by accident . . .

A frog's life was much riskier than Anya had ever considered. But now a *prince's* life was at stake.

That frog had to be found and kissed immediately!

CHAPTER TWO

Princess Anya Goes Frog Dowsing and Is Joined by a Royal Dog

Fortunately, Gotfried was back in human form, though he was still perched on one of the library desks with his black robe all puffed up around him. Before he'd become a librarian, Gotfried had been in training to become a wicked sorcerer, but the life hadn't suited him. He had very little innate wickedness, and turning into an owl when he was stressed tended to curtail supreme acts of devilry before they got started.

He was much better as a librarian, and his early magical education made him a useful resource for Anya, who had a strong interest in magic. Good magic, of course. And kind-of-gray-area magic. And, to be honest, a little bit of the evil stuff as well. But only a little bit.

"I need to make a dowsing rod to find a particular frog prince," Anya said as she shouldered the creaking library door open and slipped inside. "Denholm's got himself transformed by the Duke."

Gotfried blinked at her several times.

"You're human again," said Anya impatiently.

"Oh! Am I?" exclaimed Gotfried. He hastily slid off the desk and flexed his fingers. "Frog dowsing. You'll need some hair, fingernail clippings, or toe scrapings."

"I've got some hair," said Anya, suppressing a shudder. *Toe scrapings* . . .

"Then a forked hazel twig, dipped in pond water, the hair bound round thrice, and a simple spell," Gotfried instructed. He leaped towards a shelf, flapping his arms—and fell to his knees before recovering with some embarrassment and simply walking over. "We can find such a spell in *Divinations and Destinies,* volume two. Or volume five. Maybe six. I suggest you get the twig, dip it in the moat, and come back, Princess. I'll find the spell."

"Don't get distracted," warned Anya. "And no going owl."

"Yes, yes," said Gotfried. "It hardly ever happens twice in one day."

"*Hardly ever* is not *never,*" said Anya. "Please do hurry. It's not safe for a transformed frog in the moat. His instincts will all be wrong."

"Bah! It isn't as bad as everyone makes out," Gotfried scoffed. "I quite like being an owl."

"Better than being a frog," said Anya as she went out the door.

Finding a forked hazel twig presented no difficulty—Anya knew there were two hazel trees in the walled garden. The twigs were useful in a variety of magics, so her stepstepfather had taken pains to cultivate the trees, in the same way that he encouraged toadstools to grow on the wetter walls of the dungeon.

She was sorting through some fallen branches looking for a piece that could be broken off when an enthusiastic wuffling noise announced the arrival of one of the younger royal dogs. Named Ardent, he was still growing into his very large paws and, though officially no longer a puppy, was not much beyond that stage.

Consequently, he ran everywhere at full speed and talked too quickly.

"What are you doing?" he asked. "C-c-an I do-do-do it too?"

He barked, of course, but Anya had no difficulty understanding him or any of the other royal dogs. They had considerable magic and if they wanted humans to understand them, then the humans did. It was a mark of their disdain if you only heard barks and growls, as was the case for Duke Rikard. Over time, with practice talking to the dogs, Anya had learned to understand some other animals as well, though she had never got far with fish or amphibians. They gargled their words too much for a human to comprehend their speech.

"I am finding a stick," said Anya, and regretted it even as she spoke. *Stick* was a very important word for dogs.

"A stick!" enthused Ardent. "Th-th-row it! *Throw it!*"

"Not now," said Anya. "I need to make a dowsing rod to find Morven's Denholm, who's been turned into a frog."

"F-f-f-frog hunting! Frog hunting!" exclaimed Ardent, leaping around Anya in circles and wagging his tail.

"No, not frog *hunting*. Frog *finding*. Ah, this will do."

She held up a stick that forked two-thirds of the way along. Ardent began to leap up at it, but managed to restrain himself, only skipping forward a little bit. He pretended that was what he had intended to do all the time and looked innocently up at Anya, his tongue lolling and his mouth in a grin.

"Well done, Ardent," said Anya, knowing how difficult it was for the young dog to restrain himself. He wanted to be involved in everything. "If you promise to behave and not to eat any frogs, you can come with me to find Denholm."

"I don't eat frogs!" Ardent replied, instantly closing up on Anya's heels.

As they left the garden by what had once been a guarded and locked postern gate but was now just a hole in the wall, the dog added, "At least I don't eat frogs too often. They don't taste very nice."

"Better cooked," confirmed Anya. The bank of the moat beyond the wall was muddy and sloped quite steeply, so she had to be careful not to slide in. The moat monster was loyal, like all the occupants of the castle except for Duke Rikard, but he was also very old, inordinately deaf, and rather blind. She didn't want to get snapped up, become severely injured, and then have to sit through the monster's tearful apologies as well. "Their legs anyway. Some of the villagers catch them here and cook them up."

"Mmmmm," said Ardent. He liked cooked food. Also raw food and semicooked food, and things that might be food and so were worth chewing on for a while to make sure they *weren't* food.

Anya dipped the hazel stick in the moat. She supposed the flooded ditch would count as a pond. It was pretty stagnant and there were floating mats of what could only be pondweed. Quite a few frogs were lying on one nearby, taking it easy.

"Denholm?" called out Anya, but there was no answer, and none of the frogs moved off their weed island. "Oh, I suppose it would be too easy if he just answered when I called. Come on, Ardent. Back to the library."

It was time for a spell.

In the library, Gotfried had not gone owl. But he was perched on top of his desk over an open book, with his head craned forward oddly and his back arched.

"Princess! I have found the spell. Here."

He spun the book around so Anya could read it. Ardent reared up and put his forepaws on the desk so he could read too. The royal dogs were very smart and Tanitha, the matriarch of them all, was strict about the pups learning to read.

"Twine the hair around the pond-dipped branch . . . several minor words of power . . ." Anya followed the instructions as she read. This wasn't usually a good idea when casting spells. (You should always read all the way through first.) But she was in a hurry. Which is also not a good idea when casting spells. (Never be in a hurry. Being in a hurry makes things go wrong.)

Fortunately, it was a simple spell. Anya did everything in the right order and spoke the words of power, familiar ones she had used before. She felt a tingling in her throat as she said them, and afterwards she sneezed a few times, which was quite normal. Magic demanded a price, be it a minor allergic reaction for a small spell or a complete freezing of all good human emotion for a big spell, which was what had happened to Duke Rikard.

"I think that's done it," said Gotfried with satisfaction. "Look!"

The hazel stick was moving in Anya's hand, twisting towards the door and the moat.

"Yoicks! Tallyho!" cried Ardent, launching himself out into the corridor. Anya heard his claws scrabbling on the flagstones as he stopped and turned himself around to wait for her to show him where to actually go.

"You might need this," said Gotfried, handing Anya his butterfly net. "It should be strong enough to hold a frog, but you'd better take a bucket as well."

Anya got a bucket from the kitchen on the way, the dowsing

rod writhing and twisting in her hand in its eagerness to find the person whose hair was wound around it.

"You don't need a net or a bucket," said Ardent. "I c-c-an hold a frog in my jaws. Like this."

He demonstrated by snapping at the leg of a kitchen stool, breaking it in half. Spitting out the broken pieces, he continued, "Not exactly like that. I mean more like—"

"No," said Anya firmly. "We'll use the net and the bucket. You stay back and do not—I repeat, *do not*—even nose the frog. Any frog. Stay away from all the frogs."

"I *c-c-ould* do it."

"I know you could," Anya soothed. "I just want to do it my way. All right?"

Ardent mumbled something and spat out another small piece of wood. But he fell in behind Anya happily enough as she made her way back out through the walled garden and the hole in the wall to the moat. The dowsing rod was almost leaping from her hand, but it wasn't until it nearly pulled her into the stagnant water Anya belatedly realized that of course she would have to go in. She didn't mind swimming, but she didn't want to swim in the weed-choked, slimy water of the moat.

Kneeling down, she slapped the water with her left hand in a careful rhythm, one-two-slap-slap-slap, paused for several seconds, then repeated it.

The frogs stopped moving around on the floating weed island, and a duck that was nearby quickly launched itself into the air as a vee of ripples disturbed it, the sign of something large moving under the water.

"Moatie!" cried Ardent happily, wagging his tail.

The ancient monster's head rose out of the moat, water cascading off his long, scaly snout and spiky neck. His deep-set eyes glowed yellow like the hottest part of a candle flame. He looked extremely fearsome, an effect only slightly lessened when he opened his jaws to reveal a pink mouth and large square teeth more suitable for munching mounds of vegetable matter than rending flesh. They could still rend flesh if they had to, of course—hence only slightly less fearsome, because usually people expected really sharp teeth like those of a shark when they saw Moatie, and got a small and generally false sense of relief when they saw his square munchers.

"Time to eat the Duke?" roared Moatie in a voice that could be heard throughout the castle, the closer villages, and even the forest, a mile away. Everyone could understand the monster because once upon a time he too had been human. The details of his transformation were lost in the mists of time. Gotfried believed Moatie had done it to himself on purpose.

Moatie's threat to eat Duke Rikard was one of the things that kept the sorcerer from behaving too badly towards the princesses, at least until such a time as his sorcery grew strong enough to deal with the creature. The moat monster was admittedly extremely ancient and slow-moving, but he was also about sixty feet long, armored from head to foot, resistant to magic, and could smash down any door in the castle and slither up or down any of the stairs.

"No, not yet," bawled Anya as loudly as she could, in an attempt to overcome Moatie's deafness. "It's me, Princess Anya. Would you mind carrying me around the moat to look for a frog?"

She held up her dowsing rod close to his nearsighted eyes. The stick was twisting around, pointing at a clump of lilies about twenty yards to her right.

"Anya. I wasn't sure if it was you or Morven. Climb on."

"And me!" barked Ardent.

"And the dog, of course," said Moatie. "Which one are you?"

"Ardent. Son of Jorum and Kithlin, daughter of Fango and Goldie, daughter of Smartnose, daughter of . . . well, lots more. All the way back to Tanitha."

"Ah," said Moatie. "Come on, then, both of you."

He lowered his head and lifted up a ten-foot-long section of his neck, a broad expanse of scaly flesh. Anya climbed on carefully, balancing her bucket and butterfly net, with Ardent close behind. They found a nice flat area between some big bony plates and braced their feet.

"Over to your left," called out Anya, carefully watching where her dowsing rod was pointing. "Slowly, please!"

The huge monster moved through the water so easily he hardly sent a ripple to the shore. The frogs on the pondweed island ahead watched him suspiciously, but did not jump off.

"Even slower," Anya requested. "Stop!"

The dowsing rod was pointing directly at one particular rather-more-yellow-than-green frog who was sitting by itself, which was unusual, since the frogs generally clustered close together. Looking at it . . . him . . . Anya felt sure she could see a hint of Prince Denholm's blond hair in the frog's shiny skin.

Holding on to one of the monster's bony plates, Anya leaned down with the butterfly net and deftly scooped up the frog, before quickly transferring it, still in the net, into the bucket.

"Back to shore, please, Moatie!" she ordered, quite satisfied with having found Prince Denholm so quickly. At the same time, she had to quell a nagging sense that it had been too easy.

What if the Duke stepped in to make sure Prince Denholm stayed a frog? Sooner or later, the uneasy truce between Rikard and the princesses would be broken.

Anya growled under her breath. Ardent growled too, and looked around for enemies to bite.

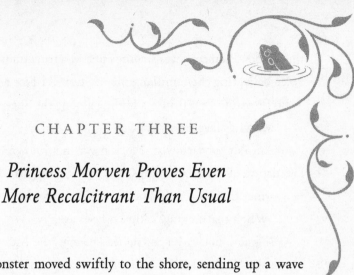

CHAPTER THREE

Princess Morven Proves Even More Recalcitrant Than Usual

The monster moved swiftly to the shore, sending up a wave that swamped all the pondweed islands and sent dozens of frogs croaking and complaining into the moat.

Anya and Ardent disembarked by the hole in the garden wall. Anya patted Moatie near one huge nostril, being careful not to get too close in case he inhaled and sucked in her hand and arm. Cleaning moat-monster snot off yourself taught a young person caution, as Anya had learned when she was six. Ardent barked his thanks.

"Tell me when to eat the Duke!" roared Moatie. "Don't forget!"

"I won't," promised Anya. "Thank you, Moatie."

She hurried through the garden, carefully holding the bucket with the net-wrapped frog. It wouldn't do if Denholm jumped out somewhere along the way. Ardent followed close at her heels, pausing only to sniff at an upside-down bug scrabbling about on the foot of the private stairs to Morven's chambers.

Anya had expected Morven still to be at least sobbing on her lounge, if not caterwauling on the carpet, so she was surprised to see her sister sitting by the tall window, looking radiant and cheerful. The explanation for this could be found in the song coming through the window. Someone was singing outside, a truly transcendent male voice delivering the familiar tune of "Loved I Not a Shepherdess Who Proved to Be a Princess Hiding among the Sheep."

Morven's favorite song.

Anya's eyes narrowed. Morven was not known for the steadfast nature of her relationships, but transferring her affections to a new prince this soon would be a record, even for her.

"Who's that singing?" Anya asked casually.

"I know not." Morven sighed, placing the back of her hand against her forehead and miming a bit of a swoon. "He is incognito, but by the purity of his voice and the two cloth-of-gold-garbed servants who are holding the music, he must be a prince."

"Well, forget about the new prince for a moment," said Anya sternly. She pulled the net out of the bucket and extracted the frog, holding it tightly in both hands. It croaked dismally and its back legs kicked in an effort to get away. "You've got to kiss Denholm!"

Morven made a gagging noise and looked away.

"I'm not kissing that!"

"Just shut your eyes and pretend to be kissing Denholm," said Anya, holding the frog closer. It kicked even more strongly, as if it objected to being kissed as well.

"I'm *not* kissing a frog!" screamed Morven. She turned determinedly to the open window and waved her hand. The singing got louder and more extravagantly phrased, with a couple of fluid trills as the prince below showed off his marvelous voice.

"You are such a selfish beast," said Anya, but she knew it was no use. Not for the first time, she wondered if perhaps it might be better to let Duke Rikard take over the kingdom after all. Morven would be such a terrible queen. But Rikard would be even worse, and he would never leave them both alive . . . or at least untransformed.

Morven ignored Anya, and continued smiling and waving.

"Now what do I do with you?" Anya asked the frog.

"Blee-blup," replied the struggling frog, which wasn't much help.

"Gotfried might know some other way to return you to your natural form," said Anya with a sigh. "Come on, Ardent."

Back in the library, Gotfried was whittling away at the door of the cupboard where he liked to sleep when in owl shape, making a large hole in the middle so he could fly out more easily.

"Morven won't kiss the frog," Anya announced. "Is there some other way to turn Denholm back into a man?"

"What? Won't kiss him?" asked Gotfried. He shook his head. "Princesses these days . . ."

"*Some* princesses," Anya corrected. "Is there another way to turn him back?"

"Yes, yes," mumbled Gotfried. He looked up at the ceiling and then across the shelves. "True love is the best dissolving agent for such spells, but there are other ways. Now, I did have a little pot of lip balm somewhere—"

"Gotfried! I really want to get this sorted out so I can go back to my reading," said Anya impatiently. "Why do you want lip balm anyway?"

"Oh, it's not for me," said Gotfried. He looked along the tall shelves again. "I seem to remember I flew with it somewhere . . ."

"Forget the lip balm! How can I transform Denholm back again?"

"Ah, but that's what the lip balm is for. It's Transmogrification Reversal Lip Balm. Almost anyone can put it on and then kiss the transformee, and it works just as if . . . well, almost as well as if there was true love involved."

"Really?" asked Anya. "It's that easy? And you've got some of this lip balm?"

"Oh, it's not easy, nor a simple mixture," said Gotfried. "It took me years to make a small jar. The ingredients are very hard to come by. The base is witches' tears, for example. It is extraordinarily difficult to get those, witches being what they are. But I like to have some on hand, in case of . . . ahem . . . difficulties in my own situation."

"It's probably in your secret hiding place," said Ardent. His legs went completely stiff and he stretched his neck out to point with his nose towards a dark corner of the library.

"What's that?" asked Gotfried nervously. A pattern of owl feathers shimmered across his face and he began to crouch.

"Not now," ordered Anya. "Get a grip on yourself!"

"Your secret hiding place," repeated Ardent. "Behind the reading chair."

"It's meant to be *secret*," hissed Gotfried.

"Just go and get the lip balm, please," said Anya impatiently. "We'll look the other way."

She turned about and grabbed Ardent's collar, dragging the dog's head away as well. He struggled for a moment, but obeyed when she scratched his ears.

Gotfried stalked over to his secret corner and made furniture-moving and rummaging noises before returning with a small bronze pot. Unscrewing the lid, he held it out to Anya. She saw a very small amount of rather dried-up looking orangey-yellow balm inside.

"Pawpaw flavor," said Gotfried. "It has quite a pleasant taste."

"Pawpaw!" exclaimed Ardent indignantly. "You make it out of paws!"

"No, no, Ardent," Anya explained. "Pawpaw is a tropical fruit. I've only read about them, though. I've never seen one."

"Help yourself," said Gotfried, proffering the pot. "Smear it across your lips and then kiss the frog."

"Hmm." Anya looked at the dried-up lip balm and then at the admittedly quite slimy frog. "Perhaps you should do it, Gotfried."

"It will work much better for a princess," said Gotfried.

Anya sighed. Everything seemed to work much better if a princess was involved, provided that princess was her. Every difficult task in the castle ultimately descended upon her shoulders. Like the cellar records, which Steward Hogar had got into a fearful muddle. It had taken Anya weeks to sort them out, in the process finding forty-eight dozen lost bottles of wine.

Luckily, she was equal to every task, but sometimes she wished someone else could share the work. It wasn't easy looking after a useless older sister, combatting an evil sorcerer's plots, and trying to get a magical education all at the same time.

Dipping her finger in the pot, she got all the remaining lip balm out and rubbed it on her lips. Though she didn't try to taste it, a little did get to her tongue, and though the flavor was quite nice there was something kind of waxy and unpleasant about the texture.

"Ugh," she said, picking up the frog. He kicked violently but she held him up to her mouth and planted a kiss on his head, immediately wiping her mouth afterwards. "Bleagh! Disgusting!"

The frog swelled in her hand. Anya put him down; there was a bright flash of rather orangey-yellow light and the smell of swamp gas. A moment later the frog exploded, and in its place stood a blond young man dressed in the rotten, sodden remnants of princely raiment in last year's fashion.

"You took your time," he said bitterly. "Do you know how long I was in that disgusting moat?"

Everyone stared at him, because he *wasn't* Denholm.

"Who are you?" barked Ardent.

Anya looked the young man up and down, working through her memory.

"You're Prince Adalbert," she said slowly. "From last year. I think you were Morven's November prince."

"Don't remind me," snapped Adalbert. He smoothed back his long blond hair and strode towards the door. "Thanks for undoing the spell and all, but the sooner I get away from this cursed castle, your mad stepstepfather, and your faithless sister, the better!"

"Wait!" cried Anya. "My dowsing rod found you. Why aren't you Denholm? And why did you resist being kissed?"

Adalbert turned around at the door.

"I have no idea why I'm not 'Denholm,' whoever he is, but part of the spell made me resist efforts to get turned back. Very thorough, the Duke. That's why I'm leaving right *now* before he shows up."

"Too late," a deep, sepulchral voice intoned. A tall figure slid out of the shadow in the corner, a theatrical trick that scared the life out of Adalbert while making Anya roll her eyes. She knew there was a narrow, unlit staircase there.

The recently frog-shaped prince made a kind of bleating noise and ran away. The evil stepstepfather turned back to Anya, swinging his rich velvet cloak wide like a raven's wing and then wrapping it around himself. Rikard always felt cold, even in midsummer.

It was a side effect of doing too much evil magic. He would never be warm again.

Ardent closed up to Anya's knee, the hair all along his back raised in a ridge and his lip curled to snarl. The princess let her hand rest lightly on his collar, taking strength from his presence. The Duke somehow made her feel even younger and smaller than she was, and Anya could feel her heart racing in fear. He would transform her one day, she knew. He was just waiting, gaining magical strength, building up his power in the kingdom, replacing loyal servants with his own people. It was only a matter of time.

"I felt someone tamper with one of my spells." The Duke's voice was cold and piercing, and made Anya's ears ache. "Really, child, you mustn't interfere with my magic. A horrible accident might occur."

"I understand," said Anya. It was always best to simply agree with the Duke.

"In fact this tendency of yours has reminded me that it is well past time you were sent away," said Rikard.

"Sent away?" This was a new and horrifying development. "You can't send me away."

"To school," said the Duke smoothly. "I have one in mind. A very good school. It is some distance away, and the journey there is perhaps a *trifle* dangerous, but that is the only drawback."

"Does my stepmother know about this?" asked Anya. "You know she promised my father I would be educated at home. A deathbed promise!"

A deathbed promise was a powerful thing. There was a good chance that the ghost of the person to whom the promise had been made would return to haunt the promiser if it was broken. But there was an even better chance that the Duke wouldn't care about that. He was very familiar with ghosts, revenants, and evil spirits of all kinds. Besides, the ghost wouldn't be haunting him, but his wife, who was rarely at home.

"I am sure my dear Yselde would agree with me, should she be here," said Rikard. "Alas, her search for the infant form of the Golden Sapsmirch Tree has proved more difficult than expected, and she will not be home for many months."

"I'm not going!"

"You will," said the Duke. "One way or another. I am your father after all."

"Stepstepfather," muttered Anya.

"It is sufficient to give me authority over you. As you well know. And who can argue with sending a child to school? Even your dogs know about the necessity of school."

Ardent growled, but very softly. School *was* important, he knew, and so he couldn't protest about that. He had been to school himself, for three whole months. In addition to reading he had learned a great many things about when to sniff, what not to sniff, how not to gulp food, how to gulp food while pretending not to, and much more.

"You can't just send me to any old school," said Anya. "I am a princess after all."

"That is why I am going to send you to the Most Select Royal Academy of Tarwicce," said the Duke. There was the trace of a smirk on his face.

"Tarwicce! But that's . . . that's almost half the world away!" protested Anya. "Six months' travel, or more, by land and sea."

"As I said, the journey there is slightly perilous. But it is the best school in the world for princes and princesses, or so I am reliably informed."

"How can something be 'slightly perilous'? I mean either it is . . . or . . . ahem . . . not," Gotfried began to say, before quailing under the Duke's stare. The white of Rikard's eyes were in fact not white, but a kind of ugly gray and his pupils were the deep red of shriveled cranberries.

"I see," said Anya quietly. "What about Morven?"

"Morven is too old to go to school," said the Duke. "She will continue in her ambassadorial duties, receiving princes from other lands, with the possibility of marriage. In fact I have high hopes a match can be arranged with her current suitor, Prince . . . ah . . . Maggers. The one with the lovely singing voice."

"Prince Maggers?" asked Anya suspiciously. "Where does he hail from?"

The Duke waved his hand vaguely. "Some kingdom in the west. Small, of course, but rich in . . . er . . . jewels and the like. He is eminently suitable."

"You've never encouraged anyone before," said Anya. "Why transform Prince Denholm into a frog, for example? He was extremely eligible—he said his father's kingdom is four times the size of ours."

"Maggers is even *more* eligible," replied the Duke with a small smile he imagined could only be felt by himself, and not seen. Anya, however, caught the tiny quirk of his left lip. It put her instantly on guard.

"Maggers is an unusual name," she said. The prince's singing had reminded her of something, some familiar sound.

"Not where he comes from," said the Duke . . . and there was that supposedly secret smile again. "It's a very common name there. Not just for princes."

Maggers. That singing, with the liquid trills . . . thoughts swirled through Anya's very sharp mind and came together in a sudden conclusion.

Prince Maggers must be a transformed magpie. The Duke was planning to marry off Morven to a magpie . . . so she would have no help from her husband, or allies from her husband's family.

"Morven will be crowned queen quite soon, in any case," said Anya, wishing that by saying this it could be true. "She can choose a husband for herself. Or not."

"*Soon* is such an imperfect term," said the Duke. "A coronation can hardly happen before your mother returns."

"Stepmother," said Anya.

"And of course, we couldn't possibly have a coronation without you, Anya. Taking into account travel time and the paucity of holidays at the school, I expect you won't be home for several years, if at—"

He stopped himself, his lips twitching. Anya knew he'd been about to say, "if at all." He just couldn't help himself. The next thing, he'd be wringing his hands together and cackling. This was yet another side effect of too much evil magic. Being cold, talking too much about plans, and eyeteeth that grew ridiculously long and sharp were all side effects. In the final stages, evil sorcerers even forgot to breathe, but sadly this didn't stop them from thinking they were still alive and carrying on as if they were.

"You can't have Morven's wedding either, in that case," said Anya. "A formal wedding would need me there too, and our stepmother."

"Oh, a *formal* wedding would, no doubt," Rikard retorted. "But one hears so often about runaway matches, a chance meeting with a well-meaning priest or a tipsy druid, happy to celebrate any wedding. It could happen tomorrow . . ."

"I won't let you marry Morven off to suit yourself," said Anya through gritted teeth.

"You won't be here. In fact, you will depart for school tomorrow morning at dawn," said Rikard, once again smiling his not-so-secret smile. "It is going to rain, so it will be suitably miserable. Do you understand?"

"I understand all right." Anya eyed one of Gotfried's paper knives on the desk. But there was no point physically attacking the Duke. He was protected by his magic from all normal weapons. The way Rikard's power was growing, she was afraid that even Moatie's great teeth might not be able to harm him now, and so their ultimate defense against him might no longer be effective.

Rikard nodded and turned to Gotfried.

"Librarian. I require a copy of the *second* volume of Tench and Watkins on the transmogrification of birds. You might recall when I spoke to you yesterday I wanted both volumes, not just the first?"

"Yes, Your Grace. I'm very sorry, Your Grace. It won't happen again, Your Grace." Gotfried was terrified of the Duke but also somewhat admiring of him, because Rikard had become the powerful sorcerer he had once wanted to be himself. "I will fetch the second volume for you."

"Bring it to my study," instructed the Duke. He turned, swirled his black cloak around behind him, and vanished into the shadowed stair.

Anya took in a shuddering breath and looked at her hands, willing them to stop shaking. She always told herself that the next time she saw the Duke would be different. That she wouldn't feel the fear.

But she always did.

CHAPTER FOUR

Princess Anya Takes Counsel from a Wise Old Dog

A nya checked the staircase after the Duke had departed to make sure he wasn't simply crouched down on the tenth step under his cloak, as he had been known to do so he could listen to what people said about him. But the staircase was empty, and the door at the top locked shut.

When she came back down, Gotfried had gone owl. He was perched on top of one of the bookcases with his head tucked under his wing.

"Oh, Gotfried!" exclaimed Anya. "I wanted to talk to you."

"Can't," said Gotfried, his voice muffled by feathers. "Have to find a book for the Duke. Have to take it to his . . . his study."

The Duke's study was a frightening place. It was impossibly tidy and the walls were very brightly whitewashed, the surface so smooth people thought all kinds of ghastly things must be hidden away behind secret doors. Anya wasn't sure there *were* any secret doors or horrible things hidden away; it was possible that the Duke was just extremely orderly. But Gotfried imagined the walls could turn on pivots to reveal a dungeon, or a laboratory so evil it would turn him into an owl forever, or perhaps turn him into an owl and then kill him on the spot, stripping the feathers and flesh from his bones to make him another skeleton in the Duke's collection.

If the Duke had a skeleton collection. Gotfried was sure he did, behind those white walls.

"Hiding your head under your wing isn't going to help," said Anya sternly.

"I'm just taking a moment to gather myself," said Gotfried. "Before I deliver the book."

Anya waited for a minute or two, but Gotfried's head did not emerge from under his wing.

"Gotfried!"

"I'm still gathering myself," mumbled the owl. "Then I'm going to get the bird transmogrification book and take it to the Duke, and then if I don't end up as a skeleton I'm going to gather myself some more."

"I need to ask you things," said Anya. "I don't know what to do! I'm going to be sent away tomorrow. At dawn! And I promised Morven I would find Denholm! A sister promise!"

Gotfried didn't answer. He shivered on his bookshelf, feathers trembling.

A soft, wet nose touched the back of Anya's hand.

"You should talk to Tanitha," said Ardent.

Relief flooded through Anya. She had panicked for a moment, losing her normal self-possession.

"Of course," she said.

Unlike normal dogs, the royal breed lived as long as humans, or even longer. No one knew how old Tanitha was exactly, but she was by far the castle's oldest inhabitant, and remembered people and dogs long since dead.

Tanitha did not move much now from her place by the vast fire in the castle's Great Hall, but a constant stream of dogs and people came by to keep her informed. Her word was law to all the dogs and other animals in the castle and beyond. Even the castle cats, a semi-independent band that primarily roved the roofs and attics, gave their allegiance to Tanitha, even if they sometimes pretended otherwise.

With the relief of knowing she could talk to someone wise, Anya's swift-thinking brain began to work properly again.

"The hair!" she exclaimed. "Morven must just add each new prince's hair to her locket. No wonder there was so much, and I got Adalbert's instead of Denholm's. Ardent, can you go to Denholm's room and find his hairbrush? And maybe you'd better get one of his socks as well. I'll have to make a new dowsing rod. Oh, I do hope he's all right in the moat. I'll go and talk to Tanitha."

Ardent barked happily, spun about on the spot, and leaped away, eager as always to carry out a job, particularly if it involved herding or fetching.

Anya followed Ardent out rather slowly, with a wistful glance back at Gotfried. The librarian was her closest ally, but he was not very dependable whenever the Duke was involved. He would be too frightened now to give her any useful advice.

"I'm not going to school," Anya whispered to herself. That one thing was certain. But how could she avoid it? The Duke had cleverly hit on a way to get rid of her. No one could object to a princess being sent to school. Even if it was very likely she would never even get there.

Many different plans went through Anya's mind as she left the library, wandered along the covered walkway through the small west courtyard, took a shortcut via the still room and its racks of drying herbs and flowers, emerged smelling of rosemary, climbed the stair to the west wall, went along it and then down another stair to the inner bailey, crossed that large courtyard, and climbed a set of stairs again to go into the keep and the Great Hall beyond the keep's iron-studded gate.

Tanitha was asleep on her personal carpet in front of the biggest of the hall's four enormous fireplaces, though as it was still summer, there was only a small fire lit. Like all the royal dogs, Tanitha was basically golden-colored with a blackish snout and back, though on her the black was shot with silver. Several other royal dogs lay around her, their heads rising and ears going up as Anya walked between the long trestle tables towards them. When the princess was several feet away, the three younger dogs got up, stiff-legged. They stretched and then bowed gracefully, lowering their heads onto their forepaws and wagging their tails.

"Thank you, Frosty, Surefoot, Gripper," said Anya, briefly scratching under collars and between ears, being sure to give the three dogs equal attention. "I want to talk to Tanitha, if I may."

"I'm awake," said Tanitha, opening one eye and emitting a minor snort. "I might not look it, but I'm awake. Sit down by me, Anya. You others, go and make yourselves useful somewhere."

The other dogs padded away as Anya collapsed gratefully by the side of the old dog and reached out to hug her around the neck. Tanitha put up with that for a minute or so, then turned her head and delivered some comforting licks to Anya's face, taking away the few small tears that had somehow leaked out despite the girl's best intentions.

"Now, now," said Tanitha. "So the Duke plans to send you away, and you're worried about Morven and this Prince Maggers, and finding Denholm the frog."

Anya nodded, not trusting herself to speak. She very rarely cried, but being brave *all the time* took an enormous amount of effort. Sometimes she just got tired of keeping everything together.

"We had better go for a walk," said Tanitha. She struggled to her feet, Anya subsiding off her like a dropped cloak. The dog's huge tail wagged, gently slapping the girl across the head as she got up. "Everything is always better for a walk. And we will talk."

"I haven't got time for a walk," said Anya fretfully. "I have to find Denholm before he gets eaten by a stork."

"There's always time for a walk," said Tanitha comfortably. "We will walk by the moat, and you can look for Denholm."

"I suppose I can remake the dowsing rod there," said Anya. "If Ardent brings me Denholm's hairbrush. But I'll need a new hazel stick to dip in the moat."

"Gripper will fetch one." Tanitha barked a command to the dogs who'd settled over by the door. Gripper answered with a short woof and circled away.

Anya and Tanitha went out via the dogs' secret tunnel, Anya bending down to follow Tanitha down the ramp that was hidden behind a hanging tapestry on the south wall. Several royal dogs on guard duty wuffled Anya's hands as she passed by, and she scratched their heads. The tunnel went deep under the keep, ran along under the kennels that were built against the inner bailey wall, then continued till it came out in the main gatehouse, the exit there hidden under a false windlass for the drawbridge. Tanitha nosed the catch and the large hatch lifted up, windlass and all, allowing the dog and girl to emerge. There were two royal dogs on guard here as well, and one of the castle cats, who held a rather strange balding mouse in his mouth.

The cat dropped this very dead mouse at Anya's feet and made a quick mewing speech.

"I didn't kill him, Princess. I mean, I would have, but he was already dead. At least, I might not have killed him if I'd realized who he was in time, but when a mouse runs out of a hole behind the big kitchen stove and falls over dead in front of you, instinct takes over, the claws go out, a little swipe this way, a little swipe that . . . I'm sorry."

Anya bent down and looked closely at the mouse. There was something about it that didn't look right. It took her a horrified moment to realize that he had an almost human face on his mouse body. An extra-cruel flourish to make when transforming a human.

He was one of the under-cooks, an oldish man named Harris. Anya had not known him well, since there were four under-cooks at any given time in the royal kitchen. But he had loyally worked for her parents, and perhaps even her grandparents, and now he was dead. Killed by the Duke, or as good as killed.

It was the first time, as far as Anya knew, that the Duke had transformed one of the castle staff. Visitors, strangers . . . but never anyone so close to herself, even someone like this under-cook who she didn't really know . . .

"I wondered what had happened to him," said Tanitha. "He burned the Duke's morning marmalade cake yesterday."

"Heart attack," said the cat professionally. Cats know a lot about death. "Couldn't take the transformation. Big to small, small to big, places a great strain on the heart."

"I didn't know that," said Anya, thinking of Denholm. This was another thing to worry about, besides him getting eaten. And then there was Gotfried. He was turning into an owl too often, being so frightened by the Duke.

"Oh yes," said the cat, licking his paws. He was a sooty kind of gray-black cat, but his paws were pure white. Anya was fairly sure his name was Robinson, but the cats never liked to admit to names. Being named might lead to being held responsible for something.

"Transformation's not good for the brain, either," continued Robinson. "It gets confused. Don't know if you're mouse or man after a while. Depends on the individual of course. Well, I must be off. There's starlings got into the observatory roof. Have to clean them out. With your permission, Your Highness, Your Dogship."

"Yes," said Anya and Tanitha together.

"Thank you for bringing Harris here," Anya called out as the cat zoomed away. "We'll . . . I'll ask Cook to organize the funeral."

"The Duke's magic is growing stronger," said Tanitha. "And he is using it more wildly. Let us go out into the world. The air is fresher where the Duke has not been at work."

"I don't like to just leave Harris," said Anya, looking down on the little curled-up, dead mouse with its bald patch between the ears. "He is . . . he was . . . one of my people, after all."

"Springer, go and tell Madame Harn what has happened, and ask her to come and put Harris in a little basket," instructed Tanitha. "He can lie with the flowers in the still room until this evening, when we will bury him. You'd better tell Cook as well."

Madame Harn was the castle's herbalist. Anya didn't like her very much, mainly because the woman was unfriendly to everyone. But she was efficient and would take care of Harris.

Anya and Tanitha crossed the drawbridge, but instead of walking down the cobbled road towards the village that lay in the valley below, they turned to walk alongside the moat, on the raised path between the flooded ditch and the water meadow that stretched beyond. There was no one else about, save a brown-shouldered kite high above, hovering in wait for some small creature in the grass.

"I don't know what to do, Tanitha," Anya confessed.

"Yes, you do," said Tanitha. She paused to sniff a clump of grass by the side of the path, squatted, and left her own remark for some later dog.

"I don't think I do. I mean apart from finding Denholm."

"That's the first thing established," said Tanitha. "Find the frog prince."

"Right . . ." confirmed Anya, her troubled brow relaxing a little. "One thing at a time. I have to find the frog prince and turn him back. Which could be difficult, since Morven won't kiss him for sure, and I used up all the lip balm . . ."

"One thing at a time. Always eat the food in front of you first, before looking for more. Ah, here comes Gripper with a hazel stick, and young Ardent with the hairbrush . . . and a sock."

Fortunately, Anya did not have to resort to looking inside Denholm's sock for a toenail clipping or scrap of skin, as there were several long golden hairs caught in the hairbrush. Denholm's name was also engraved on the back of the brush, with his coat of arms, so it seemed definite that this time the hair would be his.

It took only a few minutes to repeat the spell and re-create the frog-dowsing rod. When Anya stopped sneezing, she raised it up, expecting it to point to the moat. But the rod shook and twisted in her hands and she had to spin about to follow it, until the hazel stick was pointing with great certitude down the valley towards the village.

"Oh no," groaned Anya. "One of the villagers must have caught him to eat."

"But he is not eaten yet," said Tanitha. "Or so I presume. The dowsing rod would not point to a dead person?"

"No, I don't think so," said Anya.

At that moment, both of them caught sight of a man emerging from the water meadow and stepping onto the road that wound down to the village. He was barefoot and dressed in the traditional bright-yellow-and-green-striped cassock of a frog gatherer. He bore a staff over his shoulder that supported a dozen small wicker cages. Each cage contained at least one freshly gathered frog.

"Hey!" shouted Anya, springing off into a run, the dowsing rod quivering in her hand. "Frog Gatherer! Stop!"

Tanitha added some helpful barking and trotted along more sedately behind the princess. Ardent tried to run past her, but a nip at his tail made him fall into line behind the dog matriarch, where he added a few loud barks of his own. But the frog gatherer was some distance away, and evidently hard of hearing, for he did not turn around or answer Anya's shouts.

It took five minutes for the princess to catch up with him, and even when she called out right behind him, red-faced and puffing, he didn't turn around. In fact he didn't stop until Anya raced past him, turned on the spot, and held up one small commanding hand.

"Stop!"

The man jumped in the air, almost dropping his staff and all the frog baskets that hung from it.

"Princess Anya!" he bellowed. "What are you doing here?"

"Chasing a frog," Anya replied. She recognized him as the younger of the two main frog gatherers, a villager called Rob the Frogger. He hadn't been deaf when she'd spoken to him before.

"What?" roared Rob the Frogger.

"I'm chasing a frog!"

Rob frowned, carefully laid down his staff and the baskets on the road, and extracted two plugs of what looked like dried pond-weed from his ears.

"Sorry, Your Princess-ship," he said. "It's the croaking, I can't abide it. Gets me down, it does. Sometimes I think they're complaining about how they're going to be eaten. What was it you were wanting?"

"A frog," said Anya.

"Oh, a frog! You'd better come down to the house—I've been fattening up last week's catch. Some of 'em got legs like a chicken. Huge! Fried up with garlic, you can't beat—"

He stopped as his voice was drowned out in a sudden cacophony of frog croaking. It did indeed seem they could understand him and were complaining about their fate.

"It's one particular frog I want," said Anya, brandishing her dowsing rod. "A prince, as it happens. Transformed."

"Ugh," shuddered Rob. "Nasty. Fair gives me the horrors, that does. What if I sells a frog to someone and they're cooking it and it turns back—"

"I don't think that would happen," interrupted Anya firmly. "Only true love or strong magic can reverse a transformation. Not cooking. Or garlic. Now, if you wouldn't mind, I need to find the prince. Could you please separate the baskets and I'll dowse out which one is the prince?"

"Aye," said Rob. He bent down and began to untie the baskets, setting them out in a line next to the road. "Be quiet!"

The frogs did not stop croaking. Anya looked at them worriedly. Surely they couldn't *all* be transformed people, still able to understand human speech? As far as she knew, the Duke had only started transforming the castle staff that day, and there weren't enough visitors to account for so many frogs.

Tanitha and Ardent came up as Anya was pondering what to do with so many potential transformees. Ardent looked like he was about to explode from being forced to walk at the old dog's pace. As soon as Tanitha stopped and sat back on her haunches, he zoomed three times around the princess and four times along the line of frog baskets, sniffing wildly.

"Ardent!" Anya called out. "Calm down. And get away from the frogs."

"Have you found the prince yet?" asked Tanitha.

"I'm just about to," Anya answered. "But I'm wondering if more of these frogs are transformed humans. They seem to understand where they're headed, and they don't like it."

"Hmm," said Tanitha, getting to her feet again and going over to sniff at the frogs, while Anya restrained an indignant Ardent, who had instantly gone to copy the matriarch but with too much energy.

"There is only a faint scent of magic," said Tanitha. "I doubt more than one frog is transformed. Find the prince and separate him, and we will be able to tell."

Anya held out the frog-dowsing rod. It twisted in her hand, pointing to the middle of the line of frog baskets. She let it pull her ahead, until the end of the hazel stick smacked into the wicker sides of a basket that held a single large, somewhat yellowish frog, who flinched back from the sudden movement.

"That's him," said Anya. She bent down, detached the small basket from the carrying staff, and picked it up. Tanitha sniffed along the other cages from left to right then, to be sure, sniffed back the other way.

"No magic in the rest of them," she reported. "They must be ordinary frogs. They're probably just complaining about leaving the moat."

"You can have that one for a shilling," said Rob, indicating the transformed prince. "Normal price is a ha'penny, of course, but if he's special—"

"Whose moat did he come out of?" asked Anya. "Besides, you can't charge for a prince."

"You might even be considered a prince-napper," Tanitha pointed out. She leaned heavily against the frog gatherer's knee and looked up at him, her tongue lolling. "I should get Ardent to arrest you."

"C-can I? C-can I?" asked Ardent, bounding around in such a tight circle that he raised a small whirlwind of dust from the road.

"Oh well, can't blame a man for trying," said Rob with a sigh. "I don't suppose you want any regular frogs? Because like I said, I've got some prize ones back home."

"No thank you," said Anya. "I've got enough to do with this one."

She looked at the frog in the basket. Denholm turned and attempted to squeeze himself through the wickerwork. Duke Rikard's spell was obviously at work, and he was trying to get away from anyone who might be able to change him back into a man.

"I *will* give you a shilling, Rob," said Anya. "Because I want the basket, and Prince Denholm might have been harder to catch in the moat. But you'll have to wait for the money. The Duke doesn't give me my allowance."

"Ah, the Duke." Rob turned his head aside and spat on the grass. "You're going to take care of him, though, when the time is right? You and your sister?"

"Yes, I hope so," said Anya. She hadn't thought the villagers would be much affected by the Duke, mainly because she didn't think about anything very much outside the library and her own interests.

"There's many afeared he might set himself up as king," said Rob. "And then where would we be? It isn't like the old days, as my grandam used to say, the lawful days. Now it's them in charge doing whatever they want, and if they're sorcerers to boot, what they want is not good for any regular folk. Still, I suppose as long as there's dogs in the castle, all will be well. She used to say that too, my grandam. Anyhow, I must get these frogs down to my barrel."

He bowed, picked up his staff and the hanging baskets, and firmly pushed in his pondweed earplugs as the frogs began to croak again. "Happy to help!"

"Well, that's one thing done," said Anya as the frog gatherer marched off. She hadn't paid much attention to what Rob the Frogger had said, being intent on her more immediate problem of the transformed prince. Besides, how could there not be dogs in the castle? She couldn't imagine such a thing.

"I suppose I'll have to try to trick Morven into kissing Denholm," she added. "There's no more lip balm. And I have to work out how to avoid being sent away to school."

"Without true love, Morven's kiss will be useless. And in any case, you have something more important to do." Tanitha lay down on top of Anya's feet to indicate the significance of what she was going to say next. "The time has come when you must go on a Quest."

"A Quest! I haven't got time to go on a Quest, or even a non-capitalized little quest!" protested Anya. "I have so much reading to do—I mean when I can actually get back to it, after I sort out this frog . . . and I suppose I'll have to hide in the library somehow and get you all to bring me food—ow!"

She stopped talking because Tanitha had leisurely nipped her above the knee.

"You can't hide away," the elder dog informed Anya. "You can't even go back to the castle now. It is time that you sought help against the Duke. He grows in strength and power, and he clearly feels he can move against you and Morven now. This is your Quest: to find those who can help you defeat the Duke."

Anya was silent for a moment, thinking about this. Tanitha watched her with her wise old eyes, while Ardent snapped at a confused dragonfly that had followed the wet frog baskets from the moat.

"I suppose you're right," she said. "But I don't want to leave Morven here alone. I know you'll look after her, but . . ."

"The Duke is not threatened by Morven. He doesn't need to transform her or kill her. He will merely distract her with his magpie prince."

"I can't go back? I need to talk to Gotfried, fetch the books I'm reading . . ."

Anya's voice faltered as she caught Tanitha's eye.

"Why do I have to leave now?"

"Because it will surprise the Duke. He will expect you to hide in the library. If you go now, you may gain half a day's head start on any pursuit."

"Pursuit?" Anya did not like the sound of *that*.

"The Duke has his sorcery and controls the kingdom's wealth. He will transform weasels and stoats into human hunters, and buy the services of bandits and the like. You will be constantly in danger."

"Great!" said Anya bitterly. "I simply want to read my books and learn magic and get on with things and now not only am I saddled with a frog prince, I have to go on a Quest to save the kingdom from Duke Rikard and *I'm not even the oldest*. It's so unfair! Why do *I* have to do it?"

"You don't," replied Tanitha. She paused to worry a little point on her back, teeth harrowing her hair, before turning around to the princess again. "It is entirely your decision."

"Is it?" asked Anya. She extracted her feet with difficulty from under the dog and hunkered down next to her.

"It is," confirmed the wise old dog. "I can merely advise."

"What . . . what do you think my parents would tell me? My real parents."

"I think you know," said Tanitha softly.

"Father would tell me he trusted me to do the right thing, whatever it is," said Anya with a small sniffle. "I can't . . . I can't really remember Mother. I only sort of remember her voice. And something she said once, that I overheard. And her favorite shawl, the red woolly . . ."

"The red woolly," said Tanitha, nodding her head. "She wore it most evenings in winter, when her official work was done and she could put off the crown and the fur robes and play with you and Morven."

"What would she say?" asked Anya.

"She would want you to decide for yourself," said Tanitha. "I suppose you could even join forces with the Duke, if you really want to be a sorcerer."

"I don't want to be *that* kind of sorcerer," said Anya swiftly. "Besides, you wouldn't . . . you wouldn't love me then, would you?"

"We will always love you," said Tanitha. "But you would not know that if you become like the Duke. He has grown too cold from his magic, and has forgotten what it means to love."

"I haven't got any money, or spare clothes or food or anything," said Anya, changing the subject. "I need to prepare, to organize lots of things . . ."

Tanitha turned halfway around and pointed with her snout towards the castle. Anya looked up and saw three royal dogs trotting along the road, each carrying a small parcel in his or her mouth. She smiled tentatively, the smile getting wider as she saw an owl flying erratically along above them, a small book held in its powerful talons.

"I don't know where to go," continued Anya. "For help against the Duke, I mean. Who would help us?"

"The Good Wizard might, or perhaps a responsible dragon, a sensible knight, a great queen or king . . . You will have to seek out suitable allies," Tanitha advised. "That is why it is a Quest and not simply a matter of writing a letter or asking random visitors if they could help you out for a moment."

"I have to transform Denholm back as well," said Anya thoughtfully. "I made a sister promise. I can't forget that."

"No, you musn't break such a promise," Tanitha agreed. "But you can do several things at once."

"I suppose someone else might be able to transform—" Anya started to say, but was interrupted as Gotfried swooped low over her and dropped the book, almost on her head. She caught it just in time, by pure reflex. Gotfried did not stop, but looped around and headed back to the castle.

"Good luck, Princess! Recipe!"

Anya looked at the book. It was one of Gotfried's own notebooks, and written on the front in his familiar cursive script was *A Recipe: For the Making of Fairly Reliable Transmogrification Reversal Lip Balm.*

Anya's smile vanished and her face fell. "Oh," she said. "I'd hoped Gotfried might come with me. I suppose he's too scared of the Duke, and since it's my Quest, I have to go . . . alone!"

CHAPTER FIVE

The Questers Decide on a Direction

Alone?" repeated Tanitha. "I don't think so. Young Ardent
here also happens to be overdue for a Quest, so he can
accompany—"

"Me! A Quest!" barked Ardent, almost turning a somersault in
excitement. "With Princess Anya! Let's go!"

He tore off up the road for about ten yards, stopped suddenly,
and raced back, barking happily.

"Though perhaps someone a little older and more sedate would
serve better," mused Tanitha.

Ardent immediately stopped barking, sat down, and assumed
the position of Intently Listening Dog he'd learned at school. Paws
straight in front, ears up, and head tilted slightly to the side. Anya
bent down and hugged him, even letting him surreptitiously lick
her ear.

"I would love Ardent to come with me," she said. "Wherever
we're going. Oh, hello, Bounder, Jackanapes, and Flowersniffer. Thank
you for bringing me . . . er . . . whatever you have brought."

The three dogs dropped their burdens, which were revealed to
be silk handkerchiefs they'd carefully grabbed by the corners to

make bundles. Opening them, Anya discovered three marrowbones stolen from the kitchen; six small and very tarnished silver coins from some forgotten hoard; a dented gold-and-blue enamel snuffbox set with diamonds that Anya vaguely remembered as belonging to a duchess who had visited when Anya was small, who'd made a terrible fuss about it going missing; her own slightly torn second-best kirtle; a scrunched-up linen undershirt; a pair of woolen tights that were Morven's and hence too big; a small sheath knife, which Anya recognized as belonging to one of last year's visiting princes; and a leather water bottle with a black iron screw-thread stopper.

Anya put the coins and the snuffbox in her belt purse, tied on the sheath knife, and gathered up everything else except the marrowbones and put them into a bundle made with the three scarves tied together. The bones she gave to Bounder, Jackanapes, and Flowersniffer, despite Ardent's hungry look.

Tanitha, of course, was above accepting bones in public. She took Ardent aside and talked quietly to him. Whatever she said, it took the young dog's mind off bones. He sat completely still and listened carefully, with his tongue hanging out the corner of his mouth, indicating total concentration.

When Tanitha was finished talking to Ardent, she slowly walked over to where Anya was checking that her newly made bundle wouldn't come apart.

"Good luck in your Quest, Princess," said Tanitha. "We had best return to the castle."

The old dog lumbered forward and lifted her head. Anya hugged her. Tanitha nipped her ear gently and turned away. The other dogs bowed to the princess and followed the matriarch. Ardent forgot what he was meant to be doing for a few seconds and went along with them, before suddenly remembering and whipping back to Anya's heels.

"I suppose we'd better be off, then," said Anya. She found it hard to look away from the dogs and the castle. She'd never really been anywhere before, certainly not beyond the borders of her small kingdom. And while she was grateful to the dogs for bringing her some things, her practical mind thought that more money and fewer bones would have been better.

"Where are we going?" asked Ardent.

Anya wrinkled her forehead and looked down at Prince Denholm in his little wicker cage.

"I think first things first. Which means returning Denholm to human shape. But as Tanitha advised, I can do several things at once. So I suppose that we might as well head towards his kingdom to start with. His parents will presumably be grateful to have him back, and might aid me against Duke Rikard. Gornish is supposed to be a bigger kingdom than Trallonia."

Gornish *was* a bigger kingdom than Trallonia, but that was not saying much. Trallonia itself boasted only the royal castle, the castle village below it (known as Trallonia the Village), the fields around that, and two large expanses of forest with several small hamlets inhabited by woodcutters, foresters, and hunters.

That was it.

From what Anya could remember from Denholm's boasts, Gornish had a bigger castle and *two* villages, one of them with a small fishing harbor.

Anywhere else, neither Trallonia nor Gornish would be a kingdom. They'd barely rate as baronies. But long ago the High Kingdom of Yarrow had fallen apart when Yarrow the City was inundated by a tidal wave, and the entire royal family and government drowned. The wave was the consequence of evil magic, sadly the fault of the last High King, who had been dabbling inexpertly in very dark sorcery indeed. After the wave, all the nobles of Yarrow had declared themselves to be independent. There were now *scores* of kingdoms in what used to be the High Kingdom of Yarrow. Most of them could be crossed on foot in less than a day.

"How . . . how . . . howl!" called out Ardent. He stopped himself and asked, "How will you turn him back? With new lip balm?"

"I guess so," said Anya. She flipped open Gotfried's book and read the first few pages.

"Hmmm. It's not going to be easy," she said. Following the text with her finger, she read out the recipe for the Fairly Reliable Transmogrification Reversal Lip Balm.

"'To a pot or vessel of brass over a medium fire, add a pint of witches' tears, two feathers fresh-pulled from a cockatrice's tail, six pea-size stones of three-day-old hail from a mountaintop, four drops of blood from a retired druid . . . stir with a stirring rod made from the branch of a lightning-struck oak for four hours to reduce the mixture. After four hours, and preferably at dawn, put in lumps of beeswax until the mixture has the consistency of moat-monster snot, remove from fire, add pawpaw for flavor, continue mixing until smooth, put in a clean, dry tin lined with waxed paper, and keep out of direct sunlight. Makes sufficient for a dozen dozen applications (one gross).'"

Anya closed the book and frowned.

"A *pint* of witches' tears sounds an awful lot. None of these things will be easy to get."

"Moat-monster snot won't be too difficult," Ardent pointed out.

"We don't need any moat-monster snot," said Anya. "It just has to be mixed to that consistency."

She looked at Denholm in his little wicker cage.

"Why did you have to get yourself transformed?" she asked crossly. "If I didn't have to turn you back, this would be a much easier Quest."

"Glop," said Denholm, which probably wasn't an answer to anything.

"I suppose an alchemist might know where to get this stuff," mused Anya, after a moment's thought. "They might even have some of it in stock . . ."

"Where is there an alchemist?" asked Ardent.

"There might be one in Rolanstown," Anya answered hesitantly. Going on a Quest was all very well, but there were numerous practical difficulties. Rolanstown was the closest settlement of any size, but she had heard it was lawless and dangerous, like most towns in the former High Kingdom of Yarrow. And she might not have enough money to buy ingredients. The enameled snuffbox with the diamonds was probably very valuable but Anya knew it would be difficult to get a fair price for it.

Besides the dangers of the town, they would need food and shelter every night, and would have to protect themselves not only from whoever or whatever Duke Rikard sent after them, but also the usual bandits, brigands, robbers, thieves, cutthroats, kidnappers, monsters, strange creatures, stranger creatures, and impossibly strange creatures that infested the countryside beyond and between the remnant kingdoms. Without the High King and the knights, constables, and wardens of Yarrow, the roads and byways between the small kingdoms had not been safe for decades.

Anya knew a few spells that would be useful, and Ardent was a trained fighting dog with a brave heart. But even so, this Quest might well end with both of them dead, enslaved, or seriously hurt.

But at least it offered hope. Staying home offered only transformation, or certain death on the way to school in Tarwicce.

"It's as good a place to start as any, and it's in the right general direction for Gornish as well," Anya decided. "We will go to Rolanstown!"

"Where is it?" asked Ardent. He spun around in a circle, ready to go in any direction in an instant.

"West," said Anya confidently. She liked maps and had looked at lots of them in the library. She had yet to learn that a knowledge of maps, some drawn long ago and of dubious authority, is only the first step in actually knowing how to get somewhere. "Here, I'll show you."

She found a patch of bare earth nearby and began to draw with her finger.

"We're here, in Trallonia," she said. "Rolanstown lies beyond Trallon Forest . . . there is a good path through there, so we won't be getting into the ancient parts of the wood. Then I suppose we take what used to be the Royal Road that runs between Rolanstown and Edremorn, over the downs. From Rolanstown we would continue west towards the coast, and I think Gornish is somewhere here, to the north of Yarrow the City."

She thought for a moment, then dug her finger in again several times to indicate more points of interest.

"One of the older maps said something like 'Demesne of the Good Wizard' here," she said. "And I seem to remember a Blasted Heath around here. Bound to be lots of witches. I suppose I might have to get half a dozen crying to get a pint. That's not going to be easy."

"How far is it from here to there?" asked Ardent, indicating their current position and then Rolanstown with his nose.

"Two days' walk to Rolanstown, I think," said Anya. "We'll have to find somewhere safe tonight, to sleep. We'll still be in the forest then."

"I like the forest!" exclaimed Ardent. "We c-c-can go hunting!"

"No," said Anya. "We must try to be quiet and not draw attention to ourselves. Remember, Tanitha said the Duke will send enemies against us, and there are other dangers. You have to remember this. Quiet and careful at all times!"

"Quiet and c-c-careful at all times!" barked Ardent back at her, very loudly. Then, realizing what he had done, he repeated himself in a growling whisper. "I mean, quiet and c-c-careful, yes, Princess."

Anya nodded. She packed Gotfried's book with the other things in her bundle, picked it up, and swung it over her shoulder, then bent to lift Denholm in his frog basket.

"I'll cut a staff in the forest to balance this lot on," she said.

"I c-c-can c-c-arry the bag," Ardent volunteered, jumping up at her. "I c-c-can c-c-arry it!"

Anya considered just how much dog slobber would soak through the silk if Ardent carried the makeshift bag all the way through the forest to the road. But it would also make him be quiet. He meant well, she knew, and would try to remember to be quiet. But he was still not much more than a puppy.

"All right, you take the bag," she said, and handed it down. Ardent latched on with a snap. Anya winced as she thought of a new hole in her second-best kirtle, but let it go.

After all, a Quest was not supposed to be easy.

CHAPTER SIX

Ardent Smells Some Soup

By the time they reached the fringe of the forest two hours later, Anya had formed even more definite views on the hardships of Quests and was missing the cool quiet of the library. She had decided to stay off the road, but that had meant going through the fields by whatever farmer's tracks she could find, and they were winding and muddy, and the grass was destined to be hay in another month, so was already neck-high and annoying. If the field was pasture rather than grass then there were sheep, which meant she had to avoid treading on small pyramids of round droppings everywhere and also constantly remind Ardent he was not to go off and herd the sheep together. (He'd never had the chance to do so, and was quite eager to try.)

The sun was also high, and hot, and the frog basket was difficult to carry. All these things made Anya quite cross and irritable, so when they did reach the forest she almost plunged into the cool shade under the trees without looking. But fortunately her deep common sense made her stop and think about things before going on.

"We can't risk getting lost in the forest," she said to Ardent. "We'll have to take the road. But we'll walk on the side, and if we see anyone, we'll duck into the undergrowth and hide until they've passed."

"There are ducks in the undergrowth?" asked Ardent. He hadn't really been listening, because of the excitement of the sheep and various intriguing scents coming out of the trees ahead.

Anya took a deep breath and repeated her instructions.

She had been in the forest briefly before, but only with lots of other people, and she had not visited for quite a few years. It felt odd to be alone in the green silence, with just Ardent, and to be walking along the side of the dusty road rather than riding down the middle as part of a large company. But the dappled shade was pleasant, cutting back the heat of the summer sun, though at some points the road narrowed and the tree branches almost met overhead, forming long arched-over lanes that transformed the shade from being pleasantly cooling to dark and potentially dangerous.

They were passing through one of these overgrown lanes when Ardent dropped the bundle, sniffed the air, and growled quietly, "Smoke up ahead, Princess. C-c-could be an ogre picnic."

Anya stepped off the road and crouched down beside the pale trunk of a large ash, reviewing the few small spells she could cast. None seemed likely to be of much use against even one ogre.

"Can you smell ogres?"

"No . . ." said Ardent. "I c-c-an smell pea-and-ham soup, though. Ogres particularly like pea-and-ham soup—"

"So do people," said Anya crossly. "It's probably one of the foresters' cottages. There are few along this road. I thought the first one was farther away. We'll go ahead cautiously."

"I c-c-ould sneak ahead and take a sniff," Ardent offered.

"No, you stay with me. And don't forget the bundle."

"I won't!" Ardent turned on the spot to pick up the bundle that he had dropped and then forgotten.

The pair advanced cautiously along the edge of the road, ready to duck into the undergrowth at a moment's notice, as previously planned. As they got closer, they saw a thin stream of smoke rising up through the forest canopy, and the smell of pea-and-ham soup got stronger, now accompanied by the sound of human voices.

"I like pea-and-ham soup myself," said Anya, suddenly realizing that (a) she was hungry and (b) unlike at the castle, she would need to get food for herself somehow.

"So do I," muttered Ardent out of the corner of his mouth, almost dropping the bundle.

"It's probably foresters," said Anya. "But be ready."

She paused to remind herself of the two words of power used in a spell called The Withering Wind, which sounded like it would be truly fearsome but actually just caused a lot of shrieking wind noises in the ears of whoever it was cast on. Anya hoped this would be scary or distracting enough to enable her and Ardent to run away.

Creeping close, they saw there *was* a forester's cottage, a tumble-down affair of planked walls with a thatched roof, both walls and roof sporting holes. The smoke was from a fire that had been laid outside the cottage, with a large bronze cauldron suspended on an iron tripod above it, the source of the delicious pea-and-ham soup smell.

A woman had just added a pinch of something to the pot, and was stirring it in with a long, blackened stick. She was gray-haired and dressed much like the castle servants, in a plain undyed kirtle, with a rope around her middle instead of a belt. From that belt were suspended a large, somewhat battered ladle and an imposing knife in a buckskin sheath.

After they had watched for another few minutes, the smell of the soup was just too tempting. Anya stood up from her creeping crouch as they approached, and deliberately made more noise, treading on a few fallen sticks. The woman turned as she heard them, her hand falling to the handle of her knife.

"Good day, madam forester!" Anya called out.

"Good day to you," said the woman. Her hand didn't leave the knife.

"I was hoping we might buy a bowl of your soup," Anya went on.

"Two bowls," muttered Ardent, dropping the bundle. He snapped it back up before it hit the ground, this time definitely puncturing Anya's second-best kirtle. She winced, took it out of his mouth, and hung it on the end of the staff she had cut earlier, where Denholm in his little wicker cage was already suspended.

"Who are you?" asked the woman. She looked up at a nearby ancient oak and called out, "Hedric! There's a princess here with a frog and a dog!"

"I know," said a voice from above. Anya peered up towards the foliage, but couldn't see who was talking . . . until a large, long-bearded man in a green robe suddenly dangled from a branch, held on for a moment, then dropped to the ground.

"Ow," he added, bending down to massage his left knee. "I should know not to do that. Greetings, Princess."

"How do you know I'm a princess?" asked Anya.

"Anyone can tell you're a princess," sniffed the woman. She sounded quite unfriendly. "Fine kirtle, a belt purse, a royal dog walking alongside. And the frog. That's just showing off. You should kiss him right away, but I suppose you want an audience? Two of us enough for you?"

"That's enough, Martha," said the man. He had druidic tattoos of leafy vines winding around his hands and wrists, disappearing up into the sleeves of his robe. "Things aren't always what they seem."

"We'd just like to buy some soup, please," said Anya. "And I can't transform Denholm back. He's not the love of *my* life, he's my sister's. Well, he was . . . It's complicated. Are you a druid, by the way?"

She was thinking of the ingredients for the lip balm. Surely it would be too easy to just run into a retired druid straightaway . . .

"Yes," said Hedric. "Though I'm on a sabbatical right now. Between sacred groves at the moment, though I have the acorns and I expect I'll get around to planting one up sooner or later—"

"Later, I expect, just like everything else," said Martha. "I'm not any kind of druid, I'll have you know. *I* don't go around whispering to trees or helping hedgehogs with *their* problems, instead of helping their own sister, I can tell you that!"

"Now, Martha, I have tried—" the druid started to say, but Martha gave him a scowl so intense the words dried up in his mouth. He shrugged and pretended the fire under the soup pot needed tending, adding a few sticks and spreading things around.

Anya decided not to ask about retired druids, at least not immediately. Perhaps after they got some soup Martha's mood would improve.

"We'd just like to buy two bowls of soup," said Anya uncomfortably.

"What are you doing with that frog prince if you're not going to kiss him?" asked Martha.

"Well, I am going to kiss him eventually," Anya replied. "I have to make a special lip balm first, because, as I said, I'm not his true love. Look, don't worry about the soup. We'll just go."

"No soup?" asked Ardent mournfully.

Anya shook her head and began to walk away.

"Wait!" exclaimed Martha. "You said you had to make a special lip balm to transform him back? *Without* true love?"

"Yes," said Anya, not stopping. Ardent followed at her heels. He was still distracted by the smell of pea-and-ham soup, so his nose hit Anya behind the knees with every second step.

"No! Please! Wait!"

Martha scurried after Anya, lifting her apron so she could run faster. "I'll *give* you two bowls of soup, if you can help me! It's a matter of . . . of gruesome transformation!"

Anya stopped.

The old lady now had her attention.

CHAPTER SEVEN

The Ambitions of a Would-Be Thief

A nya turned on her heel. Ardent crashed into the front of her knees this time, pretended he hadn't, and got in a bit of a tangle with Anya's legs and his own tail.

"What do you need help with?" Anya asked the woman. "Oh, Ardent. Just sit down!"

Ardent sat. Martha wiped her face with her apron.

"I thought only true love could break a transformation spell, and no princess could love my boy, since none ever knew him before he was turned. I mean, how could even the nicest princess fall in love with a newt?"

"You have a boy who has been turned into a newt?" asked Anya.

"My son," said Martha, kneading the edge of her apron nervously.

"Who turned him into a newt?"

"A spell," said Martha. She looked away as she answered, and her voice grew a little shifty.

Anya frowned.

"How exactly did this happen to him?" she asked. "I can't . . . I won't help you unless you tell me the truth."

"He was just lost in the dark and he slipped on the roof—"

"Why was he on a roof?"

"He said he thought there were loose tiles, so he'd better climb up and fix them before they blew down and hurt someone. He slipped and fell down the chimney—"

"How could he fall down the chimney?" asked Anya. "And whose house was this anyway?"

"It wasn't exactly a *house*," said Martha. "At least I don't think anyone was living in it. More a meetinghouse. Anyway, poor Shrub was blinded—"

"His name's *Shrub*?"

"My husband was a druid too," Martha explained. She looked across at her brother, who was still fiddling with the fire and pretending he wasn't listening. She scowled. Clearly, druids were not popular with her.

"He liked the name Shrub. It's better than Acorn, which was his second favorite. Anyway, my poor boy was blinded by the soot from the chimney and bruised by the fall. He was simply trying to find his way out when the thief-taker caught him—"

"He was caught by a thief-taker inside someone's meetinghouse?"

"It wasn't his fault that when he was staggering around blinded he ran into a cabinet and it broke and the Only Stone fell out and went down the front of his tunic! He could have been badly hurt if it had hit him on the head!"

"Oh, come on, Ma!" called a strangely squeaky voice from inside the hut. "Tell the truth!"

"Who . . . or *what* is that?" asked Anya.

"That's Shrub," Martha said sadly.

"He can talk?" Whoever or whatever had transformed Martha's son wasn't as thorough as Duke Rikard. Anya looked at Denholm in his wicker cage. It would be handy if *he* could talk. He could tell her exactly where Gornish was, for a start. She knew roughly, but there were so many little kingdoms . . .

"Yes, he can talk," Martha replied. "It really wasn't his fault . . ."

"Yes, it was," said the voice from inside the cottage. The door creaked open and an enormous newt emerged, his huge bulbous eyes blinking against the sunlight. He was bright orange, the size of a large rabbit, and about the biggest and ugliest lizard-type thing Anya had ever seen.

"I'm Shrub," said the newt, to nobody's surprise. "And I was trying to steal the Only Stone. I'm training to be a thief. Or at least I *was*, until this happened."

Anya frowned. *The Only Stone . . .* She had a faint recollection of reading something about that. She could clearly remember the story of the One and Only Talking Salmon. And the Once and Forever Stone, now sadly destroyed. But try as she might, could not summon up anything useful on an Only Stone . . .

"What is the Only Stone?" she asked.

"A magical stone that protects the owner against dark magics," said Shrub. "That's why I'm so big and can talk. Even just sitting in the front of my tunic it half turned the transformation spell. If I'd been holding it, the spell would have failed completely."

Anya's interest was piqued. "Who owns the Only Stone, and who transformed you?"

"The stone is kept in the meetinghouse of the League of Right-Minded Sorcerers in New Yarrow," said Shrub. "But that's so no one good can use it. *Right-minded* just means *evil sorcerers*. The one that transformed me is called the Grey Mist, because he . . . or she . . . or it . . . is always surrounded by a cloud of choking gray mist. Or actually he-she-it *is* a cloud of choking gray mist. Are you really a princess?"

"I am," said Anya. Then she hesitated, wondering whether it was a good idea to reveal her identity or not. Ultimately good manners prevailed, possibly over good sense. "I'm Princess Anya of Trallonia. And this is the royal dog Ardent. We're on a Quest."

"Can you really transform me back into a human?" asked Shrub.

"If I can make a magical lip balm, I should be able to. But I'm not just going to transform anyone who asks. I mean, you admit you're a thief—"

"*In training* to be a thief," said Shrub. "A good one, though. You know, stealing from the rich, giving to the poor, that sort of thing. And I was trying to steal the Only Stone for a good reason."

"Why?"

"To give it to Bert," replied the newt, as if this explained everything.

"Who's Bert?" Anya was a little exasperated. After all, she'd only wanted to get two bowls of soup, not get caught up in a long conversation with a transformed newt, the newt's mother, and his druidic uncle.

"Bert is Roberta, the leader of ARR—the Association of Responsible Robbers. I want to join up with them, but she says I'm too young. I thought if I could steal the Only Stone and give it to her, that would prove I wasn't. Too young, I mean."

"How old are you?"

"I'm ten," said Shrub. "Next month. But I've been training to be a thief since I was six."

"If you change him back, I'll give you two bowls of soup and a big piece of ham to take with you, wrapped in cheesecloth," said Martha encouragingly.

"Yum," said Ardent.

"Hmmm," said Anya. "I'll buy the soup and think about this while we eat. Is one small silver enough?"

"Plenty!" said Martha, taking the proffered coin. She surreptitiously rubbed it on her apron to make sure the tarnished metal really was silver. "Please be seated. I'll get bowls and spoons."

Anya looked around and eventually sat on a half-rotten log that had fallen nearby, setting Denholm in his cage next to her. Ardent sat on her feet and leaned against her, already drooling.

"I could help you," said Shrub. He climbed up onto the log and sat next to Denholm, who eyed him balefully. Frogs and newts were not traditionally friends. "On your Quest. What are you questing for?"

"To get help against an evil sorcerer who wants to usurp the crown of Trallonia," Anya explained. "And to get the ingredients to make the lip balm to turn Prince Denholm back into a man."

"The Only Stone would be a great help against an evil sorcerer," said Shrub. He blinked as he spoke, and his long tongue came out and whisked across his eye.

"Perhaps," agreed Anya. "But as it is, I already have *one* evil sorcerer as an enemy. Why would I want to go up against a whole *society* of evil sorcerers? Particularly if one of them can turn into a gray mist. Or is a gray mist. That sounds really bad."

"No problem if you've got the Only Stone," said Shrub.

Anya sighed. This boy-turned-newt seemed to have an obsession that had clouded his thinking.

"It is a problem because we haven't got it and they do," she said. "Besides, I have to stay focused on getting the ingredients. One thing at a time!"

"Always eat the food in front of you first," said Ardent. He looked across at Martha, who was ladling soup into bowls, and licked the gathering drool off his lips.

"I still think you should . . . *mumble* . . . the Only Stone . . . *mumble* . . ." Shrub complained, his voice receding as Anya gave him one of her very stern looks. Anya's stern looks were legendary, and not something anyone wanted to experience twice.

"Here's your soup," said Martha, passing Anya a bowl and setting one down on the ground for Ardent. The dog made a slight lunge towards it, but managed to stop himself and look at Anya.

"Wait," she said to the dog, lifting her spoon. "Very well. Begin."

She had just got her first spoonful in her mouth when Ardent finished his bowl and started licking up the spots that had been spilled around by his frantic gulping.

"Greedy-guts," said Anya between mouthfuls. The soup was wonderfully good and did a great deal to improve her temper and outlook. Sitting down to eat also reenergized her mind, and for the first time since her hurried departure from the castle, Anya's brain began to work at its usual highly intelligent rate.

"I might be able to take Shrub along and turn him back when I make the lip balm," she told Martha. "If you can help me find one of the ingredients. Specifically, four drops of blood from a *retired* druid."

A sudden, shocked intake of breath from both Martha and Hedric wasn't what Anya was expecting. She lowered her spoon and looked at them.

"What?" she asked. "I just need four drops."

Hedric looked at the ground and shuffled his large feet. Martha took another deep breath and glanced quickly to the left and right, and then up at the sky.

"It's not something respectable people talk about," she whispered.

"What?" asked Anya. "The blood, or the retired part?"

"Druids don't really retire," said Martha, still whispering. She came closer to Anya and knelt down by her side. The princess leaned in close so she could hear. So did Ardent and Shrub—at least till his mother clapped her hands over his head to stop his ears. Then he tried to wriggle away.

"You behave, Shrub!" scolded Martha. She added to Anya, "It's not suitable for children to hear, you know."

"I'm a child," said Anya. "Technically."

"But you're a princess," said Martha.

"Yeeees," said Anya doubtfully. "Why is talking about retired druids unsuitable for children?"

"Druids don't retire," said Martha. "They either die with their sickles on, so to speak, or they . . ."

She took another deep breath.

"They what?" asked Anya.

"They take up with the tree spirits," mumbled Martha. "And, you know, become one."

"They become tree spirits?"

"No, they become a tree! With a tree spirit, ahem, living in it. Together."

"That doesn't sound terribly bad," said Anya. "I expect it's quite nice for both of them."

"No, no, no," said Martha. "It's not the done thing. Some of them don't even become oaks. They turn into beeches or pines or even . . . even chestnuts."

"I suppose the blood would be the sap," said Anya thoughtfully.

"Don't you talk about sap in front of my newt!" exclaimed Martha, shocked.

"He can't hear us anyway," said Anya.

"Yes I can," said Shrub, twisting out of his mother's hands.

"Well, I guess I need to get four drops of sap from a tree that used to be a druid," said Anya. "Do you know where one is?"

Martha stood up, crossed her arms, and frowned.

"I can't help Shrub otherwise," said Anya firmly.

Martha's mouth twisted about as if it was fighting itself, before finally opening.

"Oh well, I suppose he had to know sometime," she said.

"Who?" asked Anya.

"Shrub," said Martha with a sniff. "It's his own father who's become an ex-druid! He's turned into a chestnut tree and is living with a dryad called Elisandria!"

She burst into tears and fled into the cottage.

"I already knew all that," said Shrub companionably, shrugging his newt shoulders, which looked quite disturbing. "Uncle Hedric told me ages ago. I've even been to see my old dad and everything, though he don't talk much now, being a tree."

"You don't listen properly," said Hedric. "Chestnuts talk a lot, they do. Compared to an elm, say, or a willow. Willows talk so quiet, and they lisp. If you listened—"

"I'm not a druid, Uncle," said Shrub crossly. "Don't want to be one, neither. I'm a thief."

"You're a newt right now," Anya pointed out. "And likely to stay that way unless I help. Is your father nearby?"

"Edge of the forest, above the downs," Shrub answered. "Maybe five miles from here. Got to know the right path, though—he's not near the road."

"The downs are the low hills between the forest and Rolanstown, right?" asked Anya, trying to picture the map in her head. "And I suppose you know the path?"

"Course I do." Shrub raised one webbed limb. "Like the back of my hand . . . my foot."

"He does know the paths," said Hedric. "Been a wanderer ever since he was six, that boy, causing his mother no end of apprehension. If you can help Shrub, Princess, it would be greatly appreciated. Poor Martha has been beside herself, what with Dannith . . . retiring himself . . . and this transformation business."

Anya thought for a moment. She hadn't planned on recruiting a newt to their questing party, but Shrub might be useful in some way. If he could get over his obsession with the Only Stone, and if he could help her get the ex-druid's blood before they even got to Rolanstown to find an alchemist, they'd be ahead.

"Very well," she said. "But you must agree to follow my orders, Shrub. No independent thievery, you understand?"

"You'll turn me back into a boy?"

"When I get all the ingredients for the lip balm." Anya grimaced, thinking about kissing a newt. That would be even worse than kissing a frog. She also vaguely recalled that newts were poisonous, or had poison slime on their backs or something. "I will turn you back."

As she spoke, the wind shifted around the clearing, lifting the lower branches of the surrounding trees with a sudden susurration of leaves. Which is a fancy word for rustling. Ardent's nose twitched and his head turned swiftly. He let out a single sharp bark and leaped at the undergrowth, twisting around in the air to attack something hidden there.

"Princess Anya Plans to Kiss Lizard!" shouted a nervous, out-of-breath voice, accompanied by the sound of branches snapping, Ardent's deep barking, and the bark-shredding noise of someone desperately climbing a tree.

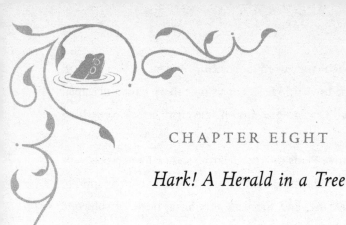

CHAPTER EIGHT

Hark! A Herald in a Tree

Anya turned around, the words for the Withering Wind spell on her lips, to see Ardent just missing out on delivering a tremendous bite to the foot of a man who was ascending a tree as if his life depended on it.

Which quite possibly it did.

"Herald Assaulted by Vicious Hound!"

Anya looked up at the long-limbed tatterdemalion who had successfully reached a fork between the trunk of the oak and a long, reaching branch. A man neither old nor young, with a thin beard and a draggling moustache, he wore a parti-colored jacket that was yellow on one side and red on the other, and his legs were encased in hose that were blue on the left and green on the right. It was not a pleasing combination, made still worse by the grubby hat he wore, which resembled a stiffened nightcap and might have been striped like a rainbow if it was clean. It was hard to tell in its current state.

Anya knew who he was, because he had been thrown out of the castle more than once in the past few years: a wandering herald, who traveled through all the little kingdoms spreading news and gossip. Most of the "news" he spread sounded to Anya as if it was entirely made up.

"Gerald the Herald," she said. "I don't suppose there is anything I can say or do that will make you forget what you've overhead?"

"Princess Tries to Suppress News!"

"Can you please stop talking like that?" asked Anya.

"Herald's Announcements All the Rage in New Yarrow!" said Gerald. He took a breath and shouted, "Death-Wish Princess Takes On Duke!"

"What do you mean by 'Death-Wish Princess'?" Anya did *not* like the sound of that.

Gerald reached inside his yellow sleeve, pulled out a slip of parchment, crumpled it into a ball, and threw it down to the princess. Anya unraveled it and saw the familiar handwriting of the Duke, with its tiny, pinched letters interspersed with grandiose capitals and emphases. It said simply:

> *Herald. Spread* WORD *to suitable Blackguards,*
> MALCONTENTS, *Assassins, rotters,*
> HOBDEHOYS, *evil witches, and No-goodniks as*
> *follows: "Huge* REWARD *for head of Princess Anya.*
> *Not* NECESSARILY *attached. 200* GOLD *Nobles.*
> *Apply Duke of Trallonia."*

"Had it by raven two hours ago," said Gerald with a sniff.

"Why show this to me?" asked Anya suspiciously. "And how did you find me?"

"I'm a herald, I am, and heralds spread the news. Knew there must be news behind this, so here I am. What's going on? Princess Flees Vengeful Stepstepfather? Anya Devotes Short Life to Transformed Amphibians?"

"How did you find me?" Anya persisted. She looked around the clearing, at all the oaks gathered close with the undergrowth so thick between them. If Gerald the Herald was already on her track, Duke Rikard's assassins might be as well. She'd thought she would at least get the rest of the day and the night as a head start.

"Nose for news," said Gerald, tapping his admittedly long nose with his forefinger. "And . . . ah . . . I was lucky. On my way to Trallonia to look into the story and thought I'd stop by Martha's for some pea-and-ham soup. That *is* pea-and-ham soup I smell, right? Sometimes she makes leek and barley and I don't like that half as much."

"Not as good as pea-and-ham soup," Ardent agreed.

It was entirely possible, Anya thought, that Gerald the Herald did have a nose for news—some inherent magic that led him to important events or people when things were happening, in much the same way that smiths could sense bad metal and could not be beaten in a fistfight fought at a crossroad.

Anya kept looking. There was something odd about Gerald's hair and moustache, and his face for that matter. He didn't quite look the same as he had the last time she'd seen him. Anya peered more intently, tilting her head on one side just like Gotfried did when he was in owl shape and thinking hard about something.

"You're wearing a wig," she observed. "And a false moustache. You're not Gerald at all!"

"Oh, yes I am!" said the man indignantly. "I am one of the three duly certified and paid-up Gerald the Heralds for Trallonia, Revania, Monstonbury, and Trallon Forest."

"What?" asked Anya. "There's more than one Gerald the Herald?"

"Hundreds," said the man. "Across the land. Always vacancies too, if you've a mind to become one. Dangerous profession, spreading the news. But honorable. Now tell me straight, Princess—what's with the transformed frog and the newt?"

"None of your business," said Anya. "Get out of that tree and be on your way!"

"News is my business," said Gerald, holding up an admonishing finger. "A princess running away with two transformed humans is news. Big news. So what's going on?"

"I can't tell you," said Anya stiffly.

"But you're going to turn them back, right?" Gerald leaned forward eagerly and almost fell. Ardent reflexively jumped up at him, snarling, before settling back to watch, as if the man was a rabbit about to emerge from a hole. "I heard you talk about a magic lip balm. You'll kiss them, right?"

"I have nothing to say," said Anya. "Ardent, let Gerald down so he can be on his way."

"Princess Anya Is the *Frogkisser!*" bellowed Gerald. "Transformees Flock to Princess for Chance to Regain Humanity!"

Anya looked at Denholm and Shrub. *Hardly a flock*, she thought. Which was just as well. She turned to Hedric.

"On second thought, perhaps we shouldn't let the herald go. Can you keep him here for an hour or two, while *we* go?" she asked. "He'll lead the Duke to us, even if he doesn't mean to."

"Aye, I can do that," said Hedric. "I've no fondness for heralds. Too loud in the greenwood, they are."

He strode over to the trunk of the oak and laid his hand against the bark. The tattoos on his arms shivered as he did so, the leaves moving as if in response to a sudden breeze.

"What are you doing?" asked Gerald nervously. "Dangerous Druid Frightens Herald!"

Hedric whispered something to the oak. A strand of mistletoe, previously unnoticed on the trunk or perhaps not even there before, shook in answer and began to twine its way up towards the herald, who squeaked and began to climb higher.

"Come on," said Anya to Ardent and Shrub. "Lead the way, Master Newt."

"What about the ham wrapped in cheesecloth?" asked Ardent anxiously, pointing with his nose towards the hut. "And shouldn't Shrub say good-bye to his mother as well?"

"Quickly, then," said Anya. "There might be assassins or hunters looking for us right now, if other Geralds have spread the news."

"Mother!" called out Shrub, not bothering to go near the hut. "I'm off now. Bring the ham!"

"Go over there and ask her nicely," said Anya. She still felt the long-ago loss of her own mother keenly and didn't approve of treating any mother in such a careless manner.

"She heard me," Shrub grumbled.

Ardent growled and lowered his head towards the newt. One bulbous eye rotated and looked up at Anya, who was frowning deeply. Her eyebrows were drawing together, the beginning of one of her stern looks forming on her face.

"I mean, I'm just going over now," he said hurriedly, then lumbered over to the hut, sliding around the half-open door with a flick of his tail.

"Badly trained puppy," said Ardent with a sniff.

"We'll fix that," said Anya. She was already having serious misgivings about taking Shrub with them and was wondering whether it might be better if she left him here and promised to stop past once she had made the lip balm. But then, he did know the way to his father, the ex-druid, and they would presumably be more likely to get four drops of blood if he was with them.

"Ble-blup," said Denholm. Anya glanced back over her shoulder to the frog in his cage hanging from the end of her staff. She'd have to catch some bugs for him to eat soon, and pour some more water over him. Which reminded her they needed a bigger water bottle. She'd already had to refill the small one twice at the streams they'd crossed, and that with only her drinking from the bottle. Ardent drank straight from the watercourses, or in fact any old puddle, but there might not be so many ahead, particularly once they were on the downs heading to Rolanstown.

Questing really does require quite a lot of equipment and preparation, Anya thought. Most of which she didn't have or had missed doing. She was having to work a lot of it out along the way.

Possibly this was the difference between an adventure and a mere expedition, considered Anya. She would have preferred the latter, with several weeks to prepare, and lists made in the comfort of the library, and things checked off.

Shrub reemerged from the hut with Martha behind him. She was sniffling into a large tartan handkerchief. Anya was relieved to see she held the wrapped piece of ham in her other hand, some distance from her dripping nose. She handed the ham over and Anya tied it to the end of her staff. It was quite heavy, and she flexed her shoulder, anticipating that it would be sore before she walked much farther.

"Princess Worn Down by Heavy Load!"

Gerald the Herald had climbed as high as he could in the oak, pursued by the slowly creeping mistletoe. But he was still true to his profession.

"You be a good boy . . . a good newt for the princess," said Martha, snuffling away. She bent down to kiss Shrub's head, flinching back at the last moment when she remembered he was poisonous.

"I will, Ma!" said Shrub, not very convincingly.

"I'll bring him back as a boy, not a newt," Anya promised. "As soon as I can. Thank you for the soup and the ham."

"Thank you," repeated Ardent. He only just managed to look away from the tantalizing lump of meat dangling above his head to bow towards Martha.

"Good fortune!" called out Martha, now moving from snuffling to full-on sobbing. "Good fortune and come back human!"

Shrub muttered something and began to head off down the road. Anya waved at Martha, then followed, with Ardent close by her heels looking up at the ham every few seconds until Anya told him to range ahead.

"This way!" called out Shrub. "We go along the road for a bit and then take the path by the fallen silver birch."

Anya followed the newt. Behind her, Gerald the Herald started up again, his voice growing fainter as they headed down the road.

"The Frogkisser Sets Forth! Herald Detained by Druid Accomplice! More News to Come! Thousands Eagerly Await Raven Dispatch from Field Correspondent!"

He paused for a breath and then added, "Deadly Duke's Killers Swarm in Search of Princess!"

CHAPTER NINE

This Never Happens to the Other Assassins

T he fallen silver birch was not much more than a faded, ancient trunk that had come down long ago. It lay by the side of the forest road, angling off into the darker interior. Shrub led the way alongside it, and then onto a path that Anya didn't think she would have noticed, or even called a path, since it was little more than relatively bare patches of undergrowth every few paces, like stepping-stones through a close green sea.

Several times as she followed along behind the lizard, Anya was tempted to ask Shrub if he was really sure he knew where he was going. But she didn't, as he seemed confident, never hesitating when other paths crossed their way, including paths that were much more distinctly formed.

Both newt and dog found it easier going than the princess. She was hampered by her staff, bundle, frog cage, and ham, and also just by her size. Unlike the others, she couldn't always slide under a fallen log or squeeze between the trunks of two trees that were practically embracing.

By the time the sun began to set, Anya was very tired, very scratched, very sweaty and dirty, and feeling ever more cross that she had been forced out of her pleasant home and her quiet library to go on not just one Quest but what was rapidly becoming a whole series of interconnected Quests. She had also drunk almost all her water and was hungry again. The soup felt like it had happened a very long time ago.

"Not far now," said Shrub. "It's starting to open up."

Anya gave a little snort of annoyed disbelief. The forest seemed as thick as ever, perhaps even thicker now that the light was fading. It was just as well Shrub was bright orange, or she could have easily lost him, and thus her way. Though Ardent would undoubtedly come back for her and track the newt by smell—

She stopped, because Ardent had stopped and *was* smelling something. His head was up in the air and he was sniffing away, moving his head from side to side.

"What is it?" whispered Anya.

"Man," said Ardent, the word half a growl. "And oiled steel. Also onions."

"You can smell a frying pan?" asked Anya.

"No, oiled steel probably a weapon," Ardent reported. "Sword or dagger. Onion on breath. He's up a tree a bit ahead."

"Shrub! Shrub!" Anya hissed at the newt, who had paused but was about to continue on his way again. She waved him back, and they hunkered down close together by the bole of a huge oak to have a hurried, whispered conference.

"There's someone up a tree ahead," said Anya. "Could be an assassin, one of Rikard's hired murderers."

Shrub shook his head.

"We're in Bert's part of the woods. There's no way she'd let any old murderer attack us."

"Maybe she doesn't know he's there," said Anya. "Ardent says he's hidden up a tree."

"She'd know," Shrub replied with some confidence.

"True," said a deep voice. All three of the questers jumped, just as there was the thrum of a bowstring, followed a moment later by a scream and the thud of someone falling out of a nearby tree.

Anya slowly stood up and turned around. A dark-skinned woman dressed in forest-green leathers with a sword on her hip and a longbow and quiver on her back was standing on one of the lower branches of a lesser tree. Another slighter woman who wore similar clothes but in a russet shade stood close behind her. There were more armed women and men on both sides of the path.

"Bert, I presume," said Princess Anya, bowing to the woman in forest green. Ardent followed her example, looking rather embarrassed that he hadn't smelled out what appeared to be a very large number of members of the Association of Responsible Robbers. (They had been downwind of him, so he was not actually derelict in his duty.)

"Yes, I am Roberta, leader of ARR. And as everyone does, you may call me Bert. I take it from the Gerald the Herald we spoke to earlier that you are Princess Anya, sworn enemy of Duke Rikard of Trallonia and defender of transformees?"

"Um," said Anya, "I *am* Princess Anya. And definitely sworn enemy of Duke Rikard, though I wouldn't call him 'of Trallonia,' much as he'd like to be. I'm not a defender of transformees, as such— I just have to change back Prince Denholm and . . . er . . . now Shrub as well."

"So you're not helping *all* transformed humans?" asked Bert.

"Well, I hadn't planned to," Anya admitted. "This just sort of happened, starting with Denholm . . ."

She stopped talking as two Responsible Robbers dragged a moaning, black-clad man through the bushes and laid him down at Bert's feet. He had been wearing a mask but it had slipped, revealing a very ordinary face, currently screwed up with pain. The cause of this was an arrow in his shoulder, a cloth-yard shaft from a longbow, undoubtedly shot by one of Bert's people.

"An assassin," said Bert. "From the city. They never learn that black isn't very sensible up a bare tree in daylight."

"I've got nothing to say," said the assassin, suppressing a groan.

"I haven't asked you anything yet," Bert pointed out. "But now that you mention it, would you like that arrow taken out and the wound dressed?"

"Yes, yes, I would," said the assassin.

"So you have got something to say," said Bert.

"You're tricky," said the assassin admiringly.

Anya rolled her eyes. He wasn't a very smart assassin.

"Oh well," the assassin went on, "I might as well talk! This never happens to any of the others. I mean, shot by a robber! We're meant to be on the same side, robbers and thieves and assassins and all. Why are you interfering in the course of my legitimate business?"

"Because we are *not* on Duke Rikard's side," said Bert. "Or on the side of anyone else involved with the League of Right-Minded Sorcerers."

"Is he?" Anya interrupted. "Rikard, I mean. Involved with those sorcerers who turned Shrub into a newt?"

"Paid-up member of the League," said Bert. "I'm surprised you didn't know. They all specialize in transformation, and they have big plans. Not just taking over little places like your Trallonia."

"What do you mean?" asked Anya.

"They want all of it," said Bert, stretching out her arms to encompass the forest, the sky, and everything beyond. "All of the old High Kingdom of Yarrow. Can you imagine everything ruled by cold sorcerers who've gone beyond any human feelings? Some of them have even gone beyond having human *bodies*, like the Grey Mist."

"So he really is just a cloud of mist?"

"She is," confirmed Bert.

"Well, if I'd known all that, I never would have taken the job," the assassin declared indignantly. "Head office never tells us anything! I just get a raven with a message to give me the job number, the target, and so on. No background—that's the trouble with the assassination business. No big picture. I never should have signed up. Should have been a public executioner like my mum. Now there's a steady, safe job—"

"Take him away," Bert ordered. "Bandage him up and drop him off on the Rolanstown road."

"Thank you kindly!" called out the assassin as he was carried away. He waved awkwardly at Anya as well. "No hard feelings, Princess. Glad I didn't get to finish you off."

"Not as glad as I am," said Anya. She looked speculatively at the leader of the robbers. Though Bert was very old from Anya's point of view, perhaps even thirty or thirty-five, she was clearly as tough a forester and highway robber as ever walked the earth. Yet she also was no ordinary robber, with her association and its ideal of only robbing from the rich to help the poor, as well as her hatred of evil sorcerers.

Her robbers were well disciplined, well armed, and, even just from the ones she could see, there appeared to be quite a lot of them. They would be perfect allies to join in the fight against Duke Rikard. Anya was just about to mention this when Bert forestalled her.

"So, Princess Anya. You know that I lead the Association of Responsible Robbers?"

"Yes," said Anya.

"We steal from the rich and give to the poor."

"Yes."

"Well, you're a princess. That puts you with the rich."

"What?" asked Anya. "I'm not . . ."

Her voice trailed off as she was hit with the sudden realization that compared to most of the folk of Trallonia she *was* rich, even when Duke Rikard didn't hand over her pocket money. She had three hearty meals a day, and good clothes, and a very comfortable place to live. There were servants who looked after her, and would do even more than that if she let them. Basically, she *was* rich.

"Um, I suppose you're right," said Anya slowly. She'd never thought about her own good fortune compared with that of the ordinary folk before, and felt a sense of unease that perhaps she *should* have made herself more aware of what was going on outside her library and beyond the castle walls.

"I don't have a lot of valuables on me at the moment, though," she continued, "and I need the ones I have for my Quest. Could you perhaps agree to rob me later? I mean, afterwards, once I've transformed Prince Denholm and Shrub back, and defeated Duke Rikard."

"Perhaps," said Bert. "The 'rob from the rich, give to the poor' is more of a general overview than a specific thing we have to do every time. It really means making sure those who have too much do some sharing with those who have too little, and it isn't always just about valuables or money or even basic things like food. It is also about sharing power and opportunities."

Anya's forehead wrinkled.

"I'm not sure I know what you mean," she said uncomfortably.

"Well, you are a princess, and thus uneducated in certain areas," said Bert. She smiled, which took a little of the sting out of her words. Anya thought of herself as highly educated. She was going to be a sorceress, after all, and had read at least two hundred books.

"We will talk about this some more," said Bert. "Later. You should come to our camp, for dinner and to sleep tonight. The forest is never really safe, and more assassins might be about. There is also someone I want you to meet."

"Thank you," said Anya. She hesitated before adding, "We accept your kind invitation."

"It's not exactly an invitation." Bert gestured at the many green- and russet-clad robbers around them, standing silently by, all of them armed to the teeth with longbows, swords, axes, daggers, and one who even had something that looked like a scythe. "I'm not giving you a choice. We may still decide to rob you after all."

Ardent growled and the hair all along his back stood up. Anya let her hand fall lightly on his head, and the rumbling in the dog's deep chest subsided. Even if Bert did take her few silver coins and the snuffbox, right at that moment Anya thought this would be a worthwhile trade for a decent dinner and the prospect of a restful sleep in some sort of bed, rather than curled up with a dog, a frog, and a cold-blooded, poison-skinned newt in a hole under a tree, which had been her likely prospect for the night.

Besides, she was curious about what Bert meant when she

talked about sharing things between those who had too much and those who had too little, and how, being a princess, she was uneducated. This was a challenge. Anya couldn't bear not knowing about something once it was mentioned. If this *was* something new to learn, then she would learn it.

"Follow me," said Bert. "Stay close. The path is tricksome. It gets dark under the trees early, and the silver moon is not up for hours."

Before too long, it was completely dark, and Anya had to hold the back of Bert's belt, stumbling along behind the leader of the robbers. Ardent followed at her heels, occasionally offering useful instructions a moment too late, like "watch out for that sticking-up tree root."

After what felt like at least an hour or even two spent stubbing her toes and shins and getting her face scratched by brambles, Anya couldn't help herself.

"Will we be there soon?" she asked.

"Very soon," said Bert. She slowed, so Anya had time to react and not crash into her, then stopped. "We will wait here for a few minutes. It will be easier . . . and safer for you . . . to go on when there is some moonglow. Look to your right."

Anya blinked off into the darkness. At first she couldn't see anything at all, not even vague shapes. She held her hand up in front of her eyes and couldn't even see her fingernails.

"I can't see a thing," she protested. "It's too dark."

"Wait, just a few moments more," said Bert softly.

Anya kept peering into the darkness. Ardent made an interested wuffling noise by her side, indicating that he saw something. Shrub made a sound too, and even Denholm let out an unexpected and slightly eerie croak.

"What?" asked Anya, irritated that they were all reacting to something she couldn't sense. "I still can't see a . . ."

Her voice trailed off. There was a shimmer in the sky above her, the delicate hint of light, slowly becoming a pearly glow. As Anya watched, the faint curve of the small moon, the silver moon, rose and split the sky into two halves, of light and darkness, delineating the horizon she couldn't see before. It continued to rise, the beautiful light beginning to etch out details. Anya saw the outlines of tall trees and tumbled rocks that looked white in the moonlight. They were fallen in a line around the edge of a bare hill, and there was a broad stair of damaged stone leading up to the crest.

"We go up, and then down," said Bert. "Only a little way now."

Robbers ranged ahead of them, not all going up the steps, but some taking the harder way up the slope, slipping between clumps of briars and thorny bushes.

Bert went carefully up the cracked and crumbling steps, Anya and her companions following. The silver moon climbed too, for it was the fast moon, crossing the horizon in a matter of hours. The larger and slower blue moon would follow, but it shed little light by comparison with its silver companion, and if it was low in the sky it could often hardly be seen.

At the top of the steps, Anya expected to find the crest of the hill, but instead she found herself on the lip of a great bowl of worked stone, with one half terraced into at least twenty or more levels going down to a large flat area some seventy or eighty feet below. There was a well-shielded fire burning down there, and Ardent was stretching out already, nose quivering at the scent of cooking meat.

"Oh!" Anya exclaimed. "It's a theater!"

She had seen drawings of the buildings left by the ancients who had preceded the current inhabitants of Yarrow, but she had never seen any firsthand. Whoever the ancients were, they had worked in stone, leaving behind a legacy of ruins dotted about the country. Many of those ruins were of amphitheaters or arenas, always semicircular in shape, with a dozen or more terraces for the audience to sit and watch the stage below.

"Yes," said Bert. "It is only one of our camps. We sleep where spectators once sat, and it is deep and hidden, so none can see our fire from afar. Come—there will be hot water for washing, and nettle tea, with roast boar and rabbit and wild yams cooked in the ashes, with honey cakes to follow."

Anya needed no encouragement, and it clearly took all of Ardent's training to keep him at her heels rather than racing ahead to snatch a piece of roasting boar straight off the spit.

"You know, since I turned into a newt, I only want to eat bugs," said Shrub conversationally as they climbed down. "I wonder if I'll still like 'em when I turn back. The shiny black ones are really nice and crunchy. I might go off and hunt some down if that's all right."

"Some bugs are good," said Ardent. "But not as good as roast boar or rabbit."

"If you could catch some bugs for Denholm too, that would be helpful," said Anya. "I don't think he gets enough from ones that go near his cage, and I can't let him out. The spell will make him run away from me."

"Don't leave the theater, Shrub," instructed Bert. "The sentries will turn you back, but I don't want them bothered. Or you shot by accident."

"I'll behave," called out Shrub, angling off along one of the terraces, already looking into the darker corners. "I promised Ma, didn't I?"

Down at the stage level, Bert showed Anya where she could lay down her staff, bundle, and frog cage. The princess offered the wrapped ham as a contribution to the dinner, but Bert refused it. Anya set it down with a firm admonishment to Ardent that he was to leave it alone.

"There is a necessary trench over that side," said Bert, pointing to the far end of the stage where the stone pavers had broken to reveal bare earth. "Take care you do not fall in, and use the small shovel to throw some dirt after your business. The barrel on the way back, there, has water and soap. It will be warm, or warmish at least. When you are ready, come to the fire for food and drink."

Anya poured some water from her bottle over Denholm before she went to the toilet herself. Ardent loped ahead to investigate, adding his own contribution. A robber brought over some steaming-hot water in a large pot and topped up the barrel just before Anya washed her face, neck, and hands, so it really was warm, and the soap, though unscented, was not the harsh, scratchy square she anticipated.

At the fire, she was handed a wooden plate loaded with roast meat, roast yams, and some wild forest greens she didn't recognize but which tasted pleasantly peppery. Ardent got a plateful too, and ate almost decorously at Anya's feet as she stood among the robbers, trying not to gulp the food down herself. When she was finished, she joined a line of robbers to wash the plates clean, and to receive a cup of nettle tea, ladled out of one of the several cauldrons that were bubbling over the long fire pit.

As Anya drank that down, one of the robbers, a young man with a mischievous face and a questionable moustache, came to talk to Bert. His hair was red, even in the moonlight, which faded most colors into shades of gray and silver.

"Music tonight, Captain?" he asked.

Bert didn't answer for a moment before she slowly nodded.

"Let's have another hand of sentries out first, Will, what with Duke Rikard up to no good with his assassins and the like. And no drums—we'll keep it a bit quieter."

Five of the robbers picked up their bows and went up the terraced side of the arena to spread out around the rim of the hill. Anya heard owl calls, and thought for a moment Gotfried might have somehow found her, before she realized they were either wild owls or more likely the robbers signaling to one another.

"Come up and sit by me," said Bert, taking up her weapons again. She climbed up to the second terrace, where a pile of new-cut ferns made a comfortable long seat upon the stone, and probably a bed later. Anya followed, with Ardent close by. Shrub was still presumably off hunting bugs.

Bert put her bow and quiver down first, before she sat, and made sure her sword was arranged not just comfortably, but so she could draw it as she stood. Anya noted her caution, and turned her own knife so she could pull it out easily even when sitting. Such caution seemed like a good idea not just for a robber, but also a princess stalked by assassins and sorcerous servants.

Down below, on the stage, other robbers were taking out instruments. Three produced lutes from their backpacks. A group of four produced wooden pipes of different lengths, though all had curved ends. Anya recognized them as crumhorn players, and leaned forward. She liked the buzzing sound of crumhorns. They were joined by two robbers on shawms, one of them already playing a soft melody, the plaintive woodwind sound suddenly the loudest noise in the whole theater.

"Music is a great balm," whispered Bert as the other players slowly joined the first shawm, building on that simple tune, reinforcing it and winding around and about it, making it both more complicated and simpler at the same time. "Another thing evil sorcerers give up. They cannot abide music, for it can conjure all human emotions, most particularly joy and happiness."

"Did someone tell you I was learning magic?" asked Anya uncomfortably. She felt rather like she was about to be lectured by a stern tutor, though she'd never really had a teacher. Apart from Gotfried, and he never lectured anyone. She had read about stern tutors in stories, though.

"I hear things," said Bert quietly. She was watching the musicians, not looking at Anya. The robbers below were smiling now, their spirits lifted by their music. The tune had become merrier and faster, like a fire given new fuel, rising higher and brighter.

Will, the robber with the red moustache, began to sing. His voice couldn't compare with Prince Maggers's, but it was warmer, more human. He sang softly. Anya couldn't make out the words, and it wasn't a tune she knew. But she liked it. She liked it a lot.

"I never want to be an evil sorcerer," said the princess firmly. She could feel the music inside her, stripping away her weariness and fear. Ardent was leaning against her leg, warm and comforting, his ears pricked up. It was probably lucky there were no trumpets, because Anya knew the dog wouldn't be able to resist joining in. Some trumpeters didn't mind, but most didn't realize Ardent was also making his own music and not protesting the noise. "I could never give up music, or . . . the things I love."

"That is a good thing to remind yourself, and to ask yourself whenever you are tempted to use magic," said Bert. "Now, we need to talk. Like I said, I hear things, but I need to know more. What is your Quest, exactly? And what is your plan?"

"Then you will decide whether to put off robbing me or not?" asked Anya.

"Then I will decide whether to *help* you or not." Now Bert did look at Anya, and her rather harsh face was momentarily transformed by a smile. "We shall see."

Anya took a deep breath, and told Bert everything.

CHAPTER TEN

In Which Princess Anya's Responsibilities Might Be Increased

So," said Bert. "You intend to find these ingredients for your magical lip balm, turn Denholm and Shrub back into humans, and also find allies against Duke Rikard. What then?"

"Well, we'll fight Duke Rikard," said Anya. "Defeat him. If I have the lip balm, his greatest sorcery will be no use because I'll be able to change back anyone he transforms. But I'll need allies to fight any soldiers he has, because he'll hire men, and transform animals into fighters, and he might have quite a lot by the time I get back."

"I meant what do you intend to happen after you defeat Duke Rikard?"

A puzzled frown gathered together across Anya's forehead.

"Morven will be queen, and I'll go back to studying in the library."

Bert nodded slowly. "Will Morven be a good queen?" she asked.

"Um," said Anya, flustered. "She's the oldest . . ."

Bert's eyes opened wider, questioningly. "And that makes her fit to rule? Tell me, in your reading, do you study history?"

"Not really," said Anya. "There isn't very much in our library. I don't know why not."

"It is because the little kings and queens of Yarrow typically don't like to be reminded that they were once merely nobles, or mayors, or sheriffs," said Bert, shaking her head and pursing her lips. "And most particularly they do not like to be reminded that once there was a code of laws that limited what they could do to their 'subjects,' who were once not subjects, but *citizens* of the kingdom."

"I don't know anything about that," said Anya uncomfortably. She didn't like admitting ignorance.

"Of course you don't," said Bert. "Very few children or even adults now know anything about the All-Encompassing Bill of Rights and Wrongs in the High Kingdom of Yarrow. But once, it laid down the rights and obligations of the ruler of the kingdom to their people, and the ordinary folk did not have to fear such as Duke Rikard or your sister. Or even yourself."

"Fear *me*?" asked Anya, astonished. "Why would they fear me?"

"If you were queen of Trallonia you could have anyone there imprisoned or executed—or you could tax them everything they own, could you not?"

"I suppose so," said Anya. "Only I wouldn't."

"What about your sister, Morven?" asked Bert. "I have heard she likes pretty things. What if she heard of a dress made from cloth of gold and trimmed with emeralds, and she didn't have enough money on hand to buy it? Would she tax the villagers and farmers to get the gold, even if it beggared them?"

Anya was silent for quite a long time.

"I think the dogs wouldn't let her," she said. "But . . . but she might try."

"The dogs may only advise. Not decide," Bert pointed out. "They would try their best, it's true. At least they remember the Bill."

She glanced over at Ardent, who had been given a bone by a kindhearted robber who missed his own dog. The royal dog was contentedly gnawing it near Anya's feet, but he was still listening.

"The All-Encompassing Bill of Rights and Wrongs?" he said now. "Have to recite it twice a year, c-c-closest full moon to midsummer and midwinter. Over at the old stone circle on the Hanging Hill. Tanitha leads the recitation and then we howl."

"I always wondered what that howling was about!" exclaimed Anya. "Why didn't I get to go? I like howling too."

Ardent shrugged.

"I don't know. It's a dog thing, the reciting. No humans c-c-ome."

"It doesn't sound like a dog thing at all!" protested Anya. "What are these rights and obligations in this All-Encompassing Bill of Rights and Wrongs?"

Ardent looked at his bone.

"You want to hear me recite it now? It isn't the time. And we aren't on the hill."

"Yes, I would like—"

"Keep your jaws for your bone," said a voice from a higher terrace. "I will recite the most important clauses of the Bill, straight from my beak."

"Ah," said Bert, half turning around to glance up. "This is who I wanted you to meet. Anya of Trallonia, greet Dehlia, the last surviving warden of the High Kingdom of Yarrow."

Anya peered up at the moonlit terraces, looking for a human silhouette, but she saw nothing till her eyes were caught by movement. She squinted, unsure what she was looking at, before Dehlia spoke again.

"Yes, I am the last warden, but there will be others again, one day."

A large white bird with an almost translucently white beak hopped down to stand next to Anya. For a moment Anya thought Dehlia must be an *albino* raven, till she noted the one sharp eye she could see wasn't red, but dark and lustrous. Nor was she entirely white. There still a few silver-wreathed black feathers in the ruff around her neck. The bird must once have been entirely black like a normal raven, and the white and silver was the result of tremendous age.

"Yes, I am very old," said Dehlia, unerringly picking out what Anya was thinking. "It is one hundred and eleven years since the Deluge and the fall of the last High King, curse his name, which shall as ever remain unspoken. I greet you, Anya, and wish you good fortune on your Quest."

The white raven dipped her head, her sharp and strangely luminous beak tapping the stone of the terrace.

"An honor," said Anya, bowing. "Uh, Your Ravenship."

"I was not always a raven," said Dehlia. "I took this shape for a number of reasons, many decades ago. They do not matter. Yet still I am a warden, even though the High Kingdom is no more, and still I uphold the All-Encompassing Bill of Rights and Wrongs and seek to enlarge others with the knowledge of it."

"Please tell me," said Anya. "I would like to know."

The raven twisted her head as if to look at Anya with her left eye. But there was no bright orb there, only a mass of scars around an empty socket. Anya's own eyes twinged. She blinked and wanted to look away, but managed not to. After a second, Dehlia turned her head, fixing her good eye on the princess again.

"First!" said the raven, her voice loud in the theater. Only then did Anya notice that the musicians had stopped playing and everyone was looking up at the ancient warden. Except for Ardent, who was chewing one end of the bone he'd managed to carefully wedge between Anya's feet.

"First," quoth the raven, "all folk are free, and may never be property, or used as such, and may stay or leave any employment at their own will.

"Second, no person shall be transformed, fined, deprived of liberty, executed, or otherwise punished save under the ancient laws as set within the Stone.

"Third, no court shall sit without a unicorn, true mirror, or oathbound seer to discern the truth of things spoken at trial.

"Fourth, the Crown shall not set, assay, or gather any tax without the assent of the Moot.

"Fifth, the Rights and Wrongs of the Bill, and the Laws Set in Stone, shall be supported, upheld, and maintained by the wardens, rangers, castellans, and dogs of the High Kingdom."

"That's us," said Ardent indistinctly, since he didn't stop chewing. "The dogs of the High Kingdom."

"I thought you were just the royal dogs of *Trallonia*," said Anya.

"Many a good dog drowned when Yarrow was flooded," said Dehlia with a gracious dip of her beak towards the gnawing dog. "But the summer kennels were at Trallonia, so there were survivors there. And some few senior hounds made it out of the inundated city, so the line continued. In fact, your ancestor 'King' Norbert of Trallonia was actually the second assistant kennel-keeper."

"No!" exclaimed Anya.

Bert and Dehlia looked at her silently. Anya thought about it for a while, then reluctantly conceded, "I suppose that *does* make sense. I always wondered why we had the huge kennel and the dog tunnels and everything . . . But this is all just history. What's it got to do with me? The High Kingdom is gone. Who cares about the Bill and the . . . the Laws Set in Stone—whatever they may be— and all the rest of it?"

"We care," said Bert, gesturing towards her band of robbers.

"I care," said Dehlia.

"So do we," said Ardent. He let the bone drop out of his mouth as if he wasn't sure how it had got there in the first place. "The dogs. One of the first things Tanitha tells us as pups. One day we'll be c-c-called on, to help put everything back together. The High Kingdom, the Bill, all that."

"But it's not possible," protested Anya. "There must be hundreds of small kingdoms now, not to mention all the bandits and evildoers and no-goodniks and monsters and evil sorcerers like Rikard and the Grey Mist and their society. How could anyone even *start* to put it all back together?"

"You start small," said Dehlia. The raven had a very particular stare. Her single eye, bright with moonshine, was focused on Anya in a very alarming way. "With a Quest to save one of those small kingdoms, and set it to rights, and have its ruler swear to uphold the Bill. Then you go on from there."

Anya looked from the raven to Bert, then back down to the robbers. They were all staring at her too.

"Oh no!" she said, scrambling to her feet. "Don't look at me. I've got enough of a Quest already!"

"It's all part of a bigger Quest," said Bert. "And we'll help with all of it. So you have found your first allies against Duke Rikard already."

"Second," corrected Ardent. "After us dogs."

"Even if I wanted to help, I could never get Morven to agree to uphold the Bill and to not raise taxes without the Moot agreeing," said Anya. "And what's a Moot anyway?"

"The Moot was the ancient parliament of the High Kingdom," said Dehlia. "Two hundred representatives gathered from all walks of life, sniffed out by the royal dogs for wisdom, patience, and cunning, tested by unicorn for truthfulness, and bound to serve their term of office by the Stone."

"The stone with the laws in it?" asked Anya.

"Yes," said Dehlia. "The Only Stone. A unique—"

She was interrupted by a sudden cry from the terrace below. The bright orange bulk of Shrub emerged from under a pile of cut ferns. He'd been practicing sneaking up on people, with considerable success.

"Did you say the Only Stone?" asked the newt. "I was going to steal it from the League of Right-Minded Sorcerers and give it to Bert, only that went wrong. Princess Anya should get it to protect her from being transformed! I could steal it for her. I'm sure I'll do better next time—"

"The Only Stone does not merely provide protection against sorcery to its wielder," interrupted Dehlia. "All the ancient laws are codified within it, including many that have been lost or forgotten. We must regain it from the sorcerers at some time. But that will be, I think, another Quest. It is beyond our power now. As Bert has said, we must start small—with Trallonia, and Princess Anya."

"All I want to do is get the ingredients for the lip balm, get enough allies to defeat Rikard, and go home!" Anya protested. "I'm not signing up to rebuild the High Kingdom, and I'm not the heir to Trallonia, so you'll have to talk to Morven about the Bill and all that."

"Oh dear," said Bert. "I guess that means we'll have to rob you after all."

"Can't you just rob me later?" asked Anya. She felt very tired all of a sudden. It had been a long and difficult day, and the prospects for tomorrow looked even worse. "Or in the morning, at least, if you absolutely can't put it off till I finish my Quest?"

Bert saw Anya's hand go up to smother a yawn. She looked across at the raven, who dipped her beak in agreement to the robber leader's unspoken question.

"Yes," she said. "We will talk in the morning. The day may bring a different view, as so often happens. The ferns are fresh cut; gather them closer together for your bed, and here is a blanket. Rest."

CHAPTER ELEVEN

Exeunt, Pursued by Weaselfolk

Anya had turned into a frog. A big, very bright green frog. She was looking at her reflection in the moat, wondering how she had become a frog, and why one so bright green? She dipped her head into the water, felt it wash over her cheek—and woke up.

Ardent was licking her face urgently.

"Wake up!" whispered the dog. "I c-c-an smell weasels. Or maybe stoats. Mixed up with people. It all smells wrong."

"What?" asked Anya blearily. It was very dark. The silver moon was long gone, and the blue moon wasn't doing much for illumination, though the sky was clear, so the stars did help.

"Weasels!" said Ardent. He let out a short, sharp bark.

"Weasel*folk*," said another voice. Bert loomed up next to Anya, a dim silhouette against the starry sky. "Weasels turned into people-size soldiers. Lots of them. We have to get you out of here!"

Anya scrabbled around for her staff, frog cage, and bundles. She had just managed to get the load balanced on her shoulder when there was a cry from somewhere high on the edge of the theater, a shout of very human pain. It was followed by the blast of a horn nearby, the sudden clash of weapons, and many decidedly nonhuman squeals, frenzied snarls, and screeches.

Bert took Anya by the elbow and hurried her down to the stage. Robbers leaped past them up the terraces, swords and axes drawn, towards the horrible screaming battle that was taking place above. Ardent turned back too, growling the fiercest growl Anya had ever heard from him, wanting to join the fray.

"No! Ardent! Stay with me!" ordered the princess. The dog growled again, but spun about to follow. Bert hustled Anya to a doorway in the low wall at the back of the stage and pushed her through, Shrub darting past her legs.

"Take the path down the hill! Shrub will show you the way to his father," Bert said very quickly. "I will meet you there. If I am . . . delayed, don't go to Rolanstown. There are no trustworthy alchemists there, and it is a dangerous place. Head towards the Good Wizard!"

Then she was gone, sword in hand. A question about where exactly the Good Wizard was located never came out of Anya's mouth; instead she stumbled down the steps beyond the stage, and from there to a narrow path between thornbushes. Shrub lolloped ahead, an orange beacon to show the way. Ardent came close at Anya's heels, turning every dozen paces to look and smell behind, the hair on his back raised in a ridge, as if he had become a razorback boar.

The sounds of fighting lessened as they reached the forest edge at the foot of the hill. Anya lost sight of Shrub for a moment and stumbled into a branch. She gasped in fright, thinking for a split second she'd been attacked, her fingers clutching at the hilt of her knife.

"Come on!" said Shrub, reappearing near her feet.

"There are weaselfolk coming down the side of the hill," Ardent reported, half growling his words.

"Come on!" repeated Shrub.

"I can't see!" Anya protested.

It was even darker under the trees.

Ardent thrust his head against her and gave her hand a comforting lick.

"Hold my collar," said the dog. He sounded less excitable than usual, more like one of the older dogs. "I can see well enough to follow Shrub."

Anya thrust her fingers through his collar. Her hand shook a little, but she quelled the tremors. She didn't want Ardent to think she was afraid, though to tell the truth, she was terrified. The darkness made everything worse, and the very idea of weaselfolk was horrifying. Which parts would be weasel, and which human? Maybe each weaselfolk was different . . .

These feelings of dread were intensified by the hideous yowling and screeching she could still hear faintly from the arena. Not to mention the shouts and screams of the wounded—possibly even dying—robbers. Anya grimaced and tried to put all that out of her mind. *You need to focus,* she told herself. *Concentrate on what's important. And what's important right now is getting away.*

"Go on, Shrub," she said quietly, though it took a great effort to keep a telltale quaver out of her voice. "Go on."

Shrub led them quickly through the forest, his pace not quite at a run but significantly faster than a walk. Anya still stumbled, and occasionally got scratched by a smaller branch, but with Ardent's help she didn't actually run into anything serious.

An hour, or perhaps two hours, later—Anya had no real feel for how much time had passed—the sun began to come up, its soft yellow light filtering in through the canopy of leaves. Anya shivered, not because she was cold, but simply because she was relieved to be able to see properly again. No matter how much she'd tried not to, she'd been thinking constantly about some half-weasel, half-human thing dropping on her in the darkness, or suddenly looming up in front of her, jaws snarling, claws reaching . . .

"We're almost there," Shrub reported. "Pity Dad doesn't make soup like Ma."

Anya slowed down and shifted her staff to her other shoulder.

"Can you smell anything, Ardent?" she asked anxiously. "Ahead or behind?"

Ardent lifted his snout and circled his head, sniffing the breeze.

"Nothing unusual," he said. Then he stiffened for a moment, frozen in place save for his nose, which quivered mightily. His head went down and forward, and he stepped one paw ahead, his tail quivering straight up.

"What is it?" whispered Anya.

"Rabbit!" barked Ardent, and he was off, a tan streak against the green of the undergrowth.

"Ardent!" Anya called hoarsely, trying to make it a whispered shout. Which isn't really possible, but people do try.

"He won't catch it," said Shrub. "Big warren around here, those rabbits have got tunnel entrances all over the place. They go out on the downs during the day. Come back into the forest at night."

Shrub was correct. A bedraggled Ardent slid out from under a sprawling but stunted hawthorn a few minutes later and plopped himself down gasping at Anya's feet.

"We're on a Quest, Ardent," Anya chastised severely. "Probably pursued by weaselfolk. This is no time for chasing rabbits."

Ardent's ears lowered and his tail drooped.

"Sorry, Princess," he said. "I'll try to remember."

He looked so woebegone that Anya forgave him. She knew that rabbits were very, very hard for a dog to resist chasing. When Ardent was older, and had more practice, he should be able to watch a fleeing rabbit with equanimity, merely lifting an ear or making a small harrumphing noise. But not now. Bending down, she scratched his head and rubbed his ears.

"You did a good job leading me in the dark, thank you," she said. "Now, we need to go get our first ingredient from Shrub's dad. And maybe have breakfast. We can eat the ham."

Even as she said that, Anya felt a twinge in her shoulder, the kind of twinge that says it is not as bad a twinge as it could be, because the burden that shoulder is supporting is lighter than it should be.

Anya looked back urgently.

The ham was gone. For a terrible second Anya thought the frog basket was as well, before her silk-scarf bundle swung a little to the right to show Denholm's prison securely behind it, farther up the staff. The frog looked at her and emitted a mournful croak. It was no life being locked up in a wicker cage and only occasionally sprinkled with water and fed moths or bugs (which were rarely the best things a frog might choose for himself).

"I must have left the ham back in the robbers' arena," said Anya sadly. She felt a sudden pang of hunger as her stomach caught up with the news.

"I should have c-c-caught the rabbit," said Ardent, equally sad.

"Plenty of bugs about," said Shrub, crunching up something, its wings falling out one side of his mouth as he swallowed.

"We'll just have to find food later," said Anya firmly. "Take us to your father, Shrub."

Shrub nodded and set off again. He hadn't gone very far before the forest began to thin out, the trees farther apart, the undergrowth more sparse. The morning sun went from sliding between small gaps in the canopy to flooding in, making everything brighter and warmer. Soon there began to be open spaces where wildflowers grew, and the trees were widely separated. Through one such gap, Anya saw they really were at the edge of the forest. Beyond lay long, low rolling hills of yellow-green grass, with only the occasional copse of trees clinging on here and there.

These were the downs, a landscape Anya had never seen before. Even the forest was somewhat familiar, but this was not. She felt both a thrill of excitement and a shiver of fear at the sight. The downs promised excitement and possibility but also danger. She hadn't forgotten the almost overwhelming terror of the weaselfolk attack in the night.

"There's my old pop!" Shrub lifted a claw and pointed to a particularly resplendent chestnut tree that overtopped several lesser companions nearby. Following his own direction, he ambled over to it and tapped several times upon the trunk.

"Pa! Pa! You got visitors!" shouted the newt.

The upper branches of the chestnut shivered in sudden movement, and not from any breeze.

"A princess!" bawled Shrub. "And a royal dog and a frog prince."

The branches moved again, making a whispering noise that Anya almost thought could be words.

"Come and put your hand . . . or paw . . . against the trunk," said Shrub. "Makes it easier to hear."

Anya and Ardent drew close to the tree and reached out to touch the grooved gray bark.

"Elisandria at home?" shouted Shrub. "No? Popped out for a bath at the spring?"

Anya almost thought she heard the ex-druid's reply to his son, the whisper of the branches louder, but still on the edge of her perception.

"Hello," she said. "I'm Princess Anya of Trallonia, and I need your help."

"Have to talk louder than that!" shouted Shrub. "He's a deaf old tree!"

"I am not, you rude boy!"

Anya heard *that* clearly, though it was still a strange whisper in the air, without any obvious source. She made a warning gesture to Shrub, not wanting him to annoy his father before she even asked for four drops of sap.

"I beg your pardon for intruding upon your peaceful . . . um . . . treeness," said the princess. She did lift her voice a little, but didn't shout. "I am on a Quest, seeking the ingredients for a magical lip balm that will let me transform this frog prince and your son, Shrub, back to their human forms. One of these ingredients is four drops of blood from a retired druid."

"Hmm," said the tree.

It was not a promising "hmm," the kind you hear before someone agrees with you or gives you a present. It sounded more like the kind of very doubtful "hmm" you get before being shown the door, which the doorkeeper regretted opening in the first place.

"Prince Denholm was transformed by the evil sorcerer Duke Rikard," said Anya hastily. "Just as Shrub was transformed by the evil Grey Mist. So you would be helping strike back against these evil sorcerers."

"Ah," said the tree.

Anya wasn't sure what this meant. Or if it had even been the ex-druid responding, because a slight breeze had come up, and now the branches of all the trees were moving and whispering.

"Just four drops," she said. "That's all. Please."

There was a long silence. Shrub cleared his throat as if to say something, but subsided as Anya gestured at him again.

"Go away," said the tree. Even via the whisper of branches, it sounded petulant.

"It is *very* important," said Anya beseechingly, still in a louder-than-normal voice.

"What's very important?"

That didn't come from tree branches rustling. Anya turned around. A green-skinned figure wearing a loose robe made from many different autumn leaves was coming towards them. She had a long back-scrubbing brush in one hand, once simply a fallen branch with just the right sticking-out twiglets, and her hair was done up inside a towel made from plaited grasses.

Clearly a dryad, come from her bath.

"I thought dryads were supposed to look like beautiful women," whispered Anya to Shrub as the tree sprite approached. Elisandria might be mistaken for a human female from a distance, but up close she looked more like someone had roughly carved a tree to resemble a woman and it had somehow got a life of its own.

"She *is* beautiful," said Shrub. "If you like trees."

"I like trees," said Ardent. "They hold the scent very well when you—"

"Quiet, Ardent," commanded Anya. She bowed as the dryad came up to them.

"You must be Elisandria. I'm Princess Anya of Trallonia, this is Ardent the royal dog, the frog in the cage is Prince Denholm, and . . . ah . . . Shrub, you know."

"Charmed, darlings," said Elisandria airily. "What's so important you need to talk to Dannith? You do know he became a tree to get out of the whole human business?"

"Uh, no," said Anya. "I didn't know why he became a tree. I don't really know anything about why druids become trees—"

"Peace and quiet," said Elisandria matter-of-factly. "Abdication of responsibility. A good long sleep. All of that."

"Well, all I wanted was four drops of blood from a retired druid," said Anya. "Sap, I guess. It's one of the ingredients to make a lip balm to turn Denholm and Shrub back into humans."

"Four drops of sap?" asked Elisandria. "Got a knife? Just make a cut on the diagonal and let it drip into the collecting vessel."

"Uh, Dannith said to go away," Anya said uncomfortably.

"Oh, don't ask him again. He won't even notice!" cried Elisandria. "He's more tree than person at the moment—I doubt he would have woken at all for anyone but Shrub. I mean, if it was a big branch or something, that'd be different, but four drops of sap? Here, I'll do it for you. Give me your knife and the bottle."

"Oh," said Anya. "I've only got a water bottle . . ."

She hesitated, wondering what to do, once again regretting that she'd had to go forth on her Quest without proper preparation.

"I guess we'll have to use that."

She put down her burdens and opened the water bottle to splash some of the precious fluid over Denholm, who croaked in gratitude. Then she poured more into her cupped hand for Ardent and drank the last of it herself, before handing over the empty bottle and her knife to the dryad.

"This won't take long," said Elisandria. She cut through the bark expertly and held the bottle underneath, quickly collecting the required four drops. "There we are."

Anya took the bottle and adjusted all her belongings along the staff.

"Nice to meet you all," said Elisandria. She yawned, revealing that the interior of her mouth was a lighter shade of green, and her teeth a kind of greenish-white. "Time for me to have a nap too."

She touched the trunk of the tree and suddenly became insubstantial, more like a waft of green smoke than a solid being. Anya could see the forest through her rapidly vanishing body and she watched in fascination as Elisandria—robe, scrubbing brush, towel-wrapped hair, and all—drifted into the chestnut tree and disappeared.

CHAPTER TWELVE

How to Make a Difficult Quest Even More Miserable

"Where do we go now?" asked Ardent.

Anya looked around. She was hungry, and thirsty as well, despite her mouthful from the bottle. Both feelings were exacerbated by knowing she had neither food nor drink.

"Bert did say to wait for her," said Anya, but not as if she thought that was the best thing to do.

"To rob us?" asked Ardent.

"I don't think so," said Anya. "Probably to talk me into their whole big Quest to restore the Bill thingie and the High Kingdom and everything."

She thought about that for a moment. Bert and Dehlia had planted the seed of thought in her mind, and it was growing away busily and putting out new shoots of thought, all of which were quite bothersome, because they were about things like responsibility and fairness, and thinking about others, and why being a princess perhaps should be about more than just having a nice library and three meals a day, particularly when other people didn't have these things . . .

Anya grimaced, forcing these thoughts back into the lower depths of her mind. But more bubbled up. Part of her wanted to wait for Bert, because then she wouldn't have to make decisions and could relax. But if she did that then they would keep on at her about the Bill of Rights and Wrongs, and she had a very guilty feeling already that she ought to be doing whatever she could to help reestablish the laws.

But that would complicate everything, would make her Quest even more difficult than it was already. If she just moved on, Anya thought, she could still be in charge and forget about the Bill of Rights and Wrongs.

She could keep her Quest simple. Or relatively simple.

"We don't need to wait for Bert," said Shrub, almost as if he could tell what Anya was thinking. "I know all the paths and roads around here. All of 'em! For leagues and leagues. Where do you want to go?"

"Bert said something else," said Anya. It had all been noise and confusion in the darkness, but she remembered. "She'd meet us here, but if delayed—"

"Go to the Good Wizard," Ardent barked happily.

"Yes," said Anya thoughtfully. Tanitha had suggested a Good Wizard would be a useful ally. A wizard might also have some of the ingredients she needed. Though she wasn't sure whether wizards used ingredients or not. She smiled wryly at the sudden thought that the best place she could have got all the ingredients in one go was from a sorcerer, and the most powerful and most likely to have everything was Duke Rikard himself.

Her smile faded as she considered her probable fate if she had tried to sneak into his secret storeroom. She would be on her way to a distant school now, or more likely dead at Rikard's agents' hands, just far enough far away from Trallonia for her friends not to know about it and cause trouble.

Anya took a deep breath and forced all her troubled thoughts about the Bill of Rights and Wrongs aside. As Tanitha had said, she had to eat the food in front of her first. That meant concentrating on getting the ingredients for the lip balm.

She wished she hadn't thought about food again.

"Do you know where the Good Wizard's demesne is from here, Shrub?" asked Anya. "I know it's somewhere on the downs, or nearby."

"Oh sure!" said the newt. "That's easy."

"Have you ever been there?" asked Anya suspiciously. Shrub had led them well through the forest, but she doubted he would know anything farther afield very well. Even if he had been "a wanderer ever since he was six," as his uncle Hedric had said.

"No," admitted Shrub. "Seen the 'Keep Out' signs, though, when I went to New Yarrow to steal the Only Stone. It's about halfway there. In fact, if we go to the Good Wizard's, we might as well keep going to the city and steal the Stone—"

"We're not stealing the Only Stone!" snapped Anya. "What do you mean 'Keep Out' signs?"

"Big signs that say 'Keep Out, Visitors to the Good Wizard by Appointment Only' and also 'Beware of the Giant.'"

"How do you make an appointment?"

Shrub's shoulders moved in the disturbing amphibian way that meant he was shrugging.

"I don't know. Don't know anything about the Good Wizard. Only from here we'd cross the downs, join the road about a league outside Rolanstown, take it towards New Yarrow, and then the path where the 'Keep Out' signs are."

"What do you know about the Good Wizard?" asked Anya.

She hardly knew anything about Good Wizards in general and nothing about the nearby one in particular. They cropped up in stories from time to time, and were wise and so on, but the stories were generally vague and just said things like "The Good Wizard also proved helpful in their quest" or "After taking counsel with the Good Wizard, the path became clearer."

She supposed that by their very nature, Good Wizards would be required to help questers like herself. Otherwise they'd be Bad Wizards. Unless, of course, the reference was to their skill at wizardry. Then a Good Wizard would be a skilled wizard, and their ethics and behavior would be up to them, and a Bad Wizard would just be incompetent, but could be quite nice.

She hoped *good* in this case meant kind, wise, and helpful.

"We need water and food," said Anya. "How long will it take to walk to the Good Wizard's demesne?"

"Rest of the day," said Shrub. "Easy peasy."

"There could be weaselfolk closing in on us already," said Ardent professionally. He stretched up and looked back the way they had come, ears up, his head slowly moving from side to side as he sniffed, the very model of a dog on guard.

"Is there somewhere on the downs or along the road we could buy food?" asked Anya. She probably could walk all day without anything to eat, but it would be very difficult. As a princess, she had never skipped a single meal before.

"We might run into a shepherd, buy some bread and cheese,"

said Shrub. "There's nothing on the road between Rolanstown and the 'Keep Out' signs. Except robbers and such."

"Bert's robbers?"

"Nah. The other kind. The ones that rob from everyone and keep it to themselves."

"We don't want to encounter any of them," said Anya. "And what are 'and such'?"

"The usual," said Shrub vaguely.

"What's the 'usual'?"

"I dunno. It's all right by day, most of the time. I heard stories about monsters at night. Maybe wolves, or a troll—that kind of thing. A cockatrice, maybe."

"A cockatrice?" asked Anya. "I need some cockatrice feathers . . . but they have to be fresh pulled, so I was thinking of getting them last, when everything else is ready."

"Not easy to pull a cockatrice's tail," said Shrub. "I wouldn't try it meself."

Anya reflected on this. She had read a little about cockatrices in Sir Garnet Bester's *Bestest Beasts and How to Best Them*, but there wasn't a lot of detail in that book. Cockatrices were basically poor cousins of dragons, with a giant rooster's head and a rather stunted dragon's body. They had weak wings, and could only flap about near the surface, not soar majestically like a real dragon. Their one real advantage was their cockatrician stare. According to Sir Garnet, they fixed their beady eyes on their prey, who would become disoriented and wobble about on the spot going "um, um, um" until the cockatrice got close enough to give them a lethal peck. So it was bestest to avert your eyes or use a mirror when stalking cockatrices.

(Sir Garnet had also mentioned the usefulness of an extra-heavy crossbow, which Anya was sadly lacking.)

"There was something else about cockatrices," mused Anya. She cast her mind back to her reading, trying to visualize the page from *Bestest Beasts*. It was a lovely book, beautifully illuminated in the margins.

"That's right!" she exclaimed. "Weasels are immune to the cockatrician stare!"

"As are stoats, ferrets, and otters," said Ardent. This was the kind of thing he'd been taught in dog school. He probably knew more about cockatrices, or at least *hunting* cockatrices, than Anya.

"Good for the weaselfolk behind us if they run into a cockatrice," said Shrub. "Dunno how it'll help *us*, though."

"Well, it might prove useful," said Anya stiffly. "Knowledge is always useful, even if . . . if it is not immediately apparent how it will be useful."

She sat silently for a minute or two, thinking about knowledge and, more to the point, exactly what she should do, while also trying to ignore the space in her stomach that was protesting the absence of breakfast.

"How long we going to wait?" asked Shrub. "Because I reckon it's going to rain."

"What?" Anya wondered how the newt could know this.

Shrub lifted his head towards the south.

"Clouds. Big dark clouds. Going to rain. Might get colder as well. If we're going somewhere, we should go there."

"If it rains, we can drink from puddles!" said Ardent. "Or you can just put your head back and let the drops fall in. That's fun!"

Anya looked to the south. There was indeed a dark line of clouds there, but it was far away and moving slowly. Perhaps if they moved quickly, they might be able to get to the Good Wizard (and shelter and food) before the rain set in.

"We'll go," she decided. "Bert can find us there as easily as here, if she really wants to. Shrub, lead the way!"

Four hours later, the rain had well and truly caught up with them.

Anya was completely sodden, cold, and starving. She was also still kind of thirsty, since she hadn't taken to drinking from puddles. And while catching raindrops with your mouth open might be fun for dogs, it wasn't very practical for a girl to get a decent drink.

Shrub also finally confessed that they were lost and he didn't know where they were, or where the road or anything else was. The clouds hid the sun, so they couldn't fix their direction by that; the heavy rain meant everything disappeared into gray fuzz fifty yards out, and even where they *could* see, every hill with its ankle-high rough grass looked exactly the same.

For all Anya knew, they'd been walking in circles ever since the weather had closed in.

On top of the current hill, with the rain so heavy they couldn't even see the *beginning* of the next hill, she called a halt to think about their position.

"I would have been fine if it hadn't started raining," complained Shrub. "Everything looks different in this weather."

Anya bit back a sharp comment. She knew it wouldn't help. She set her staff down and looked at Prince Denholm. He was the only one who seemed happy to be drenched, letting out cheerful croaks whenever a particularly heavy drop hit his cage and splintered into mist.

"I'm going to put my extra kirtle on," Anya said, shivering. She undid the bundle of silk scarves and got out the dress. It was already wet, but an extra layer did provide some warmth. She put on Morven's woolen tights as well, even though they were also wet, too long, drooped terribly around the knees, and made her smell like a damp sheep.

When she got everything approximately settled on herself, Anya retied the bundle and picked up her staff.

"I think it's that way," said Shrub, pointing with one foot.

"Hmmm," said Anya. "Ardent, can you smell anything?"

Ardent paced around them, sniffing the air.

"It's too wet; all the smells are sitting where they are," he said. "But I'll be able to tell if we cross our own path. We haven't yet."

"Oh, of course," said Anya. She'd forgotten Ardent widdled at regular intervals on suitable tufts of grass or exposed rock. So at least they hadn't been going in circles, or not completely.

Ardent sniffed the air again.

"Wait! There *is* something . . ."

He growled, deep in his chest, and turned back in the direction they'd come from. Or the direction Anya thought they'd come from. Even just in stopping, putting things down, and getting dressed, she'd managed to disorient herself.

"What is it?" she whispered.

She spoke so softly Ardent couldn't hear her over the steady beat of the rain.

"What is it?" she repeated, much more loudly.

"Weaselfolk! Err . . . or something similar . . ."

"What do you mean *similar*?" asked Anya urgently. She put down her gear again and stayed crouched, drawing her knife. It didn't feel like it would be much use against a transformed human-size weasel. Her heart was suddenly pounding, all the discomfort of her wet clothes forgotten. The words of power for The Withering Wind leaped to the front of her mind, begging to be used. "How many of them?"

"One," said Ardent. He was leaning forward, stiff-legged, nose twitching like mad. "Not exactly a weasel . . . weasel-like, but definitely transformed. There's human—"

Something human-size stood up from where it had been sneaking through the grass and held up its arms.

"Peace!" it cried in a shrill voice as Ardent barked savagely and charged forward, and the first word of power for The Withering Wind came out of Anya's lips without her even thinking about it.

"Peace! Help!"

Anya clapped her hand over her mouth to stop the rest of the spell coming out. Ardent changed direction and slid around in a circle in the muddy grass, still barking. Shrub, who had started digging a hole to hide in, stopped.

Denholm let out a croak, which might mean anything. Or nothing.

"Peace!" gasped the figure again. It wasn't much taller than Anya, and though human shaped, was covered in slick brown fur that seemed to naturally shed the rain. Its face was quite long and pointed, but was not as pointy as a weasel's. It had more rounded curves and attractive, dark brown eyes. Its hands, still held high, were webbed between the fingers and had only short claws.

"Who . . . *what* are you?" asked Anya cautiously. She still held her knife ready, and Ardent had prowled around behind the creature and was ready to lunge forward and bite a hamstring to bring it down. "Are you one of Duke Rikard's creatures?"

"Not by choice," gasped the transformed animal. "I was caught, transformed, and sent with the others. But I'm not like them. I'm an—"

"Otter!" barked Ardent suddenly. "I know that smell, I know!"

"You're an otter?" asked Anya.

"Yes, yes, my name is . . . you would say . . . ah . . . Champion Smooth Stone Oysterbreaker, I think. Of the Yarrow River clan. A stupid trapper sent me with an order of weasels and stoats to Duke Rikard, and he transformed us all at the same time without checking. But as soon as I heard about you from Gerald the Herald, I knew I had to escape. Will you turn me back to myself, please, Frogkisser?"

"Don't call me Frogkisser," snapped Anya.

"Lady Frogkisser?"

"My name is Anya," said Anya crossly. She was cold and very wet, and she really didn't need yet another transformee begging to be helped. Particularly one who wanted to be turned back into an *animal*.

Ardent circled back to Anya. The fur on his back had gone down, and he was no longer barking. Even so, he kept one eye on Champion Smooth Stone Oysterbreaker.

"They're special," the dog whispered to Anya as he drew close. "Yarrow River otters. Got magic, like us royal dogs. Used to police the river, in the old times, and serve the Bill of Rights and Wrongs."

"I don't want to know anything more about that stupid Bill," said Anya. "All I want is to get to the Good Wizard's demesne and get dry and eat something!"

"But will you help me?" asked the otter. She held out her paws beseechingly. "Look at me, I'm all stretched and horrible, and I have to walk upright most of the time! It's awful!"

"Oh yes, I suppose so," said Anya grumpily. "What's one more? I can't guarantee the lip balm will work on you, though I suppose it will. Transmogrification is transmogrification, after all, whichever way it goes."

"Oh, thank you!" cried the otter. She threw herself down at Anya's feet. "When we find a river, I will catch you a fish. Several fish!"

"I'd eat them too," said Anya. "Raw, if necessary. Oh, get up!"

The otter-maid stood up and bowed.

"Ardent the royal dog, Shrub the transformed newt, Prince Denholm the temporary frog," said Anya, introducing everyone. She looked at the otter. "We're going to need a shorter name for you, Champion Smooth Stone Oysterbreaker. How about . . . Champ?"

The otter wrinkled her nose. Her face was a disturbing mixture of human and otter, but her nose was still more like the animal's, and she had fine whiskers that quivered with that wrinkle.

"That doesn't sound right."

"Um . . . what about Smooth or maybe—"

"Smoothie!" said the otter. She clapped her hand-paws together and beamed at Anya, showing lots of fine sharp teeth. "I like it!"

She did look very smooth and sleek, Anya thought. Otters were beautiful animals, and even stretched out and made somewhat human, Smoothie had a great deal of their natural allure.

But also their fish breath, noted the princess, wrinkling her nose slightly. She hoped Smoothie didn't notice her reaction.

"Do you know if there are any weasels following us, Smoothie?" asked Anya. A nasty thought occurred to her as she said that, and she hastily added, "Or following you?"

"No, they're too stupid for that," said the transformed otter disdainfully. "I slipped away during the fighting with the robbers. They'll never find us in this rain."

Smoothie had barely finished speaking when Ardent stiffened again and whipped his head around, his ears up and nose sniffing. Even as he did that, there was a ferocious squeal and *something* erupted out of a sheet of rain and launched itself straight at Anya.

It flew through the air, a leap of a dozen feet or more over Ardent's head as he leaped up too, his jaws snapping on empty air. Anya only had time to brace herself and get her arms up before it hit her. Bowled over backwards, she found herself on the ground, desperately trying to stop her throat from being ripped open by the long, many-toothed jaws of what could only be one of the Duke's weasel soldiers.

Anya gasped and choked as the thing's horribly yellowed teeth got closer and closer, despite everything she could do. Desperately, she tucked in her chin to protect her throat, her arms shaking with the effort of holding the thing off.

From the corner of her right eye she could see Ardent, his own jaws closed tight around one of the weasel creature's taloned hands, trying to pull it back. On her left, Smoothie's sharp mouth was clamped tight on the weasel's other arm, and she was holding on with her paw-hands as well.

But even Ardent, otter, and princess together couldn't get the weasel off Anya. Its thin, furry body, stretched into a vaguely human shape, was just too strong.

Anya knew she had to do something. Her arms would be unable to keep up the strain. In a few more seconds the thing's jaws would snap shut on her throat and that would be it.

Summoning all her strength, she drew her knees up under the monster and kicked it as hard as she could with both feet, at the same time pushing back with every ounce of the remaining strength in her arms.

The weasel creature lurched back, screeching. Ardent and Smoothie let go. Anya kicked it in the stomach again, and the creature fell sideways off her. The princess scrabbled aside, and Ardent and the otter-maid landed several major bites. Screeching and hissing, bleeding from several wounds, it backed off, dog and otter circling for another opportunity to bite, wary of its slashing talons.

"We are many!" howled the creature. Its voice was very high and cruel and horrid. "We serve the Duke! We *will* find you!"

Spinning on one paw-foot, it leaped away, down the hill, and into the cloaking rain. Ardent began to pursue it, but Anya called him back.

"No, Ardent!" she croaked as she clambered to her feet. "Let it go. There might be more. We have to get away. Only which way?"

She looked around, her heart still beating what felt like a thousand times a minute, her whole body trembling with the shock. She saw Denholm was still safe in his cage. Shrub was nearby, trying to look as if he had been just about to join in her defense. Smoothie was looking back into the rain where the weasel thing had gone, her face set in a snarl.

Ardent was staring in the opposite direction.

"What is it?" snapped Anya.

"Ah!" the dog cried, leaping up and pointing, nose out, back straight, and one paw outstretched in front.

"More weaselfolk?" asked Anya urgently.

"No!" barked Ardent happily. "The road. The rain c-c-cleared for a moment, and I saw it. That way!"

CHAPTER THIRTEEN

A Giant Problem for a Small Princess

It was easier and faster walking on the road, which had once been a major royal highway. Though many of the paving stones were broken, it was still considerably broader and in better shape than any road Anya had seen before. It ran between the low hills, so there was little climbing up or down, and it even had deep, stone-lined gutters on both sides, which at the moment were running fast and spilling over, the rain continuing to come down in thick, blinding sheets.

"How far to go?" Anya asked Shrub.

She sneezed as she spoke, and then shivered. A cold was rapidly expanding its initial foothold in her nose and was getting ready to move into her chest. She was also starving and very tired. They had been walking over the dales and then along the road for hours and hours. At first they had gone as fast as they could, for fear of the weaselfolk behind them. But that pace had gradually lessened as they had grown wearier and they saw no further sign of pursuit.

It was impossible to tell what time it was without being able to see the sun, but she felt it had to be well past noon. Perhaps two or even three o'clock.

"Dunno," said Shrub. He kept licking his huge bulbous eyes as raindrops unerringly fell directly on them. "Depends where we met the road. Got to look for a milestone, or one of the Good Wizard's 'Keep Out' signs, I suppose."

"I'm looking!" barked Ardent. Despite being sodden from nose to tail, he was still cheerful, constantly running ahead and then circling back to act the advance or rear guard, in each position sniffing everywhere and rushing any small bush or tree that might harbor a (small) enemy.

Smoothie seemed happy enough too. Every now and again she plunged into one of the gutters and undulated through the water before bursting out with a shrill cry and turning over a few stones here and there to snap up beetles and worms, well before Shrub could lumber over to try to get a share.

"If I'd known I was going on a Quest I could have packed an oilskin coat," said Anya. "And a lot of other things."

"Isn't there a spell to keep off the rain?" asked Shrub.

"Of course there is!" snapped Anya. "Only I don't know it, because I'm not in my nice warm library learning magic. Instead I've had to go out in this freezing rain just so I can turn all of you back."

The truth was, as Anya knew, that even if she had been home in the library, weather magic was well beyond her abilities. It took a great deal of power to move masses of air and water vapor, and it was like sliding tiles in a puzzle, because if you moved one lot somewhere, then everything else moved. The best weather mages did things very slowly, with small nudges and encouragements, rather than wholesale shifting around of storm clouds and the like.

When weather magic was done inexpertly, storms got worse, droughts lasted longer, and snow fell out of season.

When it was both amateurish and done with evil intentions, for example trying to flood an enemy's city, it might culminate in a tidal wave that drowned your own city. As had happened with the last High King and the city of Yarrow.

It made Anya reconsider the whole idea of sorcery, just a little, thinking of things like that. A sneeze was one thing, but then there was the price Rikard had paid and was paying for his powers.

"Don't you want to turn us back?" asked Shrub. "I wonder if I stole the Only Stone now and put it in my mouth . . . maybe I wouldn't need your help at all."

"No, of course I want to turn you back," said Anya. She wiped her nose. "I'm sorry. I'm just tired and cold and wet. I'll be better once we get to the Good Wizard's. I hope I can have a hot bath."

"A hot *dinner*. Or a c-c-old one. Or lukewarm," said Ardent. "Dinner. Mmmmm."

He licked his lips and then chased his tail suddenly for a few seconds.

"Something up front," called Smoothie, who had just emerged from a gutter and was standing up very straight about twenty yards ahead. "Might be a sign. Or a person standing very still."

"I'll look, I'll look!" cried Ardent, stopping his tail-chasing to dash forward. His paws sent up huge splashes of water as he raced through the puddles. Anya almost couldn't see him as he disappeared into another curtain of heavy rain, but he emerged again very quickly, racing back so swiftly he sent a plume of water over Anya as he skidded to a halt.

"It's a sign," he said, sitting back, his tail furiously wagging backwards and forwards, splashing as much water up as was coming down. "Says 'To the Good Wizard, by Appointment Only' and 'Beware the Giant.' Different writing, though."

"Let's have a look," said Anya. Sploshing along, she tried to recall everything she'd read about giants. It wasn't much. They were generally very boastful and most were so shortsighted they were nearly blind. But they made up for this with a very keen sense of smell. They weren't very good with numbers; they could usually only count to four, and they had to do it aloud, saying, "Fee, fi, fo, fum," and then "many."

That was from their entry in *Bestest Beasts and How to Best Them*, but Anya couldn't remember much else. There were numerous categories of giants, and the book had special notes about each type. The least dangerous ones were "Somewhat Terrifying" and there were several gradations to "Truly Terrifying." The worst of all, if she remembered correctly, were "Stomach-Curling Gigantaurs." Though these latter were not strictly just giants, but very large giants that also had the heads of bulls. The stomach-curling reference was about how people felt when they first saw them.

The sign was a bit puzzling. The part about the giant had clearly been painted on, not very expertly, across the lower half of the sign. And it definitely said, "Beware the Giant," rather than "Beware *of* the Giant."

"Hmmm," said Anya. "We'll have to be careful."

She looked up and a raindrop hit her in the eye. It stung, but for the first time that day she was actually pleased it was still raining.

"The rain will help. Giants are usually very shortsighted and rely on their sense of smell."

"Do you have a plan for when we meet the giant?" asked Ardent excitedly.

"I plan to *not* meet the giant," said Anya. "We'll go slowly, keep our eyes and noses open, and if we do catch sight or sniff of the giant, we'll either go around or, if we have to, retreat back here to head along the road to Rolanstown, I suppose. We have to get food somehow."

"Plenty of bugs about," said Smoothie. "Not as good as fish or oysters, but not too bad."

Anya shuddered, sneezed, and then coughed. Weakly, she waved everybody on and shifted her staff to try to ease the ache in her shoulder. Behind her, in his dangling cage, Denholm let out a loud croak. It sounded a bit like he was laughing at her.

The road to the Good Wizard's demesne was *not* an ancient royal highway. It wasn't paved, it had no gutters, and for the most part it was really just a ten-foot-wide ribbon of mud cutting through the grassy plain. It was actually easier to walk next to the road, because the grass held the mud together, so Anya didn't sink into unsuspected holes where the mud came up to her waist and she needed Ardent and Smoothie to pull her out. Shrub was no use. He could essentially swim through the mud, but Anya didn't want to touch his poisonous hide, or have him hold on to her with his mouth.

Unfortunately, it took two sudden immersions in mud holes before Anya worked out it was better to walk next to the road, so she was not only sodden and cold, but encased in mud from roughly her armpits to her toes. The rain washed a good part of it off, but some of the extra-sticky mud remained.

The animals were also covered in mud, except for Smoothie. She got muddy all right, but in her case, it just couldn't stick to her fur. She would deliberately go for a slide along the road, making cheerful chirruping noises, stand up slathered in mud, and in only a minute or two the rain would rinse her off and she'd be as sleek as ever and ready to go mud-sliding again.

Ardent also liked the mud, though he jumped and splashed in it rather than going for a slide. Shrub was happy too. He lumbered through the mud using a curious half-swimming, half-crawling motion, and kept his mouth open, picking up lots of washed-out worms and other insects.

All three of them forgot to keep a lookout for a giant.

Mud-splattered, wearier than ever, and hungrier than she had ever been in her life, Anya forgot as well. With her head hanging down, the rain slid around her ears to join in a cascade under her chin, which then unerringly found a gap in her two kirtles to chill her rapidly weakening chest. It was all she could do to put one foot in front of the other, and her staff had slid forward so far that the bundle and Denholm's cage were essentially sitting on her shoulder rather than suspended in the air.

"FEE, FI, FO, FUM!"

The roar of the giant's voice and the accompanying blast of fetid breath instantly drew Anya's attention away from the all-consuming slog through mud, and banished all feelings of exhaustion, hunger, and cold.

The giant was right in front of them, straddling the road. He was a horrifying figure, easily twenty feet tall, with shoulders wider than a bull's. It was only a small mercy that he didn't have a bull's head, and so was not a Gigantaur. This giant's oversize human head was still no prize, with his too-wide mouth featuring uneven rows of snaggled, blackened, and rotting teeth. His nose had been broken so many times it zigzagged down his face, and his straggly blond hair was badly plaited into four ropes, knotted with human bones. Two of the plaits were tied under his chin in a kind of bow.

The giant wore massive ox-hide boots, each the size of Anya herself, and a loose smock made of bloodstained sailcloth, living up to the reputation giants had for not caring about their clothes. He held a rusted, crudely wrought cleaver the size of a small pony in his right hand, and in his left gripped a capacious leather bag that had probably started life as a knight's pavilion.

"Five!" shouted Anya, her mind continuing to rocket out of the rain-, mud-, and weariness-induced stupor she'd been in a moment before.

"WHAT?" asked the giant. He still held the cleaver high, ready to strike.

"Fee-fi-fo-fum-*five*!" shouted Anya. "There's five of us, counting the prince."

"PRINCE? I CAN'T SEE NO PRINCE," said the giant warily. He was slightly concerned. Princes as a group could potentially include the rare and very unwelcome subspecies known as giant killers.

"He's right behind me," said Anya. She waved her right hand in the air to distract the giant, urging the others to go around the giant and *keep* going with her left.

The giant peered myopically down at the road, then bent and sniffed the air above Anya's head. Giants' noses were so sensitive they could smell lies.

"Prince Denholm of Gornish," said Anya helpfully, stepping around a lie. "Right behind me. What's your name, then?"

"WHAT? I'M BEWARE THE GIANT," roared the giant. He wiped his eyes and looked around suspiciously, his bent nose snuffling wildly. He didn't pay any attention to Shrub edging past the outside of one deeply planted boot, or Smoothie sliding along on her belly between his legs. "I CAN'T SEE HIM AND I CAN'T SMELL HIM! BUT YOU SPEAK TRUTH."

"I suppose he could have one of those invisibility cloaks or maybe he's disguised," said Anya, which was basically the truth. She made another small shooing gesture at Ardent, who had stayed by her side.

The dog didn't move.

The giant sniffed the air again.

"I CAN SMELL PRINCESS, RIGHT ENOUGH. THAT'D BE YOU. AND DOG. THAT'S YOU. BUT THERE'S SOMETHING ELSE . . . SOMETHING GREEN . . ."

He bent down again, red-rimmed eyes narrowing, and sniffed very deeply.

"A FROG! YOUR PRINCE IS TRANSFORMED. HE'S NOTHING BUT A FROGGY!"

Anya gulped and thought harder still, her mind working so fast that it was surprising the raindrops weren't turning into steam as they hit her head.

"You're very smart. I suppose you must be a 'Trifle Terrifying' or . . . or even a 'Moderately Terrifying' giant?"

"WHAT?!" shouted the giant.

He stood up straight as a pine, put his head back, and roared, smashing the handle of his cleaver and the fist that held the bag against his chest. "I'M THE *TRULY TERRIFYING* GIANT BEWARE!"

"You can't be," said Anya. It took a lot of effort to stop her teeth chattering as she got this out. "You're not tall enough."

"I STAND TWELVE CUBITS TALL IN MY SOCKS!" roared Beware. He smacked his chest a few more times.

"Nah," said Anya. "You can't be more than eleven cubits, if that. Those boots have got *very* high heels on them."

"THEY HAVE NOT!" protested the giant. "I'LL SHOW YOU!"

He sat down on the road, sending a great wave of mud and water cascading over and around Anya. If it hadn't been for Ardent bracing behind her legs she would have gone over. The dog was momentarily submerged, but when the wave subsided he shook himself vigorously and looked up at the princess in admiration.

"Well done," whispered Ardent. "Do I go for his throat while he's distracted?"

Anya looked at the giant's throat. The skin there was folded and convoluted like elephant hide. It would take a two-handed axe and the muscles of a mighty forester to make even a dent in that.

"No, of course not," she whispered. "We wait until—"

"WHAT'S THAT?" roared the giant. He swung his cleaver down, the blade burying itself in the mud only a few feet away from Anya.

"I'll need something to measure you with!" Anya shouted

back. "How about the drawstring from your bag? And you'll have to lie down."

"LIE DOWN IN THIS MUD?"

"You're too tall for me to measure any other way," Anya explained. "Maybe you are eleven cubits tall after all."

"I'M TWELVE CUBITS TALL! TWELVE!" roared the giant angrily. He had one boot off already, which he threw over Anya's head. It was like a near miss from a catapulted boulder, the passage of the huge, heavy object ruffling her hair and scaring her even more, if that was possible.

"As . . . as you say, Sir Beware!" answered Anya. She didn't have to fake the trembling in her voice. Keeping it from getting out of control was the hard part. "Maybe you're even closer to *thirteen* cubits. We'll soon see, when I get measuring."

"I COULD BE!" shouted the giant. "HURRY UP!"

He pulled the drawstring out of his bag and threw it towards Anya, who jumped to one side. The drawstring was essentially a twelve-foot length of heavy-duty rope and would have badly injured her if she hadn't dodged. She picked up one end and swiftly tied a loop in it, with a slipknot.

"COME ON, THEN!" roared the giant as he settled back along the road, putting his hands behind his head. His socks were ragged and many-times patched, and his big toes stuck out. A horrible reek reminiscent of cheese left in the sun for a week or two and then mixed with sewage rolled off his feet, too strong for even the pounding rain to wash away.

"I HAVEN'T GOT ALL DAY TO GET MEASURED. I HAVE TO GET YOU BACK HOME AND COOKED UP. PRINCESS SURPRISE—MY FAVORITE MEAL!"

"Why do you call it 'Princess Surprise'?" asked Anya. She tied a loop in the other end, also with a slipknot.

"BECAUSE THEY LOOK SO SURPRISED TO BE EATEN UP!" guffawed the giant. "PRINCESSES ALWAYS EXPECTS TO GET RESCUED."

"Do they?" asked Anya mildly. "Better they should rescue themselves!"

She threw one loop over the giant's left toe and the other over his right toe, pulled both loops tight, and ran away with Ardent close at her heels.

The giant roared behind her, a great shout that she felt as much as heard. She heard him sit up, and risked a glance over her shoulder as she ran by the side of the road, far faster than she had gone any time before.

He wasn't trying to get up. He simply leaned forward from his sitting position, grabbed his cleaver—and threw it.

Anya dived for the mud, dragging Ardent with her. A huge mass of steel shot over her head, missing her by six inches at most.

Under the muddy water, Anya heard the giant roar again. She pushed herself up and launched herself away, wiping the mud from her eyes. Ardent briefly barked something but she didn't hear what he said; there was so much mud in her ears.

Behind her, Beware the Giant struggled to his feet, took one step forward, looked down in surprise, tried to take another step, turned sideways, and fell over. His huge arms cartwheeled as he fell . . . and there was a horrific snap, crackle, and pop as something very bad happened to his hip.

Anya risked another glance. The giant was howling with pain

now, clutching his left hip. She turned around and started to circle back, to get safely past the immobilized giant and join the others on his far side.

It was only at this moment that she realized she didn't have her staff, her bundle, or Denholm in his little wicker cage.

CHAPTER FOURTEEN

The Good Wizard?

I told you I c-c-could c-c-catch frogs," said Ardent, carefully dropping the disgruntled Denholm's bent-but-not-broken wicker cage at Anya's feet, the dog correctly interpreting her panicked gaze as being caused by the realization that the prince was missing.

Anya picked up the cage very carefully. Her hands were shaking violently, and it wasn't just from the cold. The giant had really frightened her. Coming so soon after the attack of the weasel creature, it had cemented just how dangerous it was to be on a Quest. It was quite different from reading about Quests, sitting in the best chair in the library, with her feet near the fireplace and a plate of honey cakes at her elbow.

Anya bit back a sob. She wished she hadn't thought about the honey cakes.

They were a good quarter league past the giant's ambush now, but they could still hear Beware howling in the distance. He'd broken his hip, Anya thought. It had looked like that from her swift glimpse as they were fleeing. If it was any lesser injury then he'd have staggered after them.

"Has anyone seen anything that might show us where the wizard is?" she asked the rest of her group. She suddenly felt even more tired, even hungrier, and even more despondent than ever, and didn't know how she could go on. The burst of energy from being terrified by the giant and having to do something was now completely gone.

Smoothie scratched her sleek head. Shrub paused for a moment, one unblinking eye looking at the princess. Then he returned to dig at something interesting in the mud. Ardent ran in a circle, sniffing.

No one replied.

Anya took a deep breath to try to steady her nerves and looked about herself, shielding her eyes against the rain. The road had come to an end, and as far as she could see—which wasn't very far—they were still in the middle of the grassy plain dotted with the same small thornbushes she'd been seeing for ages. There was no sign of any house, castle, tower, strange monolith, or anything else that might mark the presence of the Good Wizard.

"What's a demesne anyway?" asked Shrub. "I mean, to look at. In case we missed it."

"It just means the wizard's lands." Anya almost sighed, but managed to stop herself. It wasn't a habit she wanted to develop any further than she already had. "The 'Demesne of the Good Wizard' is like saying the 'Kingdom of Trallonia.' I wish I could remember anything else from the map that might help me find it. And I really wish this rain would stop!"

"It's going to stop soon," said Smoothie.

"Is it?" asked Anya. "How do you know?"

"I just know." Smoothie smiled, showing her fine sharp teeth. Her eyes twinkled. "It's a Yarrow River otter thing. It's going to stop raining, and the wind is going to come up from that direction."

She pointed one webbed hand west.

"It will be colder," she added.

Anya sneezed very violently. Her cold was already worse, without the temperature dropping. But this just made her more determined. She'd beaten a giant—she wasn't going to be beaten by a sniffle.

"We *have* to find the wizard," she said. "Let's walk on a bit farther in the direction the road was heading. It looks like it's climbing up a hill again. Maybe if the rain stops we'll get a view and can spot something."

"Would you like a grub?" asked Shrub. He'd found a decaying tree stump and had ripped it open with his claws to reveal a writhing group of white, segmented grubs.

"No thank you," said Anya. "But please, you go ahead."

Shrub needed no urging, gulping the grubs down before Ardent or Smoothie could get a look in.

Ten minutes later, just as Smoothie had predicted, it did stop raining. The wind changed direction and came back stronger and colder from the west, already beginning to clear the clouds away.

With the increased visibility, Anya saw that they had reached the top of a low ridge. She could see the road they'd left below and behind them. More important, looking ahead, the grassy plain extended to a narrow river, which had overtopped its banks and was busily flooding parts of the surrounding countryside. But there were also the remnants of a road leading to an almost-but-not-quite-submerged footbridge. On the other side the grassy plain became a meadow blessed with a great many charming yellow wildflowers, and in the middle of that meadow there was a building.

A wizard's tower, to be precise.

It was easily recognizable as a wizard's tower because it had the traditional kink in the middle and would have fallen down long since if there hadn't been some kind of magic holding it up. Counting windows, which were not mere arrow slits but fine glass windows, each of four panes, it was seven stories high, and it had a sharp-peaked, shingled roof above a narrow sentry's walk.

The stone facings were whitewashed, which did not indicate it was a Good Wizard's tower, only that the inhabitant liked white-washed walls. Plenty of Good Wizards lived in basalt-black towers, or houses painted blood red, or tents daubed with scary paintings. It was all personal taste and didn't mean a lot.

A low cloud soon rolled back across, but it didn't deliver any rain. Anya could still see the path, though the bridge and the river were now obscured by wisps of drifting white.

"Come on," she said, relief lifting her voice, visions of hot baths and food and clean clothes flitting through her head. "Let's go and meet the wizard!"

With their spirits buoyed by the prospect of food and shelter, their progress was swift. Low, wet white clouds kept blowing past, rather like a swift-moving fog. In other circumstances this would have been depressing, since they were already cold and wet, but it felt as if this was the last dash and soon all would be well.

Then, just as they came to the river, Ardent, who was in front, gave a bark of alarm.

"There's someone on the bridge!" he cried.

There *was* someone on the bridge, standing right in the middle, over the swollen river. A figure in a voluminous dark cloak, with the hood pulled right up so the face was shadowed. His or her feet were the most visible things, clad in beautifully made bright scarlet boots with curled-up toes and high heels, which were parting the shallow film of floodwater that was only just beginning to trickle over the planks of the bridge.

Anya was certain there hadn't been anyone there a moment before.

"I will c-c-lear the way!" barked Ardent, charging forward.

"No! Ardent! Stop!" shouted Anya, even as the person on the bridge raised one hand, the ring on the middle finger suddenly glowing as bright as the sun. Ardent skidded to a stop and yelped. The cloaked figure slowly lowered his or her hand.

Anya ran forward and slipped her fingers through Ardent's collar. She still couldn't see the bridgekeeper's face under the hood, but that ring was obviously magical and probably extremely dangerous.

"We'd like to see the Good Wizard, please," panted Anya.

"Dthhh ywwww hefff ahppenmen," whispered the cloaked figure.

"Ah, I'm sorry, I didn't quite catch that," said Anya nervously. She was keeping a close eye on that magic ring, desperately trying to think of what she should do if it was raised again. It probably sent out fire bolts, or maybe lightning, or at the very least caused the ground to open up beneath an enemy's feet.

A horrible gulping noise came from inside the bridgekeeper's hood. Anya stiffened, wondering what this meant and what ghastly creature was within.

"Sorry," said the bridgekeeper, pushing back her hood to reveal that she was a young woman, perhaps only ten years older than Anya. She was pretty and her luxuriant dark hair was loosely pulled back and tied carelessly with a white ribbon. "I was eating a biscuit.

Very contemplative thing to do, eat biscuits and watch floodwater. I recommend it."

Ardent made a gulping noise at the mention of biscuits.

"Do you have an appointment?" asked the woman.

"No, I'm afraid we don't. But it is very important. I'm Princess Anya—"

"Ah, the Frogkisser!" said the woman. "We heard about you from a Gerald the Herald this morning. And the dog, the frog, the newt, and the half otter-maid are all transformed humans?"

"I'm not!" said Ardent and Smoothie together, both in highly offended tones.

"Hmmm," said the woman. "And you don't have an appointment?"

"No," said Anya. Her vision of a hot bath and food started to fray at the edges, to be replaced with the image of starving in a ditch . . . with the rain coming back again, of course.

"Can't see the Good Wizard without an appointment," said the woman regretfully.

Anya thought for a moment, and looked at the red boots again. She was fairly certain she knew what they meant. Surely, only the Good Wizard herself could have such wonderful footwear. But she looked so young . . .

"Can't you make an exception?" asked Anya.

"No exceptions," said the bridgekeeper firmly. "No appointment, no seeing the wizard."

Anya thought for a few more seconds. Being very tired, very cold, and very hungry didn't help. Her mind felt extremely sluggish. She looked down at Ardent, who gazed back at her with great confidence, obviously expecting her to work something out. Shrub was looking at her in the same way, and so was Smoothie. Denholm wasn't looking at her at all; he was eyeing a mosquito that was venturing close to his cage.

She had to do something. They were relying on her to lead. She was a princess on a Quest, after all, and not just a totally sodden young girl with a cold who hadn't had anything to eat for what seemed like days.

"Could . . . could we make an appointment, please?" she asked.

"Certainly," said the bridgekeeper. She reached under her cloak and took out a dark blue leather-bound book that had *Appointments* embossed in gold type on the cover.

"Do you have anything in the next five minutes?" asked Anya.

"Certainly," said the bridgekeeper. She opened the book and wrote in it with the long, artificial nail on her forefinger. The nail turned ink-blue as she wrote and then back to pink again when she stopped writing and shut the book.

"You actually are the Good Wizard yourself, aren't you?" asked Anya.

"Her, the Good Wizard!" blurted out Shrub. He sounded very doubtful.

"Shhh," said Anya.

"I am the Good Wizard," said the woman calmly. She bent her head to meet the newt's gaze. "And you are?"

"Shrub," said Shrub. "I'm a good *thief*. I'm going to join Bert and the Association of Responsible Robbers. Just as soon as Anya changes me back. Are you sure you're even a wizard?"

"Shrub," Anya warned, seeing their appointment about to vanish before their eyes, and with it dryness, sustenance, and comfort. She sneezed violently at that thought, and the cold edged its way a bit more into her chest.

"You think I don't look like a wizard, is that it?" asked the woman.

"I'm sure you're the Good Wizard," said Anya fervently. "No one else could have such boots."

"Yes, they are nice boots," said the Wizard, if indeed she was the Wizard. She pushed one foot forward and pointed the toe. "Very nice, if I say so myself. Surprisingly waterproof too, even better than I'd hoped. But I suppose you were expecting someone more . . . ah . . . traditional, my suspicious newt?"

Shrub mumbled something. Anya could only catch the words *beard*, *staff*, and *with stars*.

"Ah, you want the full regalia," said the red-booted woman, who still might or might not be the Good Wizard. She turned her head to one side and spoke, apparently to thin air. "The complete outfit, please. Quick as you can."

She paused, as if listening to a reply. Anya could almost hear something too, but strain as she might, it was no more than a faint whistling, like some small bird in the far distance warbling in a tree.

"I don't know. In the cupboard by the front door, if you put them back properly the last time, I would suppose. Hurry along now."

"Invisible servant?" asked Anya. She had been reasonably confident from the boots, but now it was definite. Surely only a wizard could have an invisible servant.

"First-year apprentice," said the Good Wizard. "All wizarding apprentices start as invisible and *almost* inaudible servants. It's the only way. Barely heard but not seen. Leads them into temptation, and that's always a test. He'll be a while, so we might as well go on. We'll meet him on his way back. Provided young Master Newt is satisfied I'm not some imposter who'll drink your blood or something equally horrible."

"I'm not going anywhere until I see for sure," said Shrub stubbornly.

Ardent nuzzled Anya's hand. She looked down and he twitched his nose. She bent lower, and the dog whispered in her ear.

"She doesn't smell of magic, but her boots do, a lot. And her cloak, and that ring, her fingernail, and some other stuff. Shouldn't a wizard smell of magic?"

Before Anya could answer, the Wizard looked very piercingly at Ardent. She clearly had exceptional hearing, probably from having to listen to nearly inaudible invisible servants.

"What are they teaching royal dogs these days? Surely you know how wizards work?"

"I might have skipped that lesson," said Ardent. He looked at Anya guiltily. "I only missed a few. Honest."

"And what are they teaching princesses?" asked the Wizard, directing her attention to Anya.

"Nothing," said Anya. "I mean, everything I've learned I've had to learn myself. Mostly from books. And I've never really read very much about wizards."

"Then it is past time you learned," observed the Wizard. "Follow me."

"I ain't going nowhere," repeated Shrub. He plonked himself down and set his feet into the bridge, to make it hard for anyone to shift him. "Certainly not into that tower. I might never come out!"

"No one is going into the tower," said the Wizard. "It's not safe at all. Anyone can see it's only magic holding the top half up above the bend. Could fall down anytime!"

"You don't live in the tower?" asked Anya. "I thought wizards always lived in—"

"We use the lower part for storage. No one's lived in it for years, not since my predecessor's predecessor. Ah!"

She paused and half turned, nodding towards an unseen presence. Anya again thought she could almost hear something, but this time it was like muffled panting.

"He ran all the way, like a good lad. Hopefully this will satisfy your suspicious lizard."

"I'm not a lizard," grumbled Shrub. "I'm a *newt*."

"Yes, I know," said the Wizard, smiling. She really looked preposterously young, Anya thought. She had very white teeth, and amazing dark hair and lustrous dark skin. All very pretty, not like the wizards in stories. Perhaps Shrub was right to be suspicious . . . it was so overcast and foggy she could even be a vampire. Though her teeth didn't look *that* pointy, and Anya couldn't see the gill slits in her neck where a vampire sucked in extra air to create the vacuum they used to draw out their victims' blood . . .

"I don't like putting this on," said the Wizard. "But I suppose for the sake of tradition and a suspicious visitor, it must be done."

She reached into apparently empty air and drew out a pair of gold-rimmed spectacles. Putting them on, she extended her arm again, this time drawing forth a huge and very bushy mass of unruly white hair, which she threw up in the air. Craning her neck back, she looked up as it fell, the hairy bundle settling on her face. When she looked back down, the mass of hair had settled as a vast, snowy beard complete with mustachios that trailed almost to her waist.

It was a very impressive beard, for its volume and its incredible whiteness, but most of all because it looked completely real. Though odd, since attractive young women didn't normally have flowing white beards that were half as tall as they were.

"Almost there," she said, holding out her open hand, her fingers closing on a suddenly materialized hat. It was very tall, pointed, and made of a deep purple velvet liberally covered with stars, moons, and a comet, all embroidered in silver and gold wire with small ruby chips for the comet's trail.

The Wizard turned the hat upside down, reached inside, and took out a boiled sweet, striped in rainbow colors. She popped this in her mouth, put her hand in the hat again, and drew out a long staff of ebony, shod with silver at each end, and banded seven times in gold, indicating her rank as a full wizard of the seventh circle.

"There," said the Wizard, putting on her hat and stooping forward a little to lean on the staff. Her voice was male now, and very deep and sonorous. "Do you trust that I am the Good Wizard? Or must I blast you with fell lightnings?"

"No, no, I accept!" gabbled Shrub. "I'm sorry I doubted you, Lord Wizard!"

"Good," said the Wizard, her voice booming. She handed the staff back into the air. It vanished, followed by the hat and the glasses.

The beard, however, would not come off. The Wizard tugged at it several times, swore in her deep male voice, spat out the boiled sweet, swore some more in her normal voice, and stamped the bridge with her red boots, splashing muddy water everywhere.

"I hate this beard!" she said. "Trust him to play a trick on me. Just when I think I've found the last trap in it, I discover another one."

"Who's tricking you?" asked Anya carefully. She had edged away as the Wizard stamped, fearful that this sudden anger might be directed elsewhere than the beard.

"Oh, my predecessor!" said the Wizard. She gave the beard another tug, and suddenly laughed, all traces of anger gone. "It's traditional you know, to play games with things you leave for later wizards. This was his beard, naturally I mean, before he enchanted it for his heir, who turned out to be me. He was very fond of it, not least because it gave him his nickname for many decades. You would have heard of him, I expect?"

Anya shook her head.

"The long, flowing white beard," hinted the Wizard, running her hands through it to show off its properties. "Snowy, ridiculously white . . ."

Ardent's ears suddenly sprang up.

"Snow White!" he barked excitedly. "Tanitha told us. But he was the Good Wizard of all Yarrow, long, long ago. He vanished in the Deluge, drowned."

"He didn't drown!" said the Wizard. "Good gracious! Only a very incompetent wizard would let themselves drown. He just got— well, involved in a personal matter, and was caught up with things for a century or so. In a cave. And then he was tired of wizarding, so he handed over the beard and the trappings to me. You might see him later, if he's up. He does come to dinner once in a while."

"Dinner!" barked Ardent reflexively.

"Dinner," sighed Anya. She hesitated, then asked, "And is there . . . could there be . . . might I have a bath?"

The Wizard looked the muddy, bedraggled princess up and down, then across at the numerous dark streaks that gave Ardent a somewhat tigerish aspect, and the mud caked on Shrub's head.

"Baths for all of you, I think!" she pronounced. Ardent's ears and tail drooped as she went on. "Save your otter-maid, who perhaps would like a swim in the reflecting pool instead."

"A pool?" asked Smoothie, who had been watching the muddy, flooded river with her sharp eyes, noting the currents and hoping for signs of fish. "Of clean, fresh water?"

"Oh yes," said the Wizard. "Got to have a crystal-clean pool or you can't get the visions sharp enough to work out what's going on. It's fed by an underground spring. Come to think of it, you can probably get your own dinner there. Plenty of eels infest the place."

"*Eels,*" said Smoothie, her sharp-toothed smile spreading wide across her half-human, half-otter face.

"Lots of eels," confirmed the Wizard. She smiled too, but the smile vanished as a raven cawed somewhere off in the distance and was answered by another. She looked up at the sky, her eyes narrowing, and stroked her beard. Anya looked too, and caught just a glimpse of a black shape, disappearing into the low clouds.

"I like a raven with a message to come straight to the recipient," said the Wizard. "I would rather not see skulking ravens, like those two. Spies, without a doubt. Come! No point standing around here."

Anya agreed. Ravens were used as messengers by many people, but Duke Rikard had a whole bunch of particularly unsavory ravens he employed as his agents. And where the ravens were, she suspected weaselfolk would soon follow. Or assassins. Or both. Or worse.

Anya shuddered at the thought of something worse than weaselfolk, remembering those snapping jaws so close to her throat. But she forced the memory aside, and tried to think of nice things . . .

Like the prospect of a hot bath, which was now firmly fixed in her immediate future.

The Good Wizard led them up at a fast pace towards the tower but, almost within its shadow, turned sharply to the right. There was a path there, of well-rolled gravel, bordered with white-painted stones. She crunched along the graveled way with the others following, towards a huge arched gate set into the hillside.

The gate was enormous, thirty feet high and twenty feet wide, of ancient timber faced with bronze plates, tarnished dark with age. It looked as if it would take a dozen strong people to push it open, a team of oxen, or even a giant porter. But the Wizard knocked on it with her ringed hand, and the lines of a lesser door set within the gate became visible, traced in fire.

"Flashy, I know," said the Wizard, pushing this regular-size door open. "Some long-ago Good Wizard had a taste for this sort of show. When the full gate opens, there are gouts of flame and brazen trumpets, the whole works. Quite fun if you like that kind of thing, but it takes too long. Please, do come in."

There was an antechamber beyond the gate, well lit with colored lanterns that burned without smoke or visible flame. A long, highly polished mahogany bench ran down the middle of the room. There was a boot rack against one wall, on which rested two or three dozen shoes and boots of different makes and sizes, nearly all as beautifully made as the Wizard's own red boots. A line of bronze coat hooks adorned the opposite wall, most of them taken up by cloaks, over-coats, surcoats, wraps, and other outerwear, again all beautifully made with style and precision.

The majority of the coats were strangely small in length, Anya noted, though very broad in the shoulder. And many of the boots and shoes were similarly wide but short. Very few would fit the Wizard, therefore most of these items were not her own, but for some other members of the household.

The Wizard sat down on the bench and unbuttoned her boots, swapping them for a pair of elegant slippers with curled-up toes that had small bells at the very tips, so she tinkled as she stood up. She shrugged off her cloak and hung that up too, revealing an elegant robe underneath, of highly calendared dark blue wool with a silver brocade trim.

"Leave your shoes here," she said. "They will be cleaned. Take slippers from the box. I don't like muddy footprints on the carpets. They don't fly so well when they're dirty, and you never know when they might be needed with no time for cleaning."

Ardent looked down at his paws, which were undeniably muddy.

"There are dog slippers there too, Ardent," said the Wizard. "And ones for young Master Shrub and Champion Smooth Stone Oysterbreaker."

"I don't need slippers," said Smoothie. She sat down, bent double, and licked her feet clean in a few seconds.

"How do you know *all* of us?" asked Anya. Only Shrub and herself had given their names.

"I *am* a wizard." The Good Wizard pulled at her beard again, but it still wouldn't come loose. "On to baths! Robes will be provided, while your clothes are washed and . . . ah . . . mended. Or perhaps replaced?"

"That was an accident," said Ardent, noticing the Wizard looking at the holes in Anya's kirtle. "About these baths, perhaps just a shallow one; I c-c-could pop in and out? And soap . . . soap isn't really—"

"Ardent," said Anya in a firm but kindly tone. "You will have a bath. With soap."

She helped the dog on with his slippers. They were soft leather moccasins that fit perfectly over his paws and were tied with blue ribbons. Shrub's were sturdier wooden clogs with felted soles, and there was even a kind of sock that went over his tail so it wouldn't drag dirt across the floor. Or the precious carpets.

"Very good," said the Wizard. She opened the door and led them into a vast hall. Though it must have been carved out of the rocky hill, the walls were lined with paneled chestnut, as was the ceiling high above, save for the great oaken beams and braces.

The floor was entirely covered in carpets, so that whatever surface lay beneath was invisible. Dozens and dozens of carpets, of different sizes and designs and patterns, overlapping one another everywhere. In places there were raised sections where clearly three or four carpets lay beneath the visible ones, making for a rather uneven surface. The carpets were of very mixed ages: some of great antiquity, very old and faded, others vibrant, their colors strong, as if they had just been made. It was unusual flooring, Anya thought, but certainly warm and comfortable.

There was a massive fireplace at the far end, bigger than the largest one in the hall at Trallonia Castle, just as this hall was also much larger. Several logs—really the rough-hewn trunks of large trees—were burning slowly in a grate made of wrought iron in the shape of interwoven roses, with oversize thorns. Bronze firedogs that looked very much like Ardent, only larger, stood at each end of the hearth, their snouts bright from rubbing, flanks dark with the patina of great age. An iron basket held an assortment of pokers, tongs, toasting forks, and ash shovels, some bronze, some iron, and some of a silvery metal that Anya couldn't identify.

A long table of dark, polished timber dominated the hall. Only the far end was set for dinner, thirteen places in all, though the table could easily seat forty. Each setting featured half a dozen different knives and forks, Anya was very pleased to see, suggesting a quantity of food. And there were three glasses, two metal goblets, and one wooden beaker set for each diner too, indicating a great choice of drink. Anya didn't care about that, as she drank only water, but it was still impressive.

There were four ordinary-looking heavy oak doors on the left wall, and eight rather extraordinary doors on the right wall. These eight special doors were painted with scenes of craft and industry, beautiful paintings, but very old, as could be seen by some parts that were faded or obscured by decades or perhaps even centuries of collected dust and grime.

The painted doors depicted people—curiously small and broad people—hard at work, their lips curiously pursed. Not pouting, though Anya couldn't quite work out what they were doing.

One door showed a forge, bright with fire, two leather-aproned smiths hammering at an anvil; another a cobbler at a last, putting gold nails in the sole of a fancy boot; the next, weavers at a very large carpet loom; then jewelers at their desk with fine instruments; embroiderers on their stools with great spools of thread all around;

a cabinetmaker with many different timbers in front of him, a partially made screen under construction; and the seventh showed a room of many bones and tusks, with two of the short folk engaged in an intricate carving of some very long and whorled horn that Anya thought might be that of a unicorn, save that it was black and not a lustrous and pearly white.

The eighth door had the portrait of a wizard, much like the Good Wizard when she was in full regalia, with the long white beard, the starry hat, and staff. But it was not her face with those bright eyes, nor quite the same beard, and the hat was taller and had bigger stars and no comet. The staff had *nine* gold bands and a giant ruby on the end. This painting was even more clouded in darkness at the edges, a sign of great age.

"Bathhouse is through there," said the Good Wizard, pointing to the first plain door on the left. "My apprentices will help you with towels and niceties. Choose any bath you like. There should also be a small terrarium where you can place your frog prince—"

She looked to one side, tilting her head to listen to an invisible apprentice.

"Yes, it has been put there. It is quite secure, and contains a number of bugs and so forth. Please, choose your bath."

The door opened, revealing a large, steamy chamber beyond, in which nine copper bathtubs with brazen feet were arrayed in a line, each with a small table beside it laden with soaps and oils. They were already full of hot water, as evidenced by the steam. There were paper-and-bamboo screens arranged between them, which were open at present, but could be slid shut for privacy. Each of the screens was decorated with a different motif, reflecting the paintings on the doors. Anya noted the closest had small anvils, the next shoes. Clearly, the doors and bathtubs were identified for some other reason. Perhaps simply convenience, so the inhabitants of the Wizard's halls could say "the Smith's door" or "the Cobbler's bath." But it seemed to be more significant than that.

"The reflecting pool is reached by a small stair behind the fireplace, Mistress Otter," said the Good Wizard. "Just keep going down and you'll find it."

"Eels!" exclaimed Smoothie, and she was off.

"I don't like hot water," said Shrub grumpily. "Newts don't, you know."

"My apprentices will arrange the temperature according to your liking," said the Wizard. She reached under her beard and pulled out a large watch, flicking open the somewhat battered silver case. Watches were quite rare, and Anya had only seen one before. That belonged to Duke Rikard. But the Wizard's watch was not at all similar. It had too many hands and small inset windows within the main face, showing a crescent moon and a color wheel that was moving quickly from blue to red.

"Dinner in thirty minutes," said the Good Wizard, flicking the watch shut. She tugged the beard again. "I'm going to go and get this thing off."

"Are you sure we may use the baths?" asked Anya. She gestured at the doors. "They do seem to belong to particular people . . . or trades. Like the doors."

The Good Wizard's eyebrows went up.

"You really don't know anything about wizards, do you?" she asked. "The doors are to my teachers' rooms, and those are their baths. But they won't begrudge visitors using them; they only bathe once a week as a rule."

"Your teachers?" asked Anya. "There are other wizards here?"

"None save my predecessor, who does wizarding no more," said the Good Wizard. "My teachers are master artisans. They teach me their crafts."

"I don't understand," said Anya. "Like you said, I don't know anything about wizards."

"Wizards gather the stray magic left over from sorcerers' spells, witches' blessings and curses, the breath of dragons, the stab of a unicorn's horn, the swish of a mermaid's tail . . . all things that emanate magic. We then combine this magic we collect with ordinary things, which we must make. We craft items of the rarest magic entirely ourselves, like my red boots. I am a good cobbler—that is my first trade. I have practiced it for some eleven years. Now I am learning to work metal, and in time shall make magic rings and suchlike of the first order. But for things of lesser magic, I work with my teachers, putting the magic in their crafting, while also learning their craft. That is what wizards do. Oh, and be wise as well. Or attempt to be so."

"Oh," said Anya. "I had no idea. I only know about sorcery, and its cost. Does wizarding take its toll, the same as sorcery? I mean, with sniffles and colds for little spells and coldness of the spirit for the big ones?"

"It does not," said the Good Wizard gravely. "But it is slow. It takes years to learn each craft, of course, and often decades to gather the magic to put into the crafting. This is too slow for many. And there is another thing that many consider a drawback."

"What is that?" asked Anya.

"All things a wizard makes are flawed in some way. A Good Wizard, like myself, will do this intentionally. A Bad Wizard's works will have some accidental flaw, derived from their nature. All our work has some weakness."

"But why?"

"To limit the object's power," said the Good Wizard softly. "Power is always best limited. Now go and have your bath."

CHAPTER FIFTEEN

Dinner for Thirteen, One Absent

Ardent stood shivering in his bath, though it was perfectly warm. Anya, who had already had hers, stood next to it, encouraging him to get out. She was as warm as fresh-made toast, beautifully clean, wearing flannel pajamas that had been just ironed, and over them a silk dressing gown with a dragon's head embroidered on the back. Her feet were graced with sheepskin slippers lined with fleece.

The hot bath, liberally infused with rosemary, had also banished her cold, though perhaps only temporarily. At least her nose had stopped running and her chest felt clear.

"I c-c-an't get out," said Ardent. "This bath has paralyzed me. Or the soap that invisible fiend used had some paralyzing properties."

"Don't be silly," said Anya. She stepped away to avoid the expected splashing, looked to the hall door, and said, "Mmmm. I can smell dinner. I hope there's some left for us."

Ardent sprang from the bathtub and took several tottering steps towards the hall before Anya hauled him back by his collar and wrapped him in the huge towels an invisible apprentice swiftly handed to her.

"Don't worry, I'm sure the Good Wizard never runs out of food," said Anya as she vigorously toweled the dog dry. "I wonder if her teachers will come to dinner? There were thirteen places set. The Wizard, seven teachers, you, me, Smoothie, and Shrub. That's twelve . . ."

Ardent said something indistinct under the towel. Anya removed it. The dog crossed his paws in his best about-to-declaim-poetry posture and said:

> Seven dwarves, out of the west
> Seven makers, finest of the c-c-raft
> Snow White and the seven best
> I forget the rest.

"What is that?" asked Anya.

"The first three lines are from a poem story Tanitha tells the pups," said Ardent. "I really do forget the rest, though. It's all about Snow White the wizard, and the seven dwarves he worked with, and all the fabulous things they made together. Like the Magic Mirror and all that."

"Oh, I remember that too!" exclaimed Anya. As a very little toddler, she had often joined the great dog pile of puppies that writhed and wriggled about as the dog matriarch told them stories. But it had been many years since she had rolled and tumbled about with puppies on the floor, and she had forgotten most of Tanitha's stories.

"Snow White and the Seven Dwarves! No wonder they look so short and broad in the paintings on the doors. But surely it can't be the same ones? Even if Snow White the former Good Wizard is still alive? I mean, I know wizards are long-lived, but—"

"Dwarves are like rocks," said Ardent. He was unusually sedate, possibly still bath-affected, and was not trying to chase his tail or speak too quickly. "Very long-lasting, unless something breaks them. Tanitha told us that too. But I've never met any before."

"I guess we're going to meet some now," said Anya. She had been awed enough by the Good Wizard, tempered somewhat by the woman seeming to be only a decade or so older than herself. But to meet the fabled Seven Dwarves and possibly even Snow White himself . . .

"His must be the thirteenth place," she said quietly. "Snow White."

"*If* he c-c-omes. The Wizard only said he *might*." Ardent sniffed the air. "Mmm. Roast beef. You know his real name, don't you?"

"Whose real name?"

"Snow White's," said Ardent, shrugging off the towel and heading for the door. "His real name."

"No," said Anya, chasing after him.

"Neither do I. C-c-an't remember. Tanitha told us, though. There are stories about him under that name as well."

As the door swung open ahead of them, doubtless pushed by an invisible apprentice, Anya wondered where Shrub had gone. He'd climbed out of his bath earlier, protesting that the water was too clean for a newt. The last she'd seen of him was as a lump underneath a rapidly moving towel that an apprentice had thrown over him. The towel had been heading this way, so hopefully he was already at the dinner table. And Smoothie too, if she had managed to tear herself away from the eels.

Anya had spent her time in the bath thinking very deep and hard. Her hunger pangs had receded with warmth and the prospect of an imminent meal, so she had been able to think clearly for what felt like the first time in ages.

Her thoughts had naturally enough been about the recipe for Transmogrification Reversal Lip Balm, and the ingredients she needed for it, and where she might get them. But she had found her mind also inexorably drawn to the conversation she'd had with Bert the Responsible Robber and the ancient raven Dehlia, last of the wardens of the High Kingdom of Yarrow.

This in turn led to thoughts about the All-Encompassing Bill of Rights and Wrongs, and those thoughts led to the common people of Trallonia and what they deserved as opposed to what they generally got. This made her think about Morven as queen, and indeed about rulers in general and what Duke Rikard might do if he became king, which in turn led to thinking about the perils of sorcery and her own ambitions in this direction, and the curiosity that was wizardry, and back again to the problem of Duke Rikard, and thus the lip balm and finally, at long last, to a number of drawn-out sighs she hastily curtailed when she realized she was sighing them.

No matter which way she looked at it, Anya had the distinct feeling that her Quest was going to get a lot more complicated than she wanted. But short of giving up, that's the way it was going to be.

She was not going to give up.

This reminded her about the only other thing she remembered from her mother. As well as the comfort of the red woolly, she remembered the sound of her mother's voice, that soft voice telling her how much she was loved.

And she remembered one conversation between her parents in detail, though she was not absolutely sure whether she remembered it or had made it up. But it was true either way.

Her mother had been talking to her father. They had thought Anya was asleep, but actually she'd been nestled in her mother's lap, listening intently with her eyes shut.

"I will not give up. It is the right thing to do, no matter the consequences."

Anya wondered what it was that her mother had decided to do, and whether it had played some part in her early and untimely death.

"It is the right thing to do, no matter the consequences."

Now that she knew about the All-Encompassing Bill of Rights and Wrongs, she wondered if her mother's words had something to do with that. It would have been just like her mother to want to bring back the old laws and make things fairer for the people.

Anya sniffed and wiped a tear from her eye.

"Makes me c-c-ry too," said Ardent. He was staring at the table through the open door, nose up and sniffing, inhaling the scent from the platters of roast beef and roast lamb and roast pork with roast potatoes and roast sprouts and roast pumpkin and roast whole cloves of garlic, intermingled with the somewhat lesser scents (to a dog) of a salad of pungent summer herbs and watercress, a huge bowl of steamed green beans, and several long platters stacked high with fresh-baked, crusty bread.

"Come on," said Anya. "Let's eat."

She was extremely hungry, but even so she stopped short as they went through the door, and Ardent ran into the back of her legs yet again. She stopped because the *Seven Dwarves* were standing by the long table. Four male and three female dwarves, all of them wearing pajamas and silk dressing gowns like Anya's. They were no more than four feet six inches tall, but far broader in the shoulders, and their arms and legs were much more muscular.

They didn't look particularly old in face or features, but there was a quality about them that suggested great age indeed. Though each had different colored skin, in all of them that skin gave the sense of ancient, weathered stone; the deep blackness of obsidian, the pale gray of slate, the gold-red of granite, the translucence of limestone, and many shades in between.

Two of the male dwarves had long beards, neatly tied. The third had a kind of long goatee, and the fourth no beard, only a long, waxed moustache. Two of the female dwarves had short hair, beautifully cut, and one had very, very long plaited hair under a soft velvet cap that Anya immediately wanted for herself, because it was so perfect.

"Ah, the little maid and the puppy!" exclaimed the dwarf with the waxed moustache. He held up one large hand, heavy with rings, and waved them closer. "Come, let us greet you properly to these halls!"

Anya walked across the soft carpets towards the dwarves, with Ardent at her heels. She couldn't see Shrub or Smoothie, nor the Good Wizard. The dwarves were all watching her, and she felt shy and anxious, and very young all of a sudden.

"I am oldest, so I speak for us all," said the moustached dwarf. "As far as greetings go, in any case. My name is Sygror, and we welcome you younglings to this place."

He bowed carefully, from the waist, his head back, and deep brown eyes never leaving Anya's. The other dwarves did likewise.

None spilled their drinks, their movements so precise that hands holding glasses or tankards remained as steady as . . . rock.

Anya did not bow back. She just stared.

"We wore night attire like yourself in the hope that it would make you more comfortable," said one of the female dwarves. "Yet you seem disturbed? My name is Tinya, which I believe is close to your own?"

Anya blinked several times, blushed as she remembered her manners, and bowed. Ardent followed, bending his head low over his crossed paws, getting slightly off balance as he uncrossed them to straighten up.

"Yes," said the princess. "My name is Anya, so it is similar. Thank you, pajamas are good—I mean comfortable . . . I'm sorry, it is just . . . you are the Seven Dwarves of legend, and I . . . I am a little overwhelmed."

"And hungry," added Ardent. "I am Ardent. Royal Dog. Not a puppy."

"We see few younglings here," said another dwarf. "And even a much, much older dog would seem but a puppy to us. Yet we do not wish to offend you, Ardent. Let me offer my name in return. I am Gramel."

"And I, Sleipjir."

"Danash, at your service."

"Holkern."

"And last, youngest and least of my fellows, I am Erzefezonim," said the seventh dwarf, the one with the velvet cap Anya so admired. She laughed a deep, rolling laugh, and added, "Being the youngest, I must have by far the longest name. But you may call me Erzef. Come, let us sit and eat. If we wait for the Wizard, we might all become as starved as you are already."

Ardent needed no further encouragement. He jumped to a chair and looked back at Anya for permission to eat, his tongue working overtime to hold back the drool sliding from his jaws.

"Eat!" repeated Erzef. "We do not stand on ceremony."

Anya nodded to Ardent. He whipped around, forced himself to go slow, and gently leaned forward to pick up a huge slab of meat from a central platter and drop it on his own plate. From there, it vanished so quickly Anya could only just believe he'd eaten it. Already, the dog was reaching for more.

But there was plenty. More than plenty, with an additional dozen huge dishes arriving, borne on invisible hands. As Anya watched, she saw the briefest flash of a youngish man's face while one dish was descending to the table, as if a curtain had twitched aside and back again.

"Jeremy, your nose is showing! Adjust your cloak, please."

That was the Good Wizard talking, suddenly at the head of the table. She was also now in pajamas, red-and-yellow-striped pajamas, and over them a black silk dressing gown dotted with golden stars. Her hair had been newly brushed and was enmeshed in a net of silver set with diamonds and moonstones. She still wore the huge white beard, though it had been tied back with golden ribbons to make it easier for her to eat.

"Won't come off," muttered the Wizard, catching Anya's eye. "Could be worse. At least I managed to spit out the voice-changing lolly. If I'd swallowed it, the effect would last for days. Come, eat."

"Thank you," said Anya. "But I should make sure Shrub and Smoothie—"

"I'm here!" said Shrub, his voice emanating from under the table. He popped his head out. "I still only like bugs and worms and such. They've given me some under here, so as not to put you lot off."

"And your otter friend is eating by . . . or in . . . the pool," said the Good Wizard. "But it is as well that you should check. That is the mark of a leader."

"Is it?" asked Anya. She sat down. Now that there was finally all this food in front of her, she felt sort of faint and not at all hungry.

"Take it slow," said Sygror, looking at her with kindly eyes. "Small pieces to start. Chew carefully."

Anya followed this advice, and soon felt better. Well enough to take larger bites, and fill first her plate and then her stomach with food that was at least the equal of, if not better than, anything she had ever had back home.

The silence of deeply contented eating reigned for the next fifteen minutes or more, until Anya put down her knife and fork and took a deep draft of water, and Ardent slid from his chair to lie on his stomach on the floor, with a glazed expression.

The Good Wizard took a sip of her wine, set it down, and spoke to the princess.

"So, you have come to visit me, knowing almost nothing of wizards. What did you hope to find?"

"Help," said Anya. "Tanitha, the matriarch of the royal dogs, suggested you might help us. And so did Bert, the leader of the Association of Responsible Robbers."

"They are both known to us," said the Good Wizard. The dwarves around the table nodded in agreement. Most of them were still eating, though in a desultory way, picking at the dates and apricots that had replaced the main courses, and topping up their wine or beer. "Let me tell you about the help you may find here."

"Please," said Anya. The thoughts she'd had in the bath had coalesced further as she ate, and she even had the beginning, or more than the beginning, of a plan.

"First, you should know that Good Wizards never interfere directly with matters in the wider realm," said the Wizard.

"Never," said Sleipjir. He sounded a touch ironic. Anya noticed the other dwarves were hiding smiles.

"Never interfere *directly*," repeated the Wizard, waving her finger for emphasis. "But we freely give advice to those who ask. And we may give gifts. Occasionally. If we feel like it, or there's a recent birthday or something significant of the sort."

"You forgot letting visitors look in the mirror," said Erzefezonim.

"I didn't forget," said the Wizard. "I just hadn't got to that part yet. We may also allow guests to gaze into the reflecting pool, the Magic Mirror, and see what transpires far afield. Or not, depending."

"Depending?" asked Anya.

"Depending on whether it works or not," said the Wizard. "Very tricky things, reflecting pools. Got to balance the light just right, the fall of shadow. Highly technical business. I'm still getting the hang of it."

"I would very much like your advice," said Anya politely.

"Certainly," replied the Wizard. "Ask aw—"

She was interrupted by the sudden harsh alarm of a rapidly struck bell, followed by a single rather muffled bark from Ardent, whose stomach was so full it was squishing his bark-making innards.

"Front door," said Tinya.

"Without an appointment," said the Wizard, her eyes narrowing.

"Very rude," rumbled Sygror, pushing back his chair.

Suddenly all the dwarves were getting up . . . and they had much bigger and sharper knives in their hands than anything that had been laid on the table.

CHAPTER SIXTEEN

A Threatening Message Is Received

The Wizard had her head tilted to one side, in the characteristic pose that Anya recognized as her listening to one of her invisible apprentices. She raised a hand and gestured to the dwarves.

"It's only a Gerald the Herald," she said. The knives disappeared and the dwarves sat back down. Anya detected a general air of disappointment, as if they'd actually looked forward to some greater trouble.

"Bring him in," said the Wizard to the empty air. She turned to Anya. "Go on."

"I'll wait," said Anya. "I don't want a Gerald the Herald to know what I'm asking."

"Sensible," said the Wizard. "More wine?"

"I don't drink wine," said Anya. "I'm too young."

"You *are* wise. Ever thought of becoming a wizard?"

"Not before now," said Anya. "I've always wanted to be a sorcerer . . ."

Her voice trailed off as the Good Wizard raised her eyebrows.

"But not so much anymore," continued Anya.

This was true. She'd always loved reading about sorcery, and learning the small spells she had mastered so far. The sneezing and the twitches and the occasional rash that came with the sorcery had seemed a small price to pay, and she had never really looked ahead to what would come of wielding greater sorcery, denying the connection between herself and Duke Rikard. He must have started in just the same small way, many years ago.

Now she had finally realized that the path she had put her feet on would inexorably lead either to becoming something essentially inhuman like the Duke, or to being someone like Gotfried. Much as she loved her friend, she had to admit he had been badly damaged by sorcery, and not just because he kept turning into an owl. The librarian was both deathly afraid of sorcery and fascinated by it, which was not a good combination.

Anya was still very much interested in *magic*, and wanted to learn more about it and the different kinds that were practiced in Yarrow. But she had lost much of her interest in sorcery. Or so she told herself, denying that small part of her that insisted on whispering deep in her mind that it could all be worth it. *Just think of the power,* said the voice. *Think of the amazing spells you could do—*

"I might be interested in becoming a wizard," acknowledged Anya, banishing that niggling voice from going on about sorcery being so much superior to all other forms of magic.

"Frogkisser to Become Wizard!" bellowed a voice from near the door. "Princess-Wizard-Frogkisser Triple Threat!"

A Gerald the Herald in wet motley stood dripping in his guest slippers by the door. He was holding a raven under his arm, the large black bird surprisingly quiescent.

"Stop that!" called out the Wizard. "I understand you have a message for me?"

"Raven express," said Gerald. He held up the raven. "Private, not one of our messengers. Only it couldn't ring the bell, so I . . . ah . . . volunteered to help."

"What were you doing within the bounds of my demesne in the first place?" asked the Wizard.

"Wanted to ask for an appointment, Your Wiseness," said the herald, wiping his nose. "Following up the Frogkisser story. Want to make a statement?"

"No," said the Wizard. "Hand over the messenger."

"What about you, Princess?" asked Gerald. He was a different one from the herald in the forest, Anya noticed. He was taller and his hair and moustache looked real. On the other hand, his nose had been artificially lengthened by a wax extension that was coming adrift after getting too wet in the rain.

"I think you need better glue to hold your nose on," Anya advised. "You can quote me on that. Otherwise I have nothing to say."

Gerald pinched his nose to keep it together, and released the raven, which flew to the Wizard.

"Wery vell," he said, with some dignity. "As you vish. I vill vrite the story vrom over thources."

"He means he's going to repeat whatever Duke Rikard tells him," said the Wizard, who was reading the small scroll that had been tied to the raven's leg. The raven, meanwhile, was eating a long piece of pork crackling. "So off you go, Gerald. You can take this raven with you. I don't care for eavesdroppers, human or avian."

"It's raining again," said the herald rather pathetically. "And cold."

"Give him an umbrella and some food," said the Wizard to the air. She looked at the raven. "And you can take that strip of fat, Master Corvus."

The raven ruffled his neck feathers, tapped his beak on the table without letting go of the piece of crackling, and flew to the herald, who was being turned around by invisible hands.

"Wizard's Invisible Brutes Torment Truth Seeker!" shouted the herald as he was bustled out. The raven stood on Gerald's head, still eating the fat.

"Who is the message from?" asked Anya.

"Duke Rikard," said the Wizard. She read it aloud.

" 'To the Wizard known as the *Good* who resides in the Dragon Hill, greetings! Your demesne is *Surrounded* by my *weasel* soldiers and I *Demand* that you deliver to *Me* my errant stepstepdaughter the *Fugitive* princess Anya, who has run *Away* from *school*. Do so or *Else*! Duke Rikard of Trallonia, *Most* powerful Sorcerer.' "

"You won't send me out, will you?" asked Anya very anxiously.

"Of course not," said the Wizard, her words accompanied by a general round of chuckling from the dwarves. They didn't seem concerned at all, which made Anya feel a bit less shaky.

"What about his 'or else'?" said Anya. "And are we really surrounded?"

"Possibly," said the Wizard. "Let's see."

She reached inside her sleeve and took out a small bronze telescope. Pulling it open, she raised it to her eye and looked through it, apparently at the wall.

"There are weaselfolk there, sure enough," she said. "Have a look. Not for too long, though, or you'll go blind. Temporarily."

Anya took the telescope cautiously. "How long is too long?"

"Oh, more than a few minutes."

Anya looked through the telescope. Though she was pointing it at the wall, what she saw was the field outside the Wizard's front door, down to the flooded river. The sun was beginning to set outside, washing the underside of the clouds with a dull red light.

There were figures moving about near the river. Anya moved the telescope to center on one of them, and it suddenly leaped into sharper and closer focus as the magic within the lenses came into greater effect.

It was exactly like the weasel creature who had attacked her before. Perhaps six feet tall, and thin. It had an enlarged weasel's head, all sharp and ferrety, its narrow jaw filled with many sharp teeth. Its arms were long and ended in taloned paws, not fingers. It was covered in short gray fur, but also wore a kind of basic black surcoat that was crudely painted with the letter *R* in white.

For Rikard, Anya supposed. She couldn't remember whether her attacker had worn a surcoat; everything had happened so quickly.

The weasel creature looked as swift, deadly, and unforgiving as she knew they were, and there were at least thirty more of them that Anya could see, most crouched down in a line along the river, their sharp, weaselly eyes fixed on the Wizard's front door.

She lowered the telescope. Her hand shook as she gave it back, and she had to fight against a strong inclination to pull her chin down to protect her throat.

"There is little to fear while you are within these walls," said the Wizard kindly. "Tell me, was the Duke still breathing when you saw him last? Sorcerers usually only get this arrogant when they're technically dead but haven't caught on yet."

"He was breathing," said Anya. "But he looked very pale and cold."

"Hmmm, not in the final stage yet," said the Wizard. "I suppose we'd better get on with things. All done with dinner?"

"Yes, thank you," said Anya. "But what about your advice? I want to ask you—"

"We'll have a look in the Magic Mirror first," said the Wizard. "That might change your questions anyway."

She stood up, as did the dwarves. Anya followed suit. The Wizard bowed to the dwarves, who bowed back.

"While I trust my apprentices will see to the usual defenses, perhaps if you wouldn't mind pitching in, Sygror? I would not wish to become as arrogant as a nearly frozen sorcerer, or perhaps as complacent as a well-fed wizard."

"Aye, we'd be happy to!" exclaimed Sygror. He smiled broadly, an expression mirrored by the other dwarves. "It's been too long since I've felt the weight of mail on my shoulders and held an axe in my hand."

"We had arms practice yesterday," pointed out Erzef.

"Pah! That doesn't count," rumbled Sygror.

"Just don't start anything," cautioned the Wizard. "But in the unlikely event some of these weasel soldiers manage to get inside . . ."

"We'll see they regret it," Sygror vowed. There was a chorus of ayes from the other six dwarves, and they turned about, each heading towards his or her own door, evidently to change from pajamas into more warlike clothing.

Anya, Ardent, and Shrub followed the Wizard to a concealed staircase that was entered through a small door behind the great fireplace. It was narrow and tightly wound, descending into the depths like a stony corkscrew. It was dark at first, and forbidding, but as the Wizard took the first step down, the stone beneath lit up with a greenish light. From there on, every third step did the same, the glow only fading after Shrub, bringing up the rear, had slid over the edge.

At the bottom of the stair, there was a vast limestone cave. Or at least it looked like limestone at first glance, but the color wasn't quite right, or the texture when Anya gingerly touched it with her finger. It took the princess a few moments to realize that it was some kind of bone. Very white, very strong bone.

The cave was dimly lit by thousands of little greenish-white dots on the ceiling high above. They moved about constantly, and Anya felt slightly dizzy when she looked at them directly, her eyes unable to focus until she blinked several times and caught on that the dots were moving not only sideways but also up and down, flying around several feet below the strange white stone.

"Fireflies," the Wizard explained. "Atmospheric, but not bright enough for what we need. Where's that otter-maid of yours?"

Anya looked down from the ceiling. She'd thought the dark floor ahead of her was some other stone, perhaps a kind of basalt, but as her eyes adjusted she realized it was the surface of the reflecting pool. Absolutely still water that must also be very deep, to look so black.

The stillness of the dark water was suddenly broken by the ripples of a moving vee that drew closer and revealed the point to be Smoothie's head. She climbed out of the pool, sleek as ever, but with a look of dissatisfaction on her face.

"I need to be changed back soon!" she said. "This body is terrible for swimming! I could barely catch two eels and a stupid blind fish that was as slow as . . . as a toad!"

"I'll do my best," said Anya soothingly.

"Please stay out of the water now," said the Wizard. "We must let it settle while I arrange the lights."

She raised her hand, and the ring on her middle finger flashed brightly. It was answered by a thin flame on the far side of the pool, which slowly gathered strength to reveal itself as a tall candle in an iron candelabra.

Abra candelabra," said the Wizard, chuckling to herself. She winked at Anya. "Doesn't mean anything. I just like saying that."

The Wizard raised her hand again and the ring flashed. Another candle sprang alight. The Wizard's hand glided through the air, moving as if she was conducting an orchestra, and more candle flames answered.

With the extra light, Anya could see the extent of the pool. It wasn't quite as big as she had thought, perhaps fifty feet wide and thirty feet long. It was ringed with a dozen iron candelabras, each of which could hold five candles, but the Wizard wasn't lighting all of them. She was making a selection, judging the play of light and shadow.

"Almost there," said the Wizard. "Anya, stand in front of me here, on the silver scale."

Anya looked down at the strange white stone. There was indeed a silver scale there, like a fish's, but much larger, bigger than Anya's outstretched hand.

"Last of the dragon's scales," said the Wizard. "The pool lies in his eye socket, and we are standing on his cheekbone."

"This white stone," said Anya. "It's dragon bone?"

"Indeed," answered the Wizard. "Our hall is bounded by his great ribs, the bathhouse lies under the phalanges of his right wing, and so on. We stand within the bodily remains of the last of the great dragons, Karrazin the Bright, and we honor him and his gift."

"It's polite to repeat that last part," added the Wizard in a stage whisper. "Bit of a ritual, dragons never being entirely gone, as it were."

"We honor him and his gift!" Anya said quickly, followed a beat later by Ardent, Shrub, and Smoothie. The princess looked around as she spoke the words, wondering what the Wizard meant about dragons never being entirely gone. They were standing on his bare dead *skull*, after all, which seemed pretty conclusive as far as she was concerned.

"Stand on the scale," repeated the Wizard. "If I've got the light right, the pool will show you three things. Something then, something now, and something that may yet come to be."

Anya gingerly stood on the scale. It felt warm under her feet, even through her fleece-lined slippers.

"How does it work?" she asked.

"Shhh," said the Wizard. "I'll tell you later. It is about to begin. Look into the pool!"

Anya looked at the pool. It was still dark, the twinkling reflections of the candle flames not enough to lighten the deep blackness of the water. But as she kept her eyes fixed, it seemed to her the candles burned higher, their light spreading and joining, the surface of the pool slowly becoming brighter . . . and brighter still. Anya had to squint, and then shield her eyes with her hand. She would have looked away but the Wizard was behind her, suddenly gripping her head with strong fingers. The princess cried out, tears filled her eyes, and even as her cry of hurt and fear echoed through the cave, she saw three things.

The first, a vision from long ago. The hall at home in Trallonia Castle, but a warmer, more comfortable place than it was in Anya's present time. The tapestries on the walls were clean and bright, and there were carpets on the floor, not just rough flagstones. It was winter, or late autumn, for all the fires were lit, and the big one was roaring. In front of that fire, Tanitha was telling a story to a small mound of wriggling puppies . . . and a human child. A little girl in a violet robe trimmed with rabbit fur.

A very young Anya, perhaps three years old.

"The Dog with the Wonderful Nose," said Tanitha. From her tone, it was the ritual announcement of a story. All the puppies barked in excitement, and ceased most of their wriggling. Little Anya clapped her hands. It was obviously a favorite story, or a favorite character.

"The Dog with the Wonderful Nose had a truly extraordinary nose," said Tanitha. "She could tell from the smell on a footprint how tall a man was, and what he was wearing. She could smell an onion bulb growing underground from a dozen paces off. *She could even smell what was going to happen if the wind was blowing the right way.* Well, one day the Dog with the Wonderful Nose was padding along, mindful of her own past business and that of others, when—"

The reflecting pool flashed, bright as the sun.

Anya blinked, dislodging the tears that had formed from seeing a happier time, when both her parents had still been alive. Through the rainbow prism of her tears, she saw the next vision form, showing something that was happening right now.

A group of women was gathered together in a big tent. At least at first it looked like a big tent, before Anya saw that it was actually a huge piece of canvas stretched between four tall standing stones, tied on fairly haphazardly with rope. Through one open corner she could see the sun setting through patchy rain clouds, which suggested that this was happening right now.

The women were engaged in setting up a field kitchen. Some were putting out cooking utensils along a trestle table, others unpacking pots and pans and ladles and skewers and big forks, while others sharpened dozens of different knives, while more sorted and arranged boxes, canisters, and net bags of ingredients.

The women looked ordinary enough. Some were young, some middle-aged, and some old. They wore similar clothes to the villagers in Trallonia the Village, though with touches that showed they were wealthier. All of them wore brooches, for example, fancy brooches with jewels, or amber, or gold beads.

There were thirteen women, which Anya thought was significant. Their luggage was stacked up against one of the standing stones, a pile of cloak bags and valises, topped with thirteen round hat cases. This too was probably important.

"We got everything, then?" asked one of the older women, looking down the table at everything laid out on, under, and beside it.

"I think so," replied the woman next to her. She checked items off on her fingers, and other women nodded or signaled as she spoke. "Pig's coming tomorrow, but the spit is up and the fire pit is ready, isn't it, Agnes? Bread will be delivered by noon—Mollie's lad is taking care of that. Wine is coming—the cart is going slow so as not to upset the claret. Egnetha's lover boy the wine merchant chose it special, so it should be good. Greens from my own garden. My Gert will pick 'em fresh in the morn."

"None of that rampion, mind," said one of the women. "I can't abide it."

All the women laughed.

"There is something," said the first woman. "But I can't think . . . we're missing something. An ingredient? One of the herbs? I just can't put my finger . . ."

Once again, the mirrorlike surface of the pool flashed. Anya screwed her eyes shut against the brilliance, opening them slowly as the intensity of the light faded.

Gradually the third vision, the one of something that might yet come to be, coalesced on the surface of the water.

It was Trallonia again, the village this time, but not as Anya had last seen it. She was looking at the village green, which was not the well-kept square of lawn she was used to, but a small field rank with weeds. The houses across the way had holes in their thatched roofs, and ill-made shutters where once they had diamond-paned glass windows.

A villager Anya recognized, though it took her a few seconds, came skulking by the green. It was Rob the Frogger . . . but far leaner and more ragged than he had been. He had no staff over his shoulder, no suspended frog baskets, and no shoes. His feet were wrapped in dirty rags.

One of the shutters eased open, and a hoarse voice called out from the unseen darkness within.

"Get any?"

"No," said Rob, very shortly. "Not allowed anymore. *She* says all frogs are to be gathered by castle servants and sold in Rolanstown. That's the latest. We'll be eating dirt and drinking air."

He was answered by a groan, and the shutter slowly closed. As it eased shut, the vision faded, leaving Anya staring openmouthed and miserable at the pool, which now once again only showed the reflection of the candle flames and, there in the middle, the blurry image of a distressed princess, staring.

"What did you see?" asked the Wizard quietly.

Anya hesitated for a long moment.

"I think I won't tell you the third one," she said. She had been profoundly disturbed by that vision, most of all by Rob the Frogger's reference to "her." It forced the princess to confront some of the fidgety doubts that had been crawling around in her mind ever since Bert had asked about whether Morven would be a good queen. Or there was the even worse thought that the "her" Rob the Frogger mentioned might mean Anya herself—that even if she managed to defeat Duke Rikard, she'd end up as a sorcerer, and be as evil as he was anyway, or worse.

But how could she prevent that? What if it was some future *Morven* that Rob the Frogger was talking about? It was true she might be a very bad queen if she was not guided in some way. A very forceful way, since Morven wasn't one to listen . . .

"It is only something that *might* come to be," said Anya, half to herself, seeking reassurance that wasn't there. "Something I don't want to happen."

"I understand," said the Wizard. "But the first two visions? I may be able to assist you in understanding whatever the pool has shown."

Anya told her, simply describing the two visions, though it was hard for her not to cry when she talked about listening to Tanitha. She had to reach up and stop her lower lip quivering, pretending she was just wiping her mouth.

"I loved those stories about the Dog with the Wonderful Nose," said Ardent happily. "She had so many adventures, and always worked out what to do by smelling something or other. Do you remember the one about the lost sausages?"

"Not now, Ardent," said Anya, settling the dog back down and scratching his head. He'd become so excited about the story that he'd forgotten his training and jumped up at her.

"The Mirror is tricksome, and not always to be trusted," cautioned the Wizard. "But I believe this time it may have shown you things you need to know."

"How does it work?" asked Anya, repeating her earlier question. "Is it because the water is in a dead dragon's eye socket?"

"Yes . . . and no," replied the Wizard. "Yes, because the bone is a necessary raw material. But the pool as a magical object for divination was made by carving thousands of runes into the bone and investing them with magic. Everything under the surface is covered with them. It took my predecessor and the Seven Dwarves more than ninety years to make it, over three centuries ago."

"And like all magic things made by wizards, it is flawed?"

The Good Wizard bowed her head to acknowledge this.

"What is its flaw?" asked Anya.

"It sometimes shows things you *want* to see, rather than what you *need* to see," replied the Good Wizard. "This can be quite a serious drawback."

"I don't think it did that this time," said Anya. She wiped her eyes, turning the motion into a yawn. "Except maybe the first vision . . . I need to think about what it showed me. And I need to sleep. Maybe I'll work something out in my dreams. If . . . I mean, if it's all right for us to stay the night here?"

She was suddenly afraid, thinking of night falling outside, and the weaselfolk that surrounded the Wizard's demesne. She had barely escaped one of the creatures, and there were dozens out there in gathering dark . . .

"Of course," said the Wizard. "Beds have been made up for you in the library. Guests usually like to sleep there. Very handy for getting a spot of nighttime reading. We will talk in the morning, and you may choose your gift before you go."

"Gift?" asked Ardent.

At the same time, Anya said, "We have to go in the morning?"

"Wizards may give a quester a gift," said the Wizard. "If we feel like it, which I do. And yes, you do need to go in the morning. None may stay here more than a night and a day, save they be a wizard or in the wizard's service."

"Says who?" asked Shrub.

"The All-Encompassing Bill of Rights and Wrongs says so," said the Wizard. "As written on the Only Stone, which was made a thousand years ago by my predecessor's predecessor's predecessor."

"The Only Stone!" exclaimed Shrub.

"Don't get him started," warned Ardent.

"Ah," said Anya. "So it was made by wizards too. What's the Only Stone's flaw?"

"While it offers the bearer total protection against all kinds of magic, they themselves can work no magic, nor have beneficial magic cast upon them."

"And what about the laws carved in the stone? How does the Only Stone make people obey them?"

"It doesn't," said the Wizard. "They were carved in the Stone as a means of ensuring they could never be lost, the Stone being essentially indestructible, unlike paper records, or even ordinary stone tablets. No one considered that the Stone might fall into the hands of evil sorcerers and end up locked away in their fortress in New Yarrow."

"Their meetinghouse is a fortress?" asked Anya. She looked at Shrub. "Your mother didn't mention that. How did you even manage to get on the roof in the first place?"

"Told you I was training to be a thief," muttered Shrub. "I've got all the moves down, I have. Or I did when I wasn't a newt."

He hesitated, licked both eyes, and went on.

"Besides all that, I asked around. There's supposed to be a way in through the sewers as well, but I didn't fancy that, because the bloke who told me about it said it goes through the sorcerers' prison, a horrible place they call the Garden, and I heard enough about that to fair give me the blue jeebles. So I bought a ladder from a chimney sweep's boy and he showed me how to get onto the roof and told me which chimney to go down. Only it was the wrong one, and then I ended up in the Garden anyway, which would have been all right if only I hadn't got soot in my eye, and on the way out I tripped and fumbled the Stone and that Grey Mist got me. Another minute and I'd have been clean away with the loot."

"Hmmm," said Anya. She looked at the Wizard. "I was going to ask about the League of Right-Minded Sorcerers' meetinghouse."

"Indeed?" said the Wizard. There was a slight smile, just visible under her beard.

"It occurred to me—while I was in the bath, thank you—that the best place for me to find *all* the ingredients I need for a sorcerous potion is in a sorcerer's house," said Anya. "Or better still, somewhere where there are a lot of sorcerers. Am I wrong?"

"No," said the Wizard carefully. "Though you might not find *everything* you need, that is a reasonable, if dangerous, assumption."

"A pint of witches' tears might be a bit much," said Anya. "But I've an idea about that as well. From the vision. Do you know anything about witches?"

"A fair amount," said the Wizard. "Besides what we call book knowledge, my great-aunt Deirdre is a witch. I used to help her out from the time when I was a child."

"So I have some questions about witches too," said Anya. She yawned as she spoke, only just covering her mouth at the end, surprised by her own weariness. It had been a very long day, and a lot had happened, but she felt much more tired than she had only minutes before.

"Your questions can wait until morning. The Mirror's visions take their toll," said the Wizard. "Come. I will take you to the library. I suspect there will be no reading for you tonight."

Anya nodded. She was suddenly so tired she could barely stay awake, and staggered at the first step on the way out. Dimly, she was aware of the Wizard taking her arm to help her up the stairs, and Ardent talking.

"I'm not tired," said Ardent. "Have you got any books about dogs?"

CHAPTER SEVENTEEN

Three Breakfasts for a Royal Dog

Anya woke between clean sheets, under an eiderdown, with her head half on a plump goose-feather pillow. There was a heavy weight on her legs, but it shifted as she struggled to get up. She heard and felt the familiar happy thump of Ardent's tail upon the bed as he moved off her feet.

"About time you woke up," he said. "Everyone else is at breakfast already."

"But you waited," said Anya sleepily, giving him a hug.

"I did have a *first* breakfast," admitted Ardent, licking Anya's face. His breath smelled slightly of bacon. "With the apprentices. Second breakfast is with the Wizard and the dwarves."

"Oh!" said Anya, waking up properly. She let go of Ardent and looked around. Her broad and comfortable bed was in a niche on the second level of a very large room that was open in the middle like a courtyard. Galleries ran around all four sides . . . and every gallery was lined floor to ceiling with books!

Anya jumped out of bed and ran to the cast-iron railing to look up and down and across. There were four galleries above her, and above them a roof made of many octagonal glass panes set in an iron framework, allowing a considerable amount of diffuse sunlight to shine down. From the brightness and angle of the sunlight, she could tell the morning was already well advanced.

"Books," said Anya in a rather dazed little voice. This was the biggest library she had ever seen. It must contain thousands, perhaps even tens of thousands of books. She turned back towards her bed and looked at the closest shelves, those on either side of the sleeping alcove. There were small bronze plates set into the rich reddish-brown walnut shelves, identifying the subject or category of the books thereon. Anya crept closer, as if the bookshelves might vanish, and leaned in to read one of the plates.

"'Magic. Theory. General. Pre-Deluge.'"

She looked along the spines of the books. Most had titles there: type embossed, sewn, or stamped into their linen, calf, or metal cases. They all looked very interesting.

"'*The Source of Magic: An Enquiry*,'" read Anya aloud, touching that book, and then the next, "'*The Various Practices of Magic*,'" and a third, "'*Magic: My Thoughts and Analysis*.'"

"We should go to breakfast," said Ardent anxiously.

"Yes," said Anya absently. She was looking at other shelves. They were labeled *Alchemical Treatises: Old* and *Alchemical Treatises: Older* and *Alchemical Treatises: Ancient*. Moving across, an entire bookcase had only one identifying plaque: *Novels. With Magic. Worth Reading.*

Anya was just reaching for one interesting-looking novel entitled *As I Flew out One Morning* when a slight whining noise behind her arrested that movement. She turned around to find Ardent holding a shirt very carefully in his mouth.

"Breakfast right now?" asked Anya, recalled to the present. Ardent nodded.

Anya took the shirt. It was a new one, of fine linen, with the sleeves already tied on with gold ribbons. On the end of the bed, there were more new clothes, all in her size. Underclothes, leather hunting breeches, a leather jerkin with pockets, a woolen cloak that did not smell like old sheep and was a lovely dark red on one side and could be reversed to a dull green on the other, and the great luxury of silk hose. Her old shoes, belt, belt purse, and knife were the only survivors of her previous clothing, but Anya was not sorry. She didn't miss her old kirtle. Breeches were more sensible for questing anyway.

She did check her belt purse after strapping it on. The snuff-box and coins were still there. And the small water bottle that held the ex-druid's blood was with her old clothes. She tucked that in her pouch as well.

"Hurry up!" urged Ardent. "They might run out of breakfast!"

The princess got dressed with her back to the shelves, to avoid further temptation. She knew she didn't have time to read, not if they had to leave that day. Which begged the question of how they were going to leave, if the place was indeed surrounded by weasel soldiers.

But after a good night's very deep sleep, Anya felt much more optimistic about that, and about her Quest in general.

"Lead on," she said to Ardent. "I was so tired last night I can't remember how we got here."

"Two of the invisible servants c-c-carried you," Ardent explained, loping off along the gallery. "There are stairs at each end. Come on!"

Breakfast was in full swing by the time Anya reached the main hall. She stopped in the doorway, just as she had the night before, but this time it was not in awe of the Seven Dwarves. She was a little taken aback to see visitors at the table with the Good Wizard and five of the dwarves.

Bert the robber and Dehlia the warden were there, with more than a dozen Responsible Robbers. All these latter folk looked rather the worse for wear, many sporting bandages, though at least they looked like freshly applied bandages. Bert herself had two fingers on her left hand splinted and tied up, and was wielding her fork very carefully.

Anya walked over to the table, Ardent managing to stay with her and not bound ahead, even though several huge platters of just-cooked bacon were being delivered by the invisible servants.

"Ah, good morning, Anya," said the Wizard. She'd managed to lose the beard overnight. The others were all dressed, and the dwarves were even wearing armor, tough dark iron mail, and leather, but the Wizard was still in her pajamas and dressing gown. "Come, sit. Things have happened in the night, and there is much to discuss. We will talk and eat."

"Good morning," said Anya as she sat down. "Hello, Bert, Dehlia. Um, how did you get here? I thought we were surrounded by weaselfolk?"

"We fought our way through just after dawn," said Bert. "The weasel soldiers don't like the light. We've driven them off temporarily. But your stepfather—"

"Stepstepfather," corrected Anya. She didn't want to acknowledge any closer connection. Even stepstepfather was too close in her opinion.

"Duke Rikard has been busy transforming more and more weasels, and I expect they'll be back in even greater strength come nightfall," said Bert grimly. "I haven't enough robbers here for a pitched battle, even with the assistance . . . the redoubtable assistance . . . of the dwarves."

"Can't you do something?" Anya asked the Wizard.

"Wizards don't interfere directly," the Good Wizard reminded her, neatly cutting the top off her boiled egg. "As long as Rikard's creatures don't actually try to get in, I have to let them alone."

"The important thing is that they are gone for now," said Bert. "So you will be able to leave, Princess. Have you thought about where you are going to go? And about our conversation in the stone theater?"

"About the Bill of Rights and Wrongs?"

"Yes." Bert looked very serious. All the robbers looked serious. So did the raven. And the dwarves. They were all looking at Anya— only the Wizard didn't. She was eating her egg, sprinkling salt on each spoonful before she lifted it to her mouth.

"I have thought about it, and I know it's important." Anya hesitated, torn between a strong desire to commit herself to Bert and Dehlia's cause and an equally strong feeling that she had to stay focused on the Quest. "I'll do my best, my very best, to talk to Morven about it. If I survive. But I can't promise anything more."

Bert opened her mouth to speak, but the Wizard got in first.

"Can't say fairer than that!" she announced cheerfully.

"But—"

Bert started to talk, but the Wizard held up her spoon.

"No, no, can't have my guests pestered," she said. Anya wasn't sure, but she thought she saw the faintest wink cross her left eye, where Bert could see it but Anya almost couldn't. Whether it was the words, or the possible wink, or that silver spoon held up so firmly,

Bert subsided, though her mouth was set in a grim line. She exchanged a look with Dehlia. Anya could interpret that one, or thought she could. The robber and the raven were not going to give up.

"Why me?" asked Anya. "There must be tons of other princesses, or even princes in a pinch, who are actual heirs to their kingdoms. Why not choose one of them to reestablish the whole Bill of Rights and Wrongs and the High Kingdom and everything?"

"You are not the first we've tried," said Dehlia calmly. The gaze of her single eye was fixed uncomfortably on Anya again. "Nor, it seems, will you be the last."

"Eat your breakfast, Anya," said the Wizard. "And you may ask your questions. Danash and Holkern are in the treasure room, and will bring up a selection of gifts for you to choose from shortly."

Anya ate her first breakfast while Ardent galloped through a second and possibly third breakfast next to her, if you counted the two-minute pause he'd taken between polishing off a plate of fried bacon and eggs and a bowl of porridge.

"You'll get fat," she said to him as he looked longingly at a plate of freshly cooked kippers.

"I'm just making up for future lost meals," said Ardent with dignity. But he didn't take a kipper. Smoothie did, eating it slowly with her face all scrunched up, until the Wizard suggested she go to the reflecting pool and catch her own fresh eels.

Shrub was under the table again, as was evidenced by the occasional horrible crunching noise as some particularly hard-shelled insect met its end.

"Witches," said Anya when she had finally finished breakfast, toast crumbs and marmalade drops just wiped off her mouth.

"Yes?" asked the Wizard.

"I remember reading somewhere 'All witches are cooks, but not all cooks are witches.' What does that mean?"

"Cooking is the foundation of witches' magic," the Wizard answered. "They cook blessings or curses. So they must be cooks to begin with."

"The stories say they're all ugly," said Anya. "But in the vision I saw, they looked normal. I'm pretty sure they *were* witches. A coven of thirteen. I mean, some were better-looking than others, but they didn't have those horrible noses, and the hairy warts and everything."

"Ah, you didn't see them dressed up," said the Wizard. "Great-Aunt Deirdre had the most awful hairy wart. She used to put it right on the end of her chin. Ghastly! But no, they're just like you and me. The tall hats, the warts, the snake-infested hair—that's all traditional costume. Like my beard, hat, and staff."

"And in the stories I read witches are always evil," said Anya. "But again, the ones I saw seemed nice enough. Hard to tell just from that, though."

"Some witches cook more curses than blessings," said the Wizard. "Sometimes that's because they feel out of sorts with people and want to make trouble. That kind often gets called evil. But far more often the curse cookers are doing it because that's what people in their local area want. Supply and demand. They're not intrinsically evil. Or good. But witches do tend to be good at business. Sometimes they get so good at it they become confused about good and evil, measuring everything only in terms of money."

Anya nodded. This made perfect sense, and fitted in with the plan that had been forming in her head ever since her bath.

"The preparations I saw in my vision, the thirteen witches getting ready to cook something tomorrow . . . I guess today, actually . . . their kitchen was under canvas spread between standing stones. Do you know where that might be?"

The Wizard looked at Bert, who still had a very serious expression on her face.

"Probably Brokenmouth Hill in the middle of the Blasted Heath," said Bert slowly. "The standing stones look like teeth, hence the name. Witches do use it for their feasts."

"Is it far away?" asked Anya. "And is the Blasted Heath very dangerous?"

"Two, maybe three days on foot for you," Bert replied. "But the Blasted Heath is safe enough. Lots of little farms and villages, and most of the villages have their own witch."

"I thought it would be a barren wasteland," said Anya. "Inhabited by fell creatures. That's what it said on my favorite map. There were pictures of all kinds of monsters on it."

"That must be a very old map," said the Wizard. "The Blasted Heath was indeed like that long ago, but has been settled and prosperous for centuries now."

"It's too far, though," said Anya, her face a little fallen. "I thought I could get my pint of witches' tears there tonight."

"Witches don't c-c-cry," said Ardent. "I remember that. C-c-can't remember why."

"It would be more accurate to say witches don't cry from sorrow," the Wizard clarified. "Nor do they laugh. At least not in front of outsiders."

"Then how do you get witches' tears?" asked Ardent. "Bite them till they can't help c-c-crying?"

"No," said Anya. "I figured it out from my first vision. The reflecting pool *was* showing me something useful. The Dog with the Wonderful Nose could smell them growing underground, and the witches are cooks, so they use them. I think they've forgotten to get some, so I should be able to do a deal to give them some, in return for their tears."

"Give them what?" asked Ardent. "Turnips? Potatoes?"

"No, *onions*," said Anya. "I give them onions, and handkerchiefs to collect the tears they shed when they're cutting up the onions. Then I wring the handkerchiefs out to collect the tears."

"Good idea," said the Wizard approvingly. "But I suspect they'll want more than onions in return. Remember, I told you: Witches are usually very business oriented."

"But I can't get there in time anyway," said Anya. "Their feast is tonight."

"Well, we'll see about that," said the Wizard. "I might be able to help you there. Depending on which gift you choose."

"Thank you," said Anya. She looked down at herself. "Thank you for these clothes too."

"Oh, that's nothing. Not magical at all. They hardly count as gifts. But tell me, after you get the tears from the witches, which I have no doubt at all you will manage, what next?"

"We'll go to New Yarrow," said Anya. "And steal the rest of the ingredients from the League of Right-Minded Sorcerers!"

"And the Only Stone!" called out Shrub from under the table.

"No, just the ingredients," said Anya. "I'm sure they'll be less well guarded."

"Bold," said the Wizard, cutting her toast into five individual soldiers. She took another boiled egg and sat it on her eggcup. "But it could work. Ah, here come Danash and Holkern."

The two dwarves had come out of the Wizard's door, carrying a large and clearly heavy chest. They brought it over and laid it down between the Wizard and Anya.

"Let's make sure this is the right one," said the Wizard, bending down to lift up a cardboard label that was tied to one of the chest's handles with multicolored string. "Ah yes. 'Choices for Princess Anya of Trallonia.'"

She nodded to the dwarves, who threw back the lid . . .

CHAPTER EIGHTEEN

The Quester May Choose a Gift, but Only One

A nya couldn't help but crane forward. However, there were no astonishing magical treasures inside. Anya was disappointed and puzzled to see that the chest was empty, save for six small paper envelopes.

"Did I explain that it is a random choice?" asked the Wizard. "You pick one of the envelopes. You'll get whatever is written inside it."

"Can't you just give me something that would be useful?" asked Anya. "I mean, I don't want to be ungrateful—"

"Not allowed," interrupted the Wizard. "Can't interfere directly, you know. Even a random choice of a gift is stretching it a little bit."

She bent down and picked up the envelopes, shuffling them clumsily. One fell on the table. The Wizard picked it up and put it with the others, then fanned them out. But the one she'd dropped stuck out more than the rest. Anya looked at it, then up at the Wizard, who flexed her eyebrows in a way that might or might not indicate anything.

"I can tell you what the choices are for you, and their flaws."

"Please do," said Anya eagerly.

"There is the Sword of Never-Ending Sharpness. I hope you don't get that, because it is so sharp that only the highly trained can use it. I mean you can't even put it in a scabbard; it would just cut through it, so you have to carry it very carefully. Fantastic sword, though."

"Right . . ." said Anya. She hesitated before asking, "If I do get the sword, or something else I can't use, can I give it back?"

"I shouldn't worry about that," said the Wizard cheerily. "I'm sure you'll get something just right."

"Um, thank you . . . ah . . . what else is there, please?"

"The Buckler of Redoubtable Defense," said the Wizard. "A small shield, just your size. It will intercept any blow aimed at you. The drawback being it moves *very* quickly, so unless you're remarkably strong and flexible it might dislocate your arm or shoulder."

Anya nodded, not daring to speak. The Wizard waited a moment, then continued.

"A Thirty-League Flying Carpet. This is a nice one, a big flying carpet, good for thirty leagues before it needs a rest."

"What happens after thirty leagues?"

"It becomes just a carpet. Without the flying part. So you need to be sure you are on the ground before it reaches its limit."

"How can you tell?"

"You can't. The trick is to only use it from a point A to a point B that is less than thirty leagues away, leaving a good margin of error for a bad map or mistaken calculations. Or you can do a number of small flights, being sure the total distance is well under the thirty leagues. Then it needs to rest before you can use it again. Fly less than the carpet's stated distance, then let it rest till midnight— that's the basic rule."

"Ah," said Anya. "How far away is the hill in the Blasted Heath where the witches are?"

"No more than twenty leagues, I reckon," said Bert from across the table. "I'm not sure as a crow or carpet might fly. But not more than twenty, in any case."

"Carpets are also often temperamental," added the Wizard. "Won't fly on cold mornings, or in the heat of the day—that sort of thing. Even the best of them sometimes play tricks as well. You have to be sure to give them strict directions."

"Flying would be fun, though," said Anya.

"I wouldn't call it fun." The Wizard made a face. "Mostly itchy, closed in, and frightening."

Anya looked at the Wizard, wondering what she was talking about. Why would flying on a magic carpet be itchy and closed in? But there was no further explanation.

"The fourth item is a Wallet of Inexhaustible Munchings and Crunchings."

Ardent's ears pricked up at this one.

"What does that do?" he asked the Wizard.

"It provides a rather indigestible biscuit three times a day."

"And its flaw?" Anya inquired.

"The biscuit," said the Wizard with a shudder. "However, it will keep you alive."

"And the fifth possible gift?"

"Very traditional. An Ever-Filled Purse. It contains a gold coin, a silver coin, and a copper coin. A noble, a shilling, and a penny. Of the old Yarrow minting, or so they seem. If you spend it, the coin will reappear in the purse at midnight. The flaw in this case is that they're *counterfeit* coins, so using them is doubly dishonest. If you're caught with false coins, the usual punishment is death. And if you're not caught, then you'll be bilking whoever you pay."

The Wizard went on. "And the sixth choice is something I made myself; all the others were made by my various predecessors. Cloudwalking Boots. Seven leagues in a single step! Provided you step from cloud to cloud, of course."

"What happens if there are no clouds?" asked Anya. "Or they blow away while you're up in the air?"

"If you're quick enough to tell the boots to take you to the ground, then all will be well."

"And if you're not?"

"If you're not, or you try to take another step not to a cloud, then you fall."

"From the height of the cloud?"

"Yes."

"So you'd die."

"Usually. But with proper practice, focus, and bad weather, they are an admirable means of getting around. And quite fetching— lovely doeskin lined with silk, with blued steel buckles. But enough of this. It is time for you to choose."

Anya looked at the envelopes in the Wizard's hand. For all her protestations about not interfering directly, one particular envelope really stood out, and there had been that thing with the eyebrows, which seemed as good as a wink.

Anya took the sticking-out envelope.

It was sealed with a rectangular silver wax seal bearing the device of a tall hat and crossed staff. Anya slid her fingernail under the seal and broke it off, then opened the envelope. There was nothing inside, but she was used to this style of letter. Unfolding the envelope all the way, she read what was written on the inside.

"A Wallet of Inexhaustible Munchings and Crunchings."

"What? Let me see that!"

The Wizard took the opened envelope and read the message with a scowl on her face.

"Um, thank you," said Anya.

"Wasn't supposed to . . ." muttered the Wizard, her words trailing off into an incomprehensible mumble.

"It will likely be very handy," said Anya hesitantly.

"You haven't tasted the biscuit," said the Wizard, extending her hand to pull a small leather bag apparently out of thin air. But this time Anya was positioned in exactly the right place to see the invisibility cloak worn by the apprentice open and shut. In fact it was more like a small tent than a cloak. The young man underneath was wearing a strange kind of wicker work hat on his head, a pyramidal frame of thin sticks that extended out, so it supported and spread the cloak, enabling him to easily carry things and keep them invisible as well. It looked quite awkward, and doubtless would be very hot and airless in summer.

Anya took the wallet.

"Go on," said the Wizard. "Try it. You might as well know the worst."

Anya opened the small bag. There was a rather grayish, unappealing hard biscuit inside. She took it out, nibbled at the edge without making much of a dent, and put it down on the table. A moment later, Ardent's nose appeared, the biscuit disappeared, and there was a loud crunching noise reminiscent of rocks being broken with a hammer.

"You see?" remarked the Wizard. "Highly nutritious, though. You'll never starve with that. Though you might lose some teeth in the process. Now, how to get you to the witches' meeting in time? I had . . . err . . . hoped . . . you'd get the flying carpet."

"Do I get a gift too?"

The words were a little inhibited by crumbs in his throat, but Ardent's question was clear.

"I'm afraid not," said the Wizard. "I may only give questers gifts. You are a quester's helper. Shrub, Smoothie, and Prince Denholm are the beneficiaries of the Quest."

"I have a Quest too," said Ardent. "Separate from the princess's."

"You do?" asked the Wizard, brightening up. "What is it?"

"Secret," said the dog. "I c-c-an whisper it to *you*, though."

"What?" asked Anya. "What about me?"

"C-c-an't tell you, Princess," said Ardent apologetically. "Dog business. Tanitha told me not to tell."

"Hmmph." Anya was immediately burning with curiosity. What could Ardent have a Quest for? A magic bone? And why couldn't he tell her about it?

While the princess sat fuming, the Wizard bent down. Ardent stuck his nose almost in her ear and whispered just a few words.

"Good," said the Wizard as she straightened up. "That's clear. You *are* a quester, and I am delighted to offer you a gift. Now, to hurry things along, we'll just go with these envelopes I prepared earlier for Anya. Oh, my eyes are quite tired. Glasses, please."

An invisible servant handed over the same gold-rimmed glasses the Wizard had put on the day before. She sat them on the end of her nose and peered at the envelopes carefully, before fanning them out and holding them down for Ardent. Again, one was poking out a little more than the others.

Ardent sniffed them all twice, then very carefully bit down on the one that was projecting out a little, and drew it from the Wizard's hand. Putting it on the floor, he set one paw on it and opened it with his teeth. Anya leaned across to read over his shoulder.

"A Thirty-League Flying Carpet!"

"Fancy that," said the Wizard. "Now, is there anything else you need?"

"Well," said Anya with a shy glance at the dwarves, who were still busily eating their way through breakfasts that would have stunned her and might even have been a challenge for Ardent. Erzefezonim caught her eye, smiled, and nodded.

"Well," continued Anya, speaking to all the dwarves present, "I know you are all master craftsfolk, and I thought perhaps one of you might care to buy a snuffbox I have, because you'd appreciate it more and . . . and I'd get a better price than from a pawnbroker or merchant in New Yarrow. And if you did, then I'd like to buy some things from the Wizard, if they are to be had. A bag of onions, thirteen lace handkerchiefs, and a pint bottle."

"A snuffbox?" asked Sleipjir, suddenly interested. He set down the huge heel of bread smothered in gooseberry jam he'd been gnawing on and held out his hand. "Let's see it, then."

Anya produced the snuffbox from her belt purse and handed it across the table. Sleipjir had only just taken hold of it when he burst into laughter.

"Ah, it's one of mine! I made it for the Duchess of Lemmich, let me see, the one before the one before last. Or perhaps her grand-mother. A little the worse for wear, I see. Where's it been?"

"In the moat at Trallonia," said Anya. "I did come by it fair and square, or the dogs did. It was lost and found."

She suddenly thought of something and looked across at Bert, who was drinking her tea quietly, still looking very somber and thoughtful.

"You won't rob it from me now, will you?"

Bert shook her head.

"Nay. As I said, that is more a guiding principle than a rule, and in any case, only applies within the bounds we set. The Good Wizard would rightly frown on any such thing here."

"Oh good," said Anya. She looked at Sleipjir. "Will you buy it?"

Sleipjir held the snuffbox up and turned it around, to catch the light from all angles.

"I will," he said slowly. "But it's dented—that'll need fine work. And there is a diamond missing. Very hard to match. I'd have to get one in special. The resale value, oh dear, very much reduced—"

The Wizard coughed, rather meaningfully. Sleipjir looked at her and the corner of his mouth twitched.

"Ah yes," he said. "Six gold nobles and not a penny more."

"Thank you!" said Anya, beaming. That was more money than she'd ever had. You could buy a horse with a single noble. Or get a dozen very fine dinners.

"No, no, you're supposed to bargain," said Sleipjir earnestly.

"Say 'ten nobles and not a shilling less,'" suggested Erzef.

"But six is plenty," said Anya. "Unless your onions and handkerchiefs are very expensive?"

"No, no," said the Wizard. "We'll give them to you. I'm sure there are plenty of onions in the kitchen, and handkerchiefs galore in the linen room. Jeremy . . . no, who is that . . . Saralla, go and get a big bag of the most pungent onions we have and thirteen handkerchiefs. Bring them to the back door."

"Oh, and a pint bottle, please," said Anya.

"I'll give you eight and that's my final offer," said Sleipjir.

"Yes, I accept," said Anya.

"Well then, nine!" snapped Sleipjir. He reached inside the neck of his mail coat and brought out a very healthy-looking purse he wore around his neck. Opening it carefully so no one else could see inside, he counted out nine gold coins, racked them up into a column, and handed them over to Anya. She needed both hands to hold the stack, and almost spilled them putting them into her own purse.

"Have to watch out for pickpockets," said Shrub, who had crept up to Anya's side without her noticing. "If I still had my fingers, I'd have that off you in a trice."

"You can guard me against other thieves," said Anya. "I'm going to need your help in New Yarrow, for that and for getting into the League's meetinghouse. You have to forget about the Only Stone, though."

The newt nodded glumly.

"If you serve the princess well, Shrub, you may join us once you're back in human form," said Bert.

"Hey, thanks," said Shrub, suddenly brightening. He licked both his eyes and capered in a circle for a moment. "I'll be the best good thief in the business, you watch me!"

"Come," said the Wizard. "The noon hour approaches, and by deep tradition and law, you must be gone. Fetch your frog and call your otter-maid, and I will show you out the back door, in case any weasel soldiers still lurk about the place."

"What about my carpet?" asked Ardent.

"It will be there," said the Wizard. She looked around and beckoned to the air with a crooked finger. "Jeremy, make sure a good Thirty-League Carpet is brought to the back door."

"I will come and see you off," said Bert. She stood, settled a full quiver on her back, and took up her longbow, tapping the six-foot wych elm stave. "There were at least two assassins we saw among the weaselfolk, and they might try a long shot. But none can shoot as far as I."

"Or so well," added Dehlia, leaping to Bert's shoulder with a flap of her pale wings.

The sitting dwarves looked at one another and, as one, pushed their plates away and stood up, reaching behind their chairs to pick up battle-axes and swords.

"If any of Duke Rikard's creatures lie in wait, they will not to do so for long," said Erzef. She flipped her axe high in the air. It revolved three times as it fell, and she caught it by the haft. Anya flinched with every revolution and shut her eyes on the final thwap as the dwarf's hands closed on the weapon. It looked extremely heavy and extremely sharp and not at all the sort of thing that should be thrown around.

"I'll go get Denholm," said Anya. "Ardent, you fetch Smoothie."

Ardent was halfway to the stair by the fireplace when Anya shouted after him, "By fetch I mean tell her to come along!"

"I will!" barked Ardent.

Anya pushed back her chair, slowly at first and then with great determination. Visiting the Wizard had provided a welcome respite from the rigors of her Quest, but now it was time to once more go Questing!

CHAPTER NINETEEN

The Good Wizard's Predecessor Takes an Interest

The back door was reached by a very long tunnel. It seemed like a normal passage at first, paneled with the same warm reddish timber as the hall, but after a while the paneling stopped, revealing bare gray rock. Except it wasn't rock, but the petrified flesh of the dragon, and the white vertical supports and overhead beams were bones, bones that became thinner and more curved as they went along, the tunnel also narrowing.

"Dragon's tail," said the Wizard when Anya asked about the bones. "Very long, handy for a secret back exit. Quarter of a league from the front, and comes out in a little dell, hidden from view."

Eventually, the tunnel became so narrow they had to walk in single file, with the Wizard leading. There was no obvious source of light, and though it had grown darker as they walked, it didn't actually get dark. It took Anya a while to realize that the bones around them were faintly luminous.

There was a door at the end of the tunnel. The Wizard took a key out of her sleeve, but after a moment looking at the door, put it away again.

"Hmm," she said. "Unlocked already."

She pushed on the heavy oak and the door swung open, admitting a shaft of bright sunlight that washed out the pale light of the dragon bones.

"Should it be unlocked?" asked Anya.

"No," said the Wizard, though she didn't seem particularly perturbed. She walked out, with the princess close behind, looking over her shoulder. "He's just forgotten to lock it after him, that's all."

"Who?" asked Anya.

"Me," said someone as the Wizard and Anya emerged blinking into the sunlight.

Anya jumped several feet, almost dropping Denholm's cage. Her heart beat superfast as she looked wildly around for whoever had spoken.

The back door led out into a small dell, a narrow valley with a gentle slope that ran down to a marsh that was probably connected in some way with the river out the front of the Wizard's demesne. Behind them, the slope was steeper, rising up above the door to the top of the low ridge that marked the dragon's back.

Next to the door, there was a stone bench, and sitting on the bench was a very old man. He was completely bald, his yellowed skin was stretched and thin, and his eyes were very deep set and half-closed. He had a heavy woolen cloak with a fur collar wrapped tight around himself, even though now that it had stopped raining and the wind had died down, it was quite warm outside.

"My predecessor," said the Wizard. "Known to many as Snow White."

"No great snowy beard now," said the old man, fingering his smooth chin.

"You could wear the detachable one if you wanted," said the Good Wizard.

"Too hard to get off," answered the old man with a sly cackle. "Isn't it?"

"You should know—you made it that way. What are you doing out here?"

"Came to see the girl, didn't I?" said the old man. He opened his eyes wide. They were surprising. Bright green with a strong hint of mischief in them. They did not look like old, tired eyes.

"You mean me?" asked Anya.

"Of course," said the old man. He pulled a walking stick out from under his cloak, a short staff of rough bog oak, complete with the seven silver bands of a wizard, and used it to help himself up. "Not every day I get to meet the Frogkisser!"

"That's just something a Gerald the Herald thought up," said Anya with considerable embarrassment.

"How do you think I got called Snow White in the first place?" asked the old man. "Some long-nosed herald suggests a catchy name, and before you know it, everyone's using it."

"But your real name is Merlin, isn't it?" asked Ardent, who had come out and was sniffing the air. "I remember it now."

The old man smiled, and slowly bent to scratch Ardent's head.

"Yes, I was Merlin for a long time," he said. "But I have had other names. Once, even longer ago, I was known as—"

"There's something in the grass," interrupted Bert, raising her bow and nocking an arrow. "Over there."

There was a disturbance in the tall grass on the southern slope, something moving through it in a stop-start way. Whatever it was, it was small and almost completely concealed by the grass, which was generally knee-high, with taller tufts here and there.

"Don't shoot," said Merlin. "It is just a bird of some kind. I have been waiting for him to come closer. He is injured, I think, and cannot fly."

"The Duke has raven spies," Anya pointed out.

"True," said the old ex-wizard. "But this is not a raven. I have not seen him yet, but I heard him earlier, and came out to see what was going on."

"You heard a bird from inside?" asked Ardent, evidently impressed by this feat of listening, as impressive to him as the Dog with the Wonderful Nose's feats of smelling.

"Not with my ears," said Merlin. "Lower your bow, Roberta. Let him approach. It is the Frogkisser he wants, if I'm not mistaken."

"You *have* been mistaken on several occasions," said the Good Wizard. She smiled. "Though not this time, I suspect. Ah, here is your carpet, Ardent."

A rolled-up carpet, showing a bright red-and-blue pattern, appeared out the door, undulating through the air without visible support. It sagged in the middle, indicating that it was being carried by only two invisible servants, who were finding it a bit heavy.

"It does not move entirely like a natural bird," said Dehlia, who was standing on Bert's shoulder, watching the tops of the grass shifting as whatever it was hopped in a curious zigzag way towards them. "Are you sure you should let it approach?"

"I think we are guarded well enough here," said the Good Wizard drily, glancing around at the heavily armed and armored dwarves, Bert with her bow, and who knew how many invisible servants besides the ones carrying the carpet. And, Anya suddenly noticed, however many more were carrying the large sack that hung in the air near her. It smelled very strongly of onions and was far too big for her to even pick up, let alone carry anywhere.

"I don't think I need that many on—" she started to say, when Ardent sniffed twice very deeply and barked.

"It's Gotfried!"

"Gotfried?"

Even as she spoke, a small owl emerged from a clump of grass and wearily dragged itself into the open, trailing one wing. Anya and Ardent both dashed forward, ignoring Bert's cry that it might be a trap.

Within a few moments, Anya was cradling the small injured owl to her chest while Ardent helpfully leaped around her in circles.

"Gotfried!" cried Anya again. "What are you doing here? Are you hurt?"

"Yes," said the owl. "I am hurt. Badly hurt. I have been pecked near to death by the Duke's ravens. And obviously I was looking for you."

"Oh, Gotfried!" said Anya. She turned him over, checking for terrible wounds. But apart from one wing that was lacking a few feathers, he seemed to be all right. "What's happened?"

"What's happened? *Everything!*" cried the owl. "Most of it bad, I'm afraid to say."

He put his head under his undamaged wing, clearly about to gather his thoughts.

"But what exactly has happened?" asked Anya.

Some muffled and unintelligible speech came from under the wing. Anya lifted it up and saw Gotfried had tears in his eyes. As normal owls cannot cry, this was quite alarming.

"What has happened?" asked Anya again, very slowly and clearly. It had to be shockingly bad news, she knew, if Gotfried had come to seek her out.

"Morven is very sick," gabbled out Gotfried. "You have to come home."

"What?"

This was not what Anya was expecting. And Gotfried's voice didn't sound quite right.

"Morven is sick? What with?"

"Plague," said Gotfried. "Er . . . and swamp fever. Or possibly hen ague."

Anya thought about this for a few moments. Ardent stretched up, sniffing at the owl in her arms, his expression severe.

"Gotfried," Anya said heavily. "How did you know where to find me?"

It was Gotfried's turn to be silent for a while. Finally, he managed to squeak out, "I asked around. The heralds, they told me."

"He's lying," said Ardent with an angry woof. "I c-c-can smell the lies!"

Gotfried burst into full-blown crying, which was even more alarming.

"Tell me the truth," said Anya, firmly but kindly.

"The Duke made me," sobbed Gotfried. "He said if I didn't then he'd turn me into a skeleton on the spot and stick it on a spike. I'm not brave like you, Anya."

"What happened to your wing, then?"

"I just pulled some feathers out myself," cried Gotfried. He started to struggle in Anya's arms, trying to get free. "Put me down and have that archer shoot me! I'm a traitor!"

"Don't be silly," said Anya. "You're a librarian who is unlucky enough to work for an evil sorcerer, that's all. What's really happening back home?"

Gotfried stopped struggling and tried to put his head back under his wing again.

"Tell me," said Anya.

"It is bad," whispered Gotfried. "That's another reason I was so afraid."

"Tell me," said Anya.

"Moatie died the night you left," said Gotfried. His voice was so quiet Anya had to lean right down so his feathery head tickled her face. "Simply from old age, or so the cats said. He came out of the moat, roared that he was finally going to eat the Duke, and then he just . . . rolled over. That was that."

Anya sat down slowly, lowering Gotfried into her lap. The world seemed to have stopped for a moment, everything suddenly quiet, the sunshine cold. Ardent licked her ear, meaning to give comfort. Anya reached out with her free hand and scratched his head.

"The dogs left in the night," continued Gotfried. "I don't know where. Most of the servants left too, as soon as they realized the dogs were gone. The cats have gone into hiding in the top attics."

"Where did the dogs go?"

Ardent shuffled at Anya's side, but he didn't say anything.

It was difficult for Anya to speak, but she managed it. She told herself nothing had really changed. Moatie had been very old; it had always been likely that he would die, or that the Duke would grow strong enough to overpower him with sorcery. Perhaps, in his last great shout, the moat monster had believed he was killing the Duke and saving the princesses. So he would have died happy.

"I don't know," said Gotfried.

"What?" asked Anya, whose thoughts were still on the ancient moat monster. He had always been such a friend to the two little girls.

"I don't know where the dogs went," repeated Gotfried.

"And Morven?" asked Anya. "She's not sick? That was just the Duke trying to lure me home?"

"She's fine. She probably won't even realize anything's amiss," whispered Gotfried. "As long as Prince Maggers sings to her, that's all she cares about. And Bethany will never leave her, so she'll still be waited on hand and foot. I'm sure she'll be all right."

"I don't know," said Anya anxiously. Without Moatie or the dogs, Morven had to be at risk. Even if she didn't realize it herself.

"Put me down, Princess," said Gotfried. "Have your guards execute me. I deserve it."

"They're not my guards," Anya replied. "That's Snow White and the Seven Dwarves, and the current Good Wizard, and . . . some other friends I've found along the way."

"Snow White? The Seven Dwarves?" mumbled Gotfried. "Oh woe! To meet in such circumstances."

He struggled out of Anya's arms and bowed deeply to the old man and the dwarves. His trailing wing, though lacking a few feathers, seemed to have miraculously recovered.

No one bowed back.

"So you're the Trallonian librarian who wanted to be a sorcerer and botched your own transformation," said the Good Wizard. "And now you're some kind of henchman for Duke Rikard?"

"Not on purpose, Your Honor," said Gotfried miserably. "As you heard, I couldn't go through with it anyway. But better to be killed quickly than turned into a skeleton by the Duke and put on display in his white room."

"You won't be killed," said Anya. She looked at everyone else. "What was it in the Bill of Rights and Wrongs? 'No person shall be transformed, fined, deprived of liberty, executed, or otherwise punished save under the ancient laws as set within the Stone.'"

"You have remembered it well," said Dehlia. "That is good."

"The Bill of Rights and Wrongs?" asked Gotfried. "The old charter? And what's this about a stone?"

"Dehlia and Bert can explain it to you." Anya looked at the Good Wizard and said sadly, "Can you keep him here overnight? I can't take him with me. He just can't say no to the Duke."

"Make it at my invitation," said Snow White quickly to the Good Wizard. "So he won't need an appointment, and nothing on the books."

"Then as with any guest, he may stay a night and a day," said the Good Wizard.

"I want to talk to young Gotfried anyway," said Merlin, surprising everyone. "Come up to my shoulder, owl. I think I knew your great-grandfather. Did you know owls run in your family? And incompetent transformations?"

"Um, no," said Gotfried. He turned his head almost completely around to face Anya, while keeping his body straight, which always gave the princess a sympathetic twinge in her own neck. Owls, of course, can do this all night without difficulty. "Princess, can you forgive me?"

Anya bent down and lifted him so he could step onto the ancient ex-wizard's shoulder.

"Of course I forgive you. But do stay away from Duke Rikard. When you leave here, go and find the dogs. We'll meet up sooner or later."

Ardent growled something, but desisted when Anya gave him a stern look.

"I'm sure," quavered Gotfried. "How . . . how goes your quest?"

"I can't say," said Anya. She hesitated, before reluctantly adding, "You might end up back with the Duke after all, and you couldn't help but tell him. So it's better you don't know. Oh, by the way, the Good Wizard has a truly amazing library here."

"We do," said Merlin. "Let's go and look at it."

The old man went to the door, but just before he passed through, he turned back to offer Anya some parting advice.

"Good luck, Princess. Be wary of the witches. While you can trust their word, you need to listen very carefully to whatever they agree. Or don't agree. What is unsaid is as important as what is said."

"Thank you," said Anya. She wondered what he meant by that. Surely what was unsaid was difficult to consider, since it hadn't been said in the first place. But she filed his words away carefully in her mind, making sure they wouldn't be smothered by the excitement that was building up in her.

For the first time since leaving Trallonia, she felt somewhat confident about her Quest. She was clean, rested, well fed, and wearing new, better clothes. And she had a plan, which was a lot more than she'd had when she'd started out.

CHAPTER TWENTY

They're Not as Comfortable as Everyone Thinks They Are

Anya also had a flying carpet, even if it technically belonged to Ardent. It was being unrolled on the grass right at that moment. Considerably larger than Anya had expected, the carpet was at least eighteen feet long and ten feet wide. Though primarily red and blue it had some touches of black, all woven into a very attractive pattern of repeated, overlapping squares, with lines of different thicknesses. Right in the middle, there was a diamond of solid red bordered by a thick black line.

"Before you lie down, I'd better tell you the carpet's name and the words of command," said the Good Wizard, addressing both Anya and Ardent. "Make sure no one hears you using them, because otherwise they could steal the carpet by flying away with it. Of course it can be stolen simply by carrying it off, but if someone does do that, you can call it back with the correct phrase. It won't matter where it is, it will hear you and come along. Eventually. As I said, they can be temperamental. But if you treat it courteously, brush it from time to time, and don't mess it up with mud or spill coffee on it, it should be fine. Now, let me see."

The Wizard settled her gold-rimmed glasses more firmly on her nose and peered down at the corner of the carpet. Anya couldn't see anything there that was any different from any other corner, but the Wizard was clearly studying something.

"The carpet's name is Pathadwanimithochozkal," she said. "Got that?"

"No!" exclaimed Anya.

"Really?" asked the Wizard. "Thought you were training to be a sorcerer?"

She repeated the name a dozen times before Anya began to consistently get it right, though Ardent had it correct from the second time. All the royal dogs were very good at learning things by rote.

"Now, you lie down on the carpet at one end, like so," said the Good Wizard, stretching herself out on the carpet. "Then you say the carpet's name and 'Prepare for flight,' and it will roll you up—"

"Roll me up?" asked Anya. She made a rotating gesture with her finger. "You mean it'll roll up with us inside? Why?"

"So you don't fall off when it flies away," said the Wizard. She got up and stretched. "They fly very, very fast, you know. Did you think you could just sit on it?"

"That's what they do in the stories," Anya protested. "There was even a picture in one of my books—"

"*Stories*," grumbled the Wizard. "I don't know how they get started. I mean, it's simple common sense. There's nothing to hold on to, and with all that air rushing past . . . a good carpet will wrap you nice and tight so you can't even slip out the open ends if it has to do any fancy flying."

"I see what you meant about being closed in," said Anya. "And itchy. I guess you can't see anything either? I mean while you're flying along?"

"Of course you can't, because you're *rolled up in a carpet*," said the Wizard. "Anyway. Say the carpet's name, and 'Prepare for flight.' Once you're rolled up, you say the carpet's name again, possibly put in some sort of honorific like 'Oh Great Carpet known as Thingummy' and where you want to go, being as specific as possible and throwing in a few cautionary additions. For example, 'Oh Great Carpet known as Whatsit, take us safely and carefully to the top of the hill called Dragon Hill, where the Good Wizard resides.' Easy, really."

"I suppose so," said Anya dubiously as she went over the instructions in her head, hoping that she'd remember. Ardent probably would, but then he was easily distracted. "Oh, thank you for the onions too, but I shan't need a whole big sack like that."

"Of course you shan't!" exclaimed the Wizard, eyeing the sack balefully. "Jeremy, what were you thinking? Empty two-thirds of them out, you can take them back to the kitchen later. Put the sack on the carpet for the princess. Who's got the handkerchiefs? And the pint bottle?"

The pint bottle appeared from under one of the apprentices' invisibility cloaks. Anya was pleased to see it was metal and came in a leather case with a strap, so it would be very hard to break.

The Good Wizard took the stack of handkerchiefs from another apprentice and handed them over, adding an extra handkerchief from her sleeve.

"One for you too," she said, tapping the side of her nose.

"Oh, my cold's all better," said Anya. "The hot bath seemed to do the trick."

"Take it, take it," urged the Wizard. "They can come in very handy, handkerchiefs. Don't get it mixed up with the others."

Anya had been about to do just that, but now she looked at the handkerchief more closely. It was folded over, but there were marks on the inside. Something was drawn there, with writing as well. It took her a moment to recognize it must be a map.

"Put it away! Put it away! Merely a handkerchief," said the Wizard. "Magical gifts for questers, a few onions, handkerchiefs, least I could do. Now, if I were you, I'd put that newt near your feet so he doesn't poison you."

"The poison only comes out when I concentrate, and you have to actually get it in your mouth," said Shrub with considerable dignity. He thought for a moment, then added, "Or maybe up your nose or ears."

"You can completely control it?" asked Anya. This was an interesting piece of information.

"It does come out if I get scared," admitted Shrub. "It's a kind of sweat, I think."

"You might get scared flying in the carpet," said the Wizard. "I usually do."

She took her watch out of her sleeve, flipped it open, and stared at the strange dial for several seconds. "Come on, you need to be out of my demesne by twelve noon. Rules are rules."

"Can I come back?" asked Anya suddenly. "I mean, to visit? I'd like to look in your library more, and maybe . . . maybe talk to your apprentices?"

"Only one visit per quest," said the Good Wizard. "But if you're not questing, an informal drop-in is always welcome. Lie down, do! Time is fleeting."

Anya obediently lay down on the carpet, holding Denholm in his wicker cage. She looked at the frog as she settled down. He'd been uncharacteristically silent the whole time since she'd taken him out of the terrarium. She'd thought that was probably because he liked it inside the huge crystal globe that replicated a moat environment and didn't want to leave. But now that she looked more closely, Denholm had lost some of the oily sheen on his skin, and there was a hint of gray in the yellow patch on his head.

"I hope you're not sick," she said worriedly. It was very inconvenient timing. She had no idea how to treat a sick frog. Besides, it could be some side effect of his transformation.

But Anya had no time to think about this as Ardent lay down alongside her legs, with Smoothie next to him. Shrub disposed himself sideways across the carpet under Anya's feet.

"Thank you for everything," said Anya to the Wizard.

"It's nothing." The Wizard smiled, looking prettier than ever. "Visitors like you make life interesting."

"Don't forget the Bill of Rights and Wrongs," said Bert. "Remember, we will aid you in your Quest, if you will aid us in ours."

"And it's the right thing to do," Dehlia chimed in.

"I know," said Anya.

"And do be careful with the witches," added the Wizard. "My predecessor is a little biased, after his own trouble with that particular witch, you know, but he's right about their business practices in general. Be very specific with what you're offering and what you expect to get."

"If you need to sell another snuffbox or have need of our axes to hew sorcerers' necks, send word," said Erzefezonim. "Unlike the Good Wizard, we have been known to interfere directly, and perhaps that time is coming around again."

"Thank you!" said Anya. This was no small thing. Having the Seven Dwarves by her side would not only be tremendous in itself, it would attract other potential allies.

"Right," said the Wizard. "Everybody back! These carpets raise a serious whirlwind when they take off."

"Do you want to say the words, or shall I?" Anya asked Ardent.

"I will," said Ardent. "Where are we going again?"

Anya thought about that for a moment, looking up at the sky above. It was quite restful just lying on the carpet, though she did feel a little tense about what was going to happen.

"Brokenmouth Hill in the middle of the Blasted Heath, but perhaps we shouldn't go right there," said Anya. She was thinking about Merlin's advice, and the Good Wizard's. "We should ask the carpet to take us somewhere safe and hidden from view within half a league of Brokenmouth Hill."

Ardent repeated Anya's words, very slowly for him, without a stutter.

"Is everyone ready?" the dog asked.

"Ready!"

"Pathadwanimithochozkal, prepare for flight!"

The carpet twitched underneath them. Anya's hand crept across Ardent's back, hugging him closer. Smoothie inched herself closer to Ardent. Shrub let out a whimper.

The carpet suddenly rolled up. One second Anya was looking up at the sky, the next she was gasping as she was tumbled over and her nose and face were pressed against soft wool, which tickled her nose. The carpet flexed again, and Anya felt it gripping more tightly. Ardent let out a slightly disturbed whine, and Smoothie was emitting some very short, high-pitched squeaks of discomfort.

"Ask it to fly," whispered Anya.

"Oh very nice carpet known as Pathadwanimithochozkal," said Ardent. "Please take us safely and carefully to a place where we'll be hidden half a league from Brokenmouth Hill in the Blasted Heath."

"You forgot to say a *safe* place," hissed Anya. "Quick, ask it—"

At that moment, the carpet took off. Rolled into a tube, it slid horizontally along the grass for several yards, then suddenly tilted back to a near-vertical position and rocketed into the sky.

Inside the carpet, everyone screamed. Anya felt herself slip a few inches down towards the lower end of the roll, but the movement was arrested by the carpet gripping everyone more tightly.

Cold air was rushing in through the open top like an arctic gale, already freezing Anya's ears. She had no idea how fast they were traveling, but given the rush of air, it had to be very fast indeed, far faster than she had ever galloped on a horse.

"Is everyone all right?" she called out, her words muffled by the fierce blast of air and the woolen surface in her face. She could feel Denholm's wicker cage pressed against her stomach, and Ardent's warm dogskin, but Smoothie was on the other side of the dog and she couldn't feel Shrub on her feet with the carpet holding so tightly.

Ardent barked, Smoothie shouted something, but there was no reply from Shrub. Or he simply couldn't be heard over the roar of the wind rushing through.

"I forgot to ask the Wizard how long this will take!" shouted Anya. Her ears were already freezing. She turned her head sideways and pressed her left ear against the wool, but that just made her other ear and the top of her head feel even colder. She wished she'd thought to pull up the hood of her cloak. Or that the Wizard had mentioned how cold it would be.

"She said c-c-arpets are very, very fast!" Ardent shouted back.

There was no way of knowing how quickly they were traveling, apart from the howling wind that came in through the opening above Anya's head. Soon, even though she moved her head regularly to protect one side or the other, both Anya's ears felt completely frozen, and she was sure there were ice crystals in her hair. Even with her new clothes and cloak, the rest of her was very cold as well.

"I c-c-an't take much more of this!" she shouted after a while to Ardent. "It's t-too cold."

Ardent barked something back, but Anya couldn't hear him properly.

Then, just as Anya thought she might pass out from cold, the carpet suddenly tilted over and down. Anya felt the blood rush into her head, and cried out as a sudden pain ran from both ears to the middle of her forehead. She slid forward a little as well, and realized from the pressure behind her ears and eyes they were now plunging almost straight down to the ground.

This plummeting descent lasted long enough for everyone to get out a really good scream, before the carpet suddenly leveled out again and the gale that had been blowing through it eased. A few seconds later there was a jarring thud as they landed. The carpet slid along for several yards, spinning around as it did so, before finally coming to a stop. There was a horrible delay that seemed to go on for way too long, then it slowly unrolled, leaving Anya and her companions gasping and shivering face-down on the woolen surface that no longer seemed so soft, or woven in such a nice pattern.

Ardent was the first to get up. He sprang to his feet, shook himself wildly, and looked around, sniffing the air. The carpet had landed them in a grassy alley between two orderly rows of rather short, broad trees with purple flowers and fruits, with many more rows of trees stretching up a slight slope ahead.

It was an orchard of plums, shortly to be harvested from the look of the heavy fruit on the trees. In the distance, the bulk of a bigger hill loomed large.

Anya sat up very slowly, still shivering from cold. The sun was shining above them, and she could feel its warmth beginning to come through. But there was ice in her hair, and her ears felt like icicles. Rubbing her ears vigorously, she quickly checked that Denholm was still in his wicker cage and everyone else was all right. She could see Smoothie licking her hand-paws and then running them over her head, so she seemed fine.

But Shrub was still draped over Anya's feet, and he wasn't moving.

"Shrub!"

Wrapping her hands in her cloak, Anya lifted Shrub's head. His eyes were closed, and she couldn't tell whether he was breathing or not.

"C-c-cold," said Ardent, sniffing the newt. "Like a lizard, needs warmth."

"Is . . . is he dead?" asked Anya.

Ardent looked surprised.

"No! I would have said. You know the lizards by the old garden wall. They sleep through the winter in their holes when the ice starts on the moat. He'll wake up when he's warmer."

"Good," said Anya with considerable relief. She stood up and looked around properly. The orchard was quiet; no one was about. There were standing stones on the hill, which looked to be less than half a league away. A thin trickle of smoke was coming up from the middle, indicating the witches' fire, or so Anya presumed.

"No water nearby," Smoothie noted regretfully. She sniffed the air several times. "Not even a pond."

"I'm sure you'll be able to have a swim somewhere on our Quest," said Anya.

She took out the handkerchief the Good Wizard had given her and unfolded it to inspect the map. It had been drawn in a bit of hurry; there were ink splotches here and there, but it showed Trallonia, Trallon Forest, The Demesne of the Good Wizard, Rolanstown, Brokenmouth Hill, and New Yarrow, with the distances between each indicated by straight as-a-carpet-might-fly lines and a numeral for the number of leagues. Anya was surprised to see it was only nine leagues from Trallonia to Dragon Hill. It had felt much, much farther.

It was also interesting to see that New Yarrow was closer than she'd thought. Twelve leagues from the witches' meeting place. They could fly close to it, if she could steel herself to being wrapped in the carpet again.

She picked up the sack of onions and put it over her shoulder. Even with two-thirds of it emptied out, it was still heavy.

"I'm going to find the witches and trade with them," she said. "I think you should all stay here."

"What?" barked Ardent indignantly. "I go with you, Princess."

Anya shook her head.

"I need you to stay here with the carpet," she said. "And Smoothie and Shrub. I was going to leave him behind anyway, and Denholm."

"Why?"

"Eye of newt and toe of frog," said Anya.

Ardent put his head to one side, puzzled.

"It's in a song or a story about witches," said Anya. "I can't remember it that well, but I do know they like newts' eyes and frogs' toes."

"Not much meat on a frog's toe," observed Ardent dubiously. "Why would they eat just the toe and not the leg, like they do in the village?"

"I don't know if they eat them . . . it doesn't matter. We have to be careful with the witches, so it's best if you're hidden and can come and rescue me if necessary."

"Oh," said Ardent, his puzzlement replaced with satisfaction at being given an important job to do. "When do we c-c-come and rescue you?"

"If I'm not back by nightfall, come and take a very careful look," said Anya. "But I don't expect to need rescuing. I'm not that kind of princess."

"What kind of princess are you?" asked Smoothie. She was arranging herself on the carpet to get the best possible spot where the most sun managed to get through between the trees.

"Not the kind that needs rescuing," said Anya firmly. She looked around the orchard again. There was a chance that a farmer might come along, but she doubted it. They'd be picking soon, but that would already have begun if they were going to do it today. "Be careful. Try to stay hidden."

"We will," said Ardent. Smoothie nodded and rolled over, lifting her arms and legs to wriggle around so that a dinner plate–size patch of sun was firmly in place on her sleek, furry stomach.

Anya made sure she had the handkerchiefs stuffed securely down her jerkin front, picked up the pint bottle, and resettled the onion sack on her shoulder.

"Remember, don't come looking for me until nightfall," she said, and set off towards the hill and the witches, pulling the hood of her cloak up as she went. "And feed Denholm some bugs!"

CHAPTER TWENTY-ONE

In the Witches' Kitchen

The scene on the hilltop was very much as Anya had seen in the pool of the Wizard's Magic Mirror. Only it being a day later, the culinary preparations were much further advanced. A very large pig was roasting on a spit above a fire pit; there was another table set up near it on which rested two small barrels of beer marked *Mild* and *Brown*, numerous bottles of wine, and an eclectic mixture of glasses, cups, steins, and goblets, made from glass of all colors and thicknesses, silver, pewter, and even wood.

Several steel mirrors had been set up on the standing stones, and six of the witches—mostly the younger ones—were preparing themselves, jostling for room to look at their reflections as they carefully glued on hairy warts, carbuncles, and bat-shaped moles, or settled snake-wigs over their own hair.

The other seven were under the canvas roof of the kitchen, taking time out of various preparations to engage in a dispute about who was supposed to have brought the onions.

"Onions aren't greens, Shushu," said one. "I was in charge of *greens*."

"Oh, everyone knows you do onions with greens," said the

witch who was presumably Shushu. "And potatoes, and turnips, and pumpkin."

"We never use pumpkin in summer," said another witch.

"Yes, but if we did, whoever was on greens would have to bring it," said Shushu. "Now, what are we going to do without onions?"

"I got some scallions," said another witch.

"Scallions!" retorted several of the witches. Shushu, who seemed to be in charge of the cooking at least, laughed derisively and then confusingly said, "Don't make me laugh."

Anya, who had been watching from behind one of the smaller standing stones, chose this moment to step forward. Her heart quailed a little as she did so, but she knew it had to be done. On the way up the hill, she'd half seen a bird fly out of a tree, and it could have been a raven, and hence one of the Duke's spies. So there was no time to waste.

"I have onions for sale," she said loudly, brandishing the sack. "Best onions. Pungent and sharp."

All the witches turned to look at her, including the ones who'd been staring at themselves in the mirrors. For a moment Anya felt herself skewered by their gaze, like some tiny kitchen mouse suddenly noticed by a cat. Then Shushu spoke, and the gaze was broken, everyone turning back to whatever they'd been doing before, or beginning new tasks.

"Well, isn't that helpful," said the head witch with a kindly smile. She wasn't the oldest witch there, but she had to be at least in her seventies. Her hair was all white, cut fairly short, and her eyes were . . . Anya tried not to stare . . . her eyes were different colors. One was blue and the other green.

"You just happened to be passing with a sack of onions?" asked Shushu.

"Not exactly," said Anya. She was glad she'd kept her hood up, shadowing her face. "I heard you might need onions."

"Who from?"

"A Gerald the Herald," said Anya. "He heard it from a raven."

"Oh, from a raven!" exclaimed Shushu. She hadn't stopped smiling. "There's certainly enough of them about. What's your name, then?"

"Uh . . . they call me Hood," said Anya. She tapped the side of her head. "Because I like to wear my hood up."

"Not your real name, though." Shushu's eyes were very penetrating, and she was peering intently at Anya's face. The princess hoped her hood was low enough to shadow her features properly.

"No," she replied. "Look, do you want these onions?"

"Depends what *you* want for them," answered Shushu.

"I'll give them to you. If you use these handkerchiefs when you're cutting them, and give them back to me to wring out."

"Oh, I see," said Shushu. "It's witches' tears you're after. You an alchemist's brat? Or working for a sorcerer?"

"Neither," said Anya. "I work for myself."

"Going to make love potions, I suppose?"

"No!" said Anya indignantly. "I need them for something else. Do you want the onions or not?"

"Maybe," said Shushu. "Where are you from?"

"East of here," said Anya vaguely. "Does it matter?"

Both Trallonia and the Demesne of the Good Wizard were east, but then so were lots of other places, including Rolanstown.

"And you got the onions from the Good Wizard?"

"What?" asked Anya. She almost said no, but thought better of it. The witches might be able to tell if she was lying. Instead, she remained silent while she tried to think of an answer that wasn't exactly a lie.

"Your sack," said Shushu, "has *Property of the Good Wizard* stenciled on it."

"Oh." Anya held the sack out. Sure enough, those words were stenciled on the side of the sack she hadn't looked at before. "Well, yes. I did get them from the Good Wizard's kitchen."

"Hmmm," said Shushu. She was peering at Anya's face again, looking thoughtful. "The Good Wizard doesn't just hand over onions to anyone . . . Let's see them."

Anya lifted the sack to hand it over, but Shushu stepped back.

"We don't want the sack. It might be enchanted. Just tip the onions onto the table."

Anya undid the sack and poured the onions out onto the end of the table, catching the few that rolled off to put them back in the middle. They were very pungent onions, even before they were cut, their brown, papery skins crackling as Anya arranged them into a rough pyramid. When she was done, she folded the sack through the back of her belt to get it out of the way, though she doubted it was enchanted at all. The Good Wizard and the dwarves only seemed to make beautiful things, not sacks of rough hessian.

Shushu picked an onion up, tore away the crackling outer skin, and inspected the flesh beneath, holding it close to smell the sharp odor.

"We'll take them," she said. "And we will use your handkerchiefs so you can have them to wring out. Agreed?"

"If it is to be done immediately," said Anya cautiously. She didn't want to be waiting around anywhere long enough for the Duke's spies to find her.

"We need to cook them for our feast tonight, so that's no problem," said Shushu. "We'll cut them up straightaway. Is it agreed?"

"I'd like to borrow a bowl to wring the handkerchiefs out over," said Anya. "And I need your promise that I won't be harmed."

"A bowl, certainly," agreed Shushu. "And despite some stories about witches, we do not eat children. If we make gingerbread, we eat it ourselves; we don't make houses out of it to lure children to their deaths."

"I always did think that was a silly story," said Anya. "I mean, if it rained, the house would fall apart."

"You could make an icing that was proof against rain," said one of the other witches. Shushu glared at her, and she fell silent.

"Is it agreed?" asked the head witch again. "Your onions in return for our tears?"

"And my safety," said Anya.

"We will take every care that you will be safe while you are with us in the sacred grounds of our meeting place," said Shushu. "Does that satisfy you?"

Anya thought about it for a moment. She wasn't entirely sure the head witch was to be trusted, and there seemed something slightly tricky about those words. But she didn't have time to waste. If a raven spy had seen her, it might already be winging its way to report to the Duke. She needed to get the tears and get out.

"It is agreed," she said.

"Excellent," said Shushu. "We will cut the onions at once. Who will help me?"

All the witches who were not engaged with uglifying them-selves hurried over, then picked up the onions and sniffed them, rubbing their fingers to make the outer skins shred, and generally seeming very pleased with the quality of the produce. They quickly lined up along the table, selected glittering sharp knives, and began their work.

"Here are the handkerchiefs," said Anya, handing them out to the witches. Only six witches were cutting the onions, so she gave them two each and kept the thirteenth back with the extra one that had the hand-drawn map.

One of the younger witches came over as Anya watched the onion cutting. She had just fixed on a particularly horrendous wart in the middle of her forehead, but the glue wasn't dry, so it was very slowly sliding down towards the bridge of her nose.

"Want a cup of tea while you wait?" she asked. "My name's Etta, by the way."

"No thank you," said Anya. She didn't think it would be safe to eat or drink anything the witches made, even if they had guaran-teed her safety.

"Suit yourself," sniffed Etta. She blinked back some tears as a waft of cut onion passed by. "My, those onions are powerful."

"Yes, they are," agreed Anya. The witches were already wiping their eyes busily, and the first lot of handkerchiefs was looking fairly sodden. "I'd better get a bowl ready."

"Under the table, there," said Etta, pointing. She shook her head against the onion fumes, and retreated from the kitchen tent, back to the mirrors. Unfortunately, her wart flew off with her last head shake, went flying through the air, and fell onto the ground just outside the smiling arc of standing stones that gave the hill its name. Muttering curses, the witch got down on her knees and began to search for it, circling around and around, running her hands through the grass and dirt.

Anya got a large wooden bowl and began to collect the first round of handkerchiefs. By the time she'd wrung them out, the second lot was ready for collection, and the bowl was a quarter full. The princess hurried along the line of witches, swapping the damp first handkerchiefs for the completely saturated second set.

Within fifteen minutes, she had a full bowl of witches' tears and was feeling very pleased with herself as she poured it into her pint bottle. It was completely full, and there was even a little left over. Anya offered the bowl back to Shushu, but the witch held up her hands in horror.

"We never use our own tears!" she exclaimed. "The idea!"

"You want a cup of tea now?" asked Etta.

"That's very kind," said Anya hurriedly. "But I have to be going. Thank you once again."

She gave them all a short bow, which was not returned. The witches were looking at her again, with that same fixed stare. Now there seemed to be reddish glints in those eyes, somehow reflected from the fire pit.

Anya turned, her back prickling as if a dagger might suddenly sprout between her shoulder blades. She forced herself to ignore it and walked beyond the stones.

She had only gone a few paces, when smoke suddenly erupted under her feet, strange-smelling, saffron-colored smoke that wound around her knees and circled up towards her face. Anya got the slightest whiff of it and immediately felt faint. She instantly held her breath, turned her face into the inside of her cloak, and pressed the material against her mouth and nose.

"Wait till she drops," said Shushu, somewhere behind her.

Anya kept holding her breath, her mind racing. The smoke was some sort of curse, created by Etta when she'd been pretending to look for her lost wart. The witches had promised not to harm her on their hill, but evidently outside the stones didn't count. If she ran now, who knew what they might do?

Better to play along and act unconscious, Anya figured. At the worst, Ardent and the others would come to rescue her at nightfall. Or they would try, at least . . . Anya couldn't help but fear they might not be the best rescuers around.

The princess fell to her knees, put one hand out as if she was trying to push herself back up, then slowly subsided to the ground, still holding her breath.

CHAPTER TWENTY-TWO

Duke Rikard Demonstrates New and Fearful Capabilities

Anya held her breath for as long as she possibly could, and then when she absolutely had to suck in some air, tried to do it very slowly and carefully through the material of her cloak. She could hear the witches moving around, but no one had touched her yet.

A minute later, Anya felt hands on her arms. As they heaved her up, she shut her eyes and let her head hang limp, but clutched the bottle of witches' tears more tightly, hoping that they would think this was just some sort of unconscious grip.

"Put her over by the drinks table, against the flour sacks," instructed Shushu. "Who's got a Far-Speaking Pomander?"

"I don't like this," said another voice. "It's sharp practice, and she's a princess who's come from the Good Wizard."

"Who's head witch tonight?" asked Shushu. "Who cares about a no-account princess of a nothing kingdom that is already under the sway of Duke Rikard? Besides, he's a member of the League of Right-Minded Sorcerers, and you know what good customers they are."

"What about the Good Wizard?" asked yet another voice. "She's not to be trifled with, nor those dwarves neither."

"Bah! Good Wizards aren't allowed to interfere, or so they always say," said Shushu. "Who's got a Far-Speaking Pomander? We need to call the Duke and get that two-hundred-gold-noble reward."

"Two hundred? That much?" said someone greedily. "Equal shares?"

That was Etta. Anya recognized her voice. She was one of the witches holding the princess under the arms, dragging her backwards so her heels dug little furrows in the dirt. Not very carefully, they put her down against a big sack of flour. Anya let her head loll forward, then opened her eyes to the barest slits.

She was near the fire pit, and all thirteen witches were arrayed in a semicircle around it, most of them facing Shushu, who looked cross.

"I demand a vote," said one of the older witches. "Head witch or no head witch. I don't like promising safety and then doing the dirty one step outside the stones. I say she bought her tears fair and square and we let her go."

"I say she's worth *two hundred* gold nobles and we tell Duke Rikard right away," said Shushu.

"Put it to the vote," said the other old witch. "All those who favor letting her go?"

She raised her hand. Four others followed immediately, and then one very slowly.

"All those against," said Shushu, baring her teeth in a horrible grimace.

Seven hands went up, including the head witch's.

"That's settled, then. Who's got a pomander? Must I ask for everything three times?"

One of the witches produced an orange-like ball from inside her kirtle. Anya knew about pomanders—they were balls of spice and herbs and ambergris that smelled nice, and in New Yarrow and sophisticated places like that people would lift them to their nose so they wouldn't have to smell unpleasant things like open sewers or stables that hadn't been cleaned in ages.

Presumably, a Far-Speaking Pomander was something else.

Shushu grabbed it, held it up to her nose, took in a deep sniff, then threw it down at her feet. The pomander exploded into a cloud of highly perfumed smoke. The witch gestured at this cloud and called out.

"Duke Rikard! Duke Rikard! Duke Rikard!"

Nothing happened. Shushu grimaced with annoyance, then called out again.

"Duke Rikard! Duke Rikard! Duke Rikard!"

Slowly, a face formed in the smoke: the unpleasant, deathly pale face of Duke Rikard. He was wearing a high-collared black jacket that accentuated his pallor, and there were red rings around his eye sockets, which might or might not have been from the application of rouge.

"What?" he asked testily. "I'm busy. Who calls?"

"The witches of Brokenmouth Hill. I am Shushu, head witch. Greetings."

"What do you want?" Rikard's image was becoming clearer in the smoke. From the look of it, he was on top of the south tower back in Trallonia castle, which Anya found odd. Right on top, as in standing on the roof. Why would the Duke be on the roof of the south tower?

"We are calling to claim your offered reward," said Shushu evenly. "The two hundred gold nobles for the location of your runaway princess."

"You know where she is?" asked the Duke. He was getting that supposedly secret smile again, the corner of his thin-lipped mouth twitching up.

"We have her here," said Shushu. She gestured towards Anya. "You can see for yourself, if the vision is clear enough."

"It is," purred the Duke. He started rubbing his hands together and cackled a little bit before continuing. "Keep her there. I will come and collect her within the hour."

Anya suppressed the panicked leap that suddenly sparked up inside her. The Duke coming to get her? Within the hour?

"What?" asked Shushu, startled. "But you're in Trallonia, aren't you?"

"Yes," replied the Duke. He cackled again, and spread his arms wide. "But I have a new means of travel. You have called me at a most suitable time, for my power grows by the day, and my labors bear many fruit. Um, many *fruits*! Such as this one!"

The vision grew clearer around the Duke, colors and lines becoming sharper in the smoke. He wasn't standing on the roof of the tower at all, but on the deck of a strange little ship, a slender, sharp-prowed ship, all white, with a peculiar bare mast that had many kinks, as if it was made of lots of short poles stuck atop each other. Two patchwork sails made from thousands of feathers somehow woven together were furled vertically against the mast. From their position they would unfold as wings.

The little ship was perhaps thirty feet long and six feet wide, and floated in the air as easily as if it lay upon the water. It was moored to the lightning rod on the tower's roof by a thin rope that glittered in the sun like spun gold, which it very well might have been.

"Make sure you bring the money," said Shushu. But even as she spoke, the vision faded. The pieces of pomander on the ground blackened and curled, and the sweet scent of ambergris, orange, and peppermint was replaced with the foul stench of rotting food.

"I don't like this at all," said the older witch. "He's made a bone ship. And did you notice? He wasn't breathing."

"What's a bone ship?" asked one of the younger witches. At the same time another asked, "Not breathing?"

"Bah!" said Shushu. "He's a very powerful sorcerer, that's all. We were right to deal with him."

"A bone ship is made from the bones of myriad birds," said the older witch heavily. "He would have had to kill or organize the killing of a thousand or more birds, of all different sizes. The mast alone requires the femurs of thirty-nine great eagles. It is an evil construction, to make a flying craft in such a way. And if he's not breathing, he has grown totally cold, devoid of any human feelings. He has given himself completely to his own ambition, without care for anyone or anything else. That is truly evil."

"You know we do not make such judgments," said Shushu. "Business is business. We do not question whether our customers are 'good' or 'evil.'"

"Once we did," said the older witch. "When the Bill of Rights and—"

"Oh hush!" snapped Shushu. "The Bill is long gone! Gone and forgotten! Think of the two hundred gold nobles. Why that's . . . fifteen gold nobles, two shillings, and sixpence each!"

"Little enough if word gets out we sell our customers to evil sorcerers," said the old witch, with a very telling sniff. For a moment it seemed like she might spit on Shushu's feet.

Then she did. She hawked up a huge gobbet of spit and sent it straight at the head witch's clogs. It spattered on her toes with a sound like bacon hitting a hot frying pan.

Shushu howled and reached inside the pocket of her apron, drawing out a crystal potion sphere that she lifted to throw. At the same time the other witch reached in her apron and pulled out a black bottle that she uncorked and raised to pour down her own throat.

All the other witches scattered, shouting and screaming.

"Duel! A duel!"

Anya chose that moment to spring up and sprint for the closest gap in the stones, the precious bottle of witches' tears hugged to her chest. As she ran, she heard a hissing behind her, like the sound of iron being quenched by a smith, only much, much louder—and, in counterpoint to that, a noise like hail falling on a tiled roof, rat-a-tat-tat.

She didn't dare look to see what was making these sounds, but raced down the hill, zigzagging in case one of the witches threw a potion at her, or even just a rock. The noises behind her changed, the hissing suddenly replaced by a great boom, accompanied by a blast of hot air that hit Anya and helped her along her way. Presuming it had cooled from its point of origin it must have been very hot indeed back there. Behind it came a sound like dozens of animals screaming, but not any animals Anya could recognize.

She ran faster, scrambling over the low stone wall at the foot of the hill that marked the orchard's boundary. Only when she was under the shade of the plum trees did she slow down a little and chance a look back.

Coils of black, red, orange, and green smoke were rising up from Brokenmouth Hill, and there were flashes of flame between the stones. Anya saw witches running down the slope, but they weren't chasing her—they were fleeing whatever was happening in the stone circle. One witch fell over and was helped up by two others, but they didn't stop; they ran on again.

Anya ran again too, weaving between the trees, her heart pounding and breath coming in gasps. She knew that even though she'd escaped the witches, Duke Rikard was still coming in his bone ship, and he would scour the countryside looking for her. He would summon ravens and weaselfolk and bandits and assassins.

The carpet had landed in the tenth row of the orchard from the stone wall. Anya had counted on the way out, and she counted now on the way in. Bursting past the ninth row, she skidded to a stop, and looked to the left and right, expecting to see the carpet and her friends.

But there was no sign of the rich red-and-blue carpet.

Or of Ardent, Smoothie, Shrub, and Prince Denholm.

Either she'd counted wrong, or they'd disappeared.

Frantically, Anya ran to the next alley and looked up and down, then the next and the next. She ran back again in case she'd overshot, all the way to the low stone wall. Beyond that, the plumes of multicolored smoke rising from the hill were extending into huge billows, accompanied by distant explosions and strange shrieking or zinging noises. She saw no more witches outside the stone circle.

Anya sprinted back through the trees, hitting her head every now and again on a low-hanging plum, counting aloud as she ran.

"Ten!" she said at the tenth row. The princess was really beginning to panic. Rikard was getting closer with every minute she wasted looking and she was beginning to fear she would never find the carpet.

If she couldn't, she had no hope of escape.

CHAPTER TWENTY-THREE

Fly Us to the Moon

Ardent!" she screamed at the top of her voice. "Ardent!"
"What?" asked a sleepy dog somewhere to Anya's right.

"Ardent! Where are you?"

A pile of grass under a nearby tree moved, and Ardent's snout emerged, followed by the rest of him. He loped over to Anya and licked her hand. Several other lumps rose in the cut grass and proved themselves to be Smoothie and Shrub.

"Thought we'd better hide ourselves and the c-c-carpet," said Ardent, trying and failing to conceal a very big yawn. "Tanitha taught us 'surprise a superior enemy from hiding' and I thought if it's witches, they'd be superior enemies—"

Anya crouched and hugged him as best she could with the bottle of tears between them.

"Good, great, excellent idea," she babbled. "But we have to get out of here. We have to fly in the carpet again—"

"I'm not going back in that," complained Shrub. "I got so cold I couldn't even *think*, let alone wriggle my claws, and I—"

"We have to," Anya insisted. "Duke Rikard is coming in a bone ship, one that flies, and he'll be here soon. He might already be ordering his minions here as well. Get the carpet out while I look at the map."

"I'm not going to get—"

"You promised your mother!" interrupted Anya. She set the bottle of tears down and hastily unfolded the handkerchief map. "We'll ask the carpet to fly slower. Now, it was twenty leagues southeast from the Wizard's place to here, and it's twelve leagues south from here to New Yarrow—that's too far. And we can't just fly into the city anyway. Shrub, I need your knowledge now. Where can we fly to that's this side of the city? Somewhere safe?"

"I don't know," said Shrub mulishly. He blinked his eyes several times and pushed some fallen plums around with his blunt head.

"Think!" Anya urged.

"I suppose there's the Moon," Shrub said.

"What?" asked Anya. She looked up at the sky, as if either the silver or the blue moon might suddenly have appeared and be hanging low and reachable above them.

"It's an inn," Shrub explained. "On the road to New Yarrow, by the river. A couple of leagues this side. Thieves and pirates use it."

"Like Bert's robbers? Good ones?"

"Nah," said Shrub.

"It's no use if they're ordinary ones," said Anya. "They'll just steal from us. Or even kill us."

"Not if you know the passwords. They're guild thieves. And the river pirates are what d'ye call it? Fellow travelers or something. Got rules."

"Do you know the passwords?"

"Might do," acknowledged Shrub.

"*Do you know the passwords?*" shouted Anya.

"All right, no need to shout," said Shrub. "I know some. Enough so they'll leave us alone."

"Are you sure?" asked Ardent.

"Course I'm sure," said Shrub.

"That's not a good place," said Smoothie, her eyes narrowed. "Too many evildoers go there. One day we otters will clean it out."

"It's not that bad," Shrub protested.

"It'll have to do," Anya concluded. "It's a couple of leagues this side of the city?"

"I reckon," said Shrub.

"The carpet can probably fly that far. Oh, I wish I knew for sure. We'll have to ask it to land a bit short to be on the safe side. Come on!"

Smoothie had dragged the carpet out while they were talking, and was now brushing leaves off it. Anya joined her, trying to be both quick and careful. She didn't want to upset the carpet. Even as she swept busily, she couldn't help but glance up every minute or so, looking for signs of the Duke's bone ship speeding to the hill, to catch a princess and undoubtedly kill her.

As they lay down on the carpet, Anya did see it. The shadow of the ship almost passed over them as it flew over the orchard, its feather wings outstretched. The princess jumped as she saw it, then settled back down.

"Quick!" she said. "Ardent, talk to the carpet!"

"Pathadwanimithochozkal, prepare for flight!"

The end of the carpet snapped up and over, and within two

seconds everyone was rolled up tight, though not without protests from Shrub.

"What do I tell it now?" asked Ardent nervously.

"I'll do it," said Anya. She took a deep breath to collect her thoughts, after being badly rattled from the sight of the bone ship. The Duke was so close . . .

"Oh Great and Magnificent Carpet Pathidwanimithochozkal," she said. "Please fly us a little more slowly and very safely and . . . and not too high off the ground to a safe concealed landing place this side of the inn with the sign of the moon on the Yarrow River near New Yarrow, thank you very much."

Nothing happened. The carpet didn't move.

"You said the c-c-carpet's name wrong," said Ardent.

"What?" shrieked Anya. She thought about what she'd said. Instantly the carpet's name became all mixed up in her head. And there was a noise outside—was it footsteps? Was the Duke walking towards them right *now*, while she was helplessly trussed up inside a carpet?

"You say it, then!"

Ardent barked once happily, and repeated Anya's instructions, word for word, except he got the carpet's name right. He really did have an excellent memory when he put his mind to it.

In response, the carpet took off.

If it was going slower than before, Anya didn't notice. As the rug reared back and shot vertically into the air, she screamed, Smoothie screamed, and Shrub screamed. Even Denholm, who had been uncharacteristically silent, joined in with a rapid series of croaks that were probably the equivalent of a scream.

The vertical flight didn't last very long, a much shorter time than on the previous flight. The carpet leveled out, and though the airstream coming through was still cold, it was weaker than it had been before. But even though this was more comfortable, it worried Anya. What if the Duke had seen them and was giving chase in his flying ship? With the carpet going slower, he might be able to catch them.

Pressed tight in the embrace of wool, she had no way of knowing what was happening. There was also the possibility that the distances on the handkerchief map might be wrong, or she'd calculated the combined distances incorrectly and the carpet would stop flying somewhere short of their destination.

Death at the Duke's hand, or death by falling.

Anya shut her eyes and tried to think of nice things. But try as she might, she kept seeing the Duke standing in his ghastly ship of bone. Gotfried had been right all along. The white study must have had hidden doors, and behind them Rikard had been stripping birds of their feathers, collecting their bones, building his horrible craft with sorcery . . .

Ardent said something. Anya shuffled her head around to get her ear pointed at him.

"What was that?"

"Inn . . . something—*mumble*—food," said Ardent.

"You had three breakfasts!" shouted Anya.

"Just . . . something . . . keep . . . going," retorted Ardent.

"Lots of fish in the river," said Smoothie. Her higher-pitched voice was easier to hear, and her head was closer to Anya's than Ardent's. "Hard to catch with this misshapen body, though."

"It won't be too long before I can change you back!" shouted Anya encouragingly. She didn't add, "I hope." Now that she had been reminded of the Duke's powers and his sheer horribleness, she felt rather less confident about her plan to steal the remaining ingredients from the League of Right-Minded Sorcerers.

The carpet pitched downwards and everyone screamed again, except for Ardent, who barked with apparent enjoyment. It was the bark he used for chasing rabbits. He barked again as the carpet leveled out, then again, this time with surprise, as the carpet splashed down into water.

Cool water gushed in both ends of the rolled-up carpet. Anya flailed her arms, trying to get the heavy material off herself so she could get out. She pushed her face hard against the woolen fabric, desperate to keep her nose and mouth out of the water, to get one last breath before she was submerged.

The carpet unrolled. Anya lurched upwards, ready to swim for some distant surface, and found herself suddenly standing in only six inches of water. The carpet had landed in the broad shallows of a pebbly beach, on a bend in the river. The deeper, fast-running water of the Yarrow was a good thirty feet away.

Smoothie put her head in the water, held it there for several seconds, then came up smiling and shook herself, sending droplets of water over everyone. Not that it mattered, because they were already completely sodden.

Ardent picked up Denholm's cage and carried it ashore, shaking himself as he went. Shrub went after him, grumbling under his breath. Anya checked her possessions, picked up her precious bottle of witches' tears, and followed them.

The beach was quite secluded. Following the tight bend in the river for about fifty yards, it was twenty yards wide and sheltered on the land side by high riverbanks, showing the erosion of spring floods. A tangle of willows grew along the banks. Though stunted, they provided excellent cover. The questers could be seen by anyone on the river, but only if they came around the bend, and they would hear the splash of oars or the flap of a sail in time to hide among the willows. It was a very good landing spot.

"We'd better get the carpet in," said Anya. She carefully surveyed the river, but there were only some diving birds in sight. No boats, and no ravens. She looked up as well, and was relieved to see nothing but clear blue sky with a few long wisps of cloud, and the sun beginning its descent towards the west. "Where do you think the inn is?"

"Not sure," said Shrub. He peered around. One eye looked right and one looked left, then they swiveled back together again. "I remember willows along the bank, but they started farther upstream. It could be just around the bend."

Ardent was listening, his ears pricked.

"I c-c-can hear something from that direction," he said. "When the wind c-c-omes, it c-c-arries the sound. Every now and then, a kind of tock sound, wood hitting wood."

"Must be the inn," said Shrub. "They play bowls on the lawn next to the river. And bet on it. All day."

"Bowls?" asked Anya. "What's bowls?"

"It's a game where you throw wooden balls towards another wooden ball," Shrub explained. "They hit each other, knock them out of place. That's what Ardent can hear."

Anya listened, but she couldn't hear anything except the burble of the river.

"How far away?" she asked Ardent.

He thought carefully, ears slowly moving, catching the sound.

"Two or three hundred paces. Around the bend, beyond the willow border."

"We should take care to be quiet ourselves. Come on. Let's get the carpet in."

It took all of them to drag the carpet out of the water. Heavy even before its immersion, it weighted twice as much wet.

"Don't rip it," warned Anya as Ardent took a new and firmer hold with his mouth. "We'll need it later."

She thought for a moment, then added, "Because it is such a wonderful and amazing carpet. Truly we are very lucky to have . . . uh . . . Pathadwanimithochozkal in our company."

"You got the name right!" exclaimed Ardent, letting go to talk, and the sudden drop of his corner nearly made Anya's arms get torn out. Because of this, she wasn't sure whether she imagined it or not, but the carpet had seemed to wriggle in acknowledgement of her words.

They laid the carpet out to dry in a small hollow up against the high riverbank, under the trailing willow branches, where it would hopefully stay hidden. Anya draped her cloak over a long branch in the hope that it might dry too. She took stock of the situation.

"I have the ex-druid's blood and the witches' tears," she said, mostly to get it clear to herself, though everyone else was listening. "Now, here's my plan. We take a look at this inn to see if it's a safe place to hide tonight. Then we need to sneak into the city and the League of Right-Minded Sorcerers' meetinghouse, which is a fortress.

We'll steal some three-day-old hail and cockatrice feathers, get back here, and fly on the carpet to Trallonia Forest—"

Somehow saying it out loud didn't make it seem easier. In fact, it made it all sound much more difficult. But Anya couldn't think of any other plan. And they'd made it this far.

"The forest?" asked Shrub. "Why go back there?"

"So I can borrow your mother's cooking pot and stirring stick to make the lip balm," Anya replied. She'd noted Martha's bronze pot and the blackened branch, which she felt must be lightning-struck oak, given that Martha was the sister of one druid and the ex-wife of another. It was doubtless part of the reason her soup was so good.

She continued, "We can get beeswax from someone there, I'm sure; many of the foresters keep bees. Anyway, I'll make the lip balm there. We'll send messages to gather Bert's robbers and the dwarves, and when they arrive we'll carry out a surprise attack on Trallonia Castle and . . . uh . . . defeat the Duke."

"What about all his weaselfolk and assassins?" asked Ardent, who had been trained in tactics.

"We'll try to capture the weaselfolk. I'll, uh . . ."

Anya paused, a grimace forming on her face. She willed herself to assume a normal expression and continued.

"I'll . . . I'll kiss them with my lip balm on, and they'll change back and run away. Some of them might even come over to us, like Smoothie, because they want to change back."

"Weasels like blood," said Smoothie doubtfully. "Being bigger and stronger suited most of the ones in the group I was with."

"We might need more help than the robbers and dwarves," said

Ardent dubiously. "Weren't we going to go to Denholm's kingdom and get their knights and soldiers?"

"Change of plan," said Anya briskly. She looked at Denholm in his cage. The frog looked quite unwell, now a much paler shade of green. "I'm worried that something's wrong with Prince Denholm. He needs to be changed back as soon as possible. And with Moatie . . . with Moatie gone, anything could happen to Morven. The Duke is clearly getting more powerful every day, and he might decide he doesn't need even a puppet queen in Trallonia. So we have to act fast. Besides, I don't think Denholm's father, the king of Gornish, has that many soldiers anyway. We'll have to make do with whoever we can . . . um . . . enlist to the cause. The foresters might join me, and some of the druids perhaps . . ."

"We'll have to survive getting into the meetinghouse and out again in the first place," Shrub pointed out glumly. "At least they can't turn me into anything else. It'll just be death, I suppose. Or torture . . . that's always a possibility with that lot—"

"Stop it!" interrupted Anya. "Let's just focus on what we want to happen. Now, you said there was supposed to be a way into the meetinghouse through the sewers. Who could help us find that?"

"A senior thief," said Shrub. "There's probably one hanging about the Sign of the Moon. They'd want payment. More than you've got, I expect."

Anya frowned. This questing business was just full of small challenges that built up into bigger challenges, and just when she'd thought she was getting ahead—

Smoothie held up her paw-hand.

"Yes?"

"The sewers under New Yarrow? The ones from the old city? We know them. The otters, I mean. Not me personally. I never wanted to swim there, because they stink if they're too dry and they're dangerous when they're flooded. But other otters go there."

"Why?" asked Ardent.

"Because the sewers join the river and the river is our bailiwick," said Smoothie.

"What's a bailiwick?" asked Ardent.

"Like a demesne," said Anya. "An area under someone's authority."

"Oh," replied Ardent. "The same as a jurisdiction."

"Yes," said Anya impatiently. "Getting back to important matters . . . Smoothie, could you get the otters to help us find a way into the city and the League's meetinghouse through the old sewers?"

"Maybe." Smoothie's mouth was turned down, and her dark brown eyes were hooded with sadness. "But I'd have to show myself to them . . . in this twisted, awful shape . . ."

"It's only temporary," said Anya. "I'll change you back."

"Who you are is inside," said Ardent. He'd been licking his paws clean of river mud, but he stopped to look directly at Smoothie. "No sorcerer c-c-an change that, no matter what they transform the outside into. You are still a Yarrow River otter, and always will be."

Smoothie's mouth unfroze and she opened her eyes more.

"I'll go now," she said, turning towards the river.

"No, wait a moment!" said Anya. "We have to work out where to meet. I'm still not sure about this inn. The witches had heard about the Duke's reward for me. Two hundred gold nobles is a lot—"

"Oh," said Shrub. "I forgot about that. You'd better not go to the inn."

"Because someone will turn me in to the Duke?"

"They *all* would," said Shrub. "Seeing as you're only a friend of a thief, not a thief yourself. Two hundred gold nobles! I'd do it myself—"

CHAPTER TWENTY-FOUR

Shrub Finds a Boat, Smoothie Finds Some Cousins

D on't you be thinking about getting a reward for the princess," growled Ardent fiercely. He stood stiff-legged, pushing his snout into Shrub's face.

"Hey, leave off," said Shrub. "I'm a *good* thief, remember. And I promised Ma. *And* Anya is going to turn me back. Very hard to pick a lock when you're a newt, let me tell you. I can't wait to have fingers again. I was only going to say I'd do it myself *if things were different*."

"All right, all right," said Anya. "Let me think. Tell me about the meetinghouse, Shrub. Did you see anything that could be a storeroom for alchemical ingredients?"

"I didn't see much of anything inside," said Shrub with his curious shrug. "But it's what used to be the old king's castle. Half of it's fallen down, and the League has only fixed up bits of it, in the middle."

"That could be good," said Anya. "We might even be able to hide in the meetinghouse itself, and scout around."

"I suppose. It was just bad luck that when I fell down the chimney it was in one of the fixed-up parts, and they heard me. Course I got away from the first lot, but then when I got to the Garden, the Grey Mist was there—"

"The Garden?" interrupted Anya. "That's their prison?"

"Nah, that's just what people think," said Shrub. "Weren't no prisoners there. It's just the Grey Mist's private garden, I reckon. 'Spose she likes plants a bit. It's higher up from where they store stuff, though."

"So we can stay well away from it," said Anya. "I want to get in, get the ingredients, and get out as quickly as possible. Remember that, Shrub. No going off looking for the Only Stone."

"I won't go off," said Shrub. "I promised!"

"Riiiight," said Anya. She looked at the newt dubiously before she continued. "The river goes into the sewers, so we can too. But we'll need a boat, as well as an otter guide."

"I could probably get a boat at the inn," said Shrub. "I mean, by myself. Take a gold noble in my mouth, rent one. They know me there."

"Do they know you in the shape of a newt?" asked Smoothie.

"Course!" snorted Shrub. "That's where I went when I first got turned into a newt. It's not just me, you know. The way those sorcerers are in New Yarrow, you look at them wrong and you get transformed. There was a cutpurse got turned into a toad—he lives in the herb garden at the Moon now. And a baker who asked to be paid, he got turned into a rat and a big black cat et him! Mind you, it ain't all bad, I suppose. A bloke I knew a bit, he got transformed a few weeks before me, caught trying to steal some sorcerer's horse. Horses were his speciality, you know. Kenry got turned into a kind of little monkey. He was an apprentice like me . . . only a real one. I mean, he was already indentured to a master thief, that Sally Purseghoster, one of the best. Though I 'spose Bert has promised me now, so I'm kind of—"

"This apprentice," interrupted Anya. "The one who got turned into a monkey. He's at the inn?"

"Might be, I dunno," said Shrub. "Lots of thieves rest up there between jobs. Why?"

"He might be able to help us. I mean, in return for getting changed back."

"Kenry?" asked Shrub. "Like I said, it ain't always bad to get transformed. He won't want to get changed back. Being a little monkey is a dream come true for a thief. You can climb, get through really small windows, swing from yer tail, climb a leg and cut a purse and jump away. Fifty . . . no, a hundred times better than being a newt. Why, I—"

"It is a terrible thing to be changed from your own shape," interrupted Smoothie. She sounded so sad even Shrub shut up.

"True. So this Kenry might want to change back by now," said Anya. She thought for a moment, and shook her head. "No, I suppose if he really likes being a monkey, it's too much of a risk, because of the reward."

"He can't talk anyhow," said Shrub. "He understands, though."

"Never mind," said Anya. "It was just a thought."

"What do I do with a boat if I can get one?" asked Shrub. He lifted his paws. "Can't sail with these."

"Come back and report," said Anya. "Then I guess we'll have to sneak along tonight and row it away. I can row—I learned going around the moat. Oh, see if you can get some food and water put aboard as well."

"Roast beef," Ardent requested. "Or sausages."

"Shall I go now too?" asked Smoothie. "If I can find someone to guide us, I'll come back here."

"Yes," said Anya decisively. "But come back by nightfall anyway."

"Have you seen Theodric Theodricsson, the thistle-sifter's son?" asked Shrub.

"What?"

"That's the pass phrase," said Shrub. "Then if everything's all right, the inn-keeper replies, 'Nay, there's no thistle-sifting here, no, never there was.'"

"What if he doesn't say that?" asked Ardent. "Or if you get the first part wrong?"

"They knock you on the head," said Shrub. "And stick you in the river."

"Are you sure you'll be safe?" Anya was surprised Shrub was so keen to go. He hadn't seemed to be particularly brave in their previous adventures.

"Sure," said Shrub. "Like I told you, they know me there. Here, sling me a gold noble."

He opened his mouth wide. It opened a lot wider than it looked like it could or should, and the inside was a kind of an unpleasant, pallid orange. He didn't have any teeth or, as far as Anya could see, a tongue.

"How do you talk?" asked Ardent. "You haven't—"

"Here's the money!" interrupted Anya quickly. Shrub might only be able to talk because he didn't know he didn't have a tongue, but by some quirk of the transformation magic, he could still speak as if he did. If he started wondering what his tongue was doing, and felt that he didn't even have one, he might lose the power of speech.

She dropped the coin into the newt's mouth.

"Fanks," he croaked, talking around the heavy gold noble. "Back soon, I hope. Tol lol."

Rather surprisingly, Shrub returned before Smoothie. He came slithering down the bank between two huge twisted willow roots just upon dusk. Ardent, who'd smelled and heard him coming, yipped a quiet greeting. Anya, who'd been having an extra rest on the carpet, woke up, and for an instant thought something bad was happening before she realized it was just the newt.

"Got a boat," Shrub announced. "Told 'em it was for Bert, I was working for ARR, so no questions or else."

"They know Bert here?" asked Anya. She was surprised. She'd thought they were far beyond the robber's influence, which she'd presumed was local to Trallon Forest and nearby.

"Course," Shrub scoffed. "There's groups of the Association of Responsible Robbers all over the place. They call 'em chapters, like in a book. Not so many members in New Yarrow, 'cos of people being more selfish in the city, but there's some. Enough that the regular thieves and pirates take them serious and won't cross 'em. Anyhow, I got a boat, and food and water. Boat's tied up right on the end of the inn's jetty. Which sticks out from the bowling green. Where's Smoothie?"

"Not back yet," said Anya with a trace of anxiety. "I hope the otters treat her all right. She feels bad enough being half otter, half human."

"Least she's got fingers," said Shrub. "Sort of, anyway. I'm going to catch some water-skaters in the shallows."

Water-skaters were the long-legged insects that slid crazily over the surface of the water and never sank, even when they stopped.

There were always plenty on the moat back at Trallonia, and they were a staple part of the frogs' diet there.

"Catch some for Denholm, please," said Anya. She was still very worried about the frog prince. He'd continued to be very quiet in his little cage, apart from the brief bout of croaking when they'd landed in the river.

It was full dark before Smoothie returned. Shrub had caught at least a dozen water-skaters for Denholm by then, and the frog had eaten them, though not with his usual relish.

Smoothie was not alone. Two very large otters came with her. They were almost as big as Anya, far larger than any otters she'd ever seen before. She'd thought Smoothie's fine-haired hide was sleek, but these otters' hides were even sleeker. They had an almost silvery gleam about them, which was not a reflection of the moon, because the silver moon wasn't up yet, and if the blue moon was, it was so dim and low Anya couldn't see it.

Smoothie appeared to be very cheerful, Anya was pleased to notice. The half otter came gamboling up to Anya on all fours, stood up, and delivered a kind of bow. The full otters were more careful, looking around in all directions and moving in a stop-start fashion, ready to change direction and bolt back for the river if anything went amiss.

"Two of my senior cousins," said Smoothie, by way of introduction. She emitted a series of strange yowly, growly yips, then translated these as Swiftsure One Bite Salmon Slayer and Deepest Water True Diver. The otters inclined their heads as their names were mentioned, but only by a fraction, and they remained wary.

"Swiftie and Diver know the canals and the sewers," said Smoothie. "They'll lead us to the sunken rooms of the old palace;

they're cellars now, and only partly flooded. We can get into the meetinghouse above from there. Apparently, we take Bank Street from the river—"

"Bank *Street*?" asked Anya.

"It's a canal now," said Shrub, eager to show off his knowledge of the city. "You know New Yarrow is built on top of the ruins of the old Yarrow, what they called Yarrow the City? Well, in the old days, there were a couple of big canals—that's the Heavy Way and the Light Way. They're so big you can get a ship down them! But when the Deluge hit, it scoured out more canals, so lots of the old streets, they're canals now."

"We take Bank Street from the river," resumed Smoothie. "Turn right into a little canal—it hasn't got a name—where the statue without a head is. Go along that, and under the second bridge there's an outflow from the sewers. The grating's busted, so we go in there, head along a bit, and there we are."

"Sounds straightforward," said Ardent.

"I bet it isn't," Anya warned. "How far can we take the boat?"

"How big a boat?" asked Smoothie.

"Rowing dinghy," Shrub replied. He spoke slowly, and was licking his eyes, a sure sign he was thinking about something. "Twelve-footer."

Smoothie spoke to the two otters in their language. Anya tried to make sense of their reply, but couldn't, though she noticed the repetition of some particularly high-pitched squeaks. She would love to be able to speak native otter. One day, perhaps, she would be able to study otter language. Someone must have written a diction-ary or primer. There might be one in the Wizard's library . . .

"As far as the bridge," said Smoothie, interrupting Anya's momentary daydream. "Then we have to swim or you might be able to wade. They say it won't be too stinky, because the rain flushed it out last night. Or too flooded, because the rain stopped this morning."

Anya wrinkled her nose, thinking of exactly what the rain was flushing out of the sewers, into the canal and then the river. At least at Trallonia they had a proper cesspit, instead of just letting everything run into the moat. Letting it do that was very old-fashioned, and led to disease. Everyone knew that.

"All right," she said. "It's dark enough. Let's sneak around the willows and take the boat."

"There was another thing I just remembered hearing about the way into the meetinghouse through the sewers," said Shrub.

"What?" asked Anya.

"You have to watch out for a monster that guards the stairs up," said the newt.

This information was met with a deafening silence and a look of suppressed irritation from Anya that had all the hallmarks of being the precursor to one of her very stern looks.

"But thieves do get past," said Shrub. "Apparently. So it can't be *that* much of a monster."

"Do you know what kind of creature it is?" asked Anya, forcing herself to speak slowly and remain calm.

"Nope," said Shrub. "How bad can it be?"

Another, longer silence met this particular comment.

"Let's go and get in the boat," said Anya.

This time, she was unable to hold back a very long sigh.

CHAPTER TWENTY-FIVE

Into the City by River, Canal,
Sewer, and Stairs

A light wind was lifting the trailing branches of the willows as the intrepid questers followed Shrub single file along the riverbank and around the bend. The bright orange newt, as always, was much more visible than anyone else, causing Anya some concern as they came to the end of the willow-infested border and saw the long, high-roofed main building of the inn up ahead. The windows on all three stories were bright from the lantern light inside, with an occasional moving shadow indicating there were plenty of people inhabiting the place.

Shrub, however, did not hesitate, but continued on across the corner of the deserted lawn-bowls green, only just skirting a shaft of spilled light from the closest window. Anya followed on tiptoe, carefully avoiding the wooden balls that had been left higgledy-piggledy around the carefully tended lawn.

The jetty struck out into the river at a right angle from the lawn. There were at least half a dozen boats of different sizes tied up to it, but no one was in any of them. Shrub led the way over the rather alarmingly rotten and hole-peppered boards to the very end of the jetty, where one of the smaller boats swayed on the end of its mooring line. It was basically a larger version of the rowing boat

Anya was familiar with from the moat back home, though with two sets of rowlocks and oars. It didn't have a mast, unlike many of the other boats.

Anya pulled the boat in, climbed down, and held the craft against the jetty so the others could get in more easily. Smoothie handed down Denholm in his cage and the bottle of witches' tears, then boarded as if she had done it a thousand times before. Ardent jumped with precision and moved to the bow to sit like a figure-head, while Shrub paced backwards and forwards on the jetty.

"Jump down," whispered Anya urgently. She kept looking back towards the inn, expecting the sudden spill of light from a door opening at any moment, and then shouts of alarm.

"It's too far," said Shrub. "I've got short legs."

"I'll catch you," said Anya. "Come on, jump!"

Shrub hesitated before launching himself off the jetty towards the boat. Anya made no attempt to catch him, instead moving back, while still holding on to the jetty. The newt landed heavily, but without injury.

"I knew you had it in you," said Anya encouragingly. She had years of practice tricking her recalcitrant older sister into doing things.

Shrub muttered something and plonked himself down on one of the thwarts. Anya pushed them off from the jetty and sat down herself, shipping one set of oars. They were heavier and longer than she was used to, so as she began to row, she had to concentrate hard to make sure she didn't "catch a crab"—slipping the blade of the oar out of the water and cracking her chin with the other end.

"Head towards the middle of the river, where the current is strongest," Smoothie instructed. "More to your left—that's it. Swiftie and Diver will meet us there. You won't have to row much, except for direction."

"It's going to be hard coming back," said Anya. She could feel the current working on the boat. "Can you row? We'll probably need the second set of oars. I doubt I could go against the current by myself."

"I'll watch you and learn," said Smoothie. She trailed one paw-hand over the side, cupped up some water, and splashed it over her face. "Ah, I love the river! Better to be in it than on it, but this is almost as good."

It *was* beautiful on the water. The big moon was finally coming up, casting its gentle light across the water, turning the ripples from wind and current into lines of silver. The river was getting wider, spreading out, and the high banks and willows were giving way to once well-ordered farmland that, while not what it had been in the heyday of the High Kingdom, still looked neat and bucolic in the moonlight.

Looking at the moonlit land beside the river, and only needing to occasionally dip the oars to correct their way, Anya found her mind wandering, particularly with regard to the city they were heading towards. She knew that New Yarrow was built upon the ruins of Yarrow the City, which had been destroyed by the great tidal wave of the Deluge, accidentally summoned by the last High King. But that was about it.

"Who rules New Yarrow?" she asked Shrub, at least in part to make a peace offering for tricking him. Shrub was always at his best when showing off that he knew more about something than anybody else.

The newt shrugged.

"There's a mayor and a city council," he said. "But they do whatever the League of Right-Minded Sorcerers tells them to do."

"So the city's not part of any kingdom?" Anya gestured at the fields to either side of the river. There was wheat growing in long swathes off into the full darkness, but even in just the moonlight, Anya could see it was taller and thicker and closer to harvesting than back home in Trallonia. She didn't know it but these were the fabled breadbasket lands of the city, the soil unrivaled and the river providing all necessary water. The bread in New Yarrow was justifiably famous, but it owed its fame largely to the quality of the wheat from the river plains. "What about these farmlands?"

"I dunno." Shrub's bulbous eyes looked across the water without any particular interest. "I came by road. There's a few places you have to stop at the borders of little kingdoms along the way, but the city rules everywhere close, I guess. Then there's places like the inn back there—they look after themselves."

"I see," said Anya. She'd never thought much about it before, in the relative security of Trallonia. Even with the looming threat from her stepstepfather it had been a pretty safe and ordered place. But the breaking up of the High Kingdom into lots of little kingdoms and lawless areas was a thoroughly bad thing.

It made her think about the All-Encompassing Bill of Rights and Wrongs again, and the laws that were written within the Only Stone. Surely it would be a very good thing to bring back the Bill, and make sure the people in all the little kingdoms were treated fairly by their rulers.

"I suppose, if we do happen to see it . . ." she muttered half to herself.

"See what?" asked Ardent, turning his head back without shifting from his self-appointed role as a figurehead.

"Nothing!" exclaimed Anya quickly. She didn't want to say the name aloud, for fear of setting off Shrub. Or raising his hopes. "Um, can you spot the otters?"

"Of c-c-c-course," barked Ardent. "One on the left and one on the right."

Anya, who was sitting backwards to row, looked over her shoulder. Just as the dog had said, the two otters were easily keeping station with the boat, a little way ahead and to either side.

"Right a little," said Smoothie. Anya dipped her left oar, and the boat turned. The current in the middle of the river was so strong she didn't have to actually row at all, just drop in one or the other oar and hold it for a few moments.

With the boat almost steering itself, at least for the moment, Anya could devote herself to other problems. Foremost in her mind was Denholm. The frog prince had been uncharacteristically silent for a long time, and though he had eaten the water-skaters, it had not been with his usual appetite.

Anya rested the oars and picked up the little wicker cage. It was rather bent from the encounter with the giant, but still seemed all right. Denholm, however, didn't.

"He does look off-color," said Anya anxiously. She held the cage high, to get the moonlight on it. "Less green and more yellow than he did. Maybe it's just the moon—"

"No," said Smoothie. "He's definitely changing color."

Ardent came back to look. He sniffed at the cage carefully.

"Smells less like sorcery and more like a normal frog," he announced after quite a lot of snuffling.

"I hope that doesn't mean he's sickening," said Anya. "Or the transformation is having some bad effect."

Denholm let out a croaking moan and turned his back.

"I'll change you back as soon as I can," said Anya, but this didn't evoke a response. Smoothie kindly dribbled some river water on the frog, but he didn't react to this either. Anya put the cage down near her feet and took up the oars again.

"How long till we get close to the city?" she asked.

Smoothie called out across the water, and listened intently to the peeping, yowling noise that came back.

"An hour or so," she answered.

"What have we got to eat?" asked Ardent. "Besides that horrible magic biscuit?"

Anya raised an eyebrow. The biscuit had tasted like dry sawdust but she'd never known Ardent to disdain anything that was even remotely classed as food.

"Bread and meat, in the box," said Shrub.

The bread was a dozen quite small rolls, fresh baked, and the meat was an equal number of roasted chops that had already been deboned. Anya rested her oars again and assembled the beef and rolls together. She ate two herself; Ardent ate four and would have had more if Anya had let him. In fact, he would have eaten the whole lot, and kept nosing the box even after the princess had wrapped the remaining rolls in the cloth the chops had come in, saving them for the return trip. Shrub and Smoothie declined the food, claiming they'd both eaten while away on their respective missions for boat and guides.

Anya saw the lights of the city not long after they ate, while they were still quite some distance away. At first it was just a glow above the dark water of the river ahead, a glow that spread and intensified as they continued along, borne westwards by the rushing current.

The princess hadn't thought of it being light, or at least, so well lit. Gazing ahead, she realized that the glow could only be so great if almost every building and street was lit up with lanterns or torches or some other source of artificial illumination. She'd thought they could sneak along the river and canals in relative darkness and obscurity, but that was not going to be possible.

This raised the strong possibility that someone would recognize her and raise the alarm, or try to capture her themselves, in order to get the reward offered by the Duke. By now, the Duke's agents might also know about the others with her, who were all quite recognizable too.

"We have to disguise ourselves," she said. "I can keep my hood up. Smoothie . . . if you get some kind of clothes on, no one will look twice unless they're up close. Is there anything in the boat?"

"An old sail under here," said Ardent after a quick nose around. He pulled it out and dragged it back to Anya. It was just a rough piece of faded and patched canvas, but it served as a makeshift cloak for Smoothie. When it was drawn over her head, she looked like some poor beggar.

"What about me?" asked Shrub.

"You'll just have to stay low in the boat," said Anya. She couldn't think of any way to disguise a huge, bright orange newt. "Ardent, you should lie low too. And if you do have to move, act as if you're nervous and scared of being kicked. Not like a royal dog."

Anya had been right to be careful. As they drew closer to the city, they encountered other boats, mostly crossing the river rather than going up or down. The farmland on either side began to be replaced by ramshackle warehouses, small businesses, and dwellings of all sizes, from tiny huts made of reeds to once-grand four-story houses. Nearly all the buildings had their own jetties or wharves, the shoreline bristling with them at all angles.

The other boats nearly all carried red, blue, or green lanterns at stern or prow, and the buildings without exception had long strings of differently colored lanterns stretched under their eaves and across to nearby trees or poles obviously erected to hold them up.

"Is this normal?" Anya asked Shrub. "All the lanterns?"

"More than usual," said Shrub after a quick glance over the side. "Probably a festival. They have a lot of festivals in the city."

"Have we got a lantern anywhere?" asked Anya. "We don't want to look different from the other boats."

Shrub and Ardent fossicked around the bottom of the boat. Eventually, Ardent dragged a tin box over to Anya. She opened it and found several collapsed paper lanterns, a number of candle stubs, and three friction lights, or matches, as some people called them.

Anya stretched out a blue lantern, fixed the candle in place, and lit it with the second friction light. The first one had only fizzed when she dragged it along the gunwale, and smelled of sulfur. The third match she put behind her ear, in case it came in handy later on.

The blue lantern wasn't very bright, which suited their requirements. There was a little platform for it on the bow, shielded on three sides, with a peg to keep it in place. Anya fixed it there, and went back to her oars, though she didn't need to use them while the current sped the boat along.

CHAPTER TWENTY-SIX

In Which Canals Are Smelled Before They Are Seen

Soon enough Anya had to start rowing to steer the boat, Smoothie softly calling out course corrections as she watched the two otters guiding them in. It was hard work to pull out of the current, but got a bit easier as they approached the shore.

Anya kept glancing over her shoulder; though she was confident in Smoothie's directions, she wanted to see for herself as well. The line of buildings was now continual—there were no gaps at all that she could see—and there were more and more buildings behind the ones on the riverfront, outlined against the sky, or in evidence from the lanterns in their windows or roofs. Far more buildings than Anya had ever seen.

She also smelled the city now. It was like nothing she had smelled before, a mixture of smoke and odors that not only hung in the air but actively crawled up her nose and coated her tongue, occasionally intensifying to a point where the smell actually *hurt* before a slight brush of air dissipated the worst of the stench.

"You get used to the smell," remarked Shrub from his spot near Anya's feet. He'd seen her wrinkling her nose and making faces. "It's a lot worse once you get in a bit."

"Is it?" asked Ardent happily. He was crouched down as well, but his nose was up and sniffing wildly. "Fascinating! So many different combinations!"

"We're approaching the entrance to the canal," said Smoothie. "Diver is coming back for some reason . . . Slow down."

Anya eased her oars out of the water and rested her forearms on her legs, while Smoothie bent over the side and whispered in otter to her cousin.

"There's a guard on the lock gate where the river joins the canal," reported Smoothie. "The lock is open. Apparently it's always open, but there's not normally a guard."

"Bribe 'em," said Shrub from the bottom of the boat. "Hold a coin up, and as you get close, throw it to the guard."

"Oh," said Smoothie. "We didn't think of that. Swiftie's already gone to—"

Up ahead they heard a faint cry and then a loud splash.

Anya twisted around to look. It took her a few seconds to make sense of what she was looking at. A shape moving in the water resolved itself as the two otters towing an unconscious guard to the muddy shore near the canal entrance. They dragged him or her up above the tidemark of flotsam and then returned to the water, yipping victoriously.

"We can go on now," said Smoothie. Her teeth shone, moonlight reflecting from a happy smile.

Anya bent to her oars and the boat moved forward, into the canal.

It was darker almost immediately, the canal shadowed by the buildings on both sides. The lanterns, though plentiful, did not compare with the light of the silver moon. Every now and then, though, there was a line of lanterns stretched high across the canal, rather than just strung over doorways or windows. Anya hunched down as they passed under these, and tugged at her hood to keep it well forward.

There were also people. Every building had a landing with a door behind it, and some of these doors were open, as were the windows above. Though it had to be close to midnight now, there were still city dwellers looking out, or drinking on their landings, or fishing (usually while also drinking).

A few of these canal-side folk called out greetings as Anya rowed past. She didn't answer, afraid her voice would give her away, but waved with one hand. None called out in alarm or shouted about the strange occupants of the boat, but each time Anya tensed expecting trouble to begin.

No one noticed the two otters, either—and if they did, they kept it to themselves. Though the otters rarely came into the canals in the current times, people still told stories about the huge Yarrow River otters and how they had once kept the peace on the river with tooth and claw, and by extension, kept the peace everywhere the river flowed, including the city canals. If the giant otters were about, sensible people left them to their business.

Anya was particularly tense as they passed under the next bridge. It was roofed and had high sides, but it would still be possible for someone to hang over and look down straight at them, seeing Shrub. Presuming that the inhabitants of New Yarrow didn't see huge orange newts every day, this would probably lead to a commotion, would attract guards and perhaps Gerald the Heralds and then certainly raven spies and the like from the sorcerers of the League.

This made Anya belatedly wonder who those sorcerers actually were, and how many were located in New Yarrow. She knew about the Duke, of course, and had heard about the Grey Mist, but that was all.

"Hey, Shrub," she whispered after they were past the bridge. "How many sorcerers belong to the League anyway? And how many might be in the meetinghouse?"

"I dunno," said Shrub, answering with possibly his most frequent response. "Most of 'em only come in for meetings, they have 'em at the same time as the city festivals . . ."

Anya looked back at all the lanterns strung across the canal, and in the windows and doorways of every building.

"Like now?" she asked softly.

"Maybe," said Shrub. "I mean, the city has a lot of festivals. Stands to reason the League wouldn't have a meeting *every* time."

"And how many sorcerers have you heard about?"

"Let's see. There's the Grey Mist; she's kind of like the caretaker. She's always in the meetinghouse—that's why she was the one who transformed me, Then there's your Duke Rikard—"

"He's not *my* Duke Rikard," interrupted Anya.

Shrub swiveled one eyeball to look at her, then continued.

"Ahuren the Nightgaunt, he comes from the mountains. Grandmother Ghoul, oh, she's a horror. I seen her once. They say she lives in the old necropolis outside the city and she looks like they dug her up from there. Yngish, Lord of the Waves, he rules the pirates that live on the Crooked Isle in the river mouth. That's, let me see, five. I think there might be six altogether, though."

"Let's hope they're not all there right now," said Anya. "If they are, we have to avoid them. Like I said, sneak in, steal the ingredients, and sneak out."

Everyone nodded. Anya did too, very firmly. She hoped she looked more confident than she felt. The whole being-in-charge-of-a-questing-party thing was very stressful and she was really looking forward to the time when she could just curl up with her books again in the library. Different books, though. Not ones about learning sorcery.

They continued along the canal, Anya rowing slowly and carefully. She was rather disgusted by the amount of rubbish in the water. Almost every time her oars lifted, they came up with bits of rotten stuff that had just been thrown in and was so decomposed it was hard to recognize, except when a putrescent pumpkin floated past, or what was left of some large fish or perhaps a dolphin, one pallid eye bobbing just above the surface. Once, an oar got stuck and lifted up part of something she was afraid was a dead body.

"What's wrong with this city!" she hissed after disturbing a particular noxious mat of rotten vegetable peelings that was almost as big as their boat.

"Like I said," said Shrub, "no one's really in charge. Mayor and council are afraid to do anything in case the sorcerers don't like it. So they don't do anything."

"*Someone* should do something," Anya growled.

She rowed on in silence for a while after that, thinking. It was easy to say "someone should do something" but rather more difficult to put it into practice.

"Big group of people up ahead," warned Smoothie. "Small ones."

"A group of small people?" Anya looked over her shoulder. "Oh, children! Young ones. What are they doing there?"

There were half a dozen children sitting on one of the regular small landing stages that adjoined almost every canal-facing door on every building. As Anya rowed closer, one of them stood up and held out her cupped hands.

"Food, kind people. Food for the orphans?"

Anya hesitated, shipped her oars, and let the boat coast alongside the small landing till she was level with the begging child. It was a girl, aged perhaps six or seven, wearing a short robe that had once been a flour sack and still bore fading red stenciled letters that spelled out *Weshlig Mill*. The other children were no better clothed, and they all looked very undersized and scrawny.

None got up as the boat stopped, their lack of curiosity and general air of exhaustion a stark contrast from the village children Anya was used to seeing.

"Food, kind people," said the flour-sack girl again, but not as if she expected to get any.

"Here," said Anya, handing up the remnants of their bread and meat. This did attract a response, with the children moving closer and shuffling about, till they were beaten back by the flour-sack girl.

"Wait your turns," she snapped. "I'll see it divided fair."

"What are you doing here?" asked Anya. "Are you all really orphans?"

"Good as," said the girl, intently dividing the bread into tiny but equal-size portions on her lap. "Might be some who have parents somewhere, but none that are any use."

"And you stay here at night?"

"Old Jerbie, she lets us stay here," said the girl, slicing the beef now with a very blunt knife. "We work for her during the day, picking up stuff that might be useful. In the canals, and along Kneebone Street. It ain't much of a living but it's better than dying, as my old sister used to say."

Anya thought for a moment, then produced the Wallet of Crunchings and Munchings.

"What's your name?" she asked.

"Street rat, scum girl, you good-for-nought," said the child bitterly. She was still intent on carving the beef, each piece no larger than a silver penny.

"What is it really?" asked Anya.

"Truvence," said the girl. She looked across at Anya properly for the first time, and down into the boat. "Here, who are you lot?"

"Never mind that," said Anya hastily. She handed over the wallet. Truvence took it gingerly.

"That's a magical wallet," said Anya. "Three times a day, when you open it, there will be a large biscuit inside."

Truvence opened it as Anya spoke, and looked at the biscuit suspiciously.

"They're not very nice biscuits," said Anya. "But they're food, and the wallet will never run out. But you'll need to keep it secret. Don't let any others see it, or someone will steal it from you."

Truvence was still looking at the biscuit.

"Why you giving us this?" she asked.

"Because . . . because I want to make even a little difference," said Anya quietly. "Maybe later I can make a big difference."

She hesitated, then added, "People call me the Frogkisser. Remember that, because one day I'll be back to do more."

Truvence nodded mechanically, lifted the biscuit, and took a tiny bite. Anya expected her to make a face, but she didn't. She just chewed thoughtfully for a few seconds, then handed the biscuit slowly to the closest child.

"Small bite," she said firmly. "No bigger than mine, then pass it on. Bread and meat coming."

"We have to go," said Anya. "Good luck."

"Thanks, miss," said the girl. "I mean, *Frogkisser*."

The other children whispered their thanks too. Anya rowed away with a quiet chorus of "Frogkisser . . . Frogkisser . . . Frogkisser" echoing in her wake.

Anya thought Ardent might have something to say about her giving away the Wallet of Munchings and Crunchings. But he didn't. No one said anything as she rowed on, until Smoothie lifted her head at the bow and pointed.

"Turn coming up," said the otter-maid. "Sharp right, three, two, one . . . now!"

The statue without a head was some kind of gargoyle projecting from the house on the corner of the small canal. It had a chest and arms, and a broken bit where it probably once did have a head. It didn't have legs, joining the brick wall at the waist.

It was instantly darker in the narrow, lesser canal, which was so choked with garbage the water had the consistency of oatmeal and it smelled worse than the main canal, if that was possible. Even Ardent, who liked smells of all kinds, scuffed at his nose with his forepaws. Anya breathed through her mouth and tried to ignore it, telling herself that this is what she had to expect if they were going to sneak into a fortress via a sewer.

"I don't know how they can swim in this," muttered Smoothie. "You wouldn't be able to get clean for ages. Even the river would take a long time to get this muck off."

A chittering noise from the water a few seconds later seemed to confirm this assessment. Smoothie listened for a moment, then squeaked and chirruped back.

"It *is* too foul," she said to Anya. "They have to get out. The grating is under the second bridge. They wish us luck and also advise to not put your head under the water."

"Yes indeed," agreed Anya fervently. "Please give them my thanks, and if there is ever anything I can do for the otters of the Yarrow River, they have only to ask."

Smoothie repeated these words in Otterish, there were some discreet splashes, and Diver and Swiftie were gone, speeding back to the main canal . . . and from there to the clean water of the river.

The canal wasn't wide enough for Anya to row normally, so she had to dig the oars in close to the side of the boat, several times scraping the walls on the left or right. But they continued to make their way along, passing under the first narrow bridge without incident.

They stopped under the next bridge. There was a narrow tunnel leading off the canal there, which had once been barred but was now open, with only a few stubs of rusting iron left behind from the former grille.

Ardent, peering over the side, said, "It smells even more horrible. I didn't think it c-c-ould."

"We have to go up there, no matter how it smells," said Anya. She unshipped an oar and used it to probe the water, checking the depth. "It's not very deep. About up to my waist, I'd say. I can wade."

"*You* can wade," said Ardent. "I'll have to swim. So will Shrub."

"I don't mind," said Shrub. "I can't smell much anyway. No worse than mud."

"It's a lot worse than mud," said Anya. She accidentally breathed through her nose for a moment, and felt the gorge rising in her throat. "But we have to do it. You take the lead, Shrub. Look for the way into the meetinghouse. Ardent, you go next. I'll follow with Denholm. Smoothie, you bring up the rear."

Before they went over the side, Anya put the bottles of druid's blood and witches' tears down the front of her jerkin so they'd stay out of the water. She rolled up her cloak and tied it high on her back as well. The money in her belt purse and her knife would hopefully be no worse for immersion.

All that done, the princess tied the boat up to a protruding hook that stuck out of the wall and slid over the side, holding the blue lantern in one hand and Denholm in his cage high in the other hand, well clear of the polluted water.

It actually wasn't quite as bad as Anya feared. The water wasn't cold, the smell was no worse, provided she breathed through her mouth, and the lantern didn't shed enough light to see more than she cared to see floating about. She waded after Ardent, who was paddling hard, keeping his snout well up and out of the water.

Twenty or thirty paces in, Shrub called out.

"There's steps to the right! I'm going up."

The steps rose up from below the surface of the water. Anya held back as Ardent jumped up, and she turned aside just in time as he shook himself, so hundreds of droplets of disgustingly dirty sewer water flew onto her back instead of straight into her face.

"Ardent!"

"Sorry. Forgot," said Ardent.

Anya followed the dog onto the steps, almost slipping because the lower ones were covered in algae or something even worse. Smoothie followed quickly, muttering complaints under her breath about what had been done to the canal and, by connection, the river.

At the top of the steps, Shrub was studying some marks painted on the door there, a rough oak barrier that was already slightly ajar. Anya held the lantern high so she could see too. The marks looked like they were painted in blood.

"Thieves' Guild marks," said Shrub. "Don't know what they all mean, but that one is 'Beware.'"

"Like the giant," said Anya. She peered more closely at the marks, and a broad stain below them. A big puddle of dried blood.

"Is that . . . The thief must have died here!"

CHAPTER TWENTY-SEVEN

The Creature in the Cellar

N ah," commented Shrub. "That's spilled orange paint. Looks red in the blue light."

"Oh," said Anya. She started to take a deep breath of relief but managed to stop herself in time. Even breathing through her mouth the stink was almost unbearable. "Well, we have to go on. But this time, everyone really needs to be looking out, in case there is a monster guarding the way."

"What do we do if there is one?" asked Ardent. "Bite it?"

"We either sneak past or sneak back," said Anya. "Very quietly and carefully."

True to her words, she leaned over Shrub and pushed the door open as gently as she could. It creaked and groaned a little, but moved fairly easily. Shrub stuck his head around when it was open wide enough.

"All clear," he whispered. "More steps."

Anya pushed the door a little more, and squeezed through after Ardent and the newt. Her lantern was flickering now, and she regretted not bringing another candle stub from the tin box on the boat. But if it did go out, the animals would still be able to see, and they could guide her. She really hoped it didn't come to that.

At the top of the steps, Shrub halted. Ardent went to his side and crouched, sniffing. Anya came up, keeping the lantern low. Smoothie edged in behind her, so they were all crouched close together.

Ahead lay a vaulted chamber that had once been a very large wine cellar. There were still the remnants of a few huge barrels against one wall, and the collapsed timbers of a wine rack mixed in with a mound of broken bottles.

"What's that sound?" whispered Anya.

She could hear a clinking noise, like forks and spoons being put back in the cutlery chest one by one. Clink-clink-clink-clink. But there was something else as well, a strange warbling or clucking sound.

"Bluck, bluck, bluck, bluck . . ."

Ardent moved past Shrub, his ears up, tongue hanging out. Anya lifted a hand to restrain him, but then let it fall and followed him instead, walking as if in a daze. Both of them were drawn inexorably to that strange clucking sound and the clink of metal.

"What are you doing?" hissed Shrub, aghast. But they trod past him without taking any care to sneak or be quiet.

"What *are* they doing?" asked Smoothie. She stepped past Shrub to clutch at Anya's sleeve, but the princess shrugged her off and kept moving into the open cellar.

As she walked straight out, a hideous creature emerged from behind one of the decaying barrels. It had the head of giant rooster, connected to a ten-foot-long lizard-like body covered in greenish scales. Two scarred stumps on its back showed where it had once had wings, the stumps moving even now, as if in its tiny mind it still was trying to lurch forward in flight.

A thick metal chain was fixed to a manacle on its back right leg, the links rattling as it trudged forward.

Its piercing red eyes were fixed on Ardent and Anya, but it was the dreadful bluck-bluck-bluck coming from its blackened beak that kept them mesmerized.

Princess and dog continued to walk straight towards it, and the cockatrice reared back, preparing to strike with its deadly beak—straight at the defenseless Anya.

But the blow never landed.

Smoothie ran forward, and with her otterish grace, swept up a piece of plank from an old barrel and swung it like a bat at the cockatrice's head. There was a very loud squawk, an explosion of feathers, and the creature slowly subsided to the floor, its red eyes dimming.

Anya came instantly, horribly, fully aware of herself again. So did Ardent, who barked and ran first one way and then the other, biting at the air. Both of them had known what was happening, but hadn't been able to resist the compulsion to walk towards the creature.

"That horrible warbling noise," said Anya, fighting back the shakes. "I thought it was their stare that was meant to hypnotize the prey, but it was that awful sound it made!"

"Whose stare?" asked Smoothie. She had the plank ready to hit the monster again.

"That creature's," said Anya. "It's a cockatrice. Head of a rooster, body of a dragonet. Sir Garnet Bester's book never mentioned the horrible sound. It got into my head, and I couldn't get free of it . . ."

"Should I kill it?" said Smoothie unemotionally. She raised her plank.

Ardent calmed down enough to sniff at the unconscious monster. He only needed a few sniffs before he shook his head at Smoothie.

"He was human once," he said. "I c-c-an smell it, under all the magic and great age. He was transformed a long time ago. Chained here, in the dark, to guard the back door."

"We can't kill it . . . him . . . then," said Anya, correctly interpreting the look from Ardent. She hesitated, then bent down to touch the creature's head. "I'll return one day, and change you back. I . . ."

She hesitated, then added, "I promise."

Another promise. Another complication added to her Quest.

"That's nice," said Shrub. "What's to stop it eating us on the way back? Reckon it'll remember you promising to change it back?"

"We'll shorten his chain," said Anya. "For now. Oh, I must pull some feathers."

She walked to the end of the fallen creature and looked at its tail. It had a dragonish body, but its tail did end in a clump of feathers, not as abundant or as handsome as a rooster's. Anya was reaching down to take ahold of some to pull out when Ardent suddenly barked.

"Don't! They're metal. They'll c-c-ut you."

Anya hesitated. "That's harpies, isn't it?"

"Oh," said Ardent, his ears drooping. "Yes. Got them mixed up."

Even so, Anya gingerly touched the closest feather with the tip of her forefinger before proceeding. The feather felt like a chicken's, though coarser. It certainly wasn't sharp metal.

She grabbed several and pulled them out easily enough, and put them through her belt.

"I do seem to recall there's something funny about keeping cockatrice feathers," she said, looking at them. "The recipe says 'fresh-pulled.' I hope these'll last long enough. Anyway, I'll take some and we'll look for more upstairs."

"Otters must be immune to the warbling as well as the stare of c-c-cockatrices," observed Ardent, eager to regain some reputation for knowing his monster lore. "Like weasels."

"And newts," said Shrub. "It just sounded like a huge chicken to me."

Anya shuddered. She didn't like to recall how she had been so easily overcome by the creature's magic. Leaving the now rather bare tail, she followed the cockatrice's chain back to where it was connected to the wall by a huge iron staple, which despite its evident age and the rust on its surface felt very strong when Anya pulled on it. Picking up the chain, she pulled it tight and looped it back through the staple several times and then tied it in a knot, so when the cockatrice woke up it wouldn't be able to reach the lower steps.

"I suppose we'll have to send Smoothie first, with a plank, when we come back," said Anya. "Maybe it'll get the idea and shut up."

Shrub had spent the time investigating what appeared to be a pile of rubbish in one corner. It was only when Anya got closer that she saw he was digging away at a pile of old bones. A human skull rolled out and Anya pushed it aside with the toe of her shoe. Luckily, it was very old and just clean white bone.

"A thief, I reckon," said Shrub. "Not good enough to get past. Ah, I was hoping to find something like this."

He dragged out a long key.

"Take this, Princess," he said. "It was made by a wizard too, though probably not the Good Wizard."

Anya picked it up. It was very light. She'd thought it was metal, but looking at it more closely, she could see the key was carved from bone.

"Skeleton key," said Shrub. "It'll open one door and then fall into dust. I was hoping to find lock picks too, but they're all rusty and useless. I 'spose you don't know how to use them anyway?"

"No," said Anya. "It's probably something I should learn. Thank you for finding this, Shrub. And thank you, Smoothie, for saving Ardent and me from the cockatrice."

They went on through the cellar until they found another set of steps leading up. This time it ended in a locked door, but the key was in the lock on the other side, so under instruction from Shrub, Anya slid Gotfried's recipe book through the gap under the door and pushed the key out with a long splinter from a barrel. It fell on the book and Anya dragged it back to their side. A few seconds later, the door was unlocked and open.

Again, Shrub went first, to have a look around.

He returned after a few minutes to report. The questers held a quick, whispered conference.

"We're still below street level," he said. "There's a passage and lots of doors on both sides. Look like storage rooms to me, so maybe one will be full of ingredients."

"I c-c-can sniff them out," said Ardent.

"Any sign of sorcerers?" asked Anya. "Or guards?"

"All quiet," said Shrub.

"Let's go look, then," said Anya. "Ardent, sniff out what we need."

Ardent found the alchemical ingredients store behind the third door he sniffed at, and it wasn't even locked. Anya turned the handle and pushed it quietly open just enough for Shrub to go in. But he backed out almost straightaway.

"This is it!" he said excitedly. "Shelves and shelves of bottles and jars and tubs and stuff!"

Anya pushed the door open wider and slipped in. It was as Ardent had sniffed and Shrub had reported: a huge storeroom lined with shelves from floor to ceiling, and every shelf groaning with the weight of hundreds of different containers, all of them neatly labeled, though the handwriting and the faded ink indicated it had been done by many different people over a long time.

The princess put Denholm's cage down on the floor and, taking the match from behind her ear, used it to light a much larger lamp that was near the door. It was a very old bronze one that had no globe; it just burned oil from its spout. But it was full, and the flame burned clean and high and delivered a surprising amount of light.

Everyone else came in, and Smoothie carefully shut the door behind them.

"They've got everything!" Anya marveled as she read the labels. "Blind eyes, undersea terror type two. Baby basilisk teeth. Bone, powdered, wyvern. That'd be super poisonous I expect—"

"Princess!" barked Ardent, not too loudly. "We have to get what we need and get out again."

"Yes, sorry," said Anya. "I got carried away. It's alphabetical. Look for 'Hail, three day old' and maybe . . ."

She glanced down at the cockatrice feathers she'd thrust through her belt. They had lost their reddish-gold color already, and when she touched them, they turned to dust, which fell down her leg, making a horrible muddy stain on her wet trousers.

"And 'cockatrice feathers, just plucked,'" she said. "There must be a way to preserve them."

"Here's hail," said Ardent, who was standing on his hind legs at a shelf farther down. "'Hailstones, mountaintop, one day old, one doz.' and then there's more, up to a week old."

Anya went over to the dog and took down the appropriate jar. It was very cold to touch, the hailstones inside solid and unmelted. She examined the top of the jar, noting that there was some kind of spell woven into the red wax and greased paper that sealed the metal lid.

"One dozen," she said. "Twice what we need."

She wrapped the jar with the map handkerchief and put it in her belt purse. Ardent, meanwhile, had gone back to look earlier in the alphabet.

"'C-c-ockatrice feathers, freshly plucked, half doz,'" he read. "They're wrapped up well."

Anya went over to look. The cockatrice feathers were wrapped up like a parcel between boards that were wound with linen bandages. The label, in addition to identifying what was inside, carried the instruction *Do not open until immediately before use.*

Anya took a packet and thrust it through her belt.

"Right, that's it, let's get out of here," she said.

At that moment, her eye fell on Denholm's cage on the floor.

The bars were bent aside, and the frog prince was no longer there.

CHAPTER TWENTY-EIGHT

A Prince among Frogs

"Denholm!"

Anya's cry made Ardent spin around from where he'd been eyeing a very long spiral bone labeled *Narwhal horn*. Instantly taking in the empty cage, he ran forward with his nose to the floor, sniffing madly. The door to the hallway was shut, so he circled back. Catching the frog's scent, he ran along the shelves towards the back of the room. Anya ran after him, with Shrub and Smoothie close behind.

It was quite dark down the far end, away from the lamp, but there was just enough light to see a door. Ardent was scratching at the base of it, around a hole that was big enough to allow a rat to get through.

Or a frog.

"He's gone through," said Ardent.

"The transformation spell," said Anya. She tried the door, pushing and pulling on the iron ring, but it wouldn't budge. "Makes him resist anyone who can change him back. Now that I have all the ingredients, it must have got stronger. Why is *this* door locked?!"

"Use the skeleton key!" urged Shrub.

"Quickly," Ardent barked. "His scent is fading. He's moving away!"

Anya got out the key, almost fumbling in her haste. As she started to turn it, the lock groaned. Then, as it opened, it let out a shill scream, rather like one of Morven's.

Everyone jumped.

"Alarm lock," said Shrub with professional respect. "Very tricky."

Anya didn't respond. She threw the door fully open and they raced up the stair beyond.

Denholm was a dozen steps above them, hopping madly towards an open archway leading to the next floor. It clearly led to the inhabited, rebuilt part of the meetinghouse, because it was lit up.

Ardent raced ahead, leaping the steps four at a time.

"Be careful!" Anya called out as she ran after him, visions of Denholm crushed in Ardent's jaws flashing through her mind. She knew the dog could retrieve things without hurting them, but wasn't sure he would remember that in the excitement of the moment.

She burst through the archway and almost fell over Ardent, who had stopped and was sitting on his haunches. Anya didn't need to ask why—she could see for herself.

The archway led into another large chamber like the alchemical storeroom below, but this was a much stranger place. It *was* lit up, but not with lanterns. There were glowing vines that trailed down from the beams of the roof high above, and glowing fungi that was trained to grow on certain bricks in the walls.

These unusual lights illuminated a steaming tropical garden.

Ferns of all shapes and sizes and strange bushes with iridescent hanging fruit in red and yellow and green clustered in groups around cleverly sculpted ornamental pools. Tiled paths wound between the smaller pools, leading to a central square that was dominated by a single high-backed, throne-like chair of wrought iron that sat facing a much larger pool.

A pool entirely full of frogs.

Or not *entirely* full, because there was room for one more.

Denholm reached the pool with one last great leap and entered the water with a splash. Within a second Anya lost sight of him among all the other frogs that were lazing there on lily pads, swimming idly around, or gathered on the edges in quiet contemplation of their warm and comfortable home.

"I wonder how it stays so warm and clean," said Smoothie.

"Sorcery," said Shrub. He licked his eyes feverishly. "This is the Garden, the Grey Mist's hangout! That's her gloating chair, right there! We have to get out of here. Someone will have heard the lock alarm—"

"We have to collect all the frogs," interrupted Anya. She thought for a second, then reached behind her, pulled the Wizard's onion sack from her belt, and unfolded it. "We'll put them in this, make it wet so they're not too uncomfortable, take them away, and sort out Denholm later. Let's go!"

The others weren't listening. They were looking at a sudden gathering of steam or mist at the far side of the garden. It had just appeared, a cloud of thick fog that had coalesced out of nowhere and was now rolling along one of the tiled paths.

Straight towards them.

"The Grey Mist!" shrieked Shrub, and ran to the left.

Smoothie slid into the closest pool, paws searching for stones to throw.

Ardent barked once and ran forward, straight at the sorcerer.

Anya gabbled out the words of power for The Withering Wind and threw the spell at the sorcerer, at *exactly* the same time the Grey Mist cast a spell at Ardent. The spells clashed in the air, both becoming something else, not intended by the casters. This happened very occasionally in duels between sorcerers, and was generally acknowledged to be a very bad thing indeed, since the most common result was a catastrophic explosion.

This time, Anya's spell became greatly more energized. Instead of just making the target think there were withering winds howling around her, it actually created withering winds. They cut into the fog like a woodcarver whittling a stick, sending shreds of mist flying in all directions. There was an awful howl from inside the cloud, and it began to rapidly retreat, losing substance with every step as the winds did their work.

The Gray Mist's spell, typically, had been a transformation. Even before it was altered by Anya's spell it probably wouldn't have worked on Ardent, the royal dogs being so resistant to magic. But this time it bounced off his snout and landed on a nearby palm, and again would usually have done nothing. But changed as it was, it partly transformed the palm. It was unclear what the Grey Mist had been planning for, but the trunk of the palm grew eyes, and its fronds became long grasping arms. Fortunately, it didn't seem to have grown much of a brain, for the arms whipped the air without intelligence, and were easily avoided.

Ardent kept going, and disappeared growling into the fog. Anya chased after him, drawing her knife. She didn't know what else to do. At least the withering winds were still withering away, cutting off layer after layer of mist. The princess hoped it hurt the ancient sorcerer, and she couldn't help but feel some curiosity. If the winds kept going, they would reveal whether there was anything inside the cloud of mist or not.

But that curiosity was not to be satisfied. The Grey Mist reached the far end of the garden, suddenly narrowed into a thin column, and sped through a small grille low in the wall. Ardent, jumping at it, bounced off and landed badly, spinning around to look embarrassed. The withering winds, the spell fading, howled to the ceiling and were gone.

Anya cautiously inspected the grille. She could see another room on the other side, and a moment later heard a woman— presumably the Grey Mist—shouting, "Guards! Guards!"

"Bet she doesn't c-c-come back," said Ardent with satisfaction. He jumped up and licked Anya's face. "Good work, Princess!"

"She's calling for guards," said Anya. She looked back from the grille and around the Garden, her mind racing. "The only good thing is I can't hear any answering yet. We have to get out. But we still have to get the frogs first."

"There's a lot of frogs," said Ardent dubiously. "You'll never be able to c-c-arry a whole sackful—"

"Just get started! And be gentle, Ardent! Smoothie, you help. Here's the sack. Shrub! Shrub, where are you?"

"Here," said the newt, though Anya couldn't see him.

"Find all the ways out of here we could use, or the guards can get in. I want to go up if we can. Onto the roof."

"Up?" asked Shrub, emerging from under a low-hanging palm.

"Up," confirmed Anya. "And open to the air. It's past midnight isn't it?"

"Sure," said Shrub. "Must be."

"Find us a way up, and let's get these frogs."

The next five minutes were full of frantic activity. The frogs, though not as active as the ones back in Trallonia, nevertheless soon worked out what was going on, and tried to escape their captors. They also set up a massive croaking that made it hard to hear, which was unnerving, since this made it impossible to detect approaching enemies.

Anya kept putting frogs in the sack as she strained her ears for other sounds. It would be very useful to hear the guards arriving before they suddenly found themselves at spearpoint. Or transformed, if the Grey Mist was brave enough to come back. Or if one of the other sorcerers happened to be in the meetinghouse.

"This one's Denholm," said Ardent, dropping a frog carefully into the sack. "I'm pretty sure. If I had time for a better sniff . . ."

It was the third frog he'd said was Denholm, but Anya couldn't waste time looking at each frog or letting Ardent sniff them. It was much faster to take them all and be sure she'd get the prince. The weight of responsibility from her sister promise felt heavy upon her, mixed with feelings of immediate dread due to the imminent arrival of enemies and the possibility her new escape plan wouldn't work, as well as a general sense of concern about Morven and everybody else back home.

"Last one," said Smoothie, throwing a frog in. She was much faster than the frogs, and could grab one in each paw-hand, and had also once got one in her mouth, but Anya asked her not to do that. Those teeth of hers were just too sharp, even though that particular frog seemed to have survived the experience.

"Are you sure?" asked Anya. "Everyone, look around."

Everyone looked, and Ardent rummaged under every nearby fern with his snout, sniffing wildly.

"Shrub? You found a way out that's not down?"

"Yes," called the newt. "Over here."

Anya tied up the top of the sack and dippèd it in the water. It was very heavy, and she almost couldn't lift it back out again.

"Smoothie, help me with this."

Between the two of them, they carried the sack over to Shrub, who had been busy pulling vines away to reveal a very large boarded-up fireplace. The boards were old and rotten, so he'd got a few of those away as well, but only enough to make a hole wide enough for himself.

"A fireplace?" groaned Anya. "Shrub, we couldn't get up a chimney even without this sack of frogs. We'll have to go back down—"

"Someone coming up that way," interrupted Ardent, ears pricked. He growled, low and deep. "Hobnailed boots and halberd staves striking the walls. But they're going slow. Fearful, I'd say."

"I bet they are," said Shrub happily. "Having to go up against someone that sent the Grey Mist running will make 'em very cautious. Get these boards off and I'll show you, Princess."

"Show me what?" Anya was trying to think how they could scare the guards even more, to make them run away so the way back to the canal would be clear. Unfortunately, nothing was coming to mind.

"These big fireplaces here, that have the inglenook you can sit in, they have little staircases that follow the chimney up," said Shrub. "That's what I was supposed to come down when I was here last time, only I got the wrong chimney."

Before Shrub had finished talking, Anya and Smoothie had put the sack down and were tearing away the rotten boards, with Ardent's enthusiastic help. There was a very spacious inglenook behind—and, sure enough, in the right-hand corner, the beginning of a stair.

"But what do we do when we get to the roof?" asked Shrub. "With the alarm sounding, the guards will be all around the outside at street level."

"We won't go down to the street," said Anya as she lifted the sack again. "We'll go up."

Ardent, who was busily ripping a piece of glowing vine down to trail along for light, said something muffled by the vegetation in his mouth. He spat it out for a moment and exclaimed, "Ah! It's after midnight! The c-c-arpet. Good idea, Princess. If it comes when it's c-c-called."

He picked up the glowing vine again and bounded into the inglenook and up the stairs, his wagging tail dislodging a fine cloud of soot.

"Yes," said Anya. Taking up the sack with Smoothie, they followed.

Neither noticed that Shrub quickly ran back to the central pool, went to the iron gloating chair, dug something out of the tiled path directly beneath it, and ate it. Not without difficulty, his mouth stretching very wide.

He made it back and into the inglenook as the first guards poked their heads very, very cautiously through the archway from the stairs below and looked around, their crossbows rather shakily held at the ready.

CHAPTER TWENTY-NINE

Flight from the City

The questers emerged onto a flat area between two steeply arched roofs via a hatch in the huge chimney stack. They were very much blackened with soot, and Anya and Smoothie were already tired from carrying the sack of frogs. The frogs, noisy to begin with, had also quieted, which helped. Possibly the dark interior of the sack didn't encourage vocalization.

"Ardent, call your carpet," said Anya breathlessly. "I do hope it comes quickly."

"If the c-c-carpet is like its owner, it will know the importance of obeying c-c-commands," said Ardent. "We learn this as puppies, that even if you find a bone or something really good, a whistle is a whistle, and the c-c-command should never need to be given—"

"Ardent! Call the carpet!"

Ardent put his head back and called up to the stars and the distant, fleeting silver moon, which was already near the far horizon, the blue moon a slow runner-up far behind.

"Pathadwanimithochozkal! C-c-come here!"

"Say *please*," hissed Anya urgently.

"Please c-c-come here, as fast as you can, oh noble and best of c-c-carpets, my friend Pathadwanimithochozkal!"

"Don't overdo it," said Anya. "It might think you're being sarcastic."

"Praise is good," said Ardent. He looked out, up at the night sky and sniffed. "The air is better up here."

"That wouldn't be difficult," said Anya. "*We* all still stink, though."

"I don't," said Smoothie, which was true. She'd washed the stench of the sewers off in one of the Garden's ponds. So she was sooty, but didn't smell awful.

"The rest of us do," said Anya, wrinkling her nose. She had never been so filthy and stinking. Sodden from below the waist with sewer water and covered all over in soot, she didn't look or feel much like a princess.

"Here it c-c-comes!" proclaimed Ardent happily. He pointed with his nose up at a patch of sky where something flew swiftly, the light of the moon behind it.

Anya's eyes narrowed.

It wasn't the carpet.

"Down!" hissed Anya. "Everyone down and quiet. It's the Duke's bone ship!"

Everyone lay down instantly. Anya turned her head a little so she could still see the ship, now thankful for the covering of soot that would make them hard to see in the night.

The bone ship flew past them, its great feathery sails trailed out to either side. It was about fifty yards away and fifty feet higher up, descending as it passed. Anya could see the Duke standing at the stern, directing the ship simply by moving his pallid hands as if he was conducting music. There were at least a dozen weaselfolk soldiers crouched down in front of him or hanging over the sides, their red eyes fixed on the ground below.

"It's landing," whispered Ardent. "Maybe he's c-c-come for the festival, like Shrub said."

"Or he's got word we're here," said Anya grimly. "Come on, carpet!"

She searched the sky again, without getting up. As soon as the Duke landed he'd hear about the intruders, and unlike the Grey Mist, he wouldn't be so easily scared off. His weaselfolk wouldn't be as cautious as the human guards either . . .

Human guards.

Anya suddenly remembered them and crawled back to the hatch in the chimney. Sure enough, she could hear someone creeping up the steps. They were trying to be quiet, but that's difficult when you're wearing armor and hobnailed boots, and the stairway is very narrow.

"Guards are coming up," she said urgently. She looked around for some way to wedge the hatch shut, but there was nothing on the roof. "Any sign of the carpet?"

"Please, great Pathadwanimithochozkal!" called out Ardent. "C-c-come quickly!"

Anya took out her knife and, with some regret, wedged the hatch shut with it, pushing it in right up to the hilt. It wouldn't last long, but it would hold for a few minutes.

"We'll have to go across the roofs," she said. "Shrub, which way?"

Shrub made a kind of strangled noise but didn't say anything. He raised one foot and pointed over the high peak of the roof to their left.

"Choked on soot," said Ardent. "Nasty. Princess, I won't be so good on these rooftops. Leave me here as a rear guard."

"No," said Anya, thinking fast. "We couldn't get the frog sack up over that roof peak anyway. Let's tackle the first guard through. I'll take their weapon, we'll hold them off until the carpet—"

Her words were lost as a great rush of air knocked her to the ground. Pathadwanimithochozkal the carpet flew way too fast over their heads, overshot the entire building, carried on to whip around a tall spire across the street, and came back somewhat slower to plummet down on the flat area between the peaks and slide right up to Ardent's front paws.

But not without being seen from the ground.

Shouts came up from below, and there were whistles and general bellowing and carrying on of a variety that indicated a whole lot more guards and possibly sorcerers would soon be rushing up to the roof.

The carpet was too big for all of it to fit on its chosen landing spot, but there was enough space for the questers to lie down with the bulging frog sack between Anya and Smoothie.

"Where exactly are we going?" asked Ardent. "And is it less than thirty leagues?"

"The hut where Martha makes the soup in Trallon Forest," said Anya. "I think it should be less than thirty leagues. I can't remember and I can't get the handkerchief out—ah!"

The exclamation was because someone had just appeared above them, precariously balanced on the ridgeline of the nearer roof peak. Anya only just managed to grab Ardent's collar and pull him back as he tried to leap up at the intruder.

"Don't get off the carpet!" she shouted. "Say the words!"

"Frogkisser's Daring Midnight Raid on Right-Minded Sorcerers!" bellowed the intruder, yet another Gerald the Herald. She (for it was clearly a woman behind the fake beard, moustache, and wax nose-extender) put one leg over to come down, slipped a little, and decided to stay where she was. "Care to comment, Princess?"

"No!" shouted Anya as Ardent spoke the words and the carpet suddenly rolled them up, causing the hitherto silent frogs to start up a mass croaking.

"Oh greatest of all c-c-carpets, Pathadwanimithochozkal, please fly us safely and carefully to the hut of Martha who c-c-ooks soup in Trallon Forest!" gabbled out Ardent.

"Frogkisser Rescues Giant Sack of Frogs!" roared the Gerald the Herald, closely followed by "Aaargh" as the carpet took off and its slipstream blew her off the roof. Fortunately, she only slid down to another area between gables, and could lie there exulting in her exclusive news story, soon to be told to the ravens and spread to every other Gerald the Herald in the land.

Inside the carpet, the noise of the frogs competed with the howling of the wind. Since Ardent hadn't asked the carpet to go slowly, only carefully, it had gone back to its previous speed, and possibly height, though Anya didn't want to think about that. It was soon freezing again, the cold quieting the frogs.

"Shrub, you all right?" called out Anya, her teeth chattering. It was a little bit easier to bear the cold this time, because she knew they were going so fast it wouldn't last very long.

There was no answer from the newt.

The cold intensified. Anya started doing frantic calculations in her head. She thought they were about twenty-five or maybe twenty-six leagues west of the forest, but also perhaps five leagues south. So it would be quite close to thirty leagues all added up. She knew there was a formula to work this out, involving triangles, but she couldn't remember what it was or how to use it. She'd only read about it in a book, after all. No one had taught her any mathematics, not since her mother had helped her learn to count . . .

"I hope I haven't made a mistake," she said in a very small voice. She said it so quietly that none of the others had any chance of hearing. A small tear formed in the corner of her eye and trickled down, turning to ice before it was halfway down her cheek.

Anya blinked more tears away and told herself not to be silly. They had done so much already. Against great odds, they had got the ingredients for the Transmogrification Reversal Lip Balm. And she hadn't lost Denholm, even if he was mixed in with dozens of other frogs.

Nothing has gone irreversibly wrong, she thought.

Surely, all will be well.

At that moment, the carpet flipped over and nose-dived towards the ground.

Everyone screamed again, with the noticeable exception of Shrub. Even some of the frogs came out of their cold-induced stupor and added their croaks to the general expression of fear.

The dive went on and on, so long that Anya knew it had to be because the carpet had gone beyond the thirty leagues it could fly. The magic had failed and they were going to smash into the ground and be killed. Duke Rikard would triumph, and Trallonia would become impoverished and miserable and Rob the Frogger would have no food and no shoes—

The carpet leveled out with a stomach-lurching jerk that

almost made the bread they'd had on the boat reemerge from everyone's stomachs.

Even feeling sick, Anya felt a surge of relief.

They were landing after all, not crashing into the ground.

"Thank you, thank you, oh most wonderful carpet Pathadwanimithochozkal!' she cried out as they bumped down and slid to a halt. The carpet unrolled itself, spilling them out like the bowls across the green at the Sign of the Moon Inn.

Anya lay on her back, staring up at the stars that were twinkling between the great branches of an oak above her. She turned her head and saw the dim light of Martha's cooking fire, banked coals gleaming, their light reflecting from the great bronze cauldron as little dancing spots of red and yellow.

Ardent shakily got to his feet next to her and lifted his muzzle.

"Ah!" he said, sniffing deeply. "Trallon Forest!"

"Is there a lake or a river near?" asked Smoothie. "I need a proper wash again, to get this soot off."

"Lots of little streams around," said Anya. She sat up and looked over at Shrub.

"You all right, Shrub?" she asked.

"Gone dormant from the cold," said Ardent. "Like last time. He'll recover."

"I hope so," said Anya, with a nervous glance over at the hut. She doubted Martha would be pleased to find her son in this condition. Hopefully, the newt would wake up soon, because Anya was going to have to wake up Martha.

"I'm so tired," she yawned. "But there's no time to waste sleeping."

"What about eating?" asked Ardent.

"No time for that either. The Duke could be following us in his bone ship, and I don't know how fast that can go, or how quickly he might be able to find us here. I have to start making the mixture, and we need to get messengers out to Bert and the dwarves, asking them to come here. *And* to Tanitha and the dogs, if they can be found. I guess Hedric might know some *good* ravens. How are the frogs?"

Ardent was nosing the sack. There were subdued croaks coming from inside, which was a positive sign.

"I'd say they're all still alive. And grumbling."

"We can let them go into a stream once we get Denholm sorted out." Anya slowly got up. All her muscles ached from lugging the sack up the chimney steps, and she felt like she hadn't slept in ages, despite her short nap on the river beach near the inn.

"I'm going to wake Martha," she continued. "See if you can find Hedric. Where do druids sleep? Up trees?"

"Sacred groves, if they've got them," said Ardent. "But he said he hadn't. He's probably got a bed of moss nearby. I'll look!"

"Be careful," Anya warned. "Smoothie, could you please keep watch over Shrub and the frogs?"

Smoothie nodded. Anya walked over to the hut and knocked on the door.

"Hello!" she called. "Sorry to disturb you in the middle of the night. It's Princess Anya, and your son, Shrub!"

CHAPTER THIRTY

Who Forgot the Pawpaw?

T here was quite a lot of screaming, crying, and throwing arms up in the air in the next five minutes, all of it done by Martha. She'd emerged from her hut armed with a knife and ladle, ready to see off intruders, but had thrown them aside when she'd spotted Anya and then Shrub.

"Oh, my poor boy!" she exclaimed, gingerly wrapping the newt in her apron and half lifting him up. He was too heavy to lift any further.

Shrub made a noise and winked at her.

"Oh, you're alive!" exclaimed Martha. "Say hello to your mother!"

Shrub made another strange gargling nose.

"Choked up a bit on soot," said Ardent, who'd just come back with Hedric, who was wearing a nightgown made of leaves with a bark nightcap that looked highly uncomfortable.

"I need to use your cauldron, Martha," said Anya. She was already sorting out her ingredients near the fire. "And your stirring stick. It is a lightning-struck branch of an oak, isn't it?"

"Of course it is! Nothing but the best for my soup," protested Martha indignantly.

"Witches' tears, cockatrice feathers, three-day-old hail, blood from a retired druid . . . I need beeswax. Oh, and messengers!"

"To put in the pot?" asked Martha, bewildered.

"No, we need to send ravens to the dwarves in Dragon Hill to find Bert and as many Responsible Robbers as possible, and also to look for Tanitha and the Royal Dogs. Unless you know where they are, Ardent?"

"Who?" asked Ardent, who'd been distracted by a scent at the base of a nearby tree.

"Tanitha and the dogs," Anya repeated. "Do you know where they've gone?"

"Gone?" asked Ardent absently, still sniffing away.

"Oh, never mind! We'll need at least a dozen ravens to carry the messages and to search," said Anya. "Ones that can be trusted, of course, not those in the Duke's pay. Hedric, do you know any reliable ravens?"

"There is an unkindness of highly responsible ravens by the . . . not far from here," said Hedric. "I'll go to them. Is the message simply 'Princess Anya asks you to come to Martha's hut in Trallon Forest'?"

Anya thought for a moment.

"No," she said. "Ask them to say 'Anya the Frogkisser requests your aid against Duke Rikard, and asks for all her friends to gather at Martha's hut.'"

She thought again, then added, "Have the ravens tell any Gerald the Heralds they see too, and get them to spread the word."

"But the Duke will hear!" Ardent protested.

"Yes," said Anya. "But he would anyway. It's time we, I don't

314

know, told the world we're going to fight him. Raise the standard, that sort of thing, like in the stories. Oh!"

"What?" asked Hedric, who had been about to race off. "Is there more?"

"Yes." Anya took a deep breath and held it for a few seconds, her mind racing. Was she really going to commit to this?

Yes, she thought. *I am.*

Anya breathed out, drew herself up to her full height, and spoke in a clear, commanding voice.

"After the bit 'asks all her friends' add in 'and friends of the All-Encompassing Bill of Rights and Wrongs.'"

"Got it," said Hedric. "I'll tell the ravens!"

"So you've decided to begin the quest to reestablish the ancient laws!" barked Ardent. "But what will Morven say?"

"Morven will have to get used to it," Anya replied. Then she grimaced, thinking about how her sister would react to the news that her authority to be as selfish as she wanted was to be severely curtailed. "But I can't think about that now. I have to eat what's in front of me, as Tanitha would say. Let's see, I know I've forgotten something . . . pawpaw!"

She slapped herself on the side of the head.

"I bet there was some in that storeroom too," she said. "Now we'll have to use something else for flavor."

"Pea and ham?" suggested Ardent, with a longing look at Martha's ladle.

"Not for a lip balm," said Anya, making a face. She turned to Martha. "Do you have any dried fruits? Apricots, peaches, anything?"

"Got a bag of dried plums," Martha told her.

"And beeswax, mustn't forget the beeswax."

"I've got half a dozen beeswax candles. They're pure and soft."

"I'll buy them, and the plums," said Anya hastily. "Now, I need to get this to a medium fire. What would that be?"

"Hasn't anyone taught you to cook?" asked Martha. "Watch and learn, dearie, watch and learn."

She put Shrub back down and rose to her feet, rubbing her hands together with glee.

"Are you a witch?" asked Anya with interest, remembering that all witches were cooks, though not all cooks were witches.

"Well, semiretired. All that coven committee meeting stuff got on my nerves," said Martha. "But I keep up a little. Didn't you feel the blessing in my soup? Where's that recipe you're following?"

Anya showed her Gotfried's little book.

"Could you start making it?" the princess asked tentatively, her eye on the sack of frogs. She was still quite worried about Denholm. If he was really sick, it would be vital to change him back as soon as possible. Illnesses went away when you changed shape, as did most injuries, unless they were mortal wounds or caused by silver weapons.

"This?" asked Martha. "Could do it with my eyes shut and my ladle tied behind my head."

"Thank you, please do it . . . um . . . with your eyes open, though," said Anya. She went over to the frog sack, Ardent at her heels.

"I'll take them out one at a time," she said. "Take a look, you can sniff it, and we'll see which one's Denholm. Oh, I'll need another sack or a barrel or something to put the ones that aren't Denholm in. Martha, can we borrow an empty barrel?"

"Look behind the hut," said Martha, intent on feeding the fire new sticks and blowing on the coals. "Shrub, you show 'em. Couple of empties there."

Shrub, still not talking, led the way and pointed. Anya selected a medium-size barrel and rolled it around the front.

The first frog out was smaller than Denholm, Anya thought, and didn't have the yellow streak. She held it out to Ardent, who sniffed at it while it struggled mightily to get free.

"Definitely transformed," remarked the dog. "But not Denholm. Old sorcery. Years. Maybe decades."

Anya stared at the frog. Another transformee?

"Well, we'll sort you out as soon as the lip balm is made," she said gently, which made the frog struggle even harder. Anya put it in the barrel and carefully closed the lid.

The next frog was the right size and had a yellowish streak, but Anya didn't think it looked exactly the same as Denholm's streak. She couldn't remember whether his was on the left or right side of his head.

"Also transformed," said Ardent, taking no more than a single sniff.

Anya put it in the barrel and looked at the dog.

"Maybe they're all transformed," she said quietly. She looked at Shrub. "Those thieves who said the Garden was a prison were right after all. There were prisoners there. All the sorcerer's enemies, turned into frogs and put in that pond, so the Grey Mist could go there and gloat over them. You said that throne was a gloating chair, didn't you?"

Shrub did his strange shrugging thing, but didn't speak.

"We'd better sort through all these frogs," said Anya. "I still need to find Denholm and make sure he's all right. I wonder how long it will take the Seven Dwarves and the Responsible Robbers to arrive? And . . . the Duke."

"I will keep watch," proclaimed Smoothie. She had found a large smooth rock and was throwing it from hand to hand. "If I see an enemy . . . wham!"

She threw the rock at a tree. It struck at exactly head height, shearing off a huge piece of bark.

"Don't do that to the trees when Hedric's around," said Anya. "But otherwise, good idea. Shrub, what are you doing?"

Shrub had been slinking away. He turned and shrugged again.

"Maybe you need to wash your mouth out," said Anya.

"And wash the rest of you," said Martha from the fire. She was carefully adding the ingredients into the bronze pot. "I didn't want to say, but you all stink."

"We'll wash later," said Anya. "Though I suppose Shrub can go wash now. Let's get back to the frogs."

It wasn't easy sorting frogs. They didn't find Denholm for another half an hour, and every single frog Anya pulled out was a transformed human, except for one that, while definitely transformed, hadn't been human in the first place. At least, Ardent couldn't tell from the smell what it had been originally.

"The Dog with the Wonderful Nose would have been able to sniff it out," said Ardent, rather dejected.

"Your nose is wonderful too," said Anya. She'd kept Denholm separate and was holding him up to the firelight to see if the gray patch had got worse. But it was too hard to tell and he struggled so much she ended up putting him in the barrel with the others.

"I wonder who they all are," she said. "And how long they've been frogs."

"You can come and do some stirring now, Princess," said Martha. "My arms are tired."

"I'll patrol the perimeter," Ardent volunteered. Which meant he was going to wee on all the same trees he'd wet before on their previous visit, and sniff all the ones he hadn't.

"Be careful," Anya warned again. She looked up at the sky, hoping to see only stars and not the bone ship. It was a race now, to see if she could get the lip balm finished and her allies in place before the Duke got back and attacked her.

She was certain he would attack. It went with the cackle and the secret smile. Duke Rikard couldn't imagine diplomacy, or even staying on the defensive. Once he knew where Anya was, he would strike.

"Come on, everyone," she whispered to herself as she stirred the mixture. "Please come and help."

But by the dawn, none of her allies had arrived.

Only Hedric came back. He'd sent the good ravens to carry messages to the dwarves and Bert and to look for the royal dogs. He'd also sent some to see what was happening at Trallonia Castle, which was good thinking.

Anya spoke to him very seriously about the danger the Duke represented, to the forest and to the whole world, and the little she knew about the All-Encompassing Bill of Rights and Wrongs. When she was done, she asked him to gather any druids who might help her cause. After a short discussion about the rights of plants, which went nowhere because Anya felt she couldn't promise anything, Hedric agreed to help anyway and left again, to go and collect the closest druids.

By the time the first glow of the sun could be seen above the forest canopy, the lip balm mixture was ready to be removed from the fire, and the beeswax mixed in. As Anya had a much better knowledge of the consistency of moat monster snot, Martha deferred to her on the question of how much wax to stir in. They both added the dried plums, which Martha had cut up into tiny pieces.

"Now it just has to cool for a while," said Anya. She felt like she ought to be happy that she'd succeeded in her Quest. But she was too tired, and anyway, the Quest didn't feel finished. It wouldn't really be completed until she'd used the lip balm, and Denholm was a man again, and Shrub a boy, and Smoothie an otter, and all the frogs in the barrel back to being whatever they had been in the first place.

Duke Rikard also had to be defeated.

Anya had shied away from thinking about exactly what that meant, but she needed to think about it now. Before talking to Bert about the Bill of Rights and Wrongs she'd had the thought at the back of her mind that it was kill or be killed. The Duke wanted to kill her, so she would have to return the favor. Now that she had committed to at least trying to uphold the ancient laws, she supposed they'd have to capture the Duke and somehow stop him from using sorcery so he could be tried. But then they'd need to know the Laws Set in Stone, and get whatever it was Dehlia had said was required for a fair trial. A true mirror, or a unicorn, or something else.

It was all very difficult and made her head hurt.

"That'll be cool in an hour off the fire," said Martha. "You'll kiss my Shrub first, I hope?"

Anya nodded. Her eyes closed as she did so, and she caught herself almost falling asleep. Ardent appeared at her elbow and touched her hand with his wet nose.

"All quiet," he said. "Nothing happening. Not even rabbits."

"I have to sleep," said Anya. "Wake me up when the lip balm is cool, please. Or if . . . if anyone arrives. The Duke, or my friends."

"I will, Princess," said Ardent.

Anya smiled, lay down where she stood, and fell instantly asleep.

CHAPTER THIRTY-ONE

The Anti-Transmogrification Lip Balm?

A nya was awoken by a kiss. Or, more exactly, a lick. On her open mouth. Though she loved Ardent very much, this was a bit excessive. The princess pushed the grinning dog's snout aside, wiped her face with her sleeve, and levered herself up.

"What is it?" she asked crossly. The sun had hardly moved; she must have only been asleep for twenty minutes, if that. "Can't you let me sleep?"

"Weaselfolk!" Ardent cried. "One of the good ravens reported two dozen of them, c-c-coming this way along the forest road. Maybe fifteen minutes away. Advance guard for a larger army the Duke is getting ready at the c-c-astle. Hedric's got a couple of druids in though, and they're going to try to slow them down with some grasping vines and the like."

"Have any of our friends arrived?" asked Anya, suddenly very awake again, her stomach flipping in sudden fear. She gulped and tried to steady herself. "The dogs? Any Responsible Robbers?"

"No one," said Ardent. "We should retreat, go deeper into the forest. Quickly."

"But the weasels will ambush anyone coming here if we do that," protested Anya. "You said the Duke is back at the castle?"

"So the raven told Hedric. Transforming another c-c-artload of weasels. He's already got an army of them, and it looks like some at least are getting ready to march into the forest. They must know we're here."

Anya looked around. There was only Martha, Smoothie, Shrub, and a barrelful of frogs. There was no way they could fight even the advance guard. But they also couldn't easily retreat. The cauldron with the precious lip balm was too heavy, and the barrel was as well, without time to put the frogs back in a sack.

Frogs.

Anya staggered to her feet and thrust her finger into the lurid purple mixture in the very middle of the cauldron. It was still warm there, but not as hot as the stuff around the edges. She smeared some of the balm on her lips.

"Got to transform the frogs back," she said hurriedly to Ardent. "They'll fight for us. I hope. If they're not all useless princes."

She started towards the barrel, but stopped as Martha stepped in front of her.

"You said you'd kiss my Shrub first," she said.

"There's no time. I need warriors!" exclaimed Anya.

Martha didn't get out of the way. She folded her arms and glowered.

"All right, all right!" gabbled Anya. "I hope this works."

She beckoned to Shrub.

The newt didn't respond, though everyone else rushed over. Smoothie climbed up a nearby branch to get a better view of the proceedings. Ardent plumped himself down on Anya's foot. But Shrub still didn't move from the hole he'd dug for himself under a stunted hawthorn.

"Hurry up, Shrub, you're first!" called out Anya. She wondered where the safest place to kiss him would be. "Don't forget. No poison secretions, all right?"

Shrub shook his head and sat lower in his scrape.

"Shrub!" bellowed Martha. "You come here this instant! Anyone would think you want to stay a newt forever."

"What is wrong with you?" asked Anya crossly. "We're about to be attacked by weaselfolk and all you can do is sit there?"

She ran over to the newt, and despite his urgent scrambling, bent down and kissed him right between his goggly eyes.

Nothing happened.

Anya stepped back. She felt the blood draining out of her face and knew she'd gone white.

All that effort, the dangers, the difficulties they'd been through. After *everything*, the anti-transmogrification lip balm didn't work!

"We're done for," croaked Anya. "But what . . . we did everything right . . . the ingredients . . ."

"Try me!" urged Smoothie, jumping down from the branch, her paw-hands held together to beseech the princess. "It has to work! Maybe it's Shrub, not the lip balm."

Anya didn't know what else to do, so she kissed Smoothie on the top of her sleek head. Not expecting anything, she reeled back suddenly as the otter-maid exploded with a blue flash, replaced by a huge Yarrow River otter squeaking and undulating on the grass. She wove around Anya's legs, almost knocked her over, and then ran around the hut several times.

"I don't understand," said Anya. "Maybe it was still just too hot when I kissed Shrub . . . Shrub . . . where's that newt gone?"

Shrub had disappeared. Ardent dropped his nose to the ground, sniffed, then pointed with his snout and forepaw.

"Deeper under the hawthorn."

"That boy is in big trouble," said Martha as Smoothie zoomed back from the hut and did a kind of horizontal figure eight in front of Anya.

"Can you still speak human?" Anya asked the otter.

"Yersh, I shink so," said Smoothie. "Moutsh differensh. Shanks so shuch, Pchincess!"

"Right," said Anya. "Ardent and Smoothie, go watch for the weaselfolk! I'll start on the frogs. Martha, you can help."

Everyone ran. Anya and Martha moved the barrel, rolling it on its rim closer to the cauldron. Anya smeared on more lip balm and Martha plucked out the first frog. It was a big one, and it kicked and croaked as if it was about to go into a frying pan with garlic.

"Hold it away from yourself and let go as I kiss," warned Anya, leaning in to follow up her words with action.

Smooch! Bang! Green light!

A very tall, broad-shouldered woman in the tattered, rusty remnants of a mail hauberk stood before them. She overtopped Anya by two feet at least, and her impressively tattooed forearms were about as thick as Anya's waist.

"Uh, my name's Princess Anya and I've just transformed you back into a human."

Suddenly, being confronted with this huge and dangerous-looking woman, Anya wasn't so sure her plan was a good one, and her voice weakened as she added, "And I hope you'll fight for me against a wicked sorcerer?"

The woman made a croaking sound, turned her head aside to spit out what looked like part of a grasshopper, and knelt on one knee before Anya. Part of the effect was lost as more bits of her corroded armor fell off, but the intent was sincere.

"Thank you, Frogkisser," she said. "I am Sir Malorak, known as the She-Bear. I will fight for you gladly, though my arms have fallen into rust and decay."

Anya looked at her arms. They seemed very strong.

"My weapons, I mean," said the knight. She looked around the forest glade. "But if you can spare a knife, I will cut a good oaken staff to belabor the enemy."

"Here," said Martha, offering her own blade.

"Cut lots," said Anya.

"I will," Malorak vowed, glancing back at the barrel. She hesitated, then said, "How many years have passed since the Deluge and the loss of Yarrow the City?"

"About one hundred and eleven," said Anya quickly, as she applied more lip balm and gestured to Martha to bring out another frog.

"Ah," said the knight sadly. "Then my children will long be dead, never knowing what happened to their mother. Alas! But this is no time for my sorrows. Bring forth more warriors, Princess, and we shall fight!"

Anya kissed the next frog. It was another knight, a small and quick-looking man with surprisingly long hair. His leather armor was in slightly better shape than Malorak's, though again his sword was just a lump of rust in a rotting scabbard.

"Sir Havagrad, at your service," he said, bowing, as Anya

repeated her message. "Any enemy of yours is an enemy of mine. Who, ah, is that very large knight cutting oak branches?"

"Sir Malorak the She-Bear," replied Anya.

The man's eyebrows shot up.

"A legend returns! My father was one of her squires. I will go help her."

"Please do," said Anya, already applying more lip balm.

The next three frogs were a bit of a disappointment, being a singing troupe of troubadours, their stage names Xerax, Yerax, and Yomix, spoken as if Anya might have heard of them. Their colorful motley was sadly reduced to sagging greenish loincloths and all their instruments save an ebony pipe were rotten and had fallen apart. But they expressed their willingness to fight and mentioned difficulties dealt with on the road, so Anya figured they were better than nothing.

She kept kissing. Soon there were a dozen more knights, and two fighters in decayed green who declared themselves rangers, and even one thin-faced, reserved fellow who claimed to be a warden of the High Kingdom, transformed in the year immediately following the Deluge. He had been transformed the longest; his name was Parengoethes, and he had a little difficulty comprehending what was going on.

"You were a frog," Anya explained. "Now you're not. The sorcerer who transformed you, or one exactly like the sorcerer who did it, is about to attack. I need your help. Go grab a staff from Sir Malorak and wait for orders."

"Yes, yes, I see," said Parengoethes, rubbing his eyes. He made a few hopping movements towards the other soldiers, stumbled, and made himself walk. "Though I still fail to comprehend with what authority these troops have been assembled!"

He was grumbling on when Ardent came rushing back to the glade.

"Attack imminent!" he barked out. "Weaselfolk preparing to charge!"

"Form a line!" bellowed Sir Malorak, lifting the biggest, thickest staff cut so far. "On me! Protect the princess!"

"Quick, another frog!" said Anya. She shuffled around the cauldron so she could see what was happening, her heart thudding in her chest, visions of those terrible weasel teeth snapping at her throat stuck in her head.

Her newly human troops moved out into a line, old martial habits overriding the occasional frog impulse. Most of them had staves, and those who didn't had stones to throw . . . or, in one case, the propping stick from Martha's washing line.

The frog Martha held up was the one that Ardent said wasn't a transformed human, the one with the underlying scent he'd never smelled before.

Anya kissed it.

The flash this time was golden, and something much larger than a human appeared, making Anya stagger back and fall over.

At that moment, the weaselfolk burst out from under the trees, screaming their high-pitched squeals, teeth ready to rip and talons lashing the air, as they soon hoped to rend flesh.

But they found few targets. Used to scaring villagers or foresters, the weaselfolk were not prepared to be met by skillfully wielded oak staves, nor the coordinated actions of the knights working together in pairs. One would trip a weasel soldier while the other clouted it on the head, with Sir Malorak simply wading into the weasel ranks, spinning her huge staff around her like a whirlwind.

Then there was the unicorn. No one expected her, on either side. As soon as she was transformed from her frog shape, the unicorn took one glance and charged into the fray, her silvery neigh lifting the spirits of Anya's people while scaring the life out of the weasels. Her horn moved like lightning, though she didn't kill. Instead, she cut the weaselfolk's makeshift uniforms off, and trampled the clothes with their crudely painted *R* signs into the forest floor. For some reason this frightened the enemy more than anything else.

It was all over in a few minutes. Eight or nine weasels lay unconscious, a few more were probably dead, and the rest were running back through the forest, pursued by Ardent and Smoothie nipping at their heels.

"The weasel-things flee," reported Sir Malorak to Anya, wiping her sweaty brow and leaning on her staff. "Are there more?"

"Lots more," Anya replied. "And probably worse things, back at the castle with the Duke."

She was watching the unicorn out of the corner of her eye as she spoke. Anya had never seen anything so beautiful. The unicorn was like the prettiest of ponies, but with a pearly light to her white hide, and her horn shone silver, except for the bloodied tip.

The unicorn looked back at her and lowered her head to wipe her horn on the grass before turning to delicately slip away into the forest.

"Oh!" said Anya, disappointed the fabled creature was leaving.

"She will return when needed," said Sir Malorak, watching the princess's gaze. "After so long as a frog, she probably needs a gallop, as much as I needed to split heads. Are we likely to be attacked again soon?"

"We might be," said Anya. "But we have reinforcements coming, I mean besides whoever these frogs turn out to be. I suppose we'll have to have a proper big battle, since Duke Rikard will never be sensible and surrender."

"Duke Rikard?" asked Sir Malorak. "I know him not. He is the sorcerer of whom you spoke afore?"

"Yes, um, ask Ardent about the whole situation when he gets back. The royal dog. I have to keep kissing frogs."

"As you command, Frogkisser!" bellowed Sir Malorak. She seemed much more cheerful after the fight. She was also incredibly loud and very, very big. Anya was glad to have the knight on her side.

"Oh, and bring the unconscious weaselfolk over here too," said Anya. "I'll change them back so they can slip away to normal weasel life. It's not their fault, poor things."

"At once, Frogkisser!"

Anya winced to hear that name said so loudly and enthusiastically. But she had to admit it was a very accurate description of what she was doing.

Unable to repress a sigh, she put on more lip balm, leaned across to the struggling frog Martha was holding, and kissed it.

CHAPTER THIRTY-TWO

Knights and Merchants, a Prince, and a Princess

The latest frog was a young knight. She looked to be little more than twenty years old, but was built on the same impressively huge lines as Sir Malorak the She-Bear. As she bent her knee to Anya and heard the same talk the princess had given to all the transformees, the young knight looked past her and her eyes widened in shock, immediately followed by her mouth curving into the broadest of smiles.

"Yes, yes, I'll do whatever you need," said the knight. Surprising Anya, she suddenly shouted, "Mother!" and erupted into a sprint past the princess.

Anya whirled about to see Sir Malorak dropping her staff to catch the younger knight up in a great hug, both of them losing pieces of long-rusted armor in the process.

"Tilvan! I thought I'd never see you again!"

"We came questing for you," sobbed Tilvan, laughing and crying at the same time. "And fell afoul of the same sorcerers, it seems."

"You mean Solan and Soran . . ." Malorak said, looking with fierce, hungry eyes over at Anya and the barrel of frogs.

"My brothers," said Tilvan over her shoulder to Anya. "They were transformed too."

"I'm going to kiss all the frogs," Anya assured them. "As quickly as I can."

The next frog wasn't Solan or Soran, nor the next. They were a brace of confused merchants, who had been transformed for daring to ask for their long-overdue bills to be paid by the League of Right-Minded Sorcerers. But they too offered to serve Princess Anya, though they tried to negotiate particular terms.

"I haven't time for that sort of thing," said Anya. "If you want to help, good. If not, be off."

"We'll stay, Frogkisser," said the middle merchant. He was feeling along the hem of his sole remaining garment. Rotten and wet, it tore easily, and a number of gold coins fell out. "If you have an army gathering, I daresay you will need the assistance of three quartermasters, in purchasing provisions, equipment, and the like. We will happily pledge whatever coin remains on our persons to the cause. As a loan, of course."

"Good," said Anya hurriedly. "Go and talk to Sir Malorak. I have to kiss more frogs."

She put her finger in the now-quite-cool mixture and applied it again. Somehow the plum flavor was not as appealing as it had been earlier, and her face was a bit sore from puckering up so often.

The next frog was Prince Denholm. He stood blinking in the sunlight, then slowly knelt at Anya's feet.

"Thank you, Princess," he said, wiping his eyes. "I could not have stood being a frog for very much longer. I was starting to forget that I had ever been a man."

"I'm sorry you got transformed in the first place," said Anya. She hesitated, then added, "I expect you're worried about Morven.

While it is true the Duke has completely taken over Trallonia, Morven is . . . is most likely unharmed."

"Oh, Morven," said Denholm uncomfortably. "I'd rather forgotten about . . . that is, being a frog, my mind was clouded. Of course I shall not rest until Princess Morven is rescued, but . . . um . . . I might need some help."

He looked around anxiously at Anya's rather raggedy army, who were busy preparing more quarterstaves and cleaning up the battlefield, trussing live weaselfolk for kissing, and dragging the dead ones off into a clearing to make a funeral pyre.

"We're *all* going to rescue Morven," said Anya. "But first we have to gather more reinforcements. The Seven Dwarves are coming, and Bert's robbers, and I hope the royal dogs, if they can be found. We'll probably attack the castle tomorrow. If the Duke doesn't attack us first."

Denholm frowned, his handsome face troubled.

"Surely with Morven in danger, we must act!" he said resolutely. "Ah, who, by the way, are these dwarves and 'Bert's robbers'?"

"Do you not remember anything from when you were a frog?" asked Anya.

"No," said Denholm. He thought for a moment, the effort of it obvious on his face, reminding Anya that he hadn't been all that clever when he was a human. He shuddered suddenly and added, "I remember eating bugs."

"You need time to recover," said Anya thoughtfully. "Why don't you go over to Sir Malorak and cut yourself a quarterstaff?"

"Yes, but Morven!" exclaimed Denholm. His memory appeared to be coming back, as he got a kind of goofy look on his face as he said Morven's name. "My heart aches to think of my poor beauty imprisoned by that foul sorcerer Rikard."

"Try not to think about it," advised Ardent kindly. "Think about something nice instead. Like bones. Or rabbits."

"Bones or rabbits?"

"Hunting or feasting," suggested Anya. "Now you must go. I have a lot of frogs still to kiss. Go!"

Denholm went, scratching his head. He hopped a little too. Like all the others, he caught himself doing it and almost fell over with the effort of stopping. But at least he wasn't absentmindedly snapping up flies like Parengoethes.

The next frog was a princess. She was twenty-five or so, and very pretty, even in her mildewed rags, all of which made Anya acutely aware of how stinky, filthy, and young she was herself. But this princess listened politely to Anya's standard speech, looked around the clearing and the signs of battle, and raised her chin in a determined fashion.

"I'm Princess Saramin of Ulastar," she said. "I can fight, but I'm a better surgeon and doctor. Is anyone hurt? And do you have medical utensils, bandages, healing herbs, and the like?"

"No one's really hurt yet," said Anya, pleased that this older and beautiful princess was treating her as an equal. "But we will have to fight a battle again soon, I expect. Perhaps you could find whatever you can, and prepare?"

"I'll do that," said Saramin.

"There's a prince over there," said Anya thoughtfully. "Denholm. He could be a useful assistant."

Saramin raised her eyebrows, which were quite pronounced.

"He doesn't look very bright," she said dubiously.

"He's very good-natured and will do what he's told," said Anya. "Please, excuse me. I must kiss more frogs."

"Don't exhaust yourself," warned Saramin. "While not as taxing as spells, even using a magic ointment will weary you."

Anya hesitated as she lifted more lip balm to her mouth. She did feel incredibly tired, but had thought it was just from her adventures and lack of sleep.

"I have to go on," she said. "We need these frogs to fight. I don't know when my allies will get here, and Duke Rikard may attack at any time."

Saramin looked Anya over professionally.

"Pause for a minute between frogs," she advised. "Drink water and try to eat a little. Sit down to kiss them; don't stand, because you may faint. I'll go and see what I can organize in the way of a field hospital."

Anya took Saramin's advice, but she also kept kissing frogs. There were more knights, including the truly massive twin sons of Sir Malorak, whose appearance created several minutes of quite scary backslapping and hugging between all the members of that family. Anya was almost reminded of her confrontation with Beware the Giant, though they were merely very large humans and not giants themselves.

Nearly all the frogs turned out to be knights, Anya gathering from the overheard conversations as they greeted one another that most of them had been engaged in quests to rescue other knights who'd been transformed earlier. If she'd had the time and energy she would have taken a moment to feel proud that one small princess and her friends had managed to succeed where all the knights had failed.

Anya reversed the transmogrification of eighty-one frogs in total, and seven weaselfolk. The resulting weasels were released and sped off quickly enough, the slower ones a little encouraged by Smoothie and Ardent.

At the end of it, Anya slumped against a tree and could barely lift the cup of water or eat the hunk of bread and honey that was handed to her by Martha.

"Could you please scrape what's left of the lip balm into smaller containers, Martha?" asked Anya. "There should be fifty-five uses left, I think. We'll need them when we fight the Duke."

"I'll do that," said Martha. "And I'll make soup after the cauldron's cleaned. But what about my newt? I don't understand why it didn't work on him. Can you try again?"

"I will," said Anya. "Where is Shrub anyway?"

"Hiding somewhere," said Ardent, returning from weasel chasing, his tongue lolling out and sides heaving. "Do you want me to find him?"

"No," said Anya wearily. She dragged herself to her feet. "I'd better see what's happening. Any news of our allies? Anyone?"

"Hedric's just back with some other druids," said Ardent.

Anya looked across the clearing. Hedric was emerging from the undergrowth with three other druids behind him. There was also a raven on his shoulder, and he was animatedly talking with it.

Anya was just about to head over when she stopped and groaned. There, behind the extra druids, was a Gerald the Herald, looking rather tentative but still coming forward.

"That's the last thing we need," she said.

"He might know something useful," Ardent pointed out.

Sir Malorak, who had assumed a position of second-in-command under Anya, met Hedric and spoke to him briefly. Both then walked on towards Anya, with the extra druids, Gerald the Herald, and a few of the former frogs who didn't have jobs to do following along.

At several paces away, they stopped and bowed their heads.

"Don't do that," said Anya uncomfortably. "I'm just a younger princess."

"You are the Frogkisser who has saved us," said Sir Malorak. "We must offer our respect and gratitude."

"Well, keep it for later," said Anya, who was tired and grumpy. "And what's that Gerald the Herald doing here? I don't want any spies for the Duke lurking around!"

"I'm on a special assignment," said the Gerald the Herald nervously. He was skinnier and considerably younger than any of the others Anya had seen, and had not only an artificial moustache and nose, but also a very ill-fitting wig.

"You don't talk funny like the others?" asked Ardent.

"Um, I can," said the boy. "Royal Dog Questions Authenticity of Herald!"

"Don't," said Anya. "What's your special assignment?"

"I'm to stay with the Frogkisser and her army," said Gerald. "And record what happens for posterity."

"So you won't go and talk to the Duke?" asked Anya.

"Uh, no," said Gerald. "I have to stay with you until . . ."

He hesitated.

"Until what?"

"Well, the Superior Gerald told me until you're dead or transformed," he said quietly. "But I'd prefer to report your triumph over that pack of sorcerers, uh, if that's all right with you."

"Pack of sorcerers?" asked Anya sharply. "What do you mean?"

"Duke Rikard and the rest of the League of Right-Minded Sorcerers."

"This is what I came to tell you," said Hedric. He gestured to the raven. "Oddbins here, he has been visiting the castle. Duke Rikard has called for the aid of all the League, and he has sent his bone ship to collect them. By dawn tomorrow or earlier, all five sorcerers will be with his army!"

CHAPTER THIRTY-THREE

Under the Banner of the High Kingdom of Yarrow

All five sorcerers?" repeated Anya. "Rikard, The Grey Mist, Ahuren the Nightgaunt, Grandmother Ghoul, and that pirate one, Yngish?"

"That's what the Superior Gerald told me too," said Gerald. "By raven, of course. I was already in the forest, reporting on the . . . on a . . . on the lost fawn. You might not have heard about it, a pet of one of the foresters . . ."

His voice trailed off. No one was listening.

"So by dawn," said Anya heavily. "Four more sorcerers!"

This was very bad news. While the former frogs would have considerable magical resistance against being transformed again, with so many sorcerers, many more transformees would be bound to end up as amphibians again, and Anya had a limited number of uses of the lip balm. The other sorcerers might well have more awful spells to use too, like The Uproarious Gout of Flame she'd read about, or The Poisoned Pincushion of Absolute Doom, which peppered a foe with a thousand tiny poisoned arrows . . .

She took a deep breath.

"Have we had any news or word from the dwarves, or Bert, or the dogs?"

"One of the ravens saw a force of humans and dwarves marching over the downs," said Hedric. "It must be them. They should be here by dusk, or a little before."

There was a general rumble of approval at this news. Anya looked at the sun and was surprised to see it was already sinking and the afternoon well advanced. Time had flown by while she was kissing frogs.

"And the dogs?"

"No report," said Hedric.

"I wonder what they're up to," said Anya. "Are you sure you don't know, Ardent?"

Ardent shook his head and crossed his eyes, an emphatic negative.

"I wouldn't have thought they'd leave in the first place," he said.

"I think we'll have to attack as soon after dusk as we can," said Anya. "Take the castle, imprison the Duke, then . . . I don't know, either prepare to be attacked in turn by the other four sorcerers or flee back into the forest and try to hide from them. What do you think, Sir Malorak?"

"This battle has been a long time coming," said Sir Malorak. Her eyes were cold and hard. "It is not just between you and your evil stepstepfather. It is a contest between the All-Encompassing Bill of Rights and Wrongs and everything enshrined by it, and the sorcerers who would do whatever they please to whomsoever they please. I think we must take the castle and then stand and fight, whatever the enemy brings against us. Fight and win, for the Bill of Rights and for our Frogkisser!"

Everyone cheered, including the people around the clearing who couldn't have heard a word and had no idea what they were cheering for.

"We must scout out the enemy position," said Sir Malorak. "May I send a small force to do that now, Princess?"

"Of course," said Anya. "Um, I think really you should be in charge and decide that sort of thing, Sir Malorak. I mean, I'm just a . . . a youngster, and I don't really know anything about battles—"

"You are the Frogkisser, who brought us back to our human selves," said Sir Malorak. "And Trallonia is your kingdom. You must be in charge."

"It's Morven's kingdom, and I really don't know what to tell everyone to do in a battle," said Anya anxiously.

"I will take care of the details," Sir Malorak reassured. "But you will still be in charge. You need merely say 'seize that castle' and we will work out the rest."

"Oh," said Anya, brightening. "That sounds all right."

"I will send the two rangers and my sons to scout," said Sir Malorak. "And, Hedric, do you have any ravens to spare?"

"Oddbins can fly ahead and take a look," said Hedric, muttering to the raven on his shoulder. It cawed twice, then flew off to the east, towards Trallonia Castle.

"Before they go, Princess, tell me about the castle," said Sir Malorak. "If you can sketch its walls and towers in the dust here, and tell me of their condition. There is a moat, I think? And are there any secret ways in or out?"

Anya drew a plan of the castle in the dust around the fire with the stirring stick.

"The walls have fallen down in places, and there are plenty of holes," she reported. "The moat is deep, though. If they pull up the drawbridge, it will be hard to get across. As for secret ways in from outside, there's the dog tunnel, but it only goes from the hall to the gatehouse—"

"There's the *very secret* tunnel," interrupted Ardent excitedly. His tail wagged so much it created a minor dust storm. "From the lower kennels to the mound in the c-c-corner of the water meadow."

"The lower kennels?" asked Anya. "What lower kennels?"

"The ones under the upper kennels," said Ardent. "Very c-c-ozy in winter. When everyone is in the big c-c-ave it's—"

"You can lead us through this tunnel?" interrupted Sir Malorak.

"It is very secret." Ardent scratched his ear thoughtfully with his back paw. "But I suppose . . . yes."

"Good!" exclaimed the knight. "While our main force engages the weaselfolk and any other troops, a select group may enter and seize the gatehouse and let everyone else in."

"And rescue Morven," Anya added thoughtfully.

"I wantsh to shget the Dook," said Smoothie, showing her teeth. She had a lot more teeth now that she was back in full otter form.

"We'll do that as well," Sir Malorak promised. "Bind and gag him! That's my advice for dealing with a sorcerer, though as we all here can attest it's never that simple. But opening the gate must be the first priority."

"I'll go with the group in the tunnels," said Anya.

"No!" protested Sir Malorak. "We need you in the rear, ready to kiss transformees as they are brought back from the front line."

"Someone else can do that. My mouth is sore anyway."

"I believe it works better for a princess—" Sir Malorak began, before she was interrupted.

"So Princess Saramin can do it," said Anya mulishly. "She'll be staying back to treat the wounded anyway."

"I suppose that's true," admitted Sir Malorak. "But the risk—"

"Am I in charge or not?"

Sir Malorak hesitated, then bowed her head.

"Good," said Anya. "I will go with the group in the tunnel. We will sneak in, open the gate, and make sure Morven is safe."

"I'll come with you! I'll save Morven!"

Denholm's head bobbed up over Sir Malorak's mighty shoulder.

Anya opened her mouth, but no words came out.

"I've got a quarterstaff," said Denholm, holding it up. "And I know my way around the castle."

"Definitely not," said Anya. "I promised Morven I'd bring you back safe, even if she's forgotten . . . even if she may have become . . . er . . . distracted. You can help Princess Saramin, Denholm."

"But I'll c-c-come with you!" barked Ardent.

"Of course, Ardent. Smoothie too. And Shrub, I suppose, if he comes back from wherever he's lurking. It would be unfair to leave him out now."

"You must have more force," said Sir Malorak. "Tilvan, and perhaps half a dozen other knights—"

"I'll ask the Seven Dwarves," said Anya sleepily. "That ought to do it. But right now I need to lie down again and—"

She crumpled to the ground in midsentence, was caught by many hands, and was gently lowered the rest of the way.

* * *

When Anya awoke, the sun was setting. She sat up, surprised to find herself on a comfortable camp bed inside a tent. The movement also made her aware her clothes were strangely heavy. She looked down and saw that she had been washed and her clothes changed in her sleep, which must have been very deep indeed.

Now she was clad in hunting leathers, with a mail shirt over the top. There was a helmet and a short sword in a scabbard with a baldric at the foot of her bed, and a small ceramic pot. Anya stood up, put on the helmet and strapped on the baldric and sword, then opened the pot. As she had thought, it was anti-transmogrification lip balm. Perhaps enough for half a dozen uses. The bulk of the remainder from the cauldron would have gone to Princess Saramin. She slipped the pot into the top of her left boot and walked outside the tent, her mail shirt jingling.

Anya saw a very different forest clearing. It no longer looked like the shambolic site of a skirmish around a lone forester's hut. There were six more bell tents in a row next to the one she was in, and outside them were chests thrown open showing a few remaining swords and suits of mail and helmets, tossed aside as being too large or too small. There were mostly empty stands of spears next to the chests. The dwarves had come prepared to equip an army, which showed either their experience or the Good Wizard looking in her Magic Mirror and accidentally telling them what was going on, since she wouldn't have done so on purpose with the whole not-interfering thing.

Beyond the tents, along the road, there was an army drawn up in marching order, stretching out of sight into the forest in both directions.

Anya stared. The former frogs were no longer clad in rust and rags, but in shining new mail like her own, of fine dwarf-make. Some still carried quarterstaves, but most had spears or swords. They stood proudly in ranks, a regiment waiting its chance to take revenge for lives and time lost to evil sorcery.

Bert lounged against a tree, accompanied by dozens and dozens of Responsible Robbers, clad in their various shades of green and russet. All of them were armed to the teeth, their longbows most prominent. They carried extra sheaves of arrows on their backs, in addition to full quivers.

There was a cart and donkey, laden with bags, bottles, and a huge surgical chest, with Princess Saramin in the driver's seat, and the three merchants and Martha sitting behind her. Hedric and five druids sat cross-legged behind the cart, long-handled scythes laid on the ground before them. The young Gerald the Herald stood nearby, writing feverishly in his notebook.

The Seven Dwarves, clad from head to foot in articulated plate armor of their own design, were gathered close by, their huge axes at rest and their visors open. Erzefezonim caught Anya's eye, tapped her own armored chest, pointed at Anya, and smiled. The princess nodded in thanks, recognizing that it was the youngest dwarf who had cleaned and dressed her.

Behind the dwarves, Parengoethes, the oldest warden of the High Kingdom, stood with a standard, the slight breeze ruffling it open enough for Anya to see the device, a simple square of gold on a white field.

"The flag of the High Kingdom, representing the Only Stone and the All-Encompassing Bill of Rights and Wrongs," said Dehlia, landing near Anya with a flurry of her old wings.

Ardent came from behind to stand on Anya's right, putting his head under her hand. Smoothie reared up on the princess's left and made an encouraging chirruping noise. And rather surprisingly, Shrub crept out from under the hawthorn and hesitantly took up a place nearby.

Sir Malorak marched over. She had new mail and a sword, which she used to salute Anya.

"Your army awaits the order to march on Trallonia Castle, Frogkisser."

"*Our* army," said Anya. The words came out as a squeak. She took a very deep breath and spoke again, much more loudly.

"Our army! Marching under the standard of the Bill of Rights and Wrongs. Tonight we retake Trallonia and defeat the evil sorcerer Rikard!"

"Very good," said Ardent as everyone cheered. It was an amazing sound, a full-blooded cheer from hundreds of throats, which made all the birds fly out of the trees and small animals even half a league away take to their burrows.

"I hope we do defeat Rikard," said Anya very quietly. This army was impressive, but Rikard's probably was too. And he had his sorcery, which had continued to grow and grow in strength, as seen by the creation of the bone ship.

Who knew what other horrors he might have in store?

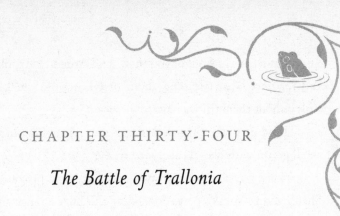

CHAPTER THIRTY-FOUR

The Battle of Trallonia

Anya was brought up to date with the latest news as the army marched out of the forest and across the fields towards the castle. The sun had set as they emerged from the tree line, but it was a clear night with many stars and the promise of the silver moon.

"The Duke has withdrawn his troops into the castle," said Sir Malorak. "The count is at least fifteen score weaselfolk, four large beasts that may be trolls or lesser stonefolk of some kind, a baker's dozen of assassins, a bandit troop of seventeen or eighteen—one may have been counted twice when she changed her hat—and the Duke himself."

"That's a lot," Anya observed.

"Twice our numbers," said Sir Malorak. "But any one of ours is worth three or four of the Duke's, save perhaps the trolls."

"Is this where I say 'seize the castle'?" asked Anya.

"You may, if you wish," said Sir Malorak. "The plan remains the same. We will draw up on the water meadow—it is dry enough—and stand ready to charge in when your party opens the gate."

"I suppose we'd better get on with it, then," said Anya. She cast an anxious look at the sky. "Particularly if those other sorcerers might arrive *before* the dawn."

"Eat what's in front of you first," said Ardent. He spoke gravely, and for once wasn't leaping about or talking too quickly. "Don't worry about them till we have to, Princess."

"Lead us to the tunnel, Ardent," said Anya. She turned to the small group with her. "Is everyone ready?"

There was a chorus of ayes and yeses and of courses! Only Shrub didn't speak. Anya looked at the huge orange newt curiously. What was he up to? His large bulbous eyes met her gaze briefly; then he looked away. Anya frowned, but she didn't have time to find out what was going on with him.

It was strange walking in the starlit night among an army getting itself ready for an attack. The dark silhouette of the castle could be seen a few hundred yards away, against the lighter sky, but there was no activity on its crumbling walls. Anya's troops went quietly to their positions, rough shapes moving with only the occasional whisper, but there was still the occasional jangle of armor or weapons as the soldiers collided by accident, stepped in a rabbit hole, or slipped in the damp mud of the water meadow.

The Duke had to know there was an enemy force getting ready out in the darkness, Anya thought. But perhaps Rikard presumed his sorcery was so powerful it didn't matter who was moving against him, and he was watching from the battlements, smiling his secret smile, a cackle about to rise in his throat . . .

Anya banished that thought, and concentrated on following Ardent. His golden coat was bright under the stars, and she let her hand fall on his back and gave him a little scratch of encouragement. His tail wagged twice, but he was concentrating too, leading them to the tunnel entrance.

"I always wondered why there was a raised mound here," whispered Anya as they reached the corner of the meadow.

Ardent didn't answer. He climbed to the top of the low mound, grasped a hidden ring in his powerful jaws, and lifted a cunningly disguised trapdoor that looked just like a square of turf. Beyond it, Anya could see the beginnings of a ramp, leading down into complete darkness.

"Best let us go first," whispered Sygror gruffly. "Dark underground is dwarf business, to be sure. We'll light a lamp for you once we're well under and the hatch closed behind."

"I'll close it," said Sir Malorak. "Good luck. Keep the Frogkisser safe!"

Sygror spoke a few quiet words in a sharp-edged tongue Anya didn't know but presumed to be Dwarvish, before he descended into the darkness. One by one the other dwarves followed him down the ramp.

Ardent went next, Anya holding his collar, then Smoothie, and finally Shrub, who scuttled in just before the trapdoor was closed by Sir Malorak, as if the newt couldn't decide where he wanted to go.

It was too dark for even Ardent to see anything, but they edged along for a few steps, the dog sniffing loudly as he went. Anya could hear the dwarves moving, and soon there was the whir and click of a clockwork firestarter, and then the bloom of light from a candle, shortly magnified by a lantern glass.

In its light, Anya saw that the tunnel they were in was lined with many small yellow bricks, quite unlike anything else in Trallonia Castle. They were mortared very tightly together, and as a consequence the tunnel was dry and well kept. It was wide enough so two dwarves, who were not narrow-shouldered, could stand abreast, and it slanted downwards quite steeply, presumably so as to pass safely under the moat.

"Onwards!" said Sygror, hefting his axe. He smiled, and the other dwarves smiled back. They seemed pleased at the prospect of battle, but Anya could only feel a twisted knot in her stomach and a kind of unpleasant fluttery feeling in her heart. She supposed this was fear, and tried to ignore it, which was a lot easier to think about than actually to do in practice.

They tramped down the tunnel, the dwarves constantly looking up, down, and to each side, as if the bricks might hide secret doors or murder holes.

Possibly they do, thought Anya, who started looking herself, nervously twitching her head from side to side and up and down.

Ardent stayed near Anya, sniffing the air constantly, but not saying anything. Smoothie came up close behind, the narrow, dry tunnel not to her liking. Shrub brought up the rear, waddling along ten paces back.

A hundred paces on or thereabouts, there was some water dripping from the ceiling. Sygror paused there, and reached up to tap the bricks. He whispered something to Gramel, who turned to whisper to Danash behind. Then Danash passed this on to Erzef, who repeated it to Anya.

"It is nothing to worry about. We go under the moat, and the tunnel is very old. But strongly built."

"I could have told you that," said Ardent indignantly.

Erzef smiled, turned to face the front, and continued.

"We'll be at the lower kennels soon," said Ardent a little later. He sniffed the air again. "I think . . . I think—"

There was a sudden bark up ahead, echoing through the tunnel. The dwarves stopped, axes raised.

"Who goes there?" growled a dog.

Anya recognized the growl. It was Gripper. All of a sudden she knew where the royal dogs had gone. Or rather where they hadn't gone. They'd never left the castle, not really. They'd simply retreated to their deep, secret kennels, to wait.

To wait for her to return.

"Gripper!" she called out, tears forming in the corners of her eyes. "It's me! Anya, with Ardent, and friends!"

"Pause, friend, be smelled and enter!" barked Gripper, in the traditional greeting of the royal dogs.

Ten minutes later Ardent was momentarily submerged by a roiling mass of his siblings and cousins, and Anya was hugging Tanitha in the center of a huge cave that was absolutely full of dogs. Magic lanterns like the ones in the Wizard's house hung from the ceiling, burning with their cool, long-lived flames, casting their light across the natural spaces and the rough-hewn edges where long ago the cave had been expanded and made more suitable for the dogs.

"We don't have much time," explained Anya to Tanitha. "These are the Seven Dwarves, the famous ones—"

"I know," said Tanitha, licking Anya's face. "We've met before."

"Indeed," said Sygror. All the dwarves bowed, the ingenuity of their armor displayed by the fact that they could easily bend in the middle and rise again, all with only the slightest clank of metal. "It is good to see you again, matriarch."

"Oh," said Anya. "Well, that's Smoothie, of the Yarrow River otters, and Shrub, who's being strange but is a transformed good thief. We're on our way to seize the gatehouse and let the army of the All-Encompassing Bill of Rights and Wrongs in—"

She paused, noting the reaction of the dogs as she mentioned the Bill. The mound centered on Ardent collapsed, and they were all drawing themselves up as if a rabbit had suddenly appeared before them, and there was that long second before a pursuit would either begin or not.

"Yes," said Tanitha. She licked Anya again. "I know. We have had reports. The cats and some of the ravens, you know. Everything is in readiness."

"In readiness?"

"Yes," confirmed Tanitha. "Frosty will lead the troop to help seize the gates. Kneegnawer will take a troop to protect Morven. Jackanapes will take another to destroy the Duke's study and any potions or suchlike there. The rest of us will wait to attack the weaselfolk in the rear when your army enters the castle."

"It seems you dogs could do it all on your own," said Sygror, his mouth quirking into a smile.

"Oh no," said Tanitha. She heaved herself up, her tail wagging slowly. "We royal dogs, we only advise and assist. We could do nothing until Anya came home."

"Thank you, Tanitha," said Anya, hugging the dog again. She felt suddenly buoyed up, the jangling of her heart steadied, the knot in her stomach lessened. It was still there, but nowhere near as bad. Her fear ebbed, to be replaced by determination.

"Let's go!"

Anya had only taken a step when she felt herself dragged back by the baldric. Twisting around, she saw Tanitha had fastened her teeth there and was holding her in place, while all around dogs were rushing towards a ramp that led upwards.

"Let me go!" protested Anya. She wriggled hard, but couldn't dislodge Tanitha's grip. The dwarves saluted her, and went to join the dogs.

"We wait," growled Tanitha, words muffled by the baldric in her mouth.

Anya gave up struggling and crossed her arms in fury.

"I've done everything so far!" she exclaimed. "And I got back here safe and sound. Stop treating me like a little girl!"

Tanitha let go.

"I'm treating you as a very important and irreplaceable person," said Tanitha. "Which you are. A castle storming is no place for a young person, or an old dog. It's too easy to be killed by accident in the first few minutes, when the fighting is fiercest. We wait."

"Shensible," said Smoothie approvingly. Even Ardent only looked after the departing dogs once, though he drew closer to Anya as if he needed to be reminded he was supposed to stay with her. Shrub crawled closer too, but as was now usual, said nothing.

They waited in silence, Anya still fuming, though she had to recognize that Tanitha was right. At first, there was no noise from up above, but very soon there came shouts and squeals and barking. Shortly after that, the first messenger dog came racing down the ramp and skidded to a halt in front of Tanitha.

"Duke's study taken," panted Shortlegs. "He wasn't there."

"Where is he, then?" retorted Tanitha. "Tell Jackanapes to destroy as much as possible but also to find the Duke. He mustn't escape."

Shortlegs nodded, twisted around on the spot, and was off again, giving the lie to his name.

"I should go up," said Anya fretfully.

"Wait," said Tanitha as another dog messenger came sprinting in. "Ah, here's Somersault. What news?"

"Kneegnawer's dead, and half the troop's out of action!" gasped Somersault. "The Duke was outside Morven's chamber. He's taken her up to the top of the south tower!"

"The best plans must change," said Tanitha. She gave out a huge sigh and then barked strongly, "To the southern stair!"

A tide of dogs surged towards the southernmost of the four arched exits to the cave, taking Anya and everyone else with it.

"Steady! Steady!" barked Tanitha, but even she could not stop the mad dash and the elder dog was soon left behind, even by the puppies who joined the rush, their minders temporarily forgetting their duties.

Anya pushed her way towards the front, sliding between dogs, Ardent nipping those who didn't move out of the way. Smoothie undulated over the top of them and Shrub slipped between their legs, keeping low to the ground.

It was slightly less crowded on the stair. As they raced up, Anya heard the crash and din of battle, the squeals of weaselfolk, and many different shouts and screams.

A minute later, they burst out onto the battlements of the south wall, beneath the tower. Below them, in the bailey, a great battle was raging, evidence that the gatehouse had already been seized, the drawbridge lowered, and the gate opened. More and more of Anya's troops were pouring in, but they were fighting a tightly massed array of weasels, assassins, bandits, and trolls.

An assassin below saw Anya and raised his crossbow, but before he could fire, an arrow sprouted in his neck. Across the courtyard, Anya heard Bert cry "He! He!" the traditional shout of an archer who has found their mark, and she saw the robber atop the gatehouse already nocking another arrow.

The dwarves were shoulder to shoulder in a wedge, driving forward towards the trolls, axes flashing. The trolls also surged to meet their ancestral foes, crushing many of their own soldiers in the process.

Finally, Anya looked up to the tower.

Duke Rikard stood in an embrasure there, with Morven balanced precariously atop one of the merlons. The only thing stopping the princess from falling to her death was Rikard's grip on the braid of her long black hair. Prince Maggers was there too, flapping his arms and circling about the Duke, but not daring to come closer than two or three paces in case the sorcerer let Morven go.

Or pushed her off.

"Surrender!" screamed Rikard, his thin, creepy voice audible even over the tumult of battle. "Surrender or Princess Morven will die!"

Adding dire punctuation to his call, Morven screamed. The loudest, most terrible scream Anya had ever heard, even from her sister.

CHAPTER THIRTY-FIVE

A Princess Is Transformed

A nya stared up at her sister and the sorcerer. It was as if everything else had disappeared from her vision; she could only see them, and all the sound and fury of the battle had faded back. All she could hear was Rikard's voice, echoing again and again through her mind.

"Surrender or Princess Morven will die!"

But she couldn't surrender, Anya knew. If she did, Rikard would kill or transform everyone. All the friends who had done so much for her. All the former frogs, who had already suffered for so many years. The royal dogs, some of whom were already slain and would be sorely missed in the kennels.

But if she didn't surrender, Morven would die . . .

"Surrender or else!" yowled Rikard again, followed by a maniacal cackle at the sky. To do this he had to put his head back, and in that moment Morven tried to escape. She leaped sideways, but the Duke didn't let go. He pulled savagely on her hair. Morven lost her footing, teetered backwards, and then with a despairing cry went over the edge.

Only Rikard's grip on her long braid kept her from falling. He held her there with unnatural strength, his skeletal white face stretched into a horrible grin as the princess swung like a pendulum against the tower wall.

"Surren . . . Oh, forget it!" screeched Rikard. He slowly opened his hand, Morven's braid slipping through his fingers like a lifeline come unstuck.

"No!" screamed Anya. She lunged forward as if she might somehow catch her sister, but she was too far away, the tower too high. There was nothing she could do.

In the moment the Duke finally let go completely, Prince Maggers leaned through an embrasure and grabbed Morven. She reached up to embrace him and for a moment it seemed the prince might be able to pull her up to safety.

Until Rikard pushed Maggers out.

Prince and princess fell together, locked in an embrace, their mouths meeting for one last kiss before they were dashed to death on the ground below.

Only they never made it to the ground. As they fell entwined, there was a flash of light. Suddenly two magpies spun out of their fall, spread their wings, and flew towards the forest, caroling their joy.

"True love," said Ardent. "Never would have thought it of Morven."

Anya watched the magpies go. She couldn't believe it either. But it must have been so, for Maggers to be transformed back to his natural form, and their love so strong that Morven also became a bird.

"Now you'll all just have to die instead!"

The thin, petulant scream from the tower drew Anya's attention back to Rikard. He had climbed to the very spire of the tower and now stood balanced on the weather vane, his face white in the moonlight and his pale, scrawny arms extended up out of his robe, so he looked rather like a disembodied head and hands from a black velvet puppet show.

An arrow arced towards him, but suddenly flew off course as it got close. Another followed, only to circle back and narrowly miss the robber who'd shot it.

"Fools! No weapons can harm me!" screamed Rikard. "And now you will pay for your discourtesy to the great, the powerful, the one and only Master Sorcerer Rikard the Omnipotent!"

He looked down at Anya on the wall, his eyes glowing red.

"You! Anya! *Frogkisser!* I will transform you into a slug! A large and juicy slug for the frogs in the moat to eat! You troublesome brat!"

He gabbled out several horrendously strong words of power and thrust one bony finger straight at Anya. She dodged, knowing it was useless. The type of spell Rikard was casting would invariably find a target.

But as a blinding green spark shot from the Duke's finger towards her, an orange shape leaped up and interposed himself!

The spark hit Shrub and disappeared, not even scorching his hide.

Rikard looked at his finger, scowled, and clenched both fists.

"Stupid newt! You may resist transformation, but you cannot resist The Blood and Bone Exploder!" screamed Rikard. He pointed again and shouted words of power that left his mouth like screaming winds.

A brilliant red spark shot from his finger, straight at the newt!

"Shrub!" screamed Anya, crouching and covering her head against the inevitable explosion and the bits and pieces of newt that would be showered everywhere.

But there was no explosion.

"Impossible!" snarled Rikard. He waved his hands around above his head, summoning his sorcery, and once more shouted out a spell, the words of this one so powerful they rattled every window in the castle with thunderous noise.

A whirlwind of swirling sparks materialized above Shrub and began to spin down, accompanied by the sound of a thousand fingernails being drawn across a thousand slates. Anya could feel the intense heat from it even a dozen paces away.

Surely, it would incinerate Shrub as soon as the whirling sparks got close enough.

But Shrub actually jumped up at the tornado with his mouth open. And then the tornado wasn't there, as if Shrub had somehow eaten it.

"No! No! No!" screeched Rikard. He started hurling spells directly at the newt. Spells of rending and mangling and spells of dis-corporation and transformation. Spells to stop a heart and freeze blood and turn people inside out and just generally kill them on the spot.

None of the spells had any effect. Anya glanced away for a moment as the Duke paused, his arms hanging down and head bowed, his sorcery depleted.

The battle below was effectively over. The forces of good were rounding up the surrendering, totally demoralized weaselfolk, assassins, and bandits. The trolls were all broken into their compo-nent rocks, the dwarves collecting the pieces in sacks to be returned to the troll homeland where they might or might not be put back together. Only criminal trolls ever left their mountains.

"This cannot be!" wailed Rikard. He drew himself together and raised his right hand, fingers clenched into a claw. "I will, I will, I will destroy you."

"No you won't!" called out Anya. "Just give up!"

"Never!" shrieked Rikard. "It seems you are proof against my spells. But *not* if I destroy myself and all with me!"

He cackled then, a fatal error, for it took several precious seconds when he could have been casting his ultimate spell. Even as he began to form the first terrible word of power there was a "Kee!" above him.

The call of a hunting owl.

Rikard looked up as Gotfried, fully owl, plummeted into his face and stuck his claws through the sorcerer's pale cheeks. The shock of the owl's impact threw the Duke backwards, one of his slippered feet coming off the crossbar of the weather vane. He teetered there for a moment and then, with a despairing cry largely muffled by feathers, he fell.

Owl and sorcerer, locked together, bounced off the battlements of the tower and plummeted all the way to the ground.

"Gotfried!"

Anya raced to the steps and rushed down, Ardent at her heels. All around the castle there was a calm, like the sudden stillness that follows a violent storm. Then people began to converge upon the spot where sorcerer and owl had fallen. Bert ran down from the gatehouse, taking four steps at a time, bow in hand, with Dehlia flying above. The dwarves laid their sacks of troll bits aside and moved together, once again in a wedge. Martha, who had been helping Princess Saramin bring the hospital cart in, left her and came running, looking for Shrub, with Hedric close behind her.

Even Sir Malorak paused in giving a constant stream of orders, clapped her daughter on the back, and declaimed, "Take charge of the perimeter," and strode through the surrendered weaselfolk, who moved aside like water parting before the prow of some great ship.

The tumbled body of Rikard was sprawled across the cobbles. He was on his back, and the owl was still stuck on his face.

"Gotfried!"

The sorcerer's body twitched. Anya, who had just leaned over to try to see if Gotfried was alive, jumped back. Rikard got to his knees, peeled the now limp body of the owl from his face, and threw it aside.

"I am not so easily defeated," he hissed. Though there were holes in his cheeks from the owl's talons, no blood was coming out. His eyes pulsed red, and when he bared his teeth, his incisors were as long as knives.

He was a terrifying sight. But when he started to stand up, Anya put her foot behind his ankle and pushed him hard in the chest.

Rikard fell back, his expression very similar to that seen on a newly stunned fish. Instantly, Ardent leaped onto his middle and pressed him flat with the dog's full weight. Smoothie clamped her jaws around the wrist of his right arm, preventing him from making any spell-casting gestures.

Finally, Shrub waddled over and draped himself over the sorcerer's mouth so he couldn't speak.

Worn out by all the spells he had cast, and shaken by the fall from the tower, Rikard only struggled once or twice, and then lay still. But his eyes blazed like dangerous coals, focused on Anya, who ignored him.

Everyone gathered in a ring around the trapped sorcerer, leaving Anya and her friends in the center with Duke Rikard.

Robbers bearing torches rushed to light the scene, and Cook came with the huge kitchen lantern.

Anya picked up the small form of Gotfried. His head hung limp, and when she held her ear close, she could hear no heartbeat.

"Broken neck," said a cat by her feet, who like everyone else had come to be certain Rikard was defeated. His sooty paws were bloodied, for the cats had fought the enemy too. Anya thought it was Robinson again, but she couldn't be sure.

"Quick and painless," added the cat. "Very brave."

"He always wanted to be brave," said Anya. She wiped away the tears that had been falling unnoticed down her cheeks. "But how did he even get here?"

"I brought him," said Merlin, stepping out of the circle around the fallen. "We came by carpet. It seemed to me he had something important to do."

"He did," said Anya sadly. "But I thought Good Wizards couldn't interfere?"

"Ah, but I'm retired," said Merlin. "Not wearing the beard, no longer Snow White. Not a Good Wizard at all. Just a concerned citizen, seeing to a few loose ends. What are you going to do with the Duke? Hard to kill him, but something could probably be worked out."

"No," said Anya. "We fought under the banner of the All-Encompassing Bill of Rights and Wrongs. He will get a fair trial."

"Well said," Dehlia and Bert replied together. "Very well said."

"I mean, I think he should be tried," Anya added. "But I suppose I'll have to go and get Morven back, and when she's queen she'll decide."

"Morven's not coming back, except to visit, or perhaps later to show off her brood," said Tanitha, slowly puffing up to Anya's side. "Why would she? She has found true love, a permanently beautiful outfit, and Maggers will sing to her always and bring her all manner of shiny jewelry, even if most of it is tinsel or broken glass. Morven will not be queen of Trallonia. Which leads us to the question: Who will be?"

Anya sat down, cradling the dead owl librarian in her lap.

"I never wanted to be queen," she said. "I think I want to be a wizard now. You can't make me be the queen."

"Who says we want to?" asked Tanitha. "Maybe someone else would be better."

Anya stared at her, shocked. The idea that someone else could be queen of Trallonia was both startling and, she was surprised to discover, rather disturbing. Perhaps she was not being entirely honest with herself about not wanting to rule the kingdom . . .

"What do you mean you might get someone else?" Anya asked. She was unable to keep a note of indignation out of her voice. "I mean, if Morven's out of the running, I'm next, aren't I?"

"That depends," said Tanitha. "Ardent! What is the result of *your* Quest?"

Ardent looked at Anya a little sheepishly.

"Success," he barked. "I found a princess suitable in all respects to be queen of Trallonia!"

"What?" gasped Anya. "Who? Where?"

"You, silly!" said Ardent. He started to get up to give her a lick, before remembering he was helping to subdue Duke Rikard.

"Me?"

"You did not know it," explained Tanitha. "But it is the royal dogs who decide who will rule Trallonia. We look first to the line of King Norbert, but should no one prove suitable, we may choose elsewhere. Morven clearly wouldn't do, even before she became a magpie, and with you there were some doubts. Your interest in sorcery was worrisome, and some feared you might end up like Duke Rikard. But if Ardent has found you suitable, then you will suffice. We'll have the coronation tomorrow."

"Maybe the day after," said Anya, accepting that she did want to be queen after all, though some small niggling thoughts were lurking in her mind about the possibility of doing other things as well. "We have to have the trial first."

She looked down at Rikard. He twitched, wriggled, and bent his baleful stare upon her. But Shrub dug in with his claws, pressing his tough and probably poisonous belly farther into Rikard's mouth, so there was no chance he could speak a spell.

That reminded Anya. Shrub's curious silence and surprising anti-sorcery properties needed to be resolved.

"I think I know why I couldn't transform you back," said Anya sternly to the newt. "And why the Duke's spells failed. You've got it, haven't you?"

"Got what?" asked Ardent.

The newt nodded, still not speaking.

"Time you handed it over, boy," said Merlin.

Shrub gave the retired wizard a what-business-is-it-of-yours look.

"I made it in the first place," said Merlin.

Anya looked at the ex-wizard. "You did? The Good Wizard said it was her predecessor's predecessor's predecessor."

"I've retired before," said Merlin. "And then came back. So that was me. Some of us take it in turns to be the Good Wizard."

He looked sternly at the newt.

"So come on. Cough up!"

Shrub tapped his forefoot against Rikard's head a couple of times.

"Oh yes, he needs to be silenced," said Anya.

Bert came forward and cut a strip off the sorcerer's robe. When the newt moved off, she quickly gagged the Duke with it.

Everyone watched in fascination and Cook raised her lantern high as Shrub waddled a few steps away, opened his mouth wide, and slowly regurgitated a cube of white stone the size of Anya's fist. It was covered in newt saliva, but even so the thousands of tiny silver letters etched in every surface could easily be seen. It also had a hole bored through its middle, for a leather strap to be put through, so it could be worn as an unruly, oversize medallion.

"So that's what it looks like!" Anya's eyes were goggling out in amazement, almost as much as the newt's did normally.

"Yep," said Shrub unhappily. "The Only Stone."

There was a collective gasp from everyone as he said the name.

"You told me to forget about it . . . but I saw it planted back in the path under that gloating chair again, and I couldn't help meself, but I *was* going to give it to Bert like I always planned, honest I was."

"I'm sure you were," said Anya. "Come here."

Shrub tentatively approached. Anya took out the small pot of lip balm and applied some to her lips, then very carefully kissed the newt on the driest patch of hide she could see.

There was a flash of greenish light and the newt exploded. In his place was a red-haired, sharp-featured boy who was rather under-sized if he really was ten. He grinned and flexed his lock-picking fingers, the grin immediately displaced as Martha emerged from the watching crowd and took him by the ear.

"Stealing again when you've been told not to!" scolded the witch. "You're going to write on your slate a hundred times 'I must only steal what I'm supposed to steal'!"

"Martha, please don't punish him," said Anya. "He's done something very important. We need the Only Stone to protect us against the other four sorcerers."

She looked up. The silver moon almost sped across the sky, the blue moon high above. It was probably only two or three hours until dawn, when the four sorcerers would arrive, and undoubtedly attack.

Merlin gingerly picked up the Only Stone and wiped it on Rikard's robe, which was coming in handy for all kinds of things. The sorcerer cringed away from the Stone—as much as he was able to with Ardent sitting on him—and made small whimpering noises.

"Oh, I doubt they'll turn up now," said Merlin. "Rikard has used up almost all his sorcery, you see. Including what was needed to keep the bone ship flying."

"So it will just fall out of the sky?"

"Perhaps," said Merlin. "More likely the magic is fading, feathers falling, bones coming unstuck. The sorcerers aboard will survive in any case. Like Rikard they surround themselves with many spells of protection. So I doubt they'll attack tomorrow. The members of the League of Right-Minded Sorcerers do not like taking real risks, and they will fear—quite rightly—that whatever or whoever defeated Rikard could do the same to them. That is not to say that they won't attack later, if they can fix the odds more in their favor."

"What will you do with the Stone, then?" asked Anya.

"That is for others to decide," said Merlin. "You among them. I am retired, after all."

He took a slim gold chain out of an inside pocket of his fur-lined robe and threaded it through the hole in the Stone. Then he fastened the chain around Anya's neck. The Stone sat on her breastbone and, despite its size, didn't feel as heavy as she'd thought it would.

"And this has all the old laws written on it?" asked Anya, turning the stone and peering at the tiny silver letters. "But they're too small to read . . ."

"You need a special prism and the sun," said Merlin. "You hold the Stone and the prism properly between the light and a whitewashed wall, and a phantasm of the writing will appear, writ large. There were quite a number of prisms about in the old days. Every warden had one. I expect you'll be able to find one in due course."

"Let's get this foul sorcerer tied up properly," said Sir Malorak. "And there's still a lot of cleaning up to be done. With your permission, Frogkisser?"

"Yes," said Anya. "Please do."

She looked down at Gotfried's quiet body.

"Were there . . . have many of our people been killed?" she asked quietly.

"A dozen at least," Sir Malorak reported solemnly. "And another score badly wounded. But we are fortunate that Princess Saramin is a true healer, and Prince Denholm has proved surprisingly useful as a nurse. It could have been many more, Anya. It would have been *many, many* more, save for your owl there. He will be remembered."

"Yes," said Anya. She slowly stood up. "I'll put him in the library, in his secret place that everyone knew. We can bury him with the others in the morning."

"I will take him," said Merlin. "We talked about his library, and I would like to see it."

He took Gotfried the owl from Anya's unresisting hands. She stood looking blankly across the courtyard at everyone working to clear up the horrible mess of battle, fortunately dim in the flickering torchlight.

"Come," said Tanitha. "Come to the Great Hall, and we will lie down with the puppies, and I will tell you a story."

"One about the Dog with the Wonderful Nose?" asked Anya. She tried to smile, but found herself crying instead. "But those are for puppies and children."

"You can never be too old for stories about the Dog with the Wonderful Nose," said Tanitha. She and Ardent closed up to Anya's legs and nudged her towards the hall. The princess let her hands rest lightly on their backs, taking comfort from the warm dogskin.

"So our Quest is done," she said in wonderment. "My sister promise is completed too. Denholm is back to being human. Allies have been found. Duke Rikard has been defeated."

"Yes," said Tanitha. "You did it, Anya. I always knew you would."

"So did I," said Ardent loyally, his tail thumping.

"Really?" asked Anya. "I didn't."

"Well, most of the time I did," said Ardent, and licked her open palm.

EPILOGUE

D uke Rikard's trial was held soon after dawn the next day, because everyone agreed that it was better to get unpleasant things out of the way early. Though no one had been able to find a prism to read the laws in the Only Stone, Dehlia, Tanitha, and Parengoethes between them could remember most of the applicable clauses. The Duke was charged with many crimes, including murder, forcible transformation, and improper cackling.

Bert, Sir Havagrad, Tanitha, Sleipjir, Holkern, and the two wardens sat as judges. They had barely gathered behind the table in the courtyard where the trial was held (since everyone wanted to watch), when the unicorn came trotting through the gate and came to stand by them. She even let Anya pat her neck, though only twice.

Rikard was brought out in chains, the dwarves not being satisfied with mere ropes. He was gagged, but the gag was removed when he sat in the single chair facing the judges. He immediately started to gabble a spell, but stopped and howled instead when Anya held the Only Stone against his back for a split second. In any case, it seemed Merlin was right about him having used up his power, because that partial word hadn't sizzled or boomed as it left his mouth.

The evidence was quickly presented. There were many witnesses to Rikard's evil deeds, so many that the counts of murder and forcible transformation were quickly proven, the unicorn confirming with a stamp of her hoof and a lift of her horn that everyone spoke truly. Except for Rikard, of course, when he talked in his own defense. The improper cackling charge was sustained on its own merits, since Rickard couldn't stop himself even during the trial.

So the Duke was found guilty, and the judges conferred on a suitable punishment. After a few minutes, they called Anya over and asked her if she had any suggestions. The options were limited, given that nearly all the old punishments were no longer possible following the Deluge. No one now knew where the Crystal Prison was, for example, where sorcerers and the like could be held harmlessly in stasis for decades.

"How about banishment?" asked Anya. "Send him to Tarwicce. No, better still, some far, distant island where no one lives. Take him there under guard in stages by flying carpet and leave him there."

The judges agreed that this was not only just, but merciful. The dwarves agreed that the Good Wizard would lend them a carpet for such a cause, though they declined to take on the job themselves, as they never traveled by carpet, even though they crafted them. Too cold and dangerous, Erzef told Anya with a shudder. But Sir Havagrad and several of the former frogs happily agreed to take on the task.

So Duke Rikard was banished to a remote island where there was very little chance he would ever be able to leave. Unless he got his sorcery back, which was very unlikely.

Though not totally impossible.

The funerals for those slain in battle came next, at the small cemetery on the lonely hill between the castle and the forest, where wildflowers grew between the graves. Hedric and the other druids spoke of the circle of life and death, the bare soil of winter and the green shoots of new life in spring. Then they sang a song that was warm and cold in turns, but ended with a gift of peace. It was all very sad, and everyone left weeping, and thinking deep thoughts, and there were many who came to the Great Hall that night to lie in a heap with the puppies and listen to Tanitha tell stories.

But the next day was a happy celebration, because it was Anya's coronation. Anya wore her best purple kirtle, her mother's red woolly, and the Only Stone. Ardent, Smoothie, and Shrub followed behind her as she walked the length of the Great Hall and up to the dais where she expected to be crowned by Hedric, since this sort of thing was normally done by a druid or a priest.

But it was the Good Wizard who stood waiting to put the simple twisted-gold-wire crown of Trallonia on her head. Anya paused for a moment when she saw her in full regalia: hat, snowy white beard, and staff. She smiled and walked the rest of the way to kneel in front of the Wizard.

"This isn't interfering," whispered the Good Wizard. She hadn't taken a voice-changing lolly, which was just as well since that deep bass voice probably couldn't whisper no matter what. She put the crown on Anya's head and tapped it a couple of times to make sure it was straight. "Just being neighborly now that all the hard work has been done by you and your friends."

"Thank you," said Anya. "Thank you for everything."

She hesitated, a vision of the vast library under the hill clear in her mind, and added, "Do you think I could still be a wizard? One day?"

"Perhaps," said the Good Wizard. "I was a princess myself once."

"You were?" asked Anya. "How—"

"Shhhh," said the Good Wizard. "That's another story. You have to stand up and wave now."

Anya stood up, turned, and waved. Everyone cheered and clapped and whistled and barked and made celebratory noises. Two magpies flew in and added their song from the rafters, and the castle cats, though they had expressed their independence by not coming down from the attics, set up a great cheerful yowling. Outside in the moat, the frogs began to croak in unison, keen not to be left out. Some of the knights inside croaked too, forgetting themselves.

Somehow, despite all this racket, the young Gerald the Herald could be heard:

"Frogkisser Crowned Queen of Trallonia! Rikard the Evil Sorcerer Defeated and Banished! Only Stone Found! All-Encompassing Bill of Rights and Wrongs Reestablished! What Could Be Next for the Frogkisser?"

ACKNOWLEDGMENTS

All authors are influenced by the work of all the writers they have read, for good or ill, and most particularly those read between the ages of say eight-ish and twenty-something. Sometimes this influence is easily observed, sometimes it is in small things not so easily spotted, sometimes it is not apparent to anyone else at all. With this book, I would like to particularly acknowledge the inspiration and positive influence that came from my youthful reading (and frequent rereading in later years) of the works of Lloyd Alexander, Nicholas Stuart Gray, Diana Wynne Jones, Robin McKinley, and T. H. White. There are many other writers who have influenced my work, of course, but I think for *Frogkisser!* these five deserve special mention.

As always, I am very grateful for the help, hard work and guidance of my agents and publishers: Jill Grinberg in New York, Fiona Inglis in Sydney, Antony Harwood in Oxford; and David Levithan at Scholastic in New York, Eva Mills at Allen & Unwin in Melbourne, and Emma Matthewson at Hot Key in London.

ABOUT THE AUTHOR

Garth Nix is the *New York Times* bestselling author of the Old Kingdom series, a modern classic of fantasy literature that includes the novels *Sabriel*, *Lireal*, *Abhorsen*, and *Clariel*. He is also the author of The Keys to the Kingdom series, *Shade's Children*, *A Confusion of Princes*, *Newt's Emerald*, and (with Sean Williams) the Troubletwisters series, among other novels. You can find out a whole lot more about him at www.garthnix.com.